ROY MACNAB

di reed

BLACK BEAST BOOKS

Royal Macnab by Di Reed

Published by Black Beast Books

First edition 2018

Printed and bound by Catford Print Centre.

Cover artwork & design by Louise Darnley at Dynam, Inverness.

Black Beast Books logo designed by Louise Darnley.

www.blackbeastbooks.com

ACKNOWLEDGEMENTS

In the eight years I cooked in the kitchens of several sporting estates on the Isles of Lewis, North Harris and North Uist, I met many people from all walks of life whose countless insights, stories and experiences informed this narrative.

Thanks to: my husband Mike, for his expertise and knowledge in all matters game fishing and fly tying; Simon Scott, manager of the Grimersta Estate, for kitchen chats and generous research assistance with the deerhounds; Debbie Millar, Grimersta's housekeeper; the Sunday Lunch Club – Claire for a ghostly encounter, Paul for an evening's boat fishing on Loch One, Daisy and Jake for a trip up the system and a carved oar; the guests and staff of Grimersta Estate, Amhuinnsuidhe Castle, The Round House and Garynahine Estate; Fergus and Anne Granville and their fishing and shooting guests; Niall Granville and Angus Alec for a day's stalking; Rosemary Shrager and the Bulmer family; Mark and Helen Bilsby; Malcolm MacPhail for the title; Tish Lockhart for her lifelong friendship, the Gaelic language and reading the draft.

Eleanor Neilson and Karen Green at Dynam.

Louise Darnley, for her terrific design skills.

DEDICATION

As ever, for Mike, Harriet, Madeleine and Al – my family rock.

NOTES

Royal Macnab is set on two fictional sporting estates, Uishall and Maglavat, on the Isles of Lewis and Harris. While they share certain characteristics of actual estates and castles on the Isles of Lewis and Harris and Skye, they are not intended to be recreations. Opinions expressed about land reform belong to the characters, and should not be attributed to actual island estates, their employees, managers, owners or guests.

To the best of my knowledge, all the characters are fictitious and should not be confused with anyone either living or dead. The fictitious Clan Macleod of Uishall and Maglavat has borrowed the tartan and badge of the Clan Macleod of Harris and Dunvegan, but that is the only connection between the two.

Not that it has much bearing on the following tale, but the events in the modern part of *Royal Macnab* take place two years after the events described in *Celtic Fringe*.

Uishall is pronounced *Ooshall*.
Eilaster is pronounced *Yellaster*.

THE ROYAL MACNAB

The concept of the Macnab originated with John Buchan's gripping adventure story, *John Macnab*. Three bored gentlemen seeking to inject some excitement into their ordered lives assume the collective pseudonym of John Macnab and, aided by a tinker boy, set about poaching a salmon, a hind and a stag between given dates, from three estates in the Scottish Highlands.

In modern times, the Macnab is defined as a brace of grouse, a stag and a salmon all taken by one hunter on the same day. This feat is only possible during September and October, when the grouse, salmon and stalking seasons coincide.

The Royal Macnab is a recent conceit, popularised by *The Field* magazine, requiring the fulfilment of the Macnab challenge, and completed by seducing the lodge cook.

PARABLE

On a sunny morning early in May, the Laird's gamekeeper came across a young lad fishing a length of river shielded by overhanging trees. Apart from the stealth required to fish the Laird's water undetected, the boy was deploying considerable guile in the casting of his line, for the water was low and clear, the fish watchful and clever, and the trees likely to snag his cast and rob him of his only hook.

"Away with you!" cried the gamekeeper, immune to the charms of the boy's skills. "This stretch of river is the Laird's, and all the fish that swim in it belong to him."

The boy looked out over the length of water. "This stretch belongs to the Laird?"

"Aye, and well you know it," said the gamekeeper grimly. "A fish caught on this beat is a fish poached, and you'll answer to the law if any you should catch."

The boy rose immediately. "Then I'll move directly," he said, and walked away with his rod.

In the evening, the gamekeeper was again patrolling the riverbank, and was astounded to see the same boy, fishing in the same place.

"Did I not warn you off this stretch of water only this morning?" shouted the gamekeeper.

"So you did," said the boy, smiling easily. "But surely the Laird cannot own the whole river? His share flowed by long ago."

THE UISHALL ESTATE,
THE CLAN MACLEOD
AND THE UGLY-BEAUTIFUL ITALIAN
MONSTER

I

Out on the West Coast of the Outer Hebridean Islands, rocky fingers of land jut out into the Atlantic, feeling their way into the wild ocean like tendrils of petrified seaweed. About halfway along the ragged shore of the main island, where the cliffs have been rent apart by the sea, leaving great expanses of white sand stretched across the wounds, an irregular chunk has been gouged out like a shark bite to form a large sea loch. This leads to the mouth of a river famous for its salmon and sea trout runs.

The land surrounding the sea loch and the river system is guarded on behalf of its English landowners, and fished by moneyed gentlemen and ladies for five months of the year. This is the Uishall Estate, ancient Macleod land, snaking away from the coast, hugging the line of the river, and then fanning out into the hills for a distance of some seven miles. Fifty thousand acres of wild country embracing dozens of lochs teeming with wild brown trout, and ending at the base of Roineabhal.

Uishall was first mentioned in the record books around 1039, when the territory was roughly double the size it is today. It belonged to the Macleods even then, and Willie, 22nd Laird of Uishall and Maglavat in the early nineteenth century, could already look back over some eight hundred years of almost continuous family ownership. In 1742, the land was passed briefly to the Clan MacInnes as part of a rich bridal dowry, and broken up between three heirs. When the eldest was killed at Culloden, the two surviving brothers put the three lumps back together again and halved the resulting mass; one took what is still called Uishall, the other made his home the other side of the Harris Mountains and called it Maglavat.

But in 1754, the MacInnes brothers were ruined by debts and gambling – easy targets for the relatively flush Macleods, who reclaimed their land with much emotion and celebration.

By 1814, Willie was a widower and his sons Alec and Ruaraidh were then young boys, destined to supervise both estates as they cast off the shackles of the old clan system and began to walk the long road in search of economic modernisation.

II

But modernisation is an ongoing process, a watchword for change, and the Clan Macleod had faced change many times before. Whatever else Willie's ancestors had got up to in the course of their turbulent and bloody history, the Clan's response to the new and different has been embodied by a fascinating piece of furniture that has stood in the dining room since the fourteenth century.

Uishall legend records that since the day it arrived, it has never been moved from its position opposite the huge stone fireplace with its great mantelpiece, its alcoves and capacious hearth where the hunting dogs traditionally doze. It is a massive oak cabinet, elaborately carved, its black, forbidding bulk offset by a soft lustre, the result of ten thousand or more polishings by generations of diligent servants. Their names have long since been wiped away, layers of history's dust not allowed to settle, but the ugly-beautiful monster they tended has survived them. Knights clash in endless battle on the backboard, lions' heads look sternly out from the corners of the top, while the doors below are heavy with bunches of grapes and twisting vines.

The story of this piece of furniture is evocative and inspirational, and as much a part of the Clan as its land and traditions. It eclipses even the romantic power of the claymore hanging above the fireplace, brandished in Jacobite fervour against the King's army by Willie's grandfather Malcolm, at the battle of Culloden in 1746.

Murdo Macleod, 12th Laird of Uishall, commissioned the piece as an extravagant wedding present for his somewhat reluctant bride in 1324. It was carved and carpentered by master craftsmen in Palestrina, northern Italy, transported on a perilously long journey across first the Alps and then the Pyrenees. Swathed in padding and protective cloths, it was hulked along in a crate that weighed twice as much as the object it carried. It was borne across the seas from Barcelona, round many a rough headland, through many a wild storm, until it was delivered triumphantly, after a three month journey, to the door of Uishall Castle.

The teller of the tale will never fail to say that when the packing crate was broken open under the forbidding gaze of the Laird, he could not find a single mark upon his costly investment, and he marvelled that it had survived its epic voyage unscathed. Only later did a servant discover a hairline crack along the side of the left-hand lion's head, by which time the exhausted carriers had departed and could not be brought to book. This tiny flaw is still visible today, and, as Alasdair Macleod once solemnly told his new wife Caitlin almost five hundred years later, reminds us that perfection is not possible when something has been exposed to such rich experience of the world.

III

At the time the Italian furniture arrived, the Clan was still living in the old castle, little more than a massive fortified tower. Its walls, six feet thick in places, were rough stone; they were hung with tapestries, and the bitter winter winds blew around the draughty halls and chambers, regardless of the great fires burning in every room. Their manners were crude, their furniture and chattels rudimentary; their clothes were rough, mostly designed to shield their wearers from the temperamental island weather, rather than inspire and build envy in the men they led. They ate roasted meat and rough bread from baskets, and had only spoons for cutlery.

The arrival of the Italian monster was nothing less than a catalyst. Murdo needed a fine space to show it off, and plates to display on its shelves. Pewter dishes arrived, a further twenty rooms were built onto the original tower over the next forty years, tables and chests and great carved chairs began to proliferate in the rooms.

With the acquisition of a single piece of European sophistication, the Clan Macleod of Uishall and Maglavat began the laborious but not unpleasant task of hauling itself into the fifteenth century, its members gradually learning to conduct themselves like the aristocratic leaders they were.

PART ONE

1823-37:
A TALE OF TACTICS

1.
FAIR GAME
AUGUST 1823

The hunter ran through the heather, his powerful strides swift and rhythmic as he leaped rocks and burns, his plaid flying, his shirt loose. The hills dipped and rose around him, the river glinting fitfully between its narrow, twisting banks like a lady tossing sly winks to her secret lover. He whooped with excitement, the thrill of the chase intoxicating him as he took gulps of the air rushing over his thin, strong frame, and realised he was gaining on his quarry. Far ahead of him she was, but not far enough. A shy creature, small and lithe, running for her life, brown eyes huge with the effort of escape.

He ran easily, with the arrogance of one who owned the land he trod. As if he had already mastered the purple hills and running deer, the sparkling river, its waters heavy with moving fish. As his speed shrank the distance between him and his prize, the early morning air was sporadically disturbed by the beating wings of the grouse. They exploded out of the heather with indignant squabbling cries, driven ahead of his thudding feet in panic.

She fled from him, her body bursting, galvanised by a kind of blind, hopeless energy. As she crested the rise, she could see the granite bulk of Uishall Castle standing at the water's edge, a good mile distant. And then, at the moment when her flight seemed at its most wild and desperate, she fell. A hidden pothole brought her down and she came crashing into the harsh, twisty arms of the heather, the breath knocked out of her, her leg smashed against a jagged rock. She let out a yell of pain; she thought he would be upon her in the instant and she struggled to her feet, crying out as she tried to put her weight on the damaged leg. She frantically scanned the landscape, but in all the wide sweep of the hills and all the way down to the shining sea, she saw that she was running towards nothing and no one, and there was no destiny for her but to be caught.

And then she heard the steady beating of his feet against the ground and the swish of his plaid over the tops of the heather. She moaned in anguish and tried to drive herself on, but the injury had crippled her. At that moment, her eyes were drawn by a flash of light. There was a dark shape moving slowly through the bracken on the hillside behind the castle, and she shouted out with heart-breaking despair:

"*An ainm an aigh, nach gabh sibh truas rium!*" [1]

She thought she saw the figure halt and turn his head in her direction, and her step faltered. But he looked like a gentleman, so even if he had heard her, he would not understand her wild cry in the old island tongue that marked her out as nothing but a poor tenant, undeserving of the help she begged.

She suddenly realised the distraction had brought her nearly to a stop; she jerked her head round to see the hunter almost upon her and threw herself forward, sobbing. When he caught playfully at her skirt, as if this were nothing more than a game of tag, it seemed as if the devil had laid his chilly hand on her heart and bid it stop. The last few agonised paces and he caught at her again, tripping her lightly with his outstretched hand as a cat will trip up a mouse. He broke the rhythm of her stumbling run, she fell again, he threw himself on top of her with a cry of triumph and she knew herself captured.

There was soft grass at her back now. He had tumbled her into a sudden clearing in the heather on top of a little knoll as if he had planned the place where he would bring about her fall. She fought him, her hands flying at his face, but he thought she was playing, and only laughed and held her. His face was alight with the thrill of seizing her.

"Who were you calling to?" he asked, looking keenly out at the green and purple hills, his body close against hers, all hot and sweating from the run. He spoke to her in Gaelic for he knew she had no English, save the little bits and pieces she had picked up from him, none of which would be useful in their present circumstances. "There is no one on the hillside but you and me, and there is no help that can come quick enough to save you from me now."

She turned her head towards the place where she had seen the shadow of a man moving, but there was no one there, just as he said, and the hope that had flared inside her was extinguished. A sharp, burning pain was shooting up from her ankle.

For a while they lay there, the sun growing stronger as they panted in the aftermath of the hunt; he held her down with a calm strength that belied the effort it cost him to keep her there.

"Be still, Janet, *mo nighean bheag*," he said at length, and translated for her, his finger touching the tip of her nose, as if improving her mind with the language of the aristocrats would improve her situation. "*My little girl*. When you fight, all you do is bring up the blood in me, and that will not help either of us."

He stopped speaking, his head thrown back, his breathing deep. He fought down his desires, for he was a young man who enjoyed the privileges of power and liked to love at leisure, and this was not a maid he wished to take in haste. She lay gasping beside him, her long red curly hair a bright, sun-spangled tangle against the grass.

He shook his head in amusement at their exhausted disarray. She was fortunate, he thought, that he was blessed with such a generous nature; a less tolerant man could have found it in him to be more than a little annoyed with her. He had already spent some considerable time in softening her up, and now it seemed he would be obliged to start that lengthy – although undeniably pleasant – process all over again. But as he looked around him, he had to concede that things had turned out better than he could have planned. Because she had bolted from him, they were now unconstrained by the risk of discovery. The fair morning, the yet fairer maid in his arms, added up to a pleasing collision of circumstances he had no mind to spoil with a show of ill humour.

Despite his best efforts at self-control, he felt the stab of rising want as he looked at her, and decided it was time to put an end to her skittishness. He leaned over her, his lips brushing her mouth. When she spat at him, he was taken aback. He wiped his face and looked at her in surprise.

"What – you are truly afraid of me, after all the smiles and tokens we've exchanged? Come, speak to me – what has happened? You seemed to like my kisses well enough before you lost your nerve."

He waited out her distressed silence with patient amusement. "No answer for me?" he mocked her. "I thought not. Your rage is misplaced, little Janet, for you have asked me often enough, without even speaking the words, to claim the bloody trophy that lies between your thighs."

She shook her head in furious denial at this outrageous declaration, and he began to accept that she was genuinely angry and afraid, and sought to calm her.

"Hush, my little frightened one," he said. "There is no need to fear. We are old friends, are we not? This wild chase, this frantic struggle, is nothing but maidenly concern for the barrier all friends must break through if they are to become lovers."

For a moment, her anger segued into uncertainty. He took his chance, kissed her, and though all her body was still hard in its defiance of him, he felt the softness of her lips.

He rested a little longer, studying her, her pretty face still heated from running, her breath rasping in her throat. The rise and fall of her breasts reminded him of the reason for their exertions. He changed his grip on her; both her small, dirty hands pinioned in one of his, while the other stroked the matted curls from her forehead and began to work open the buttons of her shirt. She struggled against him with fresh resolve, but he shook his head and pressed down on her.

"No, no," he said gently. "If you are angry and frightened, Janet, I will only hurt you. It's only life and the way of a man's love, and you must give in to me now so that we may finish our business." He opened the rough cloth, hushing her agitated protestations, and she flushed with shame as he caressed her.

"Be still for me," he said again. "Do you not like the touch of my hand?"

He saw her confusion as he stroked her, her embarrassment, her desperate rejection of him, beginning to war with other, more compelling sensations.

"Let go your anger, crabbit little maid, for there is no use in it, and no truth, either. I have waited patiently for the chance to lie with you, and so it is with you, if you will only admit it. Let me suck at those tender breasts, and you may yet see the sense of yielding to me, for what you will not give, I will take in any case."

He bent his head to her, letting go her hands in an experimental gesture of trust. There was something almost of acceptance in her face now, a realisation that it must happen as he wished, for she had no power to make it otherwise. It was the difference between them, and it would destroy the delicate bond they had woven across the social divide. He would take her now because he could, because he wanted her, and because she did not have the words to tell him that she wanted him, too, but not like this.

She looked dazed as he loosened more of her clothing, taking her sudden lack of resistance for permission to proceed, and when she was prepared to his liking, he lifted her into his arms. He tried again, kissed and fondled her, and at last his temper frayed at her failure to relent.

"What must I do, Janet? I have been patient, have I not? Must I bribe compliance out of you?" Gripping her wrist in one hand, the other groped about his plaid, and then he was holding a little leather bag above her. She turned frightened eyes towards the soft chinking sound, and his laugh was cruel with irony as he swung it in her face. "Is this what you want? A purse for granting me access – does that appease you?"

She sobbed and shook her head, snatched the purse from him and threw it violently away from her. And then he saw her helplessness, how much his taunt had hurt her, the unfair balance in his favour. He closed his eyes in disgust, for his lust had squandered all the riches this girl had given him, and made a beast of him. He did not understand what was happening between them, and in his ignorance, he felt himself shrink beside her. He did not want to force her, and yet he knew he must have her, whatever the cost. At the instant it seemed he would be overwhelmed by the conflicting drives, he felt her hand against his face.

He opened his eyes in confusion. She was weeping.

"I do not want your money," she whispered. "I have never wanted it."

His heart lunged against his ribs as she kissed him. He felt passion, relief, tenderness, pain; above them all, he knew he had won a guilty triumph, and he tried to silence the disapproval of his conscience as she held his face in her hands.

"Janet, forgive me," he said.

He clasped her to him, and this time when he kissed her, he felt the tentative touch of her tongue. His mouth began to nip and graze over her body again, and she shuddered as she felt the slow invasion of his hand. The blood beat strongly in him as he lay her down on the grass.

"Don't be afraid, Janet, now we have come so far," he said. "I will be a gentle master, because it pleases me to do you such a tender service, and because it has always been our destiny to end as lovers. Be a good girl while I prime you, relax a little and let me love you, and then you will forget your fear and feel your own desire."

He watched her face, smiling his encouragement as his hand drew up her skirts and pushed between her thighs, searching for her; when he felt the sudden rise of her hips, his oppression of her seemed vindicated, and his need came hard upon him.

"Oh, my sweet maid," he breathed, gazing down on his conquest. "You cannot know how long I have waited for you." He mounted her, slid his arm around her so that she felt his weight on her, and her heart beat fast against his chest. "Come," he said gently. "Put your arms about me now, be just a little brave for me, and I will be the first man to wound you."

And then, with gentle restraint and quiet endearments, the Laird's son, her blood brother, completed his ownership of her and changed the destiny of Uishall. The truth was that he had been stalking her for two years, and that until today, when he had finally hunted her, she had been his willing prey, flirting with the fate she knew awaited her.

For Janet, it was a confused awakening from the innocence of the friendship they had formed when desire was not yet part of the equation.

Notes:
1: "*An ainm an aigh, nach gabh sibh truas rium*!": "Pity me in my wretchedness!" (approximate translation)

2.
SPAWNING GROUNDS
MAY 1820 – JUNE 1822

I
MAY 1820

Janet lay on her belly, at right angles to the bank, then cautiously slipped her arm off the overhanging heather and into the water. Such was the guile of the movement as her hand slid downwards that even the most nervous of fish would have failed to detect her.

James sat back from the opposite bank, watching intently. His daughter had the gift, there was no doubt about it. She could tickle the brown trout when she was six, and now at the ripe old age of twelve, she could poach a five-pound salmon with her patience and tenacity, and her strong, deft hands. Her red curly hair hung down around her face as she concentrated, unmoving, only her hand slipping through the water.

Her father had identified the lie a few years ago, and knew fish rested there on their way up to the spawning grounds. He could gaff them easily enough – if they were big enough – when the occasion demanded. But while he wouldn't waste his time on what his daughter was now attempting, he liked to watch the delicate method she had adopted as her own and elevated to artistic heights.

"*Air do shocair*,"[1] he whispered, encouraging her painstaking efforts. She raised her head briefly and mouthed "Sshh," to him, grinning at his nerves.

The peaty water flowed silkily between her fingers, cold and pure, the current slow. Her hand moved upstream, an inch at a time; the fish's nose would be pointing in the same direction if he was there; James had many times told her how the salmon swam thousands of miles across the ocean, returning every year to spawn in the same river. They did not feed once they left the sea, so you caught them by net, or took your chances with the hook, or tried this, most ambitious of all. Janet preferred testing her skills to using business-like approaches that yielded more

19

certain results. She had lost countless fish, not always because she was learning, but because this method only worked on salmon. She could not tail sea-trout, of which there were many in the Uishall, because there was no wrist between tail and body, and even with her firm grip, the fish would slither away to safety. Even though she knew this was a salmon lie, there was no guarantee that she would win the fish lurking beneath her hand.

"As well we don't depend on your efforts to fill our bellies this time of year," James often said affectionately, while his young daughter practised her techniques, and she would laugh because she knew he was proud of her.

Suddenly she tensed and her arm stilled. She inched her body forward a fraction, then plunged her hand deeper. There was a bright thrashing at the surface, Janet twisted her body upright and for a second, James saw the salmon held triumphantly in her hand, before she threw it onto the heather, safely away from the water.

He shouted out delightedly, jumped to his feet and leaped the stream. Janet lay on her back, laughing with excitement, then father and daughter crouched over the silver fish and studied him. James cast about for a rock, held the fish firmly under the gills and despatched him with a single blow.

"There now," he said softly. "Another fish that won't be gracing the Laird's table."

There was no malice in the remark. While others poached for necessity as well as spite, James took the fish they needed, but had no trouble enjoying the sport of the occasion as well. The river might technically belong to the Laird, but all of them lived on the land, the river was part of that land, and the fish were for everyone.

It was a sentiment in which the Laird, Willie Macleod, concurred. While Willie dealt harshly with poachers who netted fish in large numbers and went on to sell their plunder, he had never yet prosecuted a tenant who only sought his supper from the Uishall's rich stocks.

"Even though the fish are mine," he would say, "I can never lay claim to every one of them, so why not let my tenants, within reason, take a share?"

II

Not an hour since, and only a mile or so downriver, Alec Macleod, at eighteen still three years off official manhood, had caught a salmon of his own, on a fly of his own making and design – a splendid christening for his new rod, a fine piece made of greenheart, built in three sections with a whalebone tip. His line was woven silk, an infinitely superior material to the horsehair he had previously used. For the fly, he had used hair from his deerhounds, and rubbed it in the dirt before he cast it, so it seemed river-worn and natural. He cast across the river and down, jiggling his fly in the water to attract the fish by making it look like a sand eel. He gave this information freely to Uishall's factor, Jack Macaskill, a man not known for either his generosity or his fishing skills, who was trying his luck a hundred yards further up the river. Alec's fish had been a strong fighter, and he had netted it with Jack's help after wading into the water and bracing himself against a sturdily balanced rock.

The Uishall flowed through Alec's spirit as surely as Macleod blood ran in his veins. He loved the rhythm of the sporting year – the winter stalking with his beloved deerhounds at his side, the bracing moorland hikes when he would send his hawks swooping after the grouse, the contemplative power of the river as he fished for salmon, and the stillness of the lochs where he sought the wild brown trout. He understood the water, listened to its song, knew every twist and turn in the Uishall's length as it wound its way through the hills and through the string of lochs that ended in the spreading water at the base of Roineabhal, the eastern boundary of his family's land. He knew where the fish lay, better than any poacher.

"Well now," Macaskill's young master said, as he slid the fish into his bag. "I think a walk up to the wee loch yonder might improve your chances – they have been running early this year, and you might practise your stealth around the lower banks."

The factor acceded gruffly. He was more interested in policing the river than catching from it, but the young Macleod's enthusiasm was infectious and the proposed route would take him a good way upriver – he could kill two birds with one stone.

They had been walking only twenty minutes over the rough ground when Alec's attention was caught by a movement at the surface. He nodded to the spreading ripples.

"There's your chance," he said. "You fish here, and I'll walk on to the loch. Remember what I told you, and don't lose your nerve when he takes."

With Macaskill uneasily installed in a crease in the high, uneven bank, Alec set off alone, walking towards the crest of a shallow rise that would drop away towards his destination. He hoped for a half hour alone, away from the factor's jerky casting action, which was beginning to irritate him after the time he had spent trying to coach its perpetrator into mastering a smoother action. He suddenly caught the sound of laughter and automatically dropped down and crawled towards the crest of the hill, positioning himself behind a large rock.

He watched the scene before him with fascination. It took him a little while to recognise the two figures making free with the fish in his river, for they were a good distance away and he could not risk moving closer without detection. But he carefully pulled out his telescope and soon he spotted the bright red curls of young Janet Macleod, and identified the burly mound sitting opposite her as her father.

Alec knew his river was poached, but he had never once caught anyone in the act. Even now, when he was quite within his rights to jump to his feet, shout out and stride towards them with all the indignant fire of a wronged Laird, he held back, less outraged at the theft than he was intrigued with its execution. He dropped low into the heather again and, his body flat to the ground, began to move towards them. After fifty yards or so, he looked up cautiously and his forehead creased. He could see Janet lying with her head on the bank, and her father sitting upright across from her, leaning forward. What on earth were they doing? It was the most curious sight he had come across on the Uishall, and in the end he gave up conjecture and settled himself to watch.

When Janet tailed the fish, he had to stop himself from shouting out as James did, so acute was his surprise and pleasure at the skill she showed, and so admiring was he of the trick they played. His factor, grumpily fishing away downriver, had suspected James Macleod of poaching for years, but had never caught him with a fish. James's position as community leader would make him an especially attractive prize for Macaskill, who liked to expose the hypocrisy of men who spoke intelligent words and then undercut their high moral character with common thieving. Alec could afford to be more forgiving; after all, if his factor was lax on this count, he would be failing to do his job,

22

whereas Alec, at the top of the social pile, could always choose to emulate his father's tolerance.

He watched the girl swing her fish triumphantly onto the bank and saw her father make the kill. Somewhere between them, the fish disappeared. Alec would have gladly let them make good their escape, but at that moment he glanced behind him and saw that Macaskill had tired of trying for his salmon and was set to join him. He had already come over the rise and spotted the poachers, and was almost running in their direction, his whole body an eloquent expression of malicious glee.

Alec got quickly to his feet and hailed James.

"Ho, there!" he called, and began to walk towards them.

James looked up and immediately raised his arm in greeting.

Alec sighed. The Macleod tolerance to poaching was a difficult line to tread in such a situation – it was one thing turning a blind eye, another to ignore a blatant catch. He didn't want to take the punitive line, but the vindictive Jack Macaskill breathing down his neck compromised him. It was his duty to protect his water; it wouldn't do to show a weak response to tenants who might be subsequently tempted to abuse his leniency. But as he got closer, he saw Janet's wide, frightened eyes, a vivid contrast to the elation he had seen just minutes ago, and he remembered the admiration he had felt. Shopping her to the factor would be an act of pure hypocrisy, not to mention cruelty.

"Macleod," James said heartily, shaking his hand, left with no option but to play the innocent and hope the Laird's son had not seen his daughter's catch.

"A fine day for a stroll," Alec said, and smiled at Janet, who was now staring at him with such terror that he felt pity for this little thief, and cast about for a way to calm her.

"And for the fish," James said, bold as brass, nodding at the bulge in Alec's bag. "You've had success this morning?"

"Aye," Alec said, showing him the fine fish that lay inside.

"A beauty," James said admiringly. "You caught him on fly?"

Alec smiled again and proffered the fly still tied to the catgut leader. "This one has landed me three this week," he said. "It seems the more scraggity they are, the better they catch." He glanced down at the girl still standing close to her father, unable to tear her eyes away from the Laird's son.

"You'd like to see him?" Alec said kindly, and knelt down so she could peer in. As she leaned forward, the front of her skirt seemed to drop at an odd angle against the ground, and Alec saw a silver tail slip out from a concealed pocket. He coughed suddenly, afraid he would laugh. No wonder Jack had never caught James with a fish on him. He was the perfect decoy. Janet knew instantly what had happened, her face flushing as she looked pleadingly at the Laird's son. Their eyes met over the open fishing bag; Alec could almost hear the panicked beating of her heart.

"James Macleod!" came Jack Macaskill's harsh voice across the heather. "Not one step until you answer for yourself."

Alec, still kneeling on the ground, closed the bag, reached out and touched Janet's hand, still cold and damp from the water. "It's all right, little maid," he said softly. "You must be away off home now, for the factor is a gruff man who doesn't care for little girls playing by his river."

She stared at him, not understanding why he wasn't angry, or why he appeared to be letting her off. She knew he had seen the fish, and that even though the Laird was a kind man, stealing from the Uishall was a grave offence. She glanced anxiously up at her father.

"Your father is twice the size of the factor, and can easily take care of himself," Alec said. "I will speak for him."

Still she hesitated.

"Away with you!" Alec said again, his voice low and urgent. "Quick now, before there's trouble!"

She righted her skirt, the fish slipped back out of sight, and she took off in the direction of her home as Alec stood straight and looked at James, the barest of nods passing between them.

"Explain yourself!" Jack said breathlessly, arriving at last on the scene.

"I was walking out with my daughter," James said. "It's a pleasant day, is it not?"

"And where is she off to now?" the factor said.

"She was afraid of you and ran away to her mother," Alec said, shaking his head. "And no wonder. You used that big voice of yours, and she thought you were an ogre."

Jack blustered, but refused to be distracted. "This man I have long thought was stealing from the river," he said, pointing aggressively at James. "And now it seems I have caught him at last."

Alec looked thoughtfully at the accused man. "Well, James, what say you show us your pockets? If there's a fish on you, we'll have no choice but to say you are caught red-handed. But if you are clean, we must assume matters are as you said, and you were out walking, with no thought of thievery."

James, of course, could not produce a fish, but played along gamely, even though the factor threw down his rod and ran his hands through the man's clothing himself.

"There is no other reason for you to be out here!" he shouted angrily. "I will book you in any case, for being on the river with intent to poach."

"He has no gaff," Alec said quietly. "No rod, no tackle, and in all the length of water we have walked this morning, there has been no net. How would you expect him to rob the Uishall of its fish without means?" He glanced behind him, saw Janet running nimbly away and dropped his head to conceal a grin.

"Why did she leave so quickly?" Macaskill said suddenly. "What part did she play in this business?"

"She is nothing but a frightened little girl running from a man who thinks she has done wrong," Alec said, allowing a touch of lairdly impatience to show. "Look at her, Jack. How small and slight she is! Why, any fish in the Uishall is almost bigger than she is – how would she carry it?"

"It is bad enough that men and boys are poaching, without them corrupting their innocent daughters!" the factor cried in frustration.

"Come, we have some more fishing to do before noon, and James I'm sure must be off and about his business," Alec said, openly grinning now, and gathering up his rod. He shook James' hand again and watched him walk off, whistling cheerfully.

"You take your work too seriously, Jack," he said mildly, still unable to see anything other than entertainment in the incident.

They set off, the factor surly and grumbling, annoyed that Alec had interfered, and determined that his father should hear about it. The Laird's son walked on, looking often in the direction that Janet had taken, as if he hoped she might appear again.

JULY 1821

After that day, Alec found himself drawn more and more to the shrewd girl who had come close to outwitting him. He stopped by their blackhouse from time to time, busied himself with James, talking shop about livestock and fencing, the ongoing problems of drainage. Janet was always about and after an initial period of suspicion that he planned to use his knowledge against her, she began to relax and respond when he tried to draw her into conversation. She learned quickly that her company was welcome – sometimes she would interrupt when Alec and her father were debating some point of livestock care or the politics surrounding the changing use of the land, and the Laird's son could see that she had been listening to her father and had acquired his awareness of the times they lived in.

"I had not thought you a soft touch for young tenant daughters," his brother Ruaraidh, at seventeen two years Alec's junior, said drily one day. It was a year or so after the poaching incident; they had been out riding together and Alec had paused to chat to Janet, gathering wild raspberries some distance from the peat track that cut across the hills.

Alec threw him a sardonic smile. "Nor am I," he said as their horses paused to drink from a shallow lochan on a spreading patch of grassy moorland. "But she has a spark, a lively mind and –" He stopped for a moment, not having analysed her attraction for him before. "She has that feeling for the river and the fish that swim there, that I never saw before in a lass. That's what interests me."

"Her poaching talents fascinate you," Ruaraidh said with heavy irony, and raised his eyes. "And her charming looks have nothing to do with it, I suppose?" he went on. "She is young yet, but in a year or two, she will blossom, and then you will not care a salmon's scale whether or not she has empathy with the fishes, for you will think only of possessing her." He paused. "If you have not already," he said slyly.

"It is not our place to use daughters of the land so," Alec said sharply, and there was an edge to his voice, as if an uncomfortable thought had suddenly grazed it. He turned to his brother. "What about you – you are come recently to philandering

– do you go romping with the lassies on Uishall land whenever it suits you?"

Ruaraidh laughed. "I have somewhat higher standards," he said. "I don't need to forage on the moors when there are several maids at the castle I can summon to my bed if more aristocratic fare is wanting."

Alec looked at him with distaste. The older they got, the less they seemed to have in common, and the more Ruaraidh sought to magnify those differences. The war for the opposite sex, keenly fought in the spirit of sibling rivalry, was a comparatively recent point of contention.

They had been different as children, it was true, but it was their differences that had made them close. Alec, taking seriously his responsibility as elder sibling, was always bailing his brother out of scrapes, covering for him, appeasing his suspicious mother while he begged minor medical aid in the kitchen to cover up the tell-tale signs of troublemaking. Alec was always being pressed into games of physical strength and dares, when his brother took risks that often led to severe punishment from his father. The time he wedged himself in the dining room fireplace, and dislocated his shoulder in his desperate attempts to escape before the terrifying housekeeper discovered him; the time he fell into a bog and sank up to his chest before his frantic elder brother found a branch long enough to reach across to him and haul him to safety.

When their mother died, all Ruaraidh's high spirits were forged into anger, as he raged at the world for his loss. For months, Alec was caught between the grim despair of his father and the destructive fury of his younger brother, and had no time to assimilate the magnitude of her death for himself. Willie's response was to throw himself into training his sons for the management of the estate he would one day leave them. He was a hard task master, impressing on them with all his ferocious grieving energy the enormity of the task they faced as times changed, people didn't, and the land refused to co-operate in any healing economic strategy.

The gap began to open up between the brothers when Alec proved himself the better scholar, the better at grasping business matters. Now Ruaraidh's pranks and tomfoolery were less stories that could be recalled with humour a few days after Willie had erupted, and more likely to ignite fatherly exasperation. The gradual shift in Willie's affections became more marked, until the Laird quite clearly favoured Alec over Ruaraidh, and his younger son was left with only rebellion as an option if he was to be noticed. Ruaraidh, no dunce by any means, had his intelligence blunted at every turn by his inclination to idleness; he quickly worked out that the more diligent Alec would always outstrip him, and resolved to ride on the back of his brother's talents. A touch of negative competition began to creep into their relations. Alec was a good manager of resources; Ruaraidh would test him by spending the money. Alec was a good diplomat; Ruaraidh became skilled at creating climates of dissent, then watch Alec struggle to restore even tempers. In his younger days, he had admired his big brother's talents, used them and even loved him for them; now he sneered, and felt Alec's every success as increasing evidence of his own failure.

And now they were both exerting their ability to attract the opposite sex, it was Alec who succeeded with the women Ruaraidh wanted, Alec who flirted with a lightness of touch that eluded his earthy younger brother, so that he never wanted for pretty female companionship.

These days, Ruaraidh's native instinct for risk-taking was fixed firmly on women, and he played with them whenever he had the chance, chiefly to annoy his father. The more the better, he would declare loudly over after dinner port, already teaching himself the fundamentals of excess. Willie would have turned him out of the house had he known what went on behind Ruaraidh's bedroom door when the candles were snuffed and the rest of the household asleep.

Ruaraidh's teasing about his brother's interest in young Janet Macleod had touched a nerve. She was so different from the other young women he met, who were carefully versed in fashion and etiquette, and who, anxious to find favour, transparently feigned interest in his passion for the outdoors. Amongst these refined and limited creatures, Alec was expected to seek his future wife.

Janet, young, unsophisticated and not required to play courtly games, saw no need to be anything other than honest with him. He was keenly aware of the gap between them, the breach of good conduct he risked by associating with her; yet her company pleased him; she listened to his stories about the river and wanted to know what it felt like to hook a salmon on a line and play it. She was bold, too, made him laugh out loud one day when she confessed how she had poached her salmon, and then tried to teach him the method. He had lost his temper, gone into a lairdly pet when he could not match her, but in the end had gone home laughing, with his shirtsleeve soaked, his hand numb, and her gleeful contempt for his lack of skill ringing in his ears.

Until his brother brought it up, he had not acknowledged that yes, he already desired her; and yes, he knew that she was beginning to want him, too. Once he understood the physical draw between them there was no escaping it, and instead of staying away from her as good sense demanded, he found himself moving closer, seeking deeper levels of intimacy and trust.

IV
JUNE 1822

When Janet was fourteen and Alec twenty, he came to the blackhouse one summer evening and asked James if he might borrow his daughter for an hour or two. With his permission, and his fatherly presence as etiquette demanded, the Laird's son announced he had a fishing trip in mind and would like to see her try her hand at some legitimate sport. James, busy with church matters, hesitated over giving his permission. He could see, albeit with kinder eyes than Ruaraidh, the way his daughter sparked the interest of the Laird's eldest son, and the pride she felt in the special attention he paid her. It was a potentially dangerous combination. James did not have power over the Laird's son, but in the end, he decided to trust in his strong sense of honour and propriety.

Her curiosity equalled only by her delight that the Laird's son should seek her out for a special excursion, Janet walked with him to the river and was dumbstruck when he solemnly presented her with a fishing rod.

"Spare me a surfeit of gratitude," he said quickly, "for it is not new. It is the rod I used as a lad when I was learning, and when it broke, I had no need to repair it. I have taken off some length as you are but little, and fitted it just so –" He broke off, embarrassed as she turned his gift in her hands.

"But I am not allowed to fish –"

"You may fish for trout in the lochs as your birth right dictates," Alec said. "And as you are with me at the moment, you may try for a fish while you learn the way of it."

She gazed at him for a moment, then their awkwardness vanished as her face broke into a grin of pure delight. She said,

"Show me," at the moment he said, "Come," and within a few minutes, they were standing together on the riverbank and Alec had begun to instruct her.

"And whose fish will it be should I land one?" she asked him, with consummate cheek, when she had flicked her fly somewhat clumsily into the river and was concentrating on the flow of water near the line.

The world that lay between them was in her question, and Alec had to think for a moment how he should answer.

"What say I take the fish, which would make things right and proper, and you take the credit?"

She didn't look too impressed by his offer, and said nothing while she cast out again. "But I am your guest," she said slyly, not looking him in the eye. "Would you rob a castle guest of his fish because it is the Macleods' river? I am a Macleod also, so does that not give me the superior claim?"

"A clever line to take," Alec said, laughing, but in truth a little flustered, as he always was when the issue of class came up between them. "Now cast again and we will see if you are quite as smart with a fishing line."

This time, pleased at how she had rattled him, she was over-confident, and not paying due attention.

"No, no," Alec chided her as the line landed on the water with an undignified slap. He could not conceal his annoyance, for his respect for technique meant that anything less than perfection was apt to offend him. "You threw the rod too far behind you. Here –"

He put his hand over hers, stood behind her and took control of the cast. "You feel the difference, young maid? Come, I have seen your subtle ways with the fish – this rod and line caper should not be beyond you. Too far, and the end goes quite out of control; not far enough and you might as well be throwing a bucket at your fish and dragging for him. It is just so: not too far, yet far enough."

She was vexed that he had had to correct her, and she said nothing for a while as she nursed her wounded pride and accepted his tuition with a certain grim resignation, though the rod was heavy for her arm and she tired after half an hour or so.

"Here," Alec said at last. "You have done very well. Sit and rest, and let me cast a few lines. Study closely, then you may try again a little later."

She watched intently. More than anything, she wanted to hook a fish with the Laird's son's rod, in his sight. She saw the way he concentrated, the relaxed, easy lie of the rod in his hand and the lazy curl of the line as it uncoiled itself over the water.

He fished, aware of his pupil's frustration as well as his own unfair impatience with her, wanting her to catch as much as she did. With his fifth or sixth cast, he felt a sly take from deep in the water, a pull so subtle that for a moment he thought he was mistaken. He was about to alert her to the quiet drama playing out beneath the black glassy surface, but changed his mind.

"Janet," he said. "Come, I have made a reasonable cast here, but the line is snagged. Will you take the rod while I find my knife to cut it?"

She jumped up and seized the rod while he wandered off a little, making a show of hunting through his pockets.

For a moment she looked uncertain. "Should I try – oh!"

"What? Has it come free?" Alec asked.

Her face was suddenly tense with excitement. "No. I felt something –"

"It's probably caught on the bottom," Alec said with a shrug, and turned away to hide his smile.

The rod moved violently in her hand; she almost dropped it. Alec bounded to her side.

"You have a fish!" he said with appropriate surprise and pleasure. "Now, then, keep calm. He's firmly on, and you must play him to the net."

She hauled the rod backwards.

"No, *no*, do the opposite," Alec said, as tense as she was. "Pay out some line, or he will snap you – quickly now, he is eager to be off and you will end up in there with him if you don't give him a little of what he wants."

She had forgotten her tiredness now; nevertheless, the fish tested her, and when her arm began to ache, Alec held the rod with her, controlled the line through the little brass winch that served as a reel, and they worked together to subdue the fish.

"You feel the pull?" he cried to his young companion. "He is a strong one, there is no doubt."

Eventually, the fish tired and, with Alec's guidance, Janet began to reel him in.

"Draw him towards the net slowly," Alec said, up to his knees in the water, the net sunk beneath the surface. ""Not too fast, or you will panic him. Now – lift the rod – higher – higher!"

She was too small to give him the elevation necessary, but he stepped forward instead, passed the net under the fish and lifted it quickly. With her catch secure, she promptly dropped the rod and scrambled down the bank to join him.

"Well done!" he said, looking at her, her face flushed with pride. "He is about four pounds – a handsome young grilse, and you have earned every ounce of him."

"I couldn't have landed him without you," she said.

"Or the rod," the Laird's son said, laughing. He laid the fish on the bank and pulled out the small wooden club he used for his priest. "Janet – would you like to make the kill?"

She shook her head, then changed her mind and nodded.

He was impressed with her fortitude, for the few lady fishers he had encountered had always passed the responsibility of the kill to a ghillie. He looked at her serious expression as she seized another chance to make an impact on him.

"Come," he said gently. "You are strong enough to deal the blow. The faster the better, for he has fought well and should not suffer any longer. Strike him here, hard above the eyes, and he will find his lie in fishy heaven, if such a place exists. I will hold him, if you will mind your aim and avoid my fingers."

She took the priest from him, took a firm grip and neatly despatched the fish. Both of them were silent for a moment.

"Well, there is a fisherman's tale for you to tell when you get home," Alec said. "And I think it is time to quit now – we have had our fair share of excitement for one evening."

He saw her safely home, gave her the fish, and set off for the castle. As he rode, he thought critically about the evening, Janet's progress with the rod, his own deficiencies as a tutor.

As he undressed for bed, what he remembered was his hand on hers as the rod strained beneath their grip, and the way her feelings had mirrored his own throughout the contest for the fish. He had told the tale to his father, described the incident with some animation and in the greatest detail. But what he remembered was the warmth of his hand wrapped over hers, and she was too young, and too poor, and he did not understand what he felt, and ignored the instinct that told him he should spend time working it out.

Notes
1: *Air do shocair:* go gently

3.
CATCH AND RELEASE
AUGUST 1823

I

She had always been flattered that the Laird's eldest son had taken such a fancy for her. In turn, he was curious about this girl who seemed so capable and self-contained, who played her full part in the managing of the family resources. An understanding grew between them, despite their differences, despite the guarded glances of family members on both sides.

Even before the poaching incident, he had always had a kind word for her, sometimes even a sugared almond or a small square of tablet. He taught her phrases in English, delighting to hear her struggle with the unfamiliar sounds, and then sharing her pride as she mastered them. Sometimes he even consulted her on some minor point of animal husbandry, for her gift for nursing and handling animals was well known. When one of his deerhound bitches whelped, he brought a puppy to show her, and was impressed at the gentleness with which she handled it, and how contentedly it seemed to lie in her hand. At first, her brothers had teased her, saying she should spare her shyly provocative glances for more fitting suitors – ones who shared her lowly rank for starters, ones who would be less likely to take advantage of her.

In all this, Alec was simply following family tradition. The Macleods were not as aloof as many landowners in the islands; they took an interest in their tenants and didn't always mediate through the factor. They had kept the old tongue alive in the castle, alongside the French spoken there when it was in fashion, and now hand in hand with English, which anyone going to work there had to learn.

But in the last few years Alec had taken a more personal interest in Janet's family, and it was not difficult to work out that the daughter of the blackhouse was the magnet that drew him.

As she grew older, her brothers became more protective and sometimes sent her away up the rigs[2] when the Laird's son approached, suspicious of his increasingly kind attentions.

Her mother, Rhona, became increasingly concerned at the pleasure her daughter took in attracting the Laird's son's eye, and in her anxiety to prevent a disastrous situation, she made the mistake of laying down the law to her headstrong daughter. Could she not see the danger she courted? Bad enough that he should like her and make no secret of it – worse that she should understand the charm she had, and work it on him.

With her obstinacy steadfastly glued to her youthful naivety, Janet disobeyed her, resentful of being thwarted in her desire to receive the Laird's son's gifts and compliments. Whenever she was sent away, she would creep into the byre and watch him talking with her father, and she noticed the way his eyes constantly flicked around, as if he was looking for someone.

James did not bear Alec the same dislike as his wife, although he had noticed the fondness his daughter seemed to have for him, and warned her to be careful. A man who had taken the opportunity to educate himself by means of access to a bible and occasional newspapers, James Macleod was a thoughtful man, a lay preacher and something of a spokesman for the families who occupied the neighbouring blackhouses. He had come to the conclusion that it was better to discuss problems and seek diplomatic solutions with the Laird who governed them, rather than resort automatically to insults and violence. In this, he was constantly at odds with his wife and sons, who had absorbed all the despair and hatred from the people around them and were steeped in the grim cultural history that was their legacy. They refused to believe there could ever be equal ground between Laird and tenant, and preferred nurturing their hatred to fostering tolerance. Yet in Willie, and his heir Alec, James had found people who were at least prepared to listen to grievance, if they did not always agree to act.

In their long rambles over the moorland when Janet and her father worked together to snare rabbits or poach fish from the Uishall, James talked to his daughter about the harsh realities of life and the need to find contentment within them, as the bible advised. Then, he said, one did not always live with bitterness and struggle, which steadily poisoned all efforts to live a worthwhile life. Some people were born into wealth, he said, but most were not; neither wealth nor poverty was guarantee of either a pleasant or a wretched existence – that responsibility lay with the liver of the life given, and what he or she chose to make of it. Janet had fused this aspiration to social tolerance with an acceptance of the Laird's son's superior standing, but it was an abstract concept; she didn't have the sophistication to apply it to the unspoken attraction that was steadily developing between them.

II

She didn't know what had finally made her run from him this morning, the first time that he spotted her eavesdropping in the shadows of the byre, and came for her. She had turned from the tiny, cobwebby window set deep in the stone wall to find him watching her. In that moment, the Laird's son, who was equally frustrated by the clumsy tactics that had been increasingly deployed to keep them apart, simply recognised his opportunity.

This first stage in their courtship was fairly lengthy, for the byre was dark and not likely to be disturbed by visitors at this hour. Her mother was in the blackhouse, mistaken in her confidence that Janet was busy gathering eggs, and her father and brothers had set off to help a neighbour with his livestock. Alec smiled and raised his finger to his lips, and her stillness was complete and wondering as he came towards her. She felt the first tug of an unfamiliar tension that seemed to pull downwards from her gut and charge her body with a fierce and irresistible hunger.

A kind of sensory commotion jangled through her as he gently took her hand. She understood that he intended to step over the boundary of propriety, and that when he did so, the tenor of their unlikely friendship would be altered; but her hand stayed in his, a tacit expression of consent. There was also the tiniest hint of obligation – he was the Laird's son, after all, he was not necessarily *asking* her, and perhaps she had better not cross him; then again, at this stage she did not particularly want to. Besides, she wanted to enjoy her moment of triumph as she outwitted her mother and punished her negligence. She sensed she was approaching the risky situation her mother was so anxious she should avoid, but the insistent din inside made her deaf to any warning signals.

When his lips touched the back of her hand, her stillness seemed to intensify, as if it had been only skin-deep before and had now penetrated to her centre. He turned it over and kissed her palm, opening his mouth a little so that his tongue touched it; she had never felt anything before that was so tender but so piercing, and it sent a shock-wave trembling through her. She was aware of her body, trapped and restless under her clothes.

He saw the tumult his kiss had begun, felt the deep tremor hinting at the seismic explosion to come; and he saw that she would not stop him now, not yet.

He drew her towards him, sensitive to the fact that she had not been touched like this before. He knew how alarming it could be for maids to suddenly find themselves thrust into a ferocious wrestling bout with a selfishly eager lad – all wet, sliding mouths and groping hands, brute force on the one hand and violent repulsion on the other. The Laird's son was disdainful of such coarse displays of animal lust. He did not want to frighten her; he wanted her to yield willingly and enjoy herself. So he introduced her slowly to his dry, soft kisses, dropping them like tiny flowers on her eyes and cheeks, her forehead and at last, her mouth. He did not rush her, did not touch except to hold her to him or caress her face. Soon she closed her eyes.

By and by, when her mouth began to open against his, the tip of his tongue stroked against hers. At once he felt the change in her, the sharp stab of escalating arousal, and she gripped him tighter and made her first sigh. From then on, he struggled to keep his kisses sensual and leisurely as she came vividly to life in his arms. Since she had fairly succumbed by this stage, he thought then that he would lift her and carry her in amongst the hay bales and there play gently with her and make love to her, covering her mouth with his hand if the giving up of her hymen should prove painful.

At that moment, they were both caught up in the same compulsion, to at last give expression to the powerful attraction that had always been between them. For his part, he took delight in the fervour of her girlish embraces, as she sought his mouth and the pleasures it gave. For hers, she could not even think of the complications that might arise from such a liaison. The kissing she liked fine; she liked the way he held her, so that when she was weak from the devastating thrills that ran all through her, his body hardened with the strain of keeping her pressed close against him. Janet expected the game to start and end with kissing, and the clamour boiling up inside her to abate.

But when the kissing did stop, she opened her eyes to find him looking at her flushed face with an intense, peculiar expression she had not seen before. She heard his quickened

36

breathing and her own, and she woke up with a shock as his hand settled gently on the cleft between her breasts. There was a heady beating in her body, and in the dark shine of his eyes she saw something she couldn't translate. Suddenly she remembered who he was, saw where all their flirting had been leading, the gulf they had just leaped and the wider one that still separated them. She was trembling from head to foot, but she wasn't ready yet to still the need that she had let loose in him, that he had let loose in her.

She jerked back. He was not quick enough, or he would have caught her there and then. Instead he paused, trying to give her time, and her protective training, her instinct for maidenly preservation, kicked in. Her fear overtook everything – belatedly it came, and seemingly all the stronger for its tardiness, crashing clumsily up against the frenzied desires still shouting inside her. It wrong-footed him, temporarily froze him to the spot, so addled was he by building desires at that point. He cursed his complacency as she broke away and ran from him, and then he took up the pursuit, aware of nothing but the determination that she must and would bend to his will when he finally caught up with her.

She didn't know anything. She simply ran.

Now, time had caught up with both of them. He had conquered her rebellion and as they lay together on top of the knoll, Janet understood that her actions, and the signals she had given out, had contributed to her fate.

III

All that morning, Janet lay with the Laird's son.

The first time he covered her, she strained against him, her small, strong hands gripping his wrists while he tried to open her. He soothed her, continually assured her that her patient forbearance pleased him greatly, that she had nothing to fear when they were so sweetly engaged in the business of love. It was foreign to her, his movement inside her, his body pressed against hers, his sweat between them. He was firm when he breached her maidenly defences, did not desist when she begged him, and could not stifle a groan when he broke through. His harsh breathing, the broken phrases he gasped out, only scared her more as he disappeared into an intense rapture that

37

excluded her even as it overwhelmed him; his release came swift and hard after such lengthy repression, so that she cried out with the force of it.

But once the first storm of his lust was over, he comforted her so kindly and spoke to her so gently, that she began to lose her fear and confusion, and accept the new step they had taken. Their intimacy began to feel less alien, and she began to touch her own desire as he had promised. Under his skilful handling she became aware of the heat of his skin against hers, the ebb and flow of her body under his hand; the lithe invention of his tongue, the pull and yield of his mouth as he taught her the rhythms of passion and tenderness. She began to return his embraces, to respond to his kisses and stroking, and then she found him looking at her with an odd, painful expression, as if he had caught himself out in a situation he did not expect.

Once, just once as he entered her, he looked on her with tender eyes and whispered, "*A' ghraidh*."[1] For a moment, she felt as if she had been broken open a second time and she fought the feelings that began in her. But his movements released an ungovernable ecstasy that rose up and flooded through her, sweeping all before it. A sound she had not made before broke from her mouth. He heard it, understood it, her little fist clenched against his back. He held her tightly, the pulse of her flesh around his so strong that for a few moments their separate ecstasies dissolved into each other and joined them. He whispered that it was only her body speaking the love she felt for him, as his had spoken to her, and she stopped fighting and gave herself up to him.

He did not think about the consequences of what he had done until the end of it, when she was spent and sore and bloody from his attentions, and the deep, soporific pleasure of aftermath began to recede. His manner changed as his conscience began to worm between them, and he hastily tried to recover an appropriate measure of distance. She did not understand why suddenly, he was behaving as if he had not spoken loving words to her at all, as if she had not, for a time, been made his equal by the endearments he had vouchsafed to her and the passion they had shared.

In a ludicrous parody of lairdly manners, he apologised for the first painful thrusts of his sword; but it was unavoidable, the first time a maid received love's wounding. He told her how

38

sweetly she had loved him, and how he had been moved by the pleasure she had taken in his embraces. So far, so good. But then it seemed there had been a practical purpose to his lovemaking. She was now well seasoned, he said, and thanks to his turning of her virgin soil, any attentions she received from lovers in the future would be more pleasurable. She gazed at him in confusion. He had persuaded her to yield; he had made love to her and encouraged her to love him in return; his tenderness and her eventual reciprocation had cemented the affection between them. What need had she for other lovers now?

Her bewilderment intensified when he seemed to double back, and confessed that he had watched her grow into a young woman of rough but tender beauty, and vowed that he would be the first man to claim her. He had suspected for some time that she shared those passionate feelings, and this morning she had given him, she had to admit it, a fair degree of encouragement. Her reluctance to yield had honestly confounded him after all her teasing smiles and the warmth of her kisses such a short time before.

Satisfied that he had supplied enough justification for the way he had used her, he tilted her chin and kissed her, seeking some sort of reaction to his revelation. Did that not surprise and flatter her, that such a noble man should favour such a lowly maiden with such ardent desires?

"Tell me, *mo nighean bheag,*" he coaxed her, "did I truly misread the spark of love I thought I saw dancing in those soft brown eyes?"

She turned her face away and would not answer. If there had been a world of difference between them before, there was unutterable chaos forming in the aftermath of their lovemaking.

She was reduced to crying again and he sighed at last and gave up his attempts at pleasant conversation. He truly had not wanted it to be like this, he said in his uncomfortable lairdly way; perhaps it would be best if they parted now and went their separate ways homewards.

In the course of the morning, the raw, stabbing ache in her ankle had subsided to a dull background hum, subdued by all the other sensations that had been heaped upon her. When at last he tried to lift her to her feet, she cried out and fell back onto the grass, for she had quite forgotten the injury, and had jarred it badly. Her face went white and a cold sweat started out on her forehead. It was then that he discovered the damaged ankle, and he scolded her for not drawing it to his attention sooner. He realised that half the reason for her initial wild rejection of him had been pain, not merely the frantic language of threatened modesty, and he was chastened. In his lust, he had not marked her wounds, and only now did he remember seeing the fall that had caused them before he brought her down.

He abruptly dropped his talk of physical pleasures and transformed into a solicitous Laird coming to the aid of an injured tenant, if Janet could forget that he had been the cause of all her hurting in the first place. Her ankle was black and swollen now, with an ugly red weal to the side, and she could not bear him to touch it; nevertheless, he insisted she must submit, for her own sake; he soaked a handkerchief in a nearby burn and used it to bind the injury. He cleaned a deep cut below her knee, went to some trouble to find a fresh cobweb to stem the bleeding. In the course of his search, he came upon the purse she had flung into the grass, and automatically retrieved it. She looked at him; the purse seemed to lie heavy in his hand as if it was a lump of lead between them, something neither of them wanted to carry. He hesitated, then pressed it into her hand.

"This is for you, Janet, only this time offered in the proper spirit of kindness. Take it, I beg you, and forgive me my temper before; there is no disdain implied."

She gazed at him, her pride battling with the myriad complications of necessity; nothing else he could have done would have articulated the space between them so effectively. After a moment, her fingers closed around his complicated gift and he nodded and looked away.

He was grateful, then, to be able to apply himself again to the practical problems affecting them; he dressed her with consideration, helped her carefully to her feet and supported her as they made their way back across the moorland the pair of them had galloped so energetically a few hours before. When she fainted against him from the dull, nauseating ache that shot through her leg every time she caught it on the heather, he lifted her into his arms and carried her down the last stretch of the hill.

Afterwards, she would remember being cradled against him as he strode along, the throb of his body like a sustaining pulse, a hypnotic obligato to the insistent rhythm of pain beating through her. She wondered at how safe she felt, as if he harboured both devil and angel inside him and she had met first one, and then the other. It was as if he had come upon her, broken and bleeding in the heather, and rescued her from someone else.

Rhona was at home, fretting over the disappearance of her daughter, the Laird's son's horse still tethered nearby, and the implications of the two facts placed together. Her mood switched to angry astonishment as Alec Macleod entered the blackhouse uninvited, stooping to get through the low doorway and calling out into the smoky gloom, temporarily blinded after leaving the bright sunlight outside.

"Help here, and quickly," he said, and she heard at once the agitation in his voice. "Janet is injured."

For a moment, Rhona was rooted to the spot as she stared at the figure lying limp in his arms. "*Seonaid? A' Dhia! De a thachair dhut?*"[3]

"She has taken a bad fall," he said curtly. "That will do for explanations now – fetch some fresh straw and lay it by the fire. And we will need cold water for this swelling, and a splint. I fear her ankle is broken and she might take infection."

Rhona brought hay and watched dumbfounded as the Laird's son laid Janet down and pulled her skirts delicately away, showing the wound. The movement brought her round with a low moan, and she stared at Alec with blank eyes, not recognising him. Rhona gasped, knelt beside him, then saw bloodstains higher up her daughter's leg.

"What else?" she said, aghast. "What have you done?"

"I did nothing that was not agreed between us," Alec said sharply. He met her eyes and saw that he must acknowledge her outrage, that his lairdly bluster had not deflected her focus on the ruination of her daughter. He sighed impatiently. "Her maidenhead is breached, I'll not deny it; but that she will survive. This break is more deserving of our care. Now fetch the things I asked for. She is already showing signs of fever."

He turned to Janet and briefly stroked her forehead, his voice softening. "Young maid, you must be yet braver than you have been up till now, for I must hurt you further if we are to put things right."

Rhona returned, and again found herself taking directions from the Laird's son as he bathed and better dressed the injury before setting it with the splint, which half-maddened his patient and caused her to faint again. He was a surprisingly capable physician and a tender nurse; he was also decidedly autocratic with his assistant and refused to let her touch any of Janet's injuries, judging himself to be the better qualified to handle them.

He refused to leave until Janet regained consciousness, but as soon as she did, he regretted his medical diligence, for she clutched his hand and begged him stay beside her with such piteous distress that he was thoroughly disconcerted.

"Janet, it is best I go," he said firmly. "I have done what I can, and your mother is more than capable of nursing you from here." He chafed her fingers, hot and dry with fever. "Lie quietly and rest, for my sake if that is what it takes. Don't cry now, Janet, *mo nighean bheag*, for this distress will only make the pain more sharp."

Rhona was incredulous. "How can you speak so to her, and put on such concern, when your cruel deeds are at the root of all her grief?"

"I did not mean her to be hurt," Alec said, and turned indignant eyes to her. "Don't raise your voice above her bed, it will only make things worse."

"It could not be worse if you had killed her," Rhona said angrily, watching with revulsion as Janet clung to him. "You've toyed with her for years, and put all kinds of stupid fancies in her head. Now this is the result. There's not a young man on this land that she will so much as look to for her future, thanks to your selfish flirtations and gifts. What good did you think would come of this, when you had only lustful thoughts, and made her think she might have turned your head?"

He struggled to find the authority to silence her but found he could not speak, his attention torn between raving daughter and ranting mother and his own confused thoughts impossible to hear between them. Fortunately for Rhona, he did not pay much heed to the abuse she heaped on him, because Janet's weeping had unnerved him and he could not find a way to quiet her.

"You cannot give her what she wants, and now thinks she half has," Rhona was saying violently. "So get out now, before you do more damage. You have broken her heart, foolish young maid that she is, and the lust you paraded for her as true affection may have ruined her."

In the wake of her mother's tirade, Janet became calmer, and Alec began to reassert the rightful authority that had deserted him. Satisfied she wasn't going to die on him and further muddy his already soiled reputation, he relinquished her hand and prepared to go his way. Now that her suffering was less intrusive on his over-stretched sensibilities, he recovered something of his superior standing and remembered what was right and proper for his tenants to say to him.

He was brusque with Rhona's accusations of rape as he made his way out, saying shortly that his mistress had been willing enough once he had named his price. The tag of rapist was an insult to a gentleman of his rank, he said with angry stiffness, and even though he had paid in gold for his pleasure, he would never stoop so low as to call her daughter a prostitute. He left on his dignity, and would not admit to himself afterwards how frequently he was haunted by the sight of Janet lying wounded on her bed of straw, begging him to stay.

Notes:
1: *A' ghraidh*: love, or my love
2: rigs: strips of land cultivated by peasant tenants before the formation of crofts.
3: "*Seonaid? A' Dhia! De a thachair dhut*?": "Janet? Oh God! What's happened to you?"

4.
NATIVE SPECIES
NOVEMBER 1823

I

Alec Macleod arrived too late to undo the actions of the factor. Jack Macaskill had already cut down the eldest son of the house and was now threatening to toss firebrands into the interior of the cottage to drive home the point that it would be futile to argue with his demands. The family, traumatised and resentful, had by now thrown most of their possessions onto a rickety cart, but was now pitched into the messy business of trying to administer rudimentary aid for a shallow swipe of the sword across the body.

Alec surveyed the undignified scene with grim tension. Of all the families on Uishall land, he had not wanted to make an already painful situation worse for this one. He knew that just as the head of the household was a reasonable man, so his sons were bound to cause him trouble, but he had not wanted to provoke violence with a show of clumsy force in the wake of already insensitive politics. This point he had stressed more than once to the man charged with carrying out the difficult business of eviction, and the breach of trust had clearly angered him.

"Is it not possible for you to discharge your duty under the orders I give you?" he said to Macaskill with dangerous quietude.

Both men had got down from their horses and were now facing the other two sons, while Rhona ran around fetching water and rags to tend the wounded party.

"Where is your father?" Alec asked them. "It should have been up to him to knock some sense into those thick heads, and not left to the factor."

"There are six sheep stuck fast in the bog over the way," Rhona said. "We can't afford to lose them."

Alec shook his head, partly in annoyance, partly in an attempt to diffuse the rising tempers of the two brothers still standing before him. "Further dispute will not help your brother now," he said to them. "And I would not fancy your chances, besides, if Mr Macaskill here is still of a mind to swing his blade at anyone else foolish enough to cross him."

"I had no choice," the factor protested, who looked fairly shaken by events the Laird's son had not seen. "He swung his axe at me. He has been on the whisky and thought to make a stand against me. He would have killed me had I not struck back."

Alec knelt down by the injured man, who lay groaning, whether from pain or drunkenness he could not tell. Impatience began to win out against any finer feelings, a wish to see an unpleasant task got over with, one way or another.

"Will he live? It looks more than likely that he will. It does not seem a serious wound to me."

"He is more shocked than injured," the factor said, still ruffled.

"Calum," Alec said loudly, breaking through the muttered curses and grumbling from the ground. "Listen to me. There's nothing wrong with you that can't be fixed by a day or two's rest, and a bit of contemplation to make clear within that fuddled head of yours the situation you are in. Your father has talked to you often enough, if you will not take it from me. You've brought it on yourself, for you had warning aplenty that this day would come, and all the time in the world to make arrangements."

"I swore I would fight to hold the land my family has worked these past three hundred years," Calum gasped. "It is my right to work the land that I was raised on, in the belief that it was mine."

Alec shook his head. "The scrap of Uishall your family worked never belonged to you, despite your proud claims," he said with exasperated amusement. "And whatever passion you feel for it, you never had the money, so it was no more yours than it will be the sheep's when they come to graze on it after you've gone. So nothing lost on your side but ancient pride and wrongheaded notions of ownership and rights. Ask your father some time about the history of the matter. Your emotive ties are better loosened now than tightened."

"I will not give it up," Calum groaned. "I will not cease to fight."

"Then you will die a broken man, worn out by struggle for what you cannot have." Alec put out his arm and hauled him up. "Come, get to your feet and face the facts. I am truly sorry for the notice I have had to serve. I have no quarrel with your family – we are all Macleods. It is all about whatever it takes to make the land pay. That's economics for you. The sheep will pay me better than people do; it's as simple as that, and no malice in it."

Calum staggered, and was led away by his brothers towards the blackhouse. Alec lost interest, but looked fretful. Clearing his father's land was proving more difficult than he had foreseen, and it stretched his even temper more than he cared to admit.

Willie had set the process in motion. It had not been an easy decision for him to make; it flew in the face of the interest he had always taken in the people on his land, but he had been backed into a corner by the harsh realities of trying to make a living from Uishall's wild terrain. Willie was co-founder, along with Alec's maternal grandfather, of the small and lucrative distillery and liquor merchant business on the outskirts of town. The distillery was expanding and while there would never be a shortage of customers, Willie still felt he was failing to exploit the huge resource that lay all around him; whatever profits accrued from the whisky business, they were always eroded in part by the much smaller income generated from the vast Uishall acreage, and this bald fact of life always rankled with him.

Willie was keenly aware of the turning world and the need to shed parochialism if the Clan was to prosper. Raised as a Gaelic speaker, he had learned English to facilitate the growth of his business interests, but insisted on keeping the old island tongue alive in his home; in consequence, both Alec and Ruaraidh had been raised bilingually. It seemed everyone, not just the Macleods, lived with the tensions of trying to make the old work with the new.

But although Willie loved tradition, he was not enslaved by it, and this seam of independence had always made him no one's man but his own. On the question of the land, his conclusion was that if his finances were suffering, the people had never done particularly well out of it, either – setting them free to make their own way might yield better results on both sides. Alec was not convinced, and suspected his father of philanthropic sophistry brought on by a moribund land economy; even so, he knew it would be pointless to dispute the point now the decision had been made. It was said on the island that once Willie Macleod had made up his mind about something, the rocks would crumble and the seas dry up before he would change it.

Alec looked around in the restless way he always had in this place and saw Rhona, her face tight with strain, her hands full of rags, hurrying towards the blackhouse.

"Things should not have taken such a course," he said to her. She stared grimly back at him. "I am sorry for your son's injury and will deal with the factor accordingly. But I was not to know that silver-tongued husband of yours would be wanting." He nodded in the direction of the hills, where the men were returning with a small band of draggled sheep.

"All saved?" he called to James, whose burly figure headed up the group.

"But one," James said tersely. He came down the hill and looked at his wife.

"There has been trouble?"

"Aye. Calum lies wounded in the blackhouse. The factor cut him down."

"It is not a serious wound," Alec said quickly. "Jack was provoked and admits he acted rashly."

James shook his head. "It is hard for them to take," he said heavily. "It is hard for all of us."

"I have tried to do the best I can," Alec said.

"You have done your best to mind the things you own," Rhona said, "until you saw it fit to throw us all away."

"It's a new beginning for us all," Alec said. "None of us can be certain what the future has in store."

James looked steadily at him. There was something in his eyes Alec had not seen before, a distance not usually kept between them. He was used to awkward silences between him and many other tenants, but not this one. Alec did not like the sudden implication that he had betrayed this man in some way of which he was unaware.

"The future seems pretty set, sir, from where we stand," Rhona was saying angrily.

Alec shrugged. "You are off to Eilaster, where you will be your own mistress," he said, distracted momentarily from the tension he had picked up in James. "You have no further need of the Macleods now you are free from Uishall."

She laughed bitterly. "Aye, free to pick and scrape the rough, poor land you've put at our disposal, to make us poorer than we have been thus far."

"I offered to book passage to America," he said, affronted. "It was your choice to stay with the poor land and old ways, when you might have taken a bit of a chance on a new future."

Rhona shook her head. "A pretty argument, indeed. But there's no pleasure in making choices when all the options laid before you are what another man wants."

"And there's no future in standing about discussing what might and might not be," James interrupted her, still looking at Alec. "You are right, we have set our course, and must move along it. And you have set another's course, for which you should be held accountable."

Alec stared at him, the oblique accusation confusing him.

"James," he said. "I have always depended on the straightforward discourse between us. Will you not grant me that honesty in our last conversation on Uishall ground?"

James sighed. "It is Macleod whisky that feeds the foolishness of my sons," he said with a nod towards the blackhouse, "and you have brewed other trouble with my daughter that sets us further at odds. No use to talk of honesty when your lust has made you a thief of virtue. You took from her what was not offered to you, and it's certain that now you will not accept what she is obliged to offer you in consequence. You have shamed her and your family with such conduct, and broken the trust we held between us." He turned abruptly and set off in the direction of the blackhouse, where his sons waited for him.

Alec stared after him, the shock thudding through him, as James disappeared. He turned to Rhona.

"Where is Janet?" he asked, his voice low.

"You've done enough without adding to the burden she already carries," Rhona said bitterly. "She is resting before we make the journey. It's better you don't disturb her."

He immediately strode behind the blackhouse to the low wooden door of the byre and pushed it open. Janet lay on a mound of straw, fast asleep, quite unaware of what had been happening outside. It was a full four months since he had lain with her in the heather, but it seemed as if no time at all had passed since then. As he moved towards her, he saw the small swell of her belly and something turned in him as she opened her eyes.

She started and tried to sit up, but he stopped her.

"Stay, stay," he said. "You are with child?"

"I am with *your* child," she corrected him sharply. "But since we leave your land this morning, it's no concern of yours that I carry it."

He grimaced. "You've grown up, Janet, since you became a woman."

"What is your business here?" she asked. "You did not come on account of me."

His face set as he swallowed the insult. "I came to see that all was well in hand for your move to Eilaster, but there has been a hitch. Your brother has been injured by the factor and his wounds are being bound."

He expected she would rush to the door to tend the wounded Calum, but instead she surprised him with an expression that told of his own impatient resignation, even though she began to get to her feet.

"You have taken our home from us, and a stupid boy with whisky in his veins doesn't have the wit to make a stand against you."

He shook his head in irritation, for he did not care to discuss her tiresome brother when he had been faced with such news.

"Would you have told me if I had not come this morning?"

"Why would I?" she said, her voice trembling as she tried to show her scorn for him. "What use would it have been – what use is it now that you have found out?"

He looked angrily at her. "What – you think I would abandon you –"

You have already abandoned me," she said, and burst into tears. He was still too shocked to offer anything of use, the day's business turned on its head, his guilt gnawing at him. She tried to move past him, the fact that he had seen her give way only adding to her distress.

"Janet – at least give me some chance to make amends."

"How can you make amends?" she said. "Nothing can change what happened between us, or take away what grows inside me."

"Come, don't let's part on such a cruel note. Let me give you something to help you in the weeks ahead, for winter is here and there will be little enough to sustain you until the spring."

She looked contemptuously at him as she understood that there was only one thing he could offer her, and suddenly it seemed insulting, that money was all he had to give. She couldn't articulate what else she wanted from him.

"I am so easily put right in your mind with a handful of coins, is that not so?"

He did it anyway, dug his hand in his pocket, though her words made him smart as if she had slapped him. He looked embarrassed as she stood before him clutching the coins, not wanting to accept them as much as they both knew she was in no position to refuse them.

Then quite without warning, he made bold to rest his hand against her face and though she did not stop him, her eyes sparkled dangerously.

"We loved each other one brief morning," he said. "It is neither your fault nor mine that we are kept apart by circumstances. But love it was, for my part, as I confessed, and love it was for yours, though you will still deny it and say only that you were forced."

She threw his hand away from her. "You are not brave enough to love me," she said. "It would cost you too much."

Her words hit their mark and Alec wondered why he stood and took it and did not knock her to the floor for her impudence. It was true; he could not afford to love a girl so far beneath him. He was so thrown by the sudden turn of events that he could not say with any honesty what he did feel for her, but to say he loved her – and he was surprised to realise that such a thing had left his mouth – was a waste of his breath, even if it was true. His wealth and status, his family history and expectations, would always make a prisoner of him. He flushed, stood aside and as she left, he said, "If ever you have need of anything, come to me and I will help you."

She stopped, turned and looked at him. "If I could make that same offer to you, we would be equal, and then there would be no problem between us."

He had a fleeting sense that they shared the pain of approaching separation, but like her, he did not dare dwell on it. They could not afford to add stupidity to the desolate situation they now faced. He remembered her struggles on the knoll; he saw the same struggle now, and felt her helpless rage battering against the cages his class had built for him. She was weeping now, enough for both of them, and all it did was make him angry, force him to acknowledge that he had become her victim as much as she was his. He turned his back on her and walked out.

He was numb as he climbed back on his horse and prepared to make his way homewards. He felt their eyes on him as he rode away.

The next day, he sent a cart to help transport them, because the sheep were coming, and the land would wait no longer for them.

He would have lost her anyway. That was the defiant conclusion he reached as he paced his room and stopped to gaze out over the hills towards the knoll where he had made love to his poor virgin mistress. All right, he should not have taken her, but whether he had or not, the end result would have been the same. She would still have been evicted and the bond between them severed when their relationship as landlord and tenant ended. Except that now there would be a child, and the tie could not be quite so easily cut. He had not seen her since the day he had taken her, aware of the rupture he had caused in their delicate relationship, understanding too late that in making her his temporary lover, he had destroyed something far more valuable. He missed her.

For a year or two now, he had been courting other women, noble ladies who, as he had boasted to Janet, were vying for his favours and hoped to become his wife. Sooner or later he would make his choice and life would take off in a new direction. Casual romps with pretty but socially inferior maids would become a thing of the past.

But however he blustered to himself, he could not relegate Janet to the status of a pleasing but unimportant encounter. There was too much history between them for that, something he had not thought of when he had held her in his arms and been overtaken by a powerful desire that had banished all finer notions of responsibility and respect. In the intervening months, he had avoided her, longed for her, remembered the way they had loved, but not for a moment had he anticipated the shock she would deliver. The sight of her belly growing, *with his child*, had pierced him like nothing he had ever felt. He could not face thinking about the change in James, who had always talked to him man to man with no thought of obsequiousness to taint the level ground between them. The disdain James had shown for him had both humbled and enraged him; he could still feel the rawness of Janet's pain, and wondered how much of it belonged to him.

III

"She is with child?" Willie said in disbelief, as his eldest son faced him later that evening.

"I saw her myself and James advised me of her condition –"

"*Advised you of her condition*?" Willie repeated incredulously. "Have you listened to yourself? You report it to me as coolly as if you were describing a sheep sale. Do you have any idea of what you have done? I'm sure the man was hopping with rage that you had used his only daughter so ill. I am amazed you are standing unscathed before me after facing James Macleod."

"I thought to tell you before you heard it from him," Alec said, in an abject attempt to score points for dignity.

Willie passed a hand over his eyes. "And it is yours?"

"Yes!" Alec said impatiently. "I would hardly concoct such a story to win your approval."

"She is only fifteen," Willie said. "Are there not enough young and beautiful women at your disposal, that you must rape a daughter of the land who has no means to raise a child? Who do you suppose will have her now?"

"I have behaved foolishly, I will allow you that –"

"Oh you will, will you?" His father shook his head, his anger cooling briefly into disappointment. "It is worse than foolish, Alec. It is contemptible, what you have done. You have spent time with the Macleods as I have done, we have worked together to make the best of our lot. And this is how you sought to repay their trust?"

"I did not plan to take her!" Alec shouted. "The situation became heated – she did not exactly discourage me –"

"Don't dare try my patience further by blaming her," Willie cut in. "There is not a man alive, or a woman, who would think straight in the heat of the moment." He gestured impatiently. "We have all been there, and spent our passions less wisely than we should." He sighed. "But you are the Laird's son, and Janet is your tenant, and she looked to you for leadership and example. She was your friend, Alec, and so was James. All that respect and more you have thrown away for a moment's pleasure that never had a future in it."

Alec flushed at his father's use of the word *friend*. He had always called Janet his friend because in truth, he did not know what else to call her. She occupied a unique niche in his life. But their friendship was a private matter; to hear his father speak of it seemed intrusive. Willie had used the epithet spontaneously, without self-consciousness, and Alec was exposed. The people Alec publicly called his friends were his equals. His friendship with Janet was subject to secrecy and limitations; he had abused the difference between them, and turned all his liberal notions of friendship to affectation and hypocrisy.

"I will send money —"

"You will be very careful what you choose to give that ruined young woman," Willie said sharply. "I have watched you spend time with her, and mentor her, and I said nothing, for I thought you had more sense that to press friendship on a girl who is less wise in the ways of the world than you and might mistake the meaning of your attentions. What — you would propose to her now, I suppose, to ease that guilty conscience of yours?"

Alec hesitated and then shook his head.

Willie regarded him sardonically. "No," he said. "You would not. Because you know you cannot. You bedded that girl because you could, and for no other reason —"

"I wanted her!" Alec cried in frustration, and then, in a much lower voice, "I thought I loved her."

Willie looked almost apoplectic at this. "You spoke to her of love? How dare you!" He waved his hand furiously to cut off Alec's next attempt at self-defence. "Say nothing more, for it gets worse with every word you utter." He paced behind his desk for a moment, then said, "And now she has taught you, more at her expense than yours, that it is not enough to want and simply take. She will bear the consequences of your selfishness for the rest of her life. Does that make you ashamed?"

Alec looked defiantly at his father.

"You are not fit to bear the rank of gentleman when you betray the trust of those who depend on you." He looked out of the window, running a hand through his hair in his distraction. "What can be done?" he said almost to himself. He shook his head, stared for minutes on end out at the wild lands surrounding the castle. Eventually, he turned back to his son. "You may make a gift, as it is the only thing you can do now, and it is scant enough apology for the future that girl now faces. But you will cease your friendly calls on her and give her no further cause to believe you might take deeper interest in her. And from this moment, you will seek a wife who can provide legitimately for your frustrations."

"I had not thought to marry yet —"

"And you had not thought to get young Janet Macleod with child," Willie snapped. "But so you did, and so you will do."

Alec bit his lips, the severity of his father's words forcing him into powerless silence.

"You have lost a friendship that seemed important to you," his father said after a moment. "You have reaped disrespect from your betrayal of people who expected better of your education and position, and I include myself in those disillusioned unfortunates. You have your reputation to uphold, responsibilities to the Clan, which until now you have always respected. What of those things?"

"I did not think to use her ill," Alec said in a low voice. "The passion I felt was returned, and I thought of nothing but the moment. She is a daughter of the land —"

"Oh no," Willie said sadly. "She is much more than that now. She is the mother of your child. You have walked away, for the sake of the Clan, you *must* walk away, but your seed is inside her, and if you are half the man I hope you will become, you will never be able to forget it."

5.
FOUL-HOOKED
FEBRUARY 1825

I

Janet ran to the burn that tumbled down the side of the croft, her skirts hitched around her knees as she scrambled up the steep slope. Behind her, away down near the blackhouse, the cruel and exultant voice of her mother followed her.

"You are too late, *Seonaid*. You will not save him now. He will be half gone already, and good riddance."

She had no breath for shouting back an answer, but to herself she was saying, over and over again as she climbed, "I must find him. I *will* find him. It's not too late. I will not believe it is too late."

Some fifteen minutes later, away up the back of the croft, the keen breeze already chilling her, she threw herself down at the bank side where the burn emerged from under the hill and almost immediately plunged over a rocky precipice. Her mother would have put him there – either there, where he would waste fastest and stand the least chance of being discovered, or in the pool lower down, where his agony would be slowly eked out by the more leisurely movement of the current. She thrust her hand into the icy water, her fingers running over the sharp rocks, searching for the object she sought.

The summer following their eviction from Uishall and resettlement in Eilaster Glen, Janet had delivered her bastard son after a short and violent labour. Early June was hot that year, and her confinement was uncomfortable, the nights airless and the days still. She gave birth in the blackhouse, the contractions strong, her eyes wide with pain and fear, her hand gripping tight to her mother's, who watched her grimly and could not comfort her, offering nothing throughout the trauma but brisk admonishments to bear up and be strong.

All the time, Rhona was half-hoping the child would not survive its rough ejection into the hostile world that awaited it. But over her daughter's piercing shriek as her body yielded its unwanted burden, she heard the lusty wail of a sturdy bairn, a boy who would survive, and her hatred seemed to harden like a stone inside her. Rhona picked him up, wrapped him – even then, she could hardly bring herself to touch him – and handed him to her daughter, who was sobbing with shock and exhaustion in the wake of the swift delivery. Janet snatched him into her arms, and for a minute or two all she did was clutch him against her and cry. But then she looked at him, and a knife seemed to turn inside her.

True to form, Alec sent money when he heard of his son's arrival. It was a substantial amount, and James, despite his pride and despite his loss, invested it in a fishing boat, for he saw that they must take to the sea to bolster their efforts at surviving on the land.

In October, within just a few months of Alasdair's birth, Alec had put the past behind him and married Catherine, the youngest daughter of Donald Macdonald of Skye. Janet, still struggling to cope with the demands of the new baby, still grieving for her loss, cried angry, bitter tears. Her mother chastised her, saying it was time to do as the Laird's son had done, and plan for a future without him.

Barely four months into Alec's marriage, in February, when the year had turned and winter was at its coldest, news filtered down to Eilaster Glen that he had been taken ill following a bad fall from his horse. Not serious at first, his condition had deteriorated suddenly and now he had been in danger for a week or more and there were rumours that he was close to death. Rhona made no secret of her wish that the Laird's son would be taken by the devil for his sin and her appeasement, but she kept from her daughter just how far she was prepared to go to secure an ill fate for him.

III

Janet had thought nothing of it when she had come into the blackhouse that cold February morning and found her mother hunched over the table, working something in her hands and muttering. She had gone over to the cot where her eight-month-old baby was sleeping and picked him up, which roused him at once. She sat in the rocking chair, opened her shirt and put the child to her breast, where he sucked hungrily. Whatever she gave him, it did not ever seem to be enough, and the disillusion she felt was not often lightened by the child who made increasing demands on her. And now his father was ill and Janet feared for him. Despite the way he had abandoned her and despite the surges of bitter anger that consumed her when she was low in spirits, Janet was still trapped by memories that tangled in her mind like bright, disconnected threads and bound her to him. She sat, thinking of him, wondering how he fared, looking at her mother's curved back as she concentrated grimly on her task.

"What have you there?" she asked idly. Her mother rarely spoke to her these days except to criticise her sloppy mothering, but sometimes the gloom that had settled over their home was so oppressive that even Janet, who was now set squarely at fault for increasing the family's hardship, felt obliged to try to build bridges.

For a second there was no response, and then her mother said, "I thought to make a wee clay toy for the baby. I will set it to bake when it is done."

"He will break such a thing in those strong fists of his before he has had it an hour," Janet scoffed. She sighed impatiently, setting the baby to her other breast. Her hand automatically cradled his head and her thumb made light stroking movements over his hair, because she had discovered that this soothed him.

"Why this sudden interest in making playthings for a bairn you are scarce able to hold in your arms?" she asked suddenly, raising her head and feeling the strong pull of the baby's mouth. As her mother did not attempt to justify her uncharacteristic generosity, her suspicions grew.

57

"Show it to me," she said. "Let me see this labour of love you toil at."

"It's a simple doll, that is all," Rhona said defensively. "It is far from finished. Look –"

She held up a crude figure, about eight inches high, roughly fashioned as a boy, with splayed arms and legs, the clay still wet, slicked stiffly over the palms of her hands, embedded under the nails. She would not look Janet in the eye, and her manner was impatient.

Janet sniffed. "Well, it will do for a time," she said, and her mother turned back to the table and carried on with her work.

In the course of the day, Janet noticed without much care that the doll had been set to dry above the fire.

It was later the next day when Janet was mending clothes in the rocking chair that she heard her mother stamping her feet outside, as if she was waiting for someone. It was cold and very clear, the sky a cloudless pale blue, the days just beginning to lengthen and stretch themselves against the fading resistance of winter. There would be a hard frost tonight, although the sun still felt warm and there were a couple of hours of daylight left. After a few minutes, she heard Calum come up to the door, and they stood outside, whispering, treading on the hard ground. Janet's gaze turned to the fire, then above it, and noted the absence of the clay doll. Her suspicions aroused again, she laid down her stitching and went to listen.

"Well, we have done our part," Rhona was saying, her speech rapid with excitement. "The news from the castle is that he fades hourly. This can only hasten his end. You chose a deep spot for the doll?"

Calum nodded briefly and clasped his hands together, and Janet saw through the crack in the door that they were blue with cold from his outdoors excursion. There was a tight chill in her stomach as she overheard them, and it began to dawn on her what they had done.

"He is well covered then?" Rhona nagged her son, wanting every last detail given up.

Calum nodded again. "I have put him in the burn. He will be gone soon enough, but not before he has felt the suffering we have wished on him."

"It is well done, then," Rhona said with satisfaction. "I said the words many times as I made him, as the mother told me to, when Janet could not hear what I was at."

At this, Janet threw open the door and stared at her mother and brother with an accusatory rage that made both of them cower.

"You have cursed him!" she cried. "Is that what you are whispering at, standing outside here like a pair of vagabonds, thinking I will not hear you? He is half-dead already, and you have dealt him a blow while he has no strength to protect himself. Have you no shame or pity for a sick man?"

Inside, Alasdair began to wail, and Rhona's hostility towards the Laird's son redoubled. She shook Janet by the arm. "And what pity did *he* show, raping you and leaving you with child? Yes, we have cursed him, and if our prayers are answered, he will be dead before morning, and I will be avenged for the shame he has brought my family." She paused and then said, "A curse is twice as effective if it is laid against someone who is already cut down by ill-health."

"And what does my father have to say?" Janet said. "Where is your Christian forgiveness that he tries to teach you from the bible? You think he will applaud your cruel turn, and ask for yet more unchristian acts from the woman he calls his wife?"

Rhona slapped Janet's face with a force that made her daughter gasp before she began to run towards the hill.

"Perhaps when he is dead, you will come to your senses and find a man more fitting to your station," Rhona shouted after her, as if that justified the malicious action they had taken. "That is, if there is a decent one left who will take you."

Janet stopped. "Whether he lives or dies, I will never marry, and both of us will live under your roof and eat your bread, if only to punish your wickedness for this vile act."

Her mother shook her head. "That is not all we have done," she said. "We have visited the ancient mother, and our ill wishes have been strengthened by her spiritual powers. The *droch shuil*[1] is upon him, *Seonaid*, he is damned, and I am glad of it."

Janet stared at her with hatred – and then she was gone, climbing the croft as fast as she could. The clay doll her mother had fashioned had never been meant for Alasdair. She had made it into a likeness of the Laird's son, named it, mutilated it, cursed it as she worked, and then got Calum to place it in the burn, where it would slowly dismember and dissolve as the water flowed over it, bringing destruction to the person whose identity it bore. Janet climbed faster, the image of her mother's clay-covered hands and the half-formed doll vivid and abhorrent before her. It was as if Rhona had held Alec himself in her grasp, and had the scrapings of his flesh under her nails.

She had always understood the depth of her mother's bitter malice, but it was not so straightforward for her. She was caught between remembering the terror of being pursued, the pain of being violated, and the words of tenderness and gentle handling that were mixed in with them, the surge of passionate feeling he had released, never mind the history of friendship and kindly gifts that stretched back over years to her childhood. However hard she tried, she could not hate him, so she had instead trusted to her instincts and prayed in secret for his recovery. Now, there was a more urgent task to perform if she was to save him from the dour gaze of the *droch shuil*.

The doll was not in either of the places she had first thought of, and she had lifted her face to the sky and cried aloud her frustration, for now there was no alternative but to work along the entire length of the burn as it cut its rocky way down the hill towards the river it fed at the bottom of the glen.

It took Janet an hour to find it. An hour of dipping and dragging her hand in the freezing burn, of staring through the crazed surface of the water in the fading light until her eyes were strained and playing tricks on her. When she finally came upon it, it was placed face down on a bed of rough gravel, in a deep part of the burn that undercut the bank. A cunning place to conceal him, a lie she knew from her poaching days, where the salmon would rest on their journey upstream, and now the place where Alec lay in torment, and would not be unduly hurried over his painful disintegration. The moment she saw the overhang, she knew this was where her mother had told Calum to put him, and although she could not see him at first, she put her hand down, her arm submerged almost to the shoulder before her fingers touched a cold, slimy mass.

She worked her fingers gently around and along the shape of the doll, for if it broke under her hand, she would bear the blame for destroying him. She was patient, even though her hand was aching and cramped, for Calum had pushed him firmly into the gravel, impaling him on its sharp edges. Eventually, she freed him and brought him carefully to the surface. She pulled her thin shawl tighter around her, laid him gently in her lap and studied how her mother had wounded him.

Although the water had already begun its work, she could see that the back of the doll's limbs and torso were covered with cuts and his eyes were put out, so that in the afterlife, he

60

would be forced to stumble about in darkness and would never find his way out of hell. But this was not the worst of it. In the groin, there was a lump – her mother would have been far too prudish to model a male sex in any great detail – and it had been slashed deeply with a cross. Then Calum had pinned him to the gravel, so that the front of his torso and limbs were bruised and torn with jagged holes.

Holding the doll gently, her fingers stiff and trembling in the chill air as the sun began to lose its strength, Janet smoothed out the lacerations and picked out the pieces of gravel, saying her own spells as she worked, desperately trying to restore the doll to perfection and undo her mother's evil. She kissed the eyes, telling them to see again. She used her little fingernail to prise apart the lips; then she kissed the mouth and blew into it so that he would breathe in her healing power.

"Live for us," she whispered. "Live for me."

Then she wrapped him in a rag from her apron pocket, for he was still wet and fragile, put her head in her hands and sobbed with rage and despair for what the Laird's son had brought them to, for her helplessness and for the hopeless love she still bore him.

In the morning, when the rest of the household was about their business, she set the little clay doll to bake in the ashes of a neighbour's fire, telling the same lie about its intended purpose she had heard from her mother. Then, fearful that the Laird's son still suffered, and not content that she had done enough to turn the *droch shuil* away from him, for there were two of them behind the curse and only one of her against it, she took the baby in her arms, stole all the hens' eggs, and set out to make one last barter for Alec's life.

Notes:
1: *droch shuil*: Evil Eye

6.
LIVE BAIT
APRIL 1828

Janet trudged over the wet ground through steady rain, her shawl dripping, her feet soaked through. She walked solidly, although she sustained a slight limp and her ankle, injured long ago, ached with increased intensity when it was wet and cold. A small boy trod at her side with equally dispirited steps, his fair hair sodden and plastered to his scalp, his blue eyes dulled by misery. He held his mother's hand with grudging obedience, for she had scolded him only a few minutes before for smacking his bare feet into a puddle and spattering her already muddy dress. They walked together, chained by misery and silence, by obligation and poverty, and now and again his mother glanced at him and wished her heart were not so dried and dead inside her, even though its steady beat kept her alive, mostly against her will. For all his short life, Janet had not been able to look at her small son without feeling the pain of the day almost four years ago when she had delivered him.

As soon as she had laid eyes on him, she had seen his father in the thin features. His uncanny resemblance to the Laird's son ensured that from the moment he was born, she could never forget or heal. As he grew, she saw his father's superior rank in the careless disdain he showed for everything around him, as if he understood he came from better stock, and should have been destined for finer things. Alasdair looked like him. He acted like him. He bore the marks of his father as if they were stigmata sent to wound Janet's soul for all eternity.

And she saw things in him that made her blush for shame, the shape of his mouth, the lilting smile, the sharp eyes that read the thoughts and feelings she would never admit to a living soul.

When the news had come through, over three years ago now, that the Laird's son was out of danger and had been sent to

Edinburgh to convalesce, Rhona turned on her and blamed her frantic undoing of their curse for his return to good health. Janet drew courage from the fact that her magic had been stronger than theirs, because now she knew that however humbly she had been born, she had power that could bring change.

Life resumed its miserable, unbroken rhythms as Rhona bore in silent anger her failure to despatch Alec Macleod to an early grave. To rub it in, the boy thrived, was loyal to his young mother despite her disenchantment with the whole idea of parenthood, and they were rarely seen one without the other. James was saddened at the vindictive action Rhona had taken and took greater care to show affection to Alasdair, who, he kept reminding his wife, was an innocent and could not be blamed. The boy developed a quiet, reflective personality and in his eyes there was always something a little cold, as if he feared to let down his guard.

Those first few years were hard on everyone. But time passed, some measure of normality returned to the blackhouse, and with it came a degree of acceptance, a little humility, and even, on occasion, laughter. Alasdair took his first steps, learned his first words, slowly began to acquire the skills he needed to live the life of a crofter.

Alec was more distant than ever now, separated from Janet by time and remarried after a disastrous first match. Her son continued to grow up without his father, with a mother who showed no interest in finding someone else to fill the paternal gap. James went out of his way to spend time with the growing boy, telling him stories from the bible and old fireside tales about kelpies and spirits, witches and spells. The years passed, and Janet clung stubbornly to her memories of the Laird's son, because she knew she had worked miracles to save him, and still hoped to be rewarded for the sacrifices she made every day on his account.

In Alasdair's fifth year, the rumours began.

By that time, Janet's father had the croft and the small fishing boat that he worked with her brothers, so although they struggled with poverty like all their neighbours, they were not as badly off as some. By this time, too, Janet could have married half a dozen fishermen or weavers and secured herself a life of companionable poverty and hardship to the grave, but she had refused them all. Her family was exasperated, and there were acrimonious rows about her failure to face reality. Janet was in any case viewed with rather schizophrenic judgement by the rest of the community. Some of her neighbours called her a sinful maiden who had gambled on giving herself to the Laird's son in exchange for financial support, and wouldn't touch her in any case; others saw her as a victim of the rich landowners' greed and disregard for the poor, and patronised her accordingly.

Rumours about Alec were circulating and if they were true, Rhona's vengeful trip to the spey-wife and the doll she had mutilated might not have killed him, but might have left him damaged. There was a hard, bright determination in Janet's face now, backlit by the busy workings of her mind as hope began to renew itself.

Life had been a bitter mistress since the day Alec Macleod had kissed her in the shadows of the byre. But now Janet looked down at the straw-coloured hair of her young son and began to see a way of getting her hands on some of the recompense she wanted for bearing Alec's noble-blooded son, keeping him safe, and keeping herself untouched by other suitors. He owed her something more profound – and more honest – than money. Alasdair was now the banker of more worldly ambitions and she walked steadily homewards through the drenching rain with the patient resolve of one who had learned the value of waiting.

Once again, Janet had something the Laird's son wanted, and this time a mere purse would not buy her.

7.
TANGLED
JUNE 1832

I

Alec Macleod was raging, and in his anger, his wife Iona heard the desperation of his helplessness and humiliation. She lay in the vast four-poster bed, where she had drawn the covers up to her chin in the vain hope they might protect her from his fury.

He had stopped now. The pitcher and ewer lay smashed in the hearth and her husband was standing at the mantelpiece, his head resting against his arm. Iona's face reflected his pain; she loved and pitied him, but knew the vulnerable position she was in.

His first wife, Catherine Macdonald, had been ejected from the marriage bed four years before when she had failed to fall pregnant. From the start, it had been a union rooted in political expediency and although Alec professed fondness for her, it had been duty to his father and the lure of financial gain that had driven the Macleod suit. The hasty marriage had resulted in a fruitless union that brought misery to both parties, and culminated in them approaching Willie and asking leave to separate.

As Alec expected, Willie had taken some persuading, but his father felt at least partly responsible for the unhappy situation in which his son now found himself. Willie was God's man, let no one say otherwise, but the older he got, the more he saw tensions between the wishes of God and the desires of men, and this insight marked him out as a rogue force within the strict Presbyterian faith that guided him through life. He had firm, if idiosyncratic views on marriage, and Alec and Catherine's situation obliged him to stand by them. He thought it a mockery of such a holy institution for two people to be trapped in a union that brought misery rather than joy. It was also a travesty for a marriage to be condemned to fruitlessness, and a waste of his virile son, who had the responsibility of the family fortune to bear. Wrestling with his faith, the destiny of his soul and the equally pressing concerns of his land and business interests, the Laird had eventually supported their petition, in hopes his son could make a better match.

Catherine's father was highly displeased at the insulting accusations of infertility directed at his daughter, but he could hardly grumble at the generous settlement he received for the wound to his pride. He claimed back the dowry and substantial damages, and the families were still feuding in the aftermath of the divorce, which had involved the highest levels of government and ecclesiastical intervention, and a fair amount of costly persuasion to sanction it.

Spiritual considerations aside, Willie had other, more pragmatic reasons for wanting to see his eldest son produce an heir. The old Laird had been in poor health for several years now, and of his two sons, Alec was the one he trusted to keep a grip on fiscal and management matters while the new law of the land matured.

The distillery was thriving and sales and exports were increasing. Willie had taken the advice of a trusted financier, an old friend now based in Northumberland, and a shipping office in Glasgow had opened up the overseas markets. The financial foundation Willie had laid down over the years seemed sound, but it required dedicated efforts to build on it. Alec would carry on Willie's work, but without an heir, there were new political difficulties. Willie's problems were focused on Ruaraidh, who had long since given up his interest in the management of the family's resources, and did not seem to understand that making money was only the first principle of keeping it.

If his son was profligate with money, he was yet more irresponsible in his personal life – Ruaraidh's appetite for mistresses had not waned with his wedding to the Lady Margaret Urquhart from the neighbouring Isle of North Uist. It was a match that puzzled almost everyone in a position to have an opinion on the matter. In all kinds of ways, the Lady Margaret was too good for him – such a gentle woman, so kindly and forgiving. Certainly she had turned down many other suitors – perfectly respectable, morally unimpeachable men who were attracted to her quiet virtues. In refusing them, she betrayed a surprising contrariness and an unexpected streak of determination when she accepted Ruaraidh's proposal in the face of bewildered and finally strenuous attempts to dissuade her. Perhaps she had seen the lost, angry soul in him and wanted to be his saviour.

What was even odder was that Ruaraidh really did love her. There was no doubt about it in Alec's eyes, just as there was no doubt that his brother had absolutely no idea how to communicate the way he felt. They had met at a ball in Edinburgh and Alec had seen the look that flooded Ruaraidh's eyes – a love that was so immediate and so powerful that even while he was gripped helplessly in its giddying embrace, he instantly feared it. And as Alec knew only too well, what Ruaraidh feared, he strove to either deny or oppress. Margaret might have been the mother he had lost and in consequence, even while he trembled every time he took her in his arms, he could not trust her to stay. He loved her, but he wanted to punish her – for her goodness, for the way she made him vulnerable, for the deprivation he had suffered. He did not have to conceal his torment. Margaret fell in love with him with her eyes wide open, understanding all his twisted pain, and accepting the seeds of destruction that would inevitably grow from their union.

Once she was his, he began to test her with his tempers and his infidelities. Margaret seemed to be able to grasp even that thorny branch with humility. Alec, who could not understand why his brother seemed hell-bent on abusing the very thing he most loved, began to suspect that his deteriorating behaviour was influenced by drink and the more insidious problem of the glengore[1]. Alec tried to help his brother understand the hurt he caused, but all he got in return were insults about his treatment of Janet, and his failure to make Catherine happy.

With the dissolution of Alec's marriage, Willie looked on in despair at the struggles both his sons were having with matrimony and love. But – and here was the nub of the matter – while Alec and Catherine had failed to produce a child, Ruaraidh and Margaret had two sons to their name, and therefore a stronger claim to the rich inheritance at stake. With Willie's health failing and the Macleod wealth reeling after the brutal financial impact of the divorce, the Laird wavered between the short-term advantages of putting Alec, wifeless and childless, in charge of the investment he had made, and the potentially disastrous implications of passing his wealth onto the son maintaining the family bloodline.

Then Alec fell in love with Iona Mackinnon, and hopes of a new heir being born to the new bride were renewed. She came to him from across the seas in Sutherland, with a less impressive dowry, but she was a better match for him than Catherine; she had a quick and clever mind, was a robust bedfellow and a handsome-featured young woman he genuinely loved. She was stronger and more intelligent than her predecessor and understood what it would mean if she, too, could not conceive. But she lay abed now with the most recent evidence of her empty womb a red stain on her white nightdress, and knew that the rumours were true – Alec could not give her the child she desperately wanted.

He did not see how it could be him. He had proved his fertility, however unfortunate the circumstances, all those years ago. Even the disastrous fall from his horse a few years ago had not affected his sexual performance, even though his leg had been gored by the bones of a putrefying sheep, and he had suffered a life-threatening fever.

Inescapable connections were beginning to forge themselves in his mind as he had been forced to waste his hopeful energy on first Catherine and now Iona. And when they bled every month in defiance of all their most heartfelt wishes, a persistent image had begun to torment him. He saw Janet lying beneath him in the heather, weeping with anguish, bleeding in the aftermath of his first invasion, even then the reluctant bearer of his child.

But worse for him now was not the memory of her helpless grieving, nor the way he had taunted her with money and humiliated her. What he could not suffer was the way she had yielded to his bullying, given herself as he asked, and then been forced to bear the consequences when he scorned the gifts she offered him – herself, and the son he had made with her.

Now, it seemed impossible that fate could dish up not one but two barren wives and deliver them to his bed. For his father, there was only one explanation – divine punishment had been meted out for his sin against the girl he had abused and the child he had never claimed. Alec had rejected the idea with appropriate ridicule, and asked sardonically if the small matter of his divorce might not be more of a point of contention with the Almighty. Willie had thought on this, then insisted that Alec was now paying for older sins that were at the root cause of his current difficulties. Alec had argued, but now, his father's logic was becoming more persuasive. Certainly he could not come up with a better reason. As he stood by the fireplace in the bedchamber, exhausted by the anger he had just vented, all he could think of was Janet struggling to raise the son he had given her, who did not know his father and was excluded from his privileges of land and title.

He had seen the child once, when boundary issues between Uishall and Eilaster Glen took him over that way. Alasdair was three at the time, and Alec had watched him playing a solitary and intensely involving game with a freshly cut peat bank. Into this he was carefully pressing a variety of objects, including his fingers and toes, long pieces of marram grass and heather root, to see the impressions they made in the soft, wet earth. He was absorbed to the degree that only a small child intent on learning about the world around him can be. Alec, disconcerted enough as he was, was grateful that Alasdair took no interest in the imposing stranger who idled by him. He glanced at him often, noted the physical similarities between them, and tried his best to feel the connection that bound them. The distraction did not help him take an effective part in the heated exchanges taking place over the boy's head between himself and his dispossessed ex-tenants about exactly where and where not they could graze their livestock. Janet was one of them, standing apart, staring coolly at him throughout the proceedings, defying him to look her in the eye.

II

When at last he raised his face to Iona, it was no longer rage she saw there. He came towards the bed and she held out both her hands. He sat heavily beside her and she drew him into her arms, her fair hair falling on his shoulders. She had never seen him cry before, her laughing, playful, powerful husband, and she was as shocked as she was puzzled by the strength of the emotion that came from him. He sat up at last and she kissed him.

"Now tell me what's troubling you," she said, "beyond the fact that once again I have failed to do my wifely duty."

"There is something I must tell you," he said finally. "I had thought to keep it secret, but there is my inheritance to think of, and our future together to secure, if what I have to say does not jeopardise it utterly."

"Well, tell me whatever's on your mind," Iona said. "Come, don't hold back a moment longer. What could you have to say that has such serious implications for us?"

"I have a child," he said. "A boy. He will be eight or nine by now."

Iona stared at him.

"It was many years ago, before I married," he said quickly. "A daughter of the land I had a fancy for, an Uishall tenant before her family made their lives in Eilaster." Iona drew back. "It was a morning only that I spent with this girl, and now it seems that I and those I love will be punished all our lives for one rash act."

She lay still, absorbing this potentially destructive piece of news.

"The Laird is under pressure to give the lion's share of our estate to my brother if I cannot produce an heir," Alec went on. "You know as well as I that Ruaraidh would lose everything my father has worked for in the blink of an eye." Still she did not respond. "We must face facts," he said. "It seems I cannot give you children, and that is shame enough for me to bear and an incongruous life for you, a fertile woman who must lie fallow if you are to remain my wife. But this child I could redeem from poverty and claim him as my own for us to raise. The estates would pass to me, which would secure them, even though the times we live in are not so easy as they were."

Iona sat back against the pillows and looked seriously at him. "His mother may have something to say about such a solution to your problems," she said at last. "You have seen the boy?"

"Aye. His name is Alasdair."

"And you can see he is your son?"

"Without a doubt he is the fruit of that one union."

Iona was silent.

"There is, of course, another solution," he said gently. "But in truth I could not hand you into the bed of my brother to perform the service I could not do for you myself."

Iona shook her head firmly. "I would refuse such a strategy, you know I would. There is too much danger in it."

"And I could, and should, offer you the chance of freedom and the opportunity to celebrate your fertile soil with a lustier mate than I. But I'm afraid to make you such an offer, in case you should accept it."

She kissed him fiercely at this. "If this is punishment for your sin against this girl, we will work together before God to make atonement for it. The girl – how old is she now?"

"She was fifteen then, and she is now some twenty-four years old."

"What will you offer her? I have some experience of these maids – they can be cunning if they see you at a disadvantage."

"I will offer her security and a position in my household. I cannot do more."

Iona looked at him in surprise. "I can see that you will have to bring the boy under our roof," she said. "But his mother too? Is that not asking for trouble?"

"I have thought it through," he said, and his voice was firm. "This girl suffered at my hands, and I have ignored the son she raised. If I am unable to breed because, as my father believes, there is some divine punishment at work, I may yet reverse it if I show kindness to them both." He took her hands in his and kissed them. "I would not take such a controversial course if I did not think it appropriate," he said. "But I must beg your patience in this, and your wifely trust, for it will be done as I have said."

Iona knew when her husband would brook no argument. She wrinkled her brow, trying to take comfort in the business of debating arrangements. "It's a good offer for a lowly girl." She hesitated. "How will it go with you, having in our house a wench you took to all those years ago?"

He knew what she was asking and he shook his head. "It was a fancy and no more," he said, and heard with dread the lie that crept beneath his dismissive words.

Iona was gazing solemnly at him.

"Well, we'll find out soon enough if she will take your offer," she said. "But I suspect she'll know the proper value of her son, and be inclined to barter you higher."

Notes:
1: glengore: Scottish word for syphilis

8.
TICKLED
JULY 1832

He found her at length on the croft on Eilaster Glen, high up the steep, banked hill, stacking peats with her son. His son. He had tied his horse by the croft house and walked up by the rocky crag, so she did not see his approach. For a long time he stood behind the roughcast wall and watched them, working silently at a distance. The boy looked strong, well made despite his ragged clothes and poverty. Janet – she was still the bonny lass he had lusted after, even allowing for the intervening years of hardship.

Something worked in him as he looked at her, some memory of her sweet young face before he had tumbled her to the ground and robbed her of innocence and decency. *Mo nighean bheag*, he had called her – *my little girl*. The endearments he had whispered still had the unnerving ring of sincerity when they drifted through the backwaters of his memory, and their echoes came back to him now she was before him again. *A' ghraidh*, he had called her, *my love*, and he had meant it, without understanding that he had meant it, without understanding that it was possible for him to mean it.

He had been made so painfully aware of the social chasm that divided them, but since he had made his confession to Iona, he had realised that the memories of the morning they had spent together had never lost their power to move him. He had confessed his sin to his wife, reported the act and its consequence, but hidden from her things that were far more damning. The dance of sunlight in her hair, the tremble of her body under his hand; the warmth of her back against his chest as she fished with him, the intent look on her face as she listened to him, and the delight he felt when he made her laugh. Those memories were sacred and he could never share them with anyone but her, and he was suddenly afraid of the decision he had made to bring her back into the fringes of his life.

Uishall was changing, the land broken up into large farms that paid handsome rents. The ancient rights of tenure had been overturned as times moved on and money, not tradition, became the only currency that mattered. He was a gentleman, she was *nighean an tuath,*[1] someone not worthy of him. But he had remembered her, and had been punished for his cruel neglect of her, and now he struggled with thoughts of her that did not fit with the brutal truth of the reality they inhabited.

He stood and watched her and wondered at how time had changed him. The slowly dawning knowledge that he could no longer father children had filled him with anger and shame. Poor Catherine patiently bore the force of his grieving, lying submissively night after night, sometimes crying with pain in the aftermath, while he tried to imprint her with his progeny. He had driven her from his home with desperate accusations, condemned her to a spinster's life. If he had humility enough in the future, he could yet repair that damage. The destructive struggle had only ended for him the last time Iona bled. She was still struggling to join him in the same place.

He stared across the rough grasses. And this quiet, lowly maid stacking peats with resigned fortitude on her mean croft had done what two high-born women had not managed – given him the son he craved. The bitter irony swamped him, almost made him turn his back on her. He might have done more to ease the burden he had placed on her, had he known the day would come when he would have to beg for her compassion, the way she had once begged for his. The omens were too clamorous for him to ignore.

He considered the practicalities of the situation he was now in, the demands she might make of him. He could not marry her; if that were the price she asked for his son, he would be unable to pay it. The consequences of such an uneven match would be unthinkable, especially after the expense of the divorce. Besides, he loved his wife. In certain clan circles, he was already an outcast after his disrespectful treatment of Catherine. Claiming his bastard son would make things no better. He could walk away again, make more effort to secure a more comfortable prospect for his son and erstwhile mistress, and leave it at that. But the boy obsessed him, and despite the underlying drive of his own needs, his penitential feelings were genuine. He didn't know if that would be good enough for God.

At last she stood up straight, her hands pushed in against the small of her back, and stretched herself. Still young and lithe, her body spoke to his at some distant level he could recall from years ago. He shook himself. It wouldn't do. He loved his wife. She called to Alasdair, busy cutting on a lower stretch of the bank, bid him bring the rough bread from the basket and some water from the stream. They sat together in familiar silence, and still Alec watched with fascination and did not know when to make himself known to them. But Janet's head turned at the sound of a buzzard calling as it flew overhead and she saw him, dropped her piece of bread and got hastily up from the grass, wiping her hands on her apron and urging Alasdair to his feet.

Alec was obliged at last to duck out from his hiding place and stroll towards them. Janet curtsied, her head down, but when she raised her eyes to his face, he saw the maid he had taken and the desire shot through him again, keen as a lance. He smiled ruefully.

"Well, Janet," he said softly. "How are you keeping since last we spoke?"

"Well enough, sir," she said.

Her deference embarrassed him at once, further confused him, though he understood there was irony in it as well as a need to reinforce the distance that had grown between them. They were no longer lovers, that *sir* told him, he should not complicate matters by being unduly familiar with her. He felt the hurt of being kept at a distance, and the humiliation of being put in his place.

He turned to the boy. "And you, Alasdair – do you know who I am?"

The boy shook his head, not because he didn't know the Laird's son, but because there was something about the way the question was put that made him wonder if there was something else implied by it. His sharp eyes scanned Alec's face, so like his own, and his quick mind wondered at what such a gentlemen was doing in the peat fields with the likes of them.

It was six years or more since Alec had seen him, and for a moment he was thrown by the physical similarity between them, as Alasdair had begun to grow from child towards young manhood. Like his father, he was thin but strong, and his eyes sparked with a native intelligence that Alec knew instantly he could harness. He was not staring at the ground as Alec spoke to him, but looking him full in the face, as if he spoke to his equal. A fish out of water at the moment, Alasdair would thrive in his father's domain. He would have tough mountains to climb, but in time, he would command respect. He already knew how to survive. Alec pulled himself together sharply, realising how far ahead he was leaping in his eagerness to lay claim to what was his.

The boy was watching him.

"I would speak with your mother," Alec said. "I left my horse away down at the croft house. He's had water, but some fresh grazing before we make the journey home would not go amiss." He pulled out a silver coin and the boy's eyes flickered. He nodded, glanced at his mother for confirmation that he should do as the gentleman asked, and began to make his way down the hill. Alec's eyes tracked him down the slope with reluctant envy.

"Will you sit beside me, Janet?" he asked her eventually. "I have some business to discuss."

She hesitated, then sat stiffly on a smooth low shelf offered by a rock outcrop, and he chose a rougher shelf at the same height. Sitting beside her made him feel peculiar, put him at a disadvantage. He did not feel at all that this delicate encounter was going as he wanted it to, that despite her sirs and curtseys, she still had the upper hand. He thought suddenly of all the other maids he had romped with in his youth, the careless pleasures he had taken, how he could not even recall their faces. He looked at Janet and his forehead creased. He could remember everything, and that odd, insistent feeling that he had meant everything washed through him. He struggled to keep his mind on the subject of the moment, and was at a loss where he should start.

"You have come for him, then?" she said.

He looked at her and laughed at her forthrightness, the tension between them momentarily broken.

"Can you swear he is my son?" he asked.

"You have only to look at him," Janet said.

"You have not taken any husband?"

"I am as untouched as the day I lay with you," she said bitterly.

"Janet," he said, and there was a sadness in his eyes that came to her without guile, and wrong-footed her. "I used you wrongly all those years ago, as I used many maids. And you repaid my incivility with the riches of a son, which I did not appreciate until I realised he was the only son I have, or ever will have." He threw up his hands. "There. I have laid my shame before you, and it is equal to your own. You have heard the rumours. I may be rich in land, but now you have riches I covet more. Does that not give you some advantage?"

"You have married again?"

"Aye, and she, too, will be a victim of the punishment I bear."

She was silent.

"You know what I have come to ask, Janet," he said. "I will bear the burden of raising him that you have carried up till now. He will never want for anything again. My wife will love him as her own –"

"He is *my* son too," Janet said with sudden truculence. He couldn't hear the swift and savage beating of her heart, the moment she had waited for suddenly upon her. "I've borne him, raised him, suffered for him, while you have done nothing but toss the odd few pennies in our direction. What offer will you make to *me* as part of this neat and tidy bargain?"

He dropped his head to conceal a sudden smile. Iona's warning came back to him, and he wondered if he would have made the other part of his offer if she had not asked. But she had asked, and he wondered – if she had not asked, would he have prompted her? Would he have felt disappointment instead of the relief that flowed through him now?

"I have not left you out," he said gently. "I need a manager to keep my storeroom. For that you must be trained, and you must learn to speak English, as I do, and as Alasdair must, too. The housekeeper will be your mistress, for you must learn to read and write as well, and I'll provide better for you than the position deserves. Your own apartment, bed and board, a salary and free access to your son while he is taught to be a gentleman."

She sat quietly, her back aching, her hands dirty, her eyes glittering with disappointment.

"I know what you would ask of me," he said quietly. "I will do all this, and promise faithfully on it, but I cannot secure your future with a wedding. Our son will inherit, but I cannot extend that bounty to you." When she did not respond, he said, as kindly as he could, "I love my wife, Janet. I will not give her up."

Her face tightened. "And if I do not give Alasdair up, I suppose you will take him in any case, as you once did with me?"

Alec shrugged, nettled as she touched the sensitive layers of guilt. "A boy in his position would be a fool to turn down such an offer."

76

She laughed drily. "And his mother, too, I suppose," she said.

He leaned towards her and at once she recoiled.

"Don't flinch so, Janet," he said. "I forced you once. And now I am a Laird's son obliged to beg at the feet of a poor tenant for a bastard boy I thought never to have to claim. I will not force you again. Do you not allow the possibility that I have learned from my mistakes, and am repentant? That I as well as you have been humbled by my sin?"

"Whatever you have suffered, I have borne ten times the hardship," Janet snapped.

"Well, that's fair," Alec said. "It's true I've been born more fortunate than you, but that's no reason for you to turn down the chance to make things better." He waited out her silence, then said with a sigh, "I have asked this of you and made you the best offer I can. But you may refuse it, for yourself and your son if you see it fit, and I will leave and not trouble you again."

She sat grimly, the purse of gold swinging above her. Not all she wanted from him, but a start, at least. A place in a fine house, her son's future secured without more slog on her part. It would do for now.

"Well then, take him and give him a life worth having," Janet said.

"And you will join my household?"

"We'll come to you together. It will ease the burden on my mother."

"Your family will not take kindly to such a move," he said after a moment.

"My family do not take kindly to me in any case, since you took me and hung me somewhere between Eilaster and Uishall, with no foot sure in either camp," Janet retorted. "I may as well take my chances in the castle, as remain an outcast here."

Alec nodded. "Well then. It seems your mind is set. I will make swift preparations and send a cart within a day or two." He paused. "Will you tell him who I am?"

She nodded briefly. "Aye. But he is quick of mind and has probably guessed." She sighed. "There is no shortage of people keen to whisper in his ear the secret of his parentage. Most likely I will be telling him old news."

"Janet? Can you so easily give up all your motherly responsibilities?"

"I have never loved him as I should. Look at him," she said, and Alec heard the sob she tried to fight down. "His face is yours, his manner, his expectation that life will give him whatever he wishes. Whenever I look at him I am reminded –" She broke off suddenly and turned away from him, her hands covering her face. "Go now," she said. "You have already used me, and now it suits you to use my son, and before we are finished with this sorry tale, no doubt you will see fit to use me again."

He rose and left her in confusion, the sound of her weeping following him down the croft. In it, he heard betrayal, and the sense of loss he had always felt but never understood became suddenly clear to him. He had claimed his son at last, but instead of the relief he should have felt, he rode homewards with a sense of foreboding.

Notes
1: *nighean an tuath:* a daughter of the land, tenant

9.
PLAYED
JULY 1832 - SEPTEMBER 1834

I

Janet and Alasdair arrived by cart at Alec's home one wet summer morning. They had made their farewells to the rest of the family, but there was not much heart in their parting promises to return and visit. James looked older, tired, tried to wish his daughter and grandson well, but Rhona was so angry she could not speak, and they were driven away in a silence frigid with bitter disapproval and heavy with loss.

The castle was familiar, it had been in the background all their lives, but now its great four-storeyed granite bulk seemed to loom larger than ever. They passed through the vaulted entrance hall, painted blood red and dominated by a sweeping double staircase that led to the private reception rooms and master bedrooms on the first and second floors. A spray of juniper branches, greeny-silver with fleshy needles, the badge of the Clan Macleod, hung on an iron hook. Janet stared at the silver and polished wood, glimpsed the crystal and china in the ornate cabinets, saw the uniformed servants scurrying about their work, and tried not to be overwhelmed. Alasdair simply took everything in, his eyes banking everything they saw.

They were taken to the back stairs, where they were at once given over to Alice, the housekeeper's maid. After a bewildering series of twists and turns, they were delivered to a dressing room on the second floor. Janet had brought one thing with her, a flattish object wrapped carefully in linen, which she had hidden in the pocket of her apron. In the dressing room, their clothes were thrown away and new ones given, and the linen package was slipped into her new apron pocket. With a bathtub put at their disposal and Alice to help them, they bathed, scrubbed away the years of toil and deprivation, dressed and brushed their hair. Janet tied her red curls back with a dark blue ribbon, then stood herself and Alasdair in front of the mirror. In his stiff new suit, he was a stranger already. They gazed in awe at themselves in the glass, as if they were being introduced to new people.

"When we leave this room to meet your father," she said, "you will become his son and learn new ways. It stands to reason you and I must grow apart – that's the price we pay for such a fine future."

He nodded, but said nothing.

"Kiss me, then, for luck," she said with a sigh. "You and I both will need it to survive."

At this, Alasdair grinned. "There will always be bread on the table in this house, and better bread than we are used to, at that." He looked at her. "Are you happy with this plan? That I become the gentleman, and you become a servant?"

"Take care of your own prospects," Janet said, and kissed her son's forehead. "Perhaps in time, things will change again." He looked curiously at her and she smiled. "He is rich and wants for nothing but to ease his pain," she said. "But the rich always need the poor, as you will come to learn. Without us, they are nothing, and without you, Alec Macleod has nothing."

Alasdair was entrusted to his father's care, his position explained to him, the opportunities that lay before him expounded. Even at his young age, it didn't take much for him to work it all out. The private meeting they had – Alasdair and Janet, Iona and Alec – set everything out. Iona met them in a brilliant emerald green dress, kept a formal distance, welcomed them politely and had the servant show them to their rooms. Janet went with Alice to the kitchen to begin her new life.

Later, Iona and Alec met Alasdair alone and Iona asked him through Alec – for she had no Gaelic and Alasdair had no English – if he would call her mother. With a confidence that shocked Alec, his son, only just changed into his new clothes, announced that while he was grateful for the new position in which he found himself, he could not call anyone mother but the woman who had raised him from birth. He was affronted, and not the least bit ashamed of showing it.

Iona, reading his expression if not understanding the words, turned to her husband in annoyance. "What does he say?"

Alec looked down and grimaced at the insult levelled so carelessly, but with such accurate cruelty, at his wife. It was only later that he reprimanded Alasdair for his impertinence. For the moment, he smiled kindly at Iona and said diplomatically, "It is too great an honour for him to accept at the moment. I think he means he would feel presumptuous calling so great a lady by such a familiar title."

Iona was suspicious, since the boy did not look particularly humble to her. "Are you sure that is what he says?"

Alec sighed and took her hands. "We are already asking a great deal of our new ward," he said gently. "You cannot expect him to make such a leap in the space of a morning, even for propriety's sake."

"For propriety's sake, he had better begin as he means to continue," Iona said tartly, and swept out of the room.

In the wake of her departure, Alec sat down with his son and tried to persuade him to mollify the Lady Iona, if only for a smoother passage through the difficult time ahead, but Alasdair was adamant. He would call Iona 'My Lady', if it pleased her, until such time as they had got to know each other better. Alec did not press the point and Alasdair's cool distance set the seal on his relationship with the lady of the house – it would never get any warmer.

Alasdair met Willie, who was now virtually invalided, and gazed with respectful curiosity at his grandfather. If Willie was pleased that his son had tried to atone for his past sins, he was yet unhappy with the actual form of the reparation and shared Iona's grave reservations. He was impressed with the boy, however, and immediately knew him for Alec's son. In the time he had left, he formed a gruff affection for him, admired his determination and intelligence, and marked him out as a survivor. Janet he met, too, for the first time in years, and this unsettled him. The old Laird was struck by one thing – the effect she had on his son from the moment she arrived.

Iona's distrust of the new situation was quickly realised. She found herself watching Janet closely, trying to analyse what had drawn her husband to this common girl so long ago. She was undeniably pretty, with her delicate features, her soft brown eyes offset by the untamed mass of red hair that curled and tumbled half-way down her back. She looked as if a gust of wind could knock her over, and yet she had had the strength to bear and raise a child in harder circumstances than the fortunate Iona could possibly imagine. Iona fought the jealousy that began to flower, the knowledge that this girl who was beneath her in every sense had yet risen above her by carrying her husband's child.

Iona had been raised in a home that spoke no Gaelic, so there was a further bond between Janet and her husband that she could not break. In the early days, she would come across them from time to time, and overhear a conversation that had no meaning for her, and then she would not rest until she had found some pretext to ask her husband what business he had had with his new storeroom apprentice. But she discovered a weapon; Iona spoke French, and Janet did not, and before long she was using her fluency in the language to put the daughter of the land in her place. Normally considerate towards everyone in the household, Iona was from the outset instinctively unkind to Janet, and could not modify her behaviour. She was always on her high horse, looking down on her from the great height where she sat with her husband.

Yet Janet's demeanour was respectful and irreproachable, and however unkindly Iona treated her, it seemed she could not be wounded. Another thing rankled; Iona could not detect a single trace of shame, which would have been more seemly in a girl who had committed such a sin. Janet floated like a ghost down the wide, dark corridors of the house, silent and contained, seeking no society, not even over-using the privilege of having access to her son. Iona watched like a hawk, but Janet, unlike her upstart progeny, barely made acknowledgement of Alec, cast her eyes downwards whenever he approached, would flatten herself against the wall when he passed by, rather than risk him touch her.

Even though Iona suffered, the arrangement had to be endured, for Alec would not consider any other course of action. In his house he wanted both of them, to atone for his past sins, to secure their future with an heir, and perhaps, with God's forgiveness, to grant his patient wife her own child.

II

Within a year of their arrival, Willie was dead and Alec succeeded him, his superior claim to the land agreed unwillingly by his brother. Alec shared the richest rents out fairly and reduced the possibility of sibling rivalry, so neither of them had cause for complaint. Alec took charge of the whisky and shipping businesses, a sensible arrangement for which Ruaraidh was both resentful and grateful. Both brothers and their families lived well within the new order and celebrated their prosperity.

Ruaraidh took Maglavat, supervising the final stages of the building of the new castle and waited impatiently to move in, out of the large house he had rented several miles away, where he lived with the Lady Margaret and their two sons. In more charitable moments, he hoped that a move might lift the weight of grief from his wife, who had recently suffered a miscarriage in the middle term of pregnancy, and keenly felt the loss.

The old crofters' cottages, those that had not been burned or pulled down, were already crumbling into ruins in the unforgiving climate. Sheep grazed the grasses and dotted the heather, their white bodies like giant plumes of cotton grass. Deer ran in the hills, where the new Laird and his brother hunted them with the huge, graceful deerhounds Alec loved. Most of the people were gone, cleared to the eastern side of the island, where they ran subsistence crofts as they always had, but on poorer ground, and had begun to fish the stormy waters of the Minch, diversifying their opportunities for survival. The new Laird and his brother ruled over their rough-hewn paradise, having ridden roughshod over ancient rights of tenancy that often stretched back centuries.

Ruaraidh took a malevolent interest in Uishall's new arrivals from the outset, making it clear he took a dim view of his brother's actions. There were arguments between them, Ruaraidh even investigating his legal options to challenge Alasdair's claim to his father's property. He would not speak a civil word to the child he was supposed to call his nephew and to Janet he was rude, barging her in the castle corridors, giving her curt orders, humiliating her by asking questions in English she could not answer. All the while, he let her know that he was well aware of the reason his brother tolerated her presence, and that whatever he did and however well he was taught, Alasdair would never be more than the common bastard he had been born.

If Ruaraidh hoped to intimidate him with his aristocratic bullying, he fell far short of his mark. Alasdair took to his new surroundings with the alacrity Janet had expected. He was born to be a gentleman's son. He learned quickly, cramming his mind with the essentials of schooling, language, manners and dress his father deemed appropriate. He began to learn the business of the land, too, and see it from the gentleman's perspective. And as Alec had anticipated, with just a few rudiments placed at his disposal, his son began to develop a keen commercial awareness, an appreciation of the concept of profit. Now and again he accompanied his father on business trips, broadening his horizons as far as Inverness and Edinburgh. He began to grow, up and away from the things he had known towards a future that seemed so bright with promise, he dared not look at it too closely in case it blinded him.

Janet learned too, and impressed the housekeeper with her organisational skills in the larder, the tenacity with which she applied herself to the rigours of reading, writing and arithmetic. Her English improved rapidly, and the few phrases Alec had taught her in childhood gave her initial confidence. She relished the freedom from the hardship and toil to which she had left the rest of her family and, caught up in the novelty of her employment and her advance towards being both literate and numerate, found she did not especially miss them. She bore Ruaraidh's taunting with dignity and learned to ignore the envy of her workmates. As for Alec, she spared him little of her attention and seemed closed to him.

Her room was plain but cosy and Alice lit the fire every evening when her work was done. It was a world away from the rough interior and hard labour of the blackhouse she had left. Now she slept in a bed with a lace canopy and a patchwork quilt. There was wallpaper with a delicate floral pattern, a worn rug that had once been bright with rainbow colours, curtains at the windows. A brass candleholder and a rocking chair.

As an afterthought, Alec instructed Gillies MacNicol, Uishall's woodsman, to bring down a writing table with a standish from the attic and install it by the window, together with a straight-backed chair, so that she could undertake her studies in comfort.

Gillies had heard with distaste the rumours that flew around the kitchen when it was known that a new member of staff was to join them. A large, placid, quiet man who lived alone and kept himself to himself, he pitied the tiny young woman who had come to take her place in the household, and did not envy the boy who was to live with the Laird and his Lady. Every evening, he came to Janet's room to replenish the supply of logs for the fire, and she stood at the door while he stacked them in the hearth, her body rigid with tension or dislike, he could never tell which. He saw the fear that moved in her eyes, behind the icy exterior she showed him, and he could not get past that chilly barrier. She never spoke a word to him, even though he always greeted her politely and sometimes tried to engage her in conversation with a comment about the weather, or to enquire how she was finding life at Uishall. When he stood to leave, she pointedly averted her eyes and as soon as he passed through the door, it was latched behind him.

What is she like with you? the kitchen staff always wanted to know when he returned, for they all knew what her business had been with the Laird. When he refused to give them information, they raised their eyes at his misplaced tact, and made it up for themselves. He went about his work with his usual patient diligence and kept his opinions to himself. *What was she like with him? Cold*, he thought sadly, and felt compassion for her, all walled up for her own safety, where no one could touch her. *Stiff and stark like a blasted tree.*

The privileges she enjoyed were not discussed, only tolerated by her serving peers and employers, and she hung uneasily between the two camps, at odds with both, relaxed with neither. Sometimes, when the house was quiet, she stole into the dining room, sat at the great oak table and looked at the portraits of Alec's ancestors lining the walls, and she felt the weight of history pressing at his back. She studied the grand land-owning ladies who had earned their places on the wall beside their husbands, noted their dignified carriage, elegant dress and white, unspoiled hands.

Once or twice a week, Alasdair spent the evening with her, and they would talk over the new things they had learned, practise their reading, converse haltingly in English, then relax and swap stories and servants' gossip in the old tongue. As time passed, and Janet's fluency in the new language improved, she sat more in the rocking chair by the fire, and read by the flickering light of the flames. Sometimes, as her confidence with the written word developed, she sat at the table and wrote down her thoughts for extra practise, in the hour or two she had at leisure between the close of her household duties and seeking her bed.

And every night without fail, she would bring out the linen-wrapped object she had brought with her, which she kept carefully in the top drawer of the writing table. It was the clay doll she had rescued from the burn, repaired and baked to hardness in a neighbour's fire; the doll had become a talisman, and every night she kissed it and blew her strength into its open mouth to keep him safe.

For Alec, the changes began when he first saw Janet attired for work in his household. It hit him like a blow to the stomach how close she was now. While he had not been over-conscious of her absence in the intervening years, he felt her presence now, like a reformed addict becoming suddenly re-acquainted with his previous habit. His gaze rested for too long on her and then he looked hastily away and from that day on, he tried to blank her out.

To reciprocate his careful, clumsy evasion, Janet barely even looked at him at their first, awkward meeting when Alasdair's future was laid before him, and the terms of her employment explained. For the next three years, she barely looked at him. But whenever she did, he could not cope with what he saw in those soft brown eyes, and what she made him want. She knew his weakness, as she had done when she used to flirt with him as a young girl; she let him know, without doing anything, that she had the power to overturn his misery if only he would come to her. It was a slow-acting charm she worked, but he fell surely under its spell, though not a word or a touch passed between them. While he had created a friendly working atmosphere at the castle and was usually on first-name terms with his staff, he could not relax whenever Janet was near, and made a point of addressing her formally as Mistress Macleod. But whatever he did, it didn't make much difference; she knew the source of all his pain, the failing strength of his denial. They both knew what would come, however much Alec strove to fight the dangers of the generosity he had shown her.

10.
DECOY
MARCH 1834

Iona walked swiftly through the main hall and down the corridor that led to the kitchen. Her silk dress caught and spilled the pools of light that dripped from the clusters of candles ranged along the walls. It was ten o'clock in the evening, supper had just finished and the castle guests were dozing round the fires or engaging in desultory conversation in the ground floor reception rooms before they retired for the night. In stark contrast to the relaxation of her guests, Iona's mood was irritable; her husband had been wanting at supper and had not sent word when he would next grace the company with his presence.

It was dark outside and bitterly cold, a gale howling beyond the thick castle walls. The hailstones were so large and being hurled with such force from the lowering clouds that if anyone had to step outside – as the unfortunate Gillies MacNicol was obliged to do, if the fireplaces were to be kept roaring – they were instantly attacked with savage ice shot.

"Where is Mistress Macleod?" Iona demanded when she reached the kitchen.

Most of the servants shook their heads apologetically, but Alice stepped forward.

"She has been called away on an errand," she said.

"Really?" Iona said, raising an eyebrow. "And by whose authority has she been removed from her usual duties?"

Alice looked uncomfortable. "The Laird asked for her," she said. "He came down some two hours since, and asked leave of the housekeeper to borrow her for some special task."

Iona flushed. "Why was I not informed?"

"If you please, my lady," Alice said quickly, "the Laird sent a message via one of the stable boys, but he could not find you to deliver it."

"How long will this task take?"

"The Laird did not say what she was to do," Alice said wretchedly. "I'm sorry, my lady, I don't know any more."

"I see." She sighed impatiently. "My difficulty will have to wait until the Laird sees fit to release her back into my charge." She hesitated a moment longer, then began to make her way back towards the main drawing room. She had not thought to ask where in the castle this mysterious task might be taking place, and just as the thought occurred to her, she heard footsteps hurrying behind her, and turned to see Alice.

"My lady, Tom says he has just come from the stables, and there is a light burning in the hay store. He thinks he saw the Laird going in there with blankets and a lamp not half an hour since."

Iona seemed to go still at these words. "Well, he is found, then," she said, her voice trembling slightly. "In that case, I will don my cloak and investigate."

A few minutes later, Iona was hurrying across the stable yard, shielding herself from the volleying hailstones and screaming wind. She threw herself into the stables and the horses shied, unsettled by the violent weather beating against the roof and walls. She slipped the hood from her head. At the far end there was a large barn area stacked with hay bales, and she could see the dim glow of lamplight. She walked cautiously towards it, afraid of what she might find. When she was within a few yards of the entrance, she heard the murmur of voices and stopped. She leaned against one of the stalls and listened. Her husband's voice came first, then Janet's. They whispered, as if they could not risk being overheard, and it was the old tongue they spoke, the language she could not understand. Her hands had formed themselves into tight fists as she walked through the doorway and confronted them.

They were at the back of the hay store, tucked into the corner, both sat on a blanket, apart from each other. Their concentration was focused on something in front of them and she caught Alec's expression, tired, strained, almost exhausted. She took a step forwards and he turned and saw her.

He got to his feet at once, came towards her and took both her hands in his. Janet did not react, or even seem to realise she was there.

"My darling," he said, and hearing the tone of his voice as he spoke the words, her suspicions foundered. "Here you are at last. Did you not receive my message?"

She shook her head.

He gazed at her, her worried eyes, her unspoken accusation that he had excluded her from some ugly secret.

"What must you think of me?" he said.

He pulled her into his arms and she embraced him. He seemed to need the comfort as much as she did and it was some time before they pulled apart.

"What are you doing out here?" she asked him eventually. "And why is Mistress Macleod with you?"

He touched the tip of her nose with his finger, a gentle reprimand for her jealousy. "Bridie is whelping," he said. "I did not tell you, or anyone, as it is so tiresome for me and wearing for the bitch to have inquisitive maids peeping in and out to try to get a glimpse of the pups. And you are so squeamish about these things, that it would have been sheer misery for you to spend the afternoon here."

He cocked his head at her and smiled, soliciting her agreement. She hesitated, and then gave it with a wan smile. She had never been fond of the deerhounds. They were too big, too intimidating when they frisked about her, and she could never relax in their company. As Alec invariably took them with him on his countryside excursions, she had taken to riding instead, and felt safer atop her horse with the gangling might of the dogs below her. And she was so relieved to find an innocent explanation for his disappearance that she did not mind him drawing attention to one of her failings.

"Janet is an old hand in these matters and I enlisted her without first asking your permission, for Bridie was about her business before I could do anything correctly. So forgive me. And the last two pups have not come easy. This last is stuck fast, and if there is anyone on this land who can save it, it is Janet." He smiled. "She delivered the rest with those clever, gentle hands of hers and I am hoping now she will perform me one last miracle."

He took Iona's hand again, not noticing how she had withdrawn from him slightly at his glowing praises of the young woman she had always seen as both her inferior and her adversary. Now she saw that Janet was bending over the deerhound bitch, her hands on the wet, slippery birth sac of a puppy struggling to make its entrance into the world. Iona swallowed. She would never have been able to touch the bitch in these circumstances, let alone the half-delivered pup. Three other pups, eyes tight shut, were curled by their mother.

"The mother – is she all right?"

"Aye, but tired now," Alec said. "She has been delivering all afternoon, they have been slow to come, and this last is proving the most difficult of all."

"She cannot push as strongly as before," Janet said in Gaelic, glancing up at Alec, showing no interest in his wife. "You will not lose her, but the pup may suffocate. It has been too long."

"Tear the sac," Alec said, automatically reverting to the old language, letting go his wife's hand and kneeling at Janet's side. "His nose is out, is it not?"

Janet sighed. "I will pull one last time," she said. She laid her hand on the bitch's stomach, felt the muscles harden into another contraction.

"Do it," Alec said, nodding at her. "If he does not survive, it will not be because you have not done everything in your power to make it otherwise."

Janet bent over the bitch again and took the half-delivered pup in her hands. She tore the sac away from its face and then eased her fingers a little inside the mother. Iona grimaced and turned away, a hand to her mouth. Janet pulled gently, shook her head, murmured something and Alec spoke back. Iona turned and saw Janet looking at the Laird with pity and sadness before she applied herself to the task and pulled more firmly. The bitch whined a little and her rear end lifted before the tiny body suddenly slithered out a little further, one of its shoulders freed.

Alec went still and Janet relaxed suddenly, withdrew her hands and sat back on her heels. Iona joined them, her hand on her husband's shoulder.

"No use?" he whispered to Janet, his hand automatically reaching up to cover his wife's.

"Wait," she said. "His mother may finish the job herself now."

With the next contraction, the pup was delivered and the bitch turned and licked away the sac, pushing him with her nose. Alec watched, barely breathing, waiting for signs of life. Then the pup's nose lifted slightly and he wriggled.

The Laird rose to his feet, caught Iona in his arms and whirled her round in his excitement. She laughed, the tension in the hay store dispelled, the new life in it all preserved. Janet looked up at Alec, smiling, and looked quickly back at the bitch and her litter when she saw the way he celebrated with his wife.

"This has been a long and weary evening, and your Laird has not had one bite of food since breakfast," Alec said, with sudden energy, his normal speaking voice sounding loud in the wake of all the hushed tones that had preceded it. "Come, we must leave our new mother to tend her young and get some well-earned rest."

"I'll gather up the blankets," Janet said, getting to her feet before the Laird thought to help her. There was only the barest moment of awkwardness as he looked at her, and he seemed to have difficulty phrasing his thanks in the appropriate manner.

"You have saved a life today, Mistress Macleod," he said, opting for his attitude of gracious lairdly benevolence, "and you should be proud of it. Run in now and beg some supper from the cook, and mind you tell me if she gives you trouble over it."

He threw his arm around Iona's shoulders, she put hers about his waist, and they strode away towards the stable door and the wild weather beyond it, for the moment a relieved and happy man that his beloved dogs were all safe and well. He ate a hearty supper, roused the company from their after-dinner torpor and spent a convivial hour with them, apologised profusely for his absence, then took Iona to bed and made love to her with the passionate fervour of a man who considered himself well-blessed in his marriage partner.

But he woke in the night after confused dreams and his arm was stretched out before him, reaching for the phantom images his wakefulness had chased away. He had seen Janet's hand laid close and warm against the bitch's flank and he was reaching for it, wanting to possess that hand for himself, and feel those strong, gentle fingers pressed against his own flesh.

11.
MIRED
APRIL – JUNE 1834

I
APRIL

The London specialist regarded his gentleman patient with appropriate gravity. From the distant Scottish islands he had come, anxious to avoid detection at a treatment centre closer to home ground. The man was already in the secondary stage of disease, and while the specialist's compassion was genuine, it was wedded to a certain calculating knowledge that he could charge handsome fees for his treatment. The money was not always enough compensation, however, for the hostility he took from the rest of the medical profession. His colleagues judged him to be as morally corrupt as his patients for wishing to help them overcome the physical and moral degradation that was syphilis.

"You understand the nature of your disease?" he said.

Ruaraidh nodded tersely. "I have been caught by the French pox, and had I been more concerned with French letters, I might have escaped it." He sighed. "Your name came to me by private recommendation, as the best man in London to help me be rid of it."

The specialist shook his head. "Your recovery will not be easily got. You know the only course I can propose, and the dangers that accompany it?"

Ruaraidh stood and paced the room. Behind him, seven hundred miles distant, lay Uishall and Maglavat and his wife, grieving for the loss of yet another baby, conceived in the womb but not able to survive the full term of pregnancy. He did not like to think of Margaret's suffering, the pain she endured when she lost them, and the grief that enveloped her afterwards. Three miscarriages she had borne in the last two years, one an almost full-grown bairn, a little girl who took two days to deliver, and was handed to her dead. He had two sons; Ciaran, the eldest, was sickly and wasted, often ill and not expected to survive his teens. The other, Jamie, was stronger, but sensitive and not much good for the harsh landscapes that were his birth right. In his favour, he had a degree of aptitude for business. He was not as gifted as his uncle, but he was steady and shrewd enough to become an effective, if unimaginative manager of the land.

On top of all Ruaraidh's fatherly cares, he was now forced to undertake a four-month absence from his lands. He had already caught the disease once, and been cured of it with a less challenging treatment programme than the one he was facing now; but his experiences had not deterred him from returning to his former habits, with the same depressingly predictable result. He looked grimly at the specialist.

"Aye, I know. You will give me mercury. I have heard of it."

"It is a severe treatment, and will affect you grievously," the specialist said. "You must stay here to complete the course, then convalesce for several weeks, for you will have no strength for the long journey home. And you must abstain from further pleasures of the flesh until your cure is made good." He paused. "How does your wife?"

"My wife is well," Ruaraidh said coldly. "But she is not charged upon your account, and therefore you should not concern yourself with her wellbeing or otherwise. Spare your humbug and your lecturing for more penitent ears than mine."

He looked away, and heard the specialist's tired sigh. His guilt bore down on him, for his own physician had warned him of the likelihood that his wife would fall prey to his disease if he insisted on siring her. Margaret seemed well enough at the moment, and did not bear obvious signs, as he did, of the sibbens[1]. He tried not to bother her with his needs, but after all, she was his wife, his legitimate bedfellow, and it was her duty to satisfy his drives when no other solution presented itself. Besides, the more children she lost in the womb, the more desperately she craved a sibling for her two surviving sons, and her grieving would not be appeased by any other means. It stood to reason, then, that from time to time he must take his own wife, if only to try to ease her suffering, as any good husband would.

Before he left Maglavat, he had been honourable as far as Margaret was concerned, and had not taken her in the two weeks leading up to his journey. He had instead comforted himself with the tender flesh of a young chambermaid, Annie, a shy, nervous girl neither he nor anyone else had tried before, whose struggles and tears had somewhat dampened his ardour before he had finally solicited her compliance with threats. Ruaraidh ran a hand through his hair, distracted by uncomfortable thoughts that underlined his inability to withstand the natural urges that were now ruining other lives.

"As you wish," the specialist said curtly. "Well, is your course set? For there are papers to sign if it is, and one half of the costs to be paid in advance."

Ruaraidh hesitated, but his fate seemed sealed. The cost of the treatment, the journey, the expenses of recovery, would all add to the debt already carried by Maglavat, and the sense of failure he had always felt in the shadow of his luckier, more virtuous and more gifted elder brother. Alec would bear the burden of making good the deficit made on his account. He feared the treatment, but if he did not proceed, he would face an early death, and that was worse than dealing with the censure of Alec and the exhausted forgiveness of his wife, who still did not know – or refused to acknowledge – that her husband was stricken with the glengore.

II
JUNE

Alec pushed open the door and walked cautiously into the room. The smell hit him first. The windows were curtained so that very little light penetrated the gloomy interior. His brother's bed was against the wall – except that on first sight, Alec did not recognise the wasted individual that lay sleeping between the sheets, a jaundiced, ghastly, cadaverous echo of the powerful, thickset man who had left Maglavat barely three months before. He stood over him, appalled, then leaned forward and gently shook his arm.

"Ruaraidh. I am come. It is your brother."

Ruaraidh opened his eyes and stared at Alec for a moment before giving him a tired and sardonic smile.

"Well," he said. "A familiar face at last. It seems that if the glengore does not finish me, then the doctors will."

He raised himself slightly against the pillows, groped for a large white handkerchief and opened his mouth over it to drain a rush of saliva. The fetid smell rose to Alec's nostrils, its note sharp and rank above the underlying stench and he grimaced

94

involuntarily and jerked his head back. Ruaraidh tutted disapprovingly at his lack of tact.

"I didn't realise you were so sensitive, brother," he said with heavy sarcasm. "I am sorry for offending you – it is a foul stench, is it not, but you will soon be rid of it, where as I have lived with it for three months, and must endure it for at least a few more weeks. The doctors like to see me drooling – they say it draws the poison out of my body." He paused for a moment. "Well it may do, but it almost took my teeth as well, and my mouth is sore beyond measure with ulcers."

Alec recovered himself, strode over to the window and threw it open, allowing the mild summer air to drift in and lighten the stink in the room. "What in God's name have you agreed to?" he said. "You look far sicker to me than when you took your leave."

Ruaraidh flicked his hand. "My symptoms were progressing," he said. "The course of action was either drastic, or not worth taking."

"Is it finished?"

Ruaraidh shook his head. "I wish it were," he said. "There is another month of this torment, I think."

Alec regarded him grimly. "Another month of this will end it for you," he said. "What are they doing?"

"Mercury," Ruaraidh whispered. "It is the devil's medicine, I'll tell you that."

He looked away suddenly and Alec saw with horror that his brother was weeping. He shifted uncomfortably, turned his gaze to a painting on the wall, giving Ruaraidh time to compose himself. His throat tightened as he realised he could not comfort him; he felt the distance between them thrown into sharper relief than ever, the years separating the brother he had mentored when they were young, and the painful enmity between them as men, that even sickness could not overcome.

"Forgive me, brother," Ruaraidh said after a moment, his voice hoarse. "Forgive my weakness. I swear to you, I had never known true wretchedness until I came to this place."

Alec sat on the bed and took in the changes that the treatment had visited on him. His hair was thin and had lost much of its black, lustrous sheen. His teeth were yellow, his skin ashen, his flesh had fallen away. His hands trembled and his eyes darted nervously about him.

"I could not eat a month," he said at last, when he had got himself under control. His eyes were red and watery and he wiped distractedly at them. "The sickness, Alec, it was frightful, and the pains in my mouth and throat – unspeakable. They gave it me by mouth, just to start with, and then it is rubbed into the most troublesome sores every day. They cover me with blankets to make me sweat." He shook. "There is a treatment room, unbearably hot, where they purge and bleed me, then heat my bed and tent it in so I can breathe the vapours. It feels as though my head has been possessed – such nightmares I suffer, such exhaustion I have never known. I am now so weak I cannot leave this bed, and I cannot even last a conversation without forgetting the subject of it."

He stopped, trying to control the desperation he knew was coming out, then sighed and smiled bitterly. "But there, this is the worst of it. The specialist says the dosage has been reduced, for they dare not give me all they planned to, and then I have but to rest and recover." He shook his head. "That is the way of it, to all but poison me to kill the poison that was there in the first place."

"You cannot let Margaret see you like this," Alec said.

"I will stay here for the summer. There is a rest home by a pleasant park, where I will be tended until I am well." He stopped speaking, for the effort had tired him. There was silence for perhaps twenty minutes, while he slipped into a fitful doze. When he woke, Alec was sitting in the chair by the window, seemingly lost in other worries of his own.

"How does my Lady Margaret?" his brother's voice eventually said into the half-light. The sound was thin and vexing, like the weak rasping of a saw against dry wood. "Is she faithful to her absent Laird?"

"Aye, more so than you have ever deserved," Alec said. "Don't think to curry sympathy from me. You know my feelings on the matter." He sighed impatiently. "It's true you suffer now, but you have brought it on yourself, and put the Lady Margaret at risk. If it is God's will that this monstrous treatment will effect a cure, you still must practise chastity with her to keep things right."

Ruaraidh sneered. "You set such store on faithfulness, even when your wives cannot give you the children Uishall needs. What of your common little mistress, whose child you have been forced to borrow back? Does she not warm your bed from time to time, and heat your cock with promises of heirs?"

Alec flushed. His brother's capacity for pleasantness, even when sick, still had paltry limits. "It seems your memory serves you when it suits you," he said.

"Peace, brother," Ruaraidh said, his words placatory but his smile unkind. "I did not mean to anger you. It is my mind, sometimes it seems my thoughts are not my own."

"Iona is my wife. She warms my bed and I would have no other in it," Alec said stiffly.

Ruaraidh tossed his head. "But she still has her eye on you, that low-born maid you took. Be on your guard, or she will have her way."

"We are not all so easily led to sin as you," Alec said, and knew he sounded pompous, and a hypocrite. "I learned the value of monogamy, and wish you would come to value it in turn, if only for the Lady Margaret's sake."

Ruaraidh glanced at him ironically. "Perhaps one day I will, when I am cured of wanting every sweet-faced maid I see." He closed his eyes. "But all the same, you should not judge me. You might think me dissolute, but you are a liar, and in consequence our sins weigh equal. Is it not so, brother?"

He smiled; he was even beginning to feel a little better, knowing he was touching raw nerves. "It is ironic, is it not, how our sins show two sides of the same suffering?" he said. "Both of us bear the scars of Venus, but mine are visible and come from surfeit, while yours are hidden and come from denial."

Alec went to the window and looked out over the elegant square, trying to close out his brother's voice.

"You still want her," Ruaraidh said, his voice weak. "And you think you can deny her by swearing devotion to your wife. Well, if I can see the way your eyes follow her, then it's certain Iona can."

"You have the devil in you, even more so than usual," Alec said.

Ruaraidh let out a low, derisive laugh. "You are not alone in your desires, you may take comfort in that," he said. "Oh, she is very proper with you, with her polite manners and evasive eyes, her little curtseys and careful distances, but she is no less eager to win her place back in your bed than you would be to have her there."

When Alec failed to rise to his provocations, he sighed fretfully. "Common though she is, she is yet a pretty one," he conceded slyly. "If you will persist in your humbug and denials, why, I might have a turn at her myself, if such an opportunity presents itself."

At this, Alec walked over to the bed and bent over his brother, his face pale with temper. "You will not lay so much as a finger on her while she works within my house and under my protection," he said.

Ruaraidh grinned, his fatigue and nausea temporarily and sweetly relieved. "Tsk, tsk," he said and wagged an admonitory finger. "You are too easily roused on her behalf, brother. It saddens me to see it, such misplaced passion."

Alec resumed his place at the window. There was a tense and lengthy silence before he said, "You wish me to stay in London, or accompany you anywhere?"

"No, no, you must not trouble yourself further on my account. You have business here? I thought so. I have arrangements made for the short journeys I must undertake during convalescence. But I would appreciate the presence of our physician's apprentice when I start for home. The specialist has warned me I am not likely to be at full strength for some time."

Ruaraidh sank back further into the pillows, the handkerchief held against his mouth. His chin was raw and chapped from constantly mopping away the excess spittle. "You have done your duty by me, brother, and now I would you were gone," he said. "By God, I'll be glad to be rid of this constant running at the mouth."

Notes:
1: *sibbens*: Highland slang for syphilis

12.
CORNERED
AUGUST 1835

She was looking for the oranges, and her hand was shaking as she sorted quickly and with increasing impatience through the fruit baskets in the storeroom. They should be there, and their absence made her uneasy. Something was wrong. She had sensed it in the tense and awkward atmosphere in the dining room and again in the kitchen, where the staff were quieter than usual and had looked on her with more sly spite than usual when she entered. She was flustered and they knew it, tossing furtive, unkind smiles between them as she unlatched the storeroom door and went inside. Some distrustful instinct told her that they knew the reason for her agitation and were waiting for something.

Despite the privileges she had come to enjoy as a member of Alec's household, Janet's was not an easy life. The underhand, jealous looks of her kitchen comrades, the resentment of the privileges she enjoyed, were bad enough. The way all of them taunted her by aping the Laird's uncomfortable relations with her and calling her Mistress Macleod. The disdain of the Lady Iona, who never had a kind word for her. The stable boys and other men who watched her with hostile cunning, knowing she had once lain with the Laird, and wondering what their own chances with her might be – all these things Janet had to bear in the course of carrying out her duties.

Fortunately, Alice, an energetic girl of only nineteen, was her chief workmate, and she and Janet shared a steady companionship which had developed into friendship. Alice was more of a chatterbox, taller than Janet and broadly built, with a strong sense of right and wrong, and a touching loyalty towards her storeroom companion. Aside from Alice, Janet had only her son for company, but she was never so despairing that she wished herself back where she had started.

Ruaraidh was especially fond of oranges. Whenever he came to dinner he insisted that one be served to him with a sharp knife, during desserts. He would make long, thin slices through the skin, with the concentration of a surgeon about to perform an operation. He would smell the zest and fastidiously peel away every last trace of pith, then eat the juicy segments one by one, with salacious glances at the ladies at table, showing them his tongue. Everybody knew about the oranges. It was one of the first things Janet had learned when her job began: every time Alec's objectionable brother came for dinner, she was responsible for making sure there were oranges. And it was a duty regularly required of her; Alec, Laird of Uishall, and Ruaraidh, recently become the proud first occupant of Maglavat's finally completed castle, ate dinner together often, tied by business necessities and the customs of sharing Clan blood.

Tonight, when Alice had been forced to return to the dining room empty-handed, Ruaraidh had at once demanded, with the bullish illogic that only makes sense to the inebriated, that the mistress of the storeroom be sent for. Janet's superior being away to her bed, it was she who had become the object of the summons. Alec protested impatiently that his brother, drunk at table as usual and embarrassing everyone, especially his wife, should let the subject drop. Why not instead content himself with one of the fine apples already gracing the table?

Alec glanced with pity at the Lady Margaret, who had found the whole meal something of a trial. She had been only just well enough to make the journey from Maglavat the day before, and had spent most of the visit resting in her room. It seemed that as soon as Ruaraidh had begun to recover his strength, Margaret had begun to lose hers, and Alec put it down to the infant losses she had suffered and the exhausting grief that accompanied them. In recent months, the physician had been called out to her more and more often, to treat a succession of complaints that had everyone baffled. Tonight, a lingering infection of the gums had made eating a misery for her – everything seemed to irritate them, and she was struggling to swallow even the softest dishes on the table. The physician, an old family friend, was one of the party, as he had thought it unwise for her to travel without recourse to medical support.

Ruaraidh had not helped matters, his mood swinging between showing concern for his wife's difficulties, then annoyance at her picking and toying with the excellent food. She had offended him earlier, he had said, to the astonishment and discomfort of the company, by being unable to eat some of her favourite chocolates that he had had shipped to her at great expense. What business had she, showing such ingratitude, when he took such pains to gratify her every whim? Alec, who had long since ceased to be amazed at his brother's complete disregard for form when he was in this frame of mind, heard the prick of hurt beneath his anger. An image flashed into his mind – his little brother standing in the stables the day after his mother's funeral, rhythmically kicking the door of his mother's favourite mare, the animal growing increasingly distressed as Ruaraidh methodically beat out the pulse of his rage, his face dark with controlled fury. At the table, Margaret, embarrassed, had tried patiently to explain that she could not eat the chocolate because it hurt her to put anything in her mouth, but by that time, Ruaraidh had stopped listening and was brooding over her unkindness. He had resorted at last to bullying her, and the more Alec remonstrated with him, the worse he got.

It was less than a year since he had returned from the savage treatment given him at great expense and physical cost in London. In the succeeding months, he had recovered most of his strength, his hair had thickened and recovered its colour and lustre, his flesh had built up around his bones, and the disease seemed to be in abeyance at least. But his temperament had altered, he was moodier than ever, prone to outbreaks of furious rage for little reason, and still saw fit to torment the serving girls at his home with his rampant sexual needs. Alec had tried to understand the changes he saw at work in his troubled brother, but there were circumstances, such as had arisen today, when it seemed no excuses could be made for him.

Alec was angry, had been all day. His brother's drinking and boasting, his ill-judged womanising stories, which had forced Alec to reprove him more than once for his lack of tact. All these things had sorely tried the Laird's patience. He had kept his temper, but only just, for the sake of the poor Lady Margaret, the rest of the company and Iona, who was looking increasingly uncomfortable with the loaded remarks being made about Ruaraidh's diminished inheritance thanks to the late appearance of Alasdair. The object of his disgruntled remarks being still too young to join the adults at dinner, Ruaraidh was casting around for fresh outlets for his ire, and the oranges had all the makings of handsomely fitting the bill.

"An orange is what I want, and an orange is what I'll have," he said, his voice thick with drink and the temper beginning to blacken his eyes. The other guests shifted uncomfortably in the heavy silence. "If they have been ordered for me as you say, then they must be found and got out."

Alice hovered, not sure who she should listen to. Her nervous glance fell on Ruaraidh's meaty right hand, still relaxed on the arm of his chair. The thick gold ring set with a large ruby glistened dully on his little finger, catching the flickering light of the fire like a devil's eye. The juniper logs spat and crackled in the grate as they released their resiny scent.

Alec waved his hand impatiently. "Be gone, Alice," he said to her. "If you cannot find the oranges, then it's certain they are not there. There is no point disturbing another member of the household to discover again what we already know to be the case. The oranges are missing, but we'll survive somehow without them."

He might have got away with this if he had left it at that, but some demon inside made him continue. "It will do my brother good to taste apple instead of orange for a change, just as it would do his fellow diners good to see him sober at table instead of drunk." He knew better than to nettle him, but Ruaraidh had been worse than usual this evening, positively dangerous when they were shooting earlier and sullen since their return. He had disappeared just before the bell announced dinner, and it was twenty minutes before he reappeared and they could be seated.

Ruaraidh dropped his head, but Alec saw him smile, a dangerous, reptilian smile that undercut the quietness of his voice. Alec was immediately uneasy and regretted his provocations. He had seen that look a thousand times before and knew it meant trouble. His brother was up to something. Ruaraidh looked again at Alice, who, despite her robust constitution, was frightened of his frequent tempers.

"Maid, go and fetch the mistress of the storeroom, or it will be the worse for you," he said, and his voice was very soft, albeit laced with threat. When she hesitated, he shouted "Now!" so suddenly and so loudly that she jumped with fright.

Alice fled and sought out Janet in her room, who laid aside her reading by the fire and hastily donned her apron and cap. Alice was upset, fearing retribution, and Janet tried to calm her anxious chatter as they made their way back downstairs. It would be best if she handled this herself, she told the young girl, and sent her back to the kitchen to await developments. If Ruaraidh were to lose his temper, as he seemed to have a mind to do, better he had only one servant to vent his rage on. Like Alec, she trusted Alice; if she couldn't find the oranges, someone had moved them, for whatever reason, and she could not conceal her unease as she approached Ruaraidh's chair.

"You sent for me, sir."

He looked testily at her. "Where is my orange, mistress?"

"I laid them ready," she said. "And I showed Alice where to find them." When he raised his eyes in mocking irritation at her incompetence, she said, "I will check the place at once."

She left the dining room, struggling with agitation and annoyance in equal measure as she hurried to the storeroom. Something about Ruaraidh's manner troubled her. And even though the kitchen staff were still busy with dishes and scrubbing in the next room, she felt vulnerable in the gloomy light as she held the candle and began to hunt for the missing fruit. She knew she had to get out quickly, with or without them. She searched, trying to keep a clear head, trying to think what could have happened.

The soft click of the storeroom door closing behind her made her freeze in mid-movement. The door was solid and the storeroom was large, and she was well inside it. She turned around to find Ruaraidh standing a few steps away, something held in his hand.

"Is it this you seek, mistress?" he said softly.

He held the orange towards her, a glint in his eye.

"Where were they?"

"Where I hid them," he said, and laid the orange on the nearest shelf between them.

"For later," he said, and winked at her.

Janet's eyes flicked towards the closed door. She knew the kitchen staff had colluded in his little practical joke, and their betrayal devastated her. They had been waiting for him and now she was trapped. Before she could do anything, he was upon her, his hand over her mouth. His chunky fingers smelled powerfully of gunpowder, the grease of gun barrel oil and cooking, rare game sauced with juniper, and faint traces of orange zest.

"So you're the wench my brother took such a shine to," he said, pushing her past the baskets. "And the bastard boy you whelped had a hand in turning round my inheritance, did he not?"

Janet tried to fight, but it felt as though her limbs had turned to water. The same fear washed through her that she had felt when Alec felled her in the heather, and the memory forged a sudden, hideous link between the brothers. She smelled whisky on Ruaraidh's breath, was suddenly aware of the danger she was in. He was much stronger than she was, but tonight his strength was dulled by liquor. Feeling her wilt beneath his grip, he relaxed for a moment and Janet took her chance and sank her teeth into his hand.

Ruaraidh shouted out and struck her across the face. Janet screamed with the force of the blow and the deep scratch of the ruby ring at the side of her face. Beyond the door, the muffled sounds of kitchen chatter, the dull clatter of the dinner dishes in the wooden sink, and the scraping of saucepans in the pot sink, fell silent.

"Little evil bitch," Ruaraidh said. "You think they are going to help you?" He pushed his face close to hers. "They don't like you, Janet – what you did, or the foolish way my brother treats you. They're all thinking, *she spread her legs for one brother – why not do it with the other*?"

He cupped his hand and pressed it against her skirts, until he felt the shape of her, and grunted with malicious satisfaction. "The rumour is no man has touched you since my brother got you with child. So it would be fitting, would it not, if I were the one to break that long fast?" He smiled at her. "Yes. It's high time our prim little mistress learned some humility at the hands of the brother she has wronged." He tried to kiss her and was not quick enough to avoid the nip of her teeth.

He swore, grabbed at her hair, saw the hatred in her eyes and grinned again, even though he tasted blood on his lip. "Still of a mind to fight me? I wonder if you gave my brother so much trouble?" He brought her head back with a swift, violent movement and banged it hard against the wall; the pain exploded inside her skull, and this time she staggered and her cry was muted. She half-fell against him, a little blood from the cut oozing onto his ruffled collar, so that he was obliged to push her up against the cold stone and hold her there.

"Well now," he said, his lips against her ear. "That's better. Now you are nicely subdued, let's see what you are made of, and whether or not I can divine what draws my brother's lust so strongly."

He had unbuttoned his breeches and begun to hoist up her skirts when the door flew open, admitting a stream of yellow light from the kitchen. Ruaraidh was wrenched backwards and thrown to the floor, and she fell forward, gasping. She vaguely saw the white-faced Alice standing in the doorway, frightened half out of her wits, and understood that it was she who had gone to get help.

104

"You will not treat my employees in this fashion," Alec was saying, his voice shaking with rage. "The rules your maidservants are made to live by at Maglavat do not apply here."

Ruaraidh struggled to his feet, surveying his brother with cool contempt. "I never understood what you saw in her," he said. "And I was just about to find out." He shook his head. "I'm amazed you got anywhere near her. See how she has bitten me. All of them are sluts, but this one is savage with it."

Aware they had an audience, with all the kitchen staff staring at the three of them in shocked fascination, Alec tried to collect himself, but failed when he saw his brother's taunting smile. Grabbing him by the throat, Alec shoved him out of the storeroom, and watched with grim satisfaction as Ruaraidh fell again.

"Your drunkenness, your debauchery, your disease – all of them shame me. You have wasted a fortune in London to end up worse than you were. Up, get up on your feet at once. Get out – now." He seized his arm, crushing it so that Ruaraidh flinched, and then whispered, "If you have succeeded in violating her, you will answer to me. And if she is diseased, I will kill you."

Ruaraidh shrugged. "You will have to ask her whether or not she considers herself defiled. For myself, I will tell you I was thwarted, and did not come within a hair of getting what I sought."

"I will hear it from her lips before I am satisfied."

Ruaraidh's smile was cold with cruel intelligence. "And you will tell your wife, if your gossiping servants do not get there first, how fiercely you have just fought for her rival." He paused. "Admit it, brother, had I succeeded, and she had been with child, you would have thanked me, would you not? You should think on the consequences of *that* before you come running to me with your duelling pistols."

As Ruaraidh left the kitchen, Alec turned to Alice. "Call for my brother's carriage at once - he is to be driven home. Then go to the dining room and speak to the Lady Margaret's physician. It is too late for her to make the journey back across the mountains. She is to stay here until she feels strong enough to undertake the trip. See she is escorted kindly to her chamber, and when she is settled, the physician is to attend Mistress Macleod in her room. He will need directions."

Alice nodded and ran from the storeroom. Alec paused, his eyes moving to the staff grouped around the door. "None of you will take a single order from him, if ever he tries to set foot in this house again."

By this time, Janet had got to her feet and was brushing down her skirt, still leaning against the wall to steady herself.

"You are hurt?" he asked, and all the kitchen saw that his formal stance, the way he stood back from her, was at odds with the tenderness in his voice.

"No sir, only startled." She was trembling, the smell of Ruaraidh still on her clothes, and her vision still fogged. Her hand moved involuntarily to the sore place where Ruaraidh had hit her and Alec, still fighting to keep his distance, lost the battle when he saw the short, deep cut where she had been struck.

He went to her; he could not help it, and saw the warning flash in her eyes as she ducked away. He stopped, confused, inhibited, still angry, the eyes of all the kitchen staff upon him. His arm dropped to his side and he turned on them with renewed outrage.

"I had better not hear which of you aided my brother in this assault," he said, "or you will be forced to seek employment at Maglavat, where as we all know, the standards are not so high as here, and the servants are expected to gratify my brother's every whim, without question."

"I will help you to your room," he said to Janet, his voice suddenly quiet again.

She shook her head. "It's not necessary, sir," she said. "Sleep will repair any damage done."

"What has happened?"

Alec turned to find Iona in the storeroom doorway, her face betraying concern and distrust. "The physician has just taken the Lady Margaret to her chamber. Is Ruaraidh to make the journey home so late?" She looked questioningly at her husband.

"I have turned my brother out of the house. He has attacked Mistress Macleod in the course of carrying out her duties. I will talk with Margaret in the morning."

Iona glanced coolly at Janet. "He is a man with little enough in the way of self-control," she said, her tone slightly patronising. "If you provoked him even a little, he would rise to the bait."

It took Janet a moment to understand that she was being accused. "My Lady, I did not –" she began, but was interrupted before she could defend herself. Alec was staring at his wife as if he could hardly believe his ears.

"Wait – wait. Are you suggesting it is *Janet* who is at fault? That she was somehow hoping that drunken boor would have her in full view of all the kitchen staff? Do you think she *asked* for this?"

Iona recoiled. "I only meant –"

"Not another word," he said harshly. "Whatever you meant, it was neither kind nor just. My brother has just shamed me by treating my staff like common whores. My staff stood by and did nothing while Janet was shut up in the storeroom. And now my wife is behaving just like them, by making accusations and giving in to bigotry."

He broke off as he saw Iona's bewilderment.

"You would defend her over me?" she whispered.

"I would defend anyone who has been accused of another's crime!" Alec shouted, and a shocked silence succeeded his outburst.

He passed a hand over his eyes. It was as if all the petty unkindnesses his wife had heaped on Janet had fused into this moment of vindictive cruelty; it demeaned her, reducing her to someone who had suddenly aroused his contempt. The sensation was as powerful as it was fleeting, as nakedly real as it was vigorously repressed. He could not look at Iona for the anger and disappointment he felt. He could not look at Janet for the feelings that would engulf and betray him if he was forced to gaze again on the wounds inflicted by his brother. The silence strained against the weight of the Laird's rage. It seemed the whole household hung on his next words.

In the hiatus, Janet took an uncertain step towards the door. Alec rounded on her.

"Stay," he said sharply. "You are not fit to make the journey to your room when you are shaking so badly you can hardly stand." He glanced behind him, saw a stool against the far wall and seized it. "Sit a moment," he said. "We will get to the bottom of this once and for all." He broke off, snatching up the orange Ruaraidh had discarded on the shelf. "This is what you came to seek. Where were they? Why could Alice not find them when she came?"

"I don't know, sir," Janet said. "The gentleman followed me here and he held it in his hand. He said he had hidden it."

"The door was closed," Alec persisted. "Did my brother shut you in?"

She shook her head.

"Tell me the truth, Janet," he said. "You have my word you will not suffer for your answer."

She hesitated. "Sir, the door cannot be closed from within," she said at last. "It must be latched from the other side."

Alec nodded, rose and turned to his wife. "That is answer enough for you," he said.

Iona swallowed. "Well then, the mistake is mine." She inclined her head briefly. "My apologies, mistress," she said to Janet with chilly formality. "I see now that you have been wronged, and I must submit to being made an example of before my entire household."

"No," Alec said, his anger at last relenting. "The entire household has been made an example of. We have all joined in my brother's game."

Iona was still staring at him, her eyes full of tears. Too late, Alec was moved to pity and remorse.

"Now here's a bad end to a hard day," he said. "I am not worth these tears, and neither is my brother, who has caused them." He took her hands in his and kissed her, a public display of reconciliation. "I am sorry for my anger. Let's to bed and start a better day tomorrow. Go up to our chamber now, and I will bid our other guests goodnight and follow shortly, when I see that all is well."

Iona nodded, subdued, but he knew she was hurt beyond measure at the way he had embarrassed her. She cast a swift glance at Janet, and left.

Alec sighed again, then turned to his staff. "All of you are shamed by what has happened here tonight," he said coldly. "Now set to work, for there are still tasks to be done before you seek your beds."

With the dispersal of the kitchen staff, he turned again to Janet.

"I beg you sir, I am marked out enough without you making me more of a special case."

"They sought to hurt you." He looked at her with genuine bewilderment. "If Alice had not come –" he said, and broke off. "Has it always been like this? Who will you count on, if I am not here?"

Janet rose, still idling miserably on the whim of her employer. "Tell me one thing," she said. "Did Alice know what they planned to do?"

Alec shook his head. "Only when she saw Ruaraidh follow you. She guessed at once and ran to the dining room."

Janet smiled. "Well then, it seems I have one friend besides you."

He looked at her. "And now you must tell me something in return," he said. "I must ask, for your sake as well as mine. Did he –?"

"No, sir. You came in time."

His eyes closed for a moment. "Come, this episode is at an end." He took a step towards her and she moved back hastily.

"I am better on my own," she said again.

"You have leaned on me before," he said. "Why not now?"

"Please sir, I know you mean to show me kindness, but it's better that I go alone."

He looked at her in exasperation. "Alice!" he called into the kitchen. "Leave your duties and help Janet to her chamber." He smiled at her. "It is thanks to you a much worse situation has been avoided. Now Janet, go and sit by your fire and await the physician. No, mistress, you will not remonstrate with me. Alice, see her safely installed, then put together some whisky, honey and hot milk, and stay with your patient on the physician's bidding."

Janet was glad of the sturdy Alice at her side, for she felt faint and sick as soon as she began to move. She knew that Alec followed, at a distance, until he saw them both safely to the stairs that led to her room. None of them saw Iona standing in the shadows as they passed, and did not know she had heard every word that passed between them.

Once Janet was safely in her room, Alice left for the kitchen; a few moments later, there was a gentle knock.

Janet called out, "Come," expecting the physician, but it was Gillies MacNicol who entered the room, and for a moment, she panicked.

He halted, distressed. "Peace, Mistress Macleod," he said hastily. "I mean you no harm. I thought only to bring you some extra logs to stoke the fire. If you would rather, I will quit your room at once."

She shook her head and watched him as he walked carefully towards the fireplace and set two logs on the fire and a further four in the hearth. She sat, not cold and stiff, but vulnerable and frightened of him, shrinking under the blanket. If he saw the tears that began to run from her eyes, he did not acknowledge them. He swept up the ashes, keeping his head down as he worked. He did not look at her, made no pleasant comment as he usually did, no attempt to draw her out in conversation.

On his way out, he surprised her by saying, "The man is a beast to treat you as he did."

Janet barely had time to register his words before the physician arrived. He tended her efficiently, making no comment on the cut to her face except to tut under his breath. She endured the sting of iodine and the strong smell of witch-hazel as he cleaned the wound and bound it, finding bruising and abrasion at the back of her head, and gave orders that she was to rest the following day, for she had taken some rough blows and suffered concussion, and would feel quite out of sorts come the morning. He gave her a sleeping draught and instructed Alice to watch over her until she slept.

The medicine was strong, but Janet spent a restless, fevered night. At length, she dreamed she felt a cool cloth on her forehead and heard a soft voice stealing through the edges of the darkness, until it reached her, wrapped her and comforted her. It spoke to her in the old tongue, the lilt of it sweet and soothing, and she heard the words *a'ghraidh*, whispered in a broken voice, and she seemed at last to fall out of fever and into sleep, cradled in safe, strong arms.

In the morning, she woke bathed in sweat and overwhelmed by loneliness. Her fire was usually only lit in the evenings, but a comforting blaze greeted her, and a new supply of wood stacked neatly by the grate. Some of the precious juniper logs, reserved usually for the dining room and principal drawing rooms, were burning in her grate, their scent pleasingly astringent. Her eyes drifted listlessly above the fireplace and lighted on a small posy of wild orchids set in a little earthenware pot on the mantelpiece. The touching gift broke through the miasma of painful images and she was comforted. Her head ached with savage intensity, but what hurt most of all was that Alec had almost touched her, which caused as much anguish as the unasked handling of his brother.

13.
RUBBY-DUBBY
OCTOBER 1835

I

Iona sat at the rough wood table in the tiny circular stone hut, her hands laid on a large, smooth oval stone, and wept. Thus far, she had shown a dignified face to the world; indeed she had been positively haughty on this occasion, when she was admitted to the low room and had attempted to look with disdain on her mean surroundings. Her shoes were soaked through and muddy, the hem of her travelling dress limp and heavy with wet grass and trails of peat. Her fair hair, coiled simply around her head, was lank and draggled after her journey. But her need was too strong for her to pretend the hut was beneath her for long. When the crone sitting opposite had bid her touch the stone and show her true feelings to it, Iona had given way, the dam of pride broken open within minutes of her arrival.

Around the walls, over the fireplace and above her head hung bunches of dried herbs and flowers, roots and seeds, weaving their pungent odours into a tapestry of scent that was as seductive as it was repellent, as redolent of desperation as it was of hope. Iona flinched when she saw the withered juniper berries, still on their branches, festooned with sharp needles, the old evil medicine for prompting abortion. She drew back on her stool, as if just being in the room with them would further blight her already negligible chances of conceiving and carrying a child. It seemed cruel indeed that juniper was the badge of the Clan Macleod of Uishall, as if she and Alec were doomed to labour fruitlessly under a curse handed down by his ancient forebears. The more her miserable condition weighed on her, the more she sought omens and symbols in the details of her everyday life, reasons for why she must bear this terrible burden. It seemed powerful indeed that not only was her husband infertile, but that the very symbol of his Clan seemed to drive home the message that even

111

if he were not, she would still have to struggle against a family icon that repelled the idea of children.

It was a measure of her painful sorrow that had brought her on the punishing journey into the mountains to seek the advice of this ancient mother, renowned for her mystical and healing gifts. She was reputed to be over a hundred years old, a shape-shifter with the power to turn into a hare and keep at bay evil spirits by leading them away from the ordinary mortals they would otherwise torment. Iona had sent for her, wanting to receive her at Uishall, but the old woman had refused – a tactical manoeuvre she often employed as a test – not of faith, but of need. The very fact that the Lady Iona was prepared to humble herself by making the journey, told her the depth of suffering in which her seeker was mired.

The old woman watched silently as her grand visitor poured out her grief. She saw that Iona was failing in strength, succumbing to the strain of continual denial of what she most wanted. Her pale face, the suffering so thinly veiled by her attempts to play her public role with conviction, the knotting of her hands in her lap when she first sat down. The prolonged torrent of weeping was as good a starting point for healing her as anything. Her hands lay on the stone and before long her forehead rested on it too, and the old woman did nothing, said nothing, until the worst of her grieving had been spent.

At last, Iona sat back from the table and lifted her eyes to the healer. God in his wisdom had so far turned a blind eye to her suffering, and she was still not carrying the child she longed for. Her monthly bleeding made a mockery of her strenuous efforts to compensate for her husband's sin, as if God was throwing her faith, her heartfelt supplications, back in her face. Alec had increased his devotions, made his own atonement to the boy and his mother, to no good effect. God was either pitiless or sadistic and now Iona, miserable in her barrenness, crucified by her failing faith, had rejected the stern Christian beliefs she had been raised in. The pagan route might prove to be a clearer path to the objectives she sought.

The old woman drew the stone across the table towards her, and laid her own hands upon it.

"There is anger in these tears, child," she said. "And fear, too. I sense another element in this that adds to your struggle."

Iona's face darkened. "He has brought a witch into my house," she said, her voice trembling. "She does nothing and yet I feel her power, as if she has touched him."

"He is bewitched?"

"Aye, but he will not listen to me. He says he has not touched her, but she – " Iona stopped, steeled herself. "She has borne his child, twelve years since, and whatever prayers I make to God, I cannot do the same for him."

"She has made you jealous, then," the old woman said. "And jealousy will destroy your heart as surely as any other poison."

Iona stared at her as if she had just been hit by a falling truth. "Yes. She has poisoned me," she said, seeing with fresh clarity the twisted relationship she had with Janet. "I feel hate for her, and it saps my strength."

"You were brought into the Christian fold when you were young," the old woman commented with a sniff. "Do you still have faith?"

Iona shook her head. "God watches my struggle and it seems that he finds amusement in it, for every time I renew my petitions, he finds some new way to twist his knife. I took no part in my husband's sin, and yet God continues to punish us both. And now it is not only the lack of a child I fear, but the waning affections of my husband. Is this how my faithfulness is to be rewarded, by having suffering piled on top of pain?"

The healer watched her, nodding slowly. "God is not strong enough to work his miracles in so magic a place as this," she said softly. "The old faiths still hang their charms like cobwebs about the land, and they repel him."

"That's why I am here," Iona whispered. "I am losing my husband because I cannot give him what he knows he has already got from another." She broke down again. "Help me, mother, for if I cannot conceive and win back my husband's love, I am better dead."

"There is fight in you yet," the healer said firmly. "Come, stand, let me look properly on you and see where you need strength. You cannot wage war with a wasted body, and you cannot outwit your witch with a broken mind and spirit."

When she left an hour or two later, Iona was exhausted, but filled with new resolve. The old woman gave her a strong garlic infusion to build up her blood, stag-horn jelly for her health, and performed the charm of the three threads to protect her from the *droch shuil*. Iona wept through most of the proceedings, paid handsomely for her cure, and left clutching a bag of medicines and a rock crystal, charmed to keep Janet's baleful influence at bay. On the long journey homeward, she saw several times a hare flashing ahead of her on the path.

II

When Alec came to their chamber a few nights later, Iona was waiting for him, standing shyly at the foot of their bed, her white nightdress loose, her fair hair down over her shoulders. She held a bunch of greenery in her hand, tied up with a white ribbon, and her smile was welcoming, but bashful. He saw the charm, recognised it, and went to her, drawing her into his arms and kissing her tenderly.

"What, you are turning to the old ways to help us now?" he asked.

"I have prayed until my hope has turned bitter," she said. "If God will not take heed of my requests, then he will not take heed when I make my pleading to another. There can be no harm in seeing what our local powers can do."

Alec sighed and stroked her hair away from her face. "In the end there may be no powers we can draw on except those we find within ourselves," he said. "You have the will to try to make a child with me, but do you have the strength to give it up if no child ensues? Can you love me if I cannot give you what you want?"

"I am not alone in this," Iona said, her voice sharpening as her grip tightened on the charm she held. "We may both have to learn to accept what we cannot have, and let go what we most want." She paused, and when she spoke again, there was a hint of pleading in her voice. "But agree with me at least that we must not give up the fight until we have spent all our efforts and there is nothing more to be done."

He nodded, kissed her, and her arms came around him. "Well then, offer them to me," he said. "And I will accept and take you and we will see what we will see."

Wild carrot she gave him, embarrassed to hand it to him when they had been so long practised in loving each other. The thin roots hung down from the tender, ferny heads like skinny parsnips, and he took them, kissed them, and made her laugh by holding them against his sex. Then he placed the charm on the bed beside her, stripped off his clothes and came to her. Their passion fuelled by hope again, Alec held his wife close against him and whispered his devotion. He prayed for fertile seed as he pushed his way inside and tried to touch her stubborn womb.

14.
DISPLAY
HOGMANAY 1835

I

The Great Hall at Uishall Castle was hung with Macleod tartan banners and huge white satin bows. The bold blue, green and black checks of the tartan, crossed through with narrow bands of red and yellow, gave a distinguished backdrop to the occasion. Bunches of dried flowers and heather, holly wreaths bright with red berries and spiky, silvery-green juniper branches, were tied up together with blood-red ribbon to deck the walls and ceilings. Juniper logs burned in the fireplaces, giving out their clean, cedar-like fragrance, edged with the keen, distinctive scent of the berries that were harvested in the autumn. There was a festive atmosphere as music played and the gentry and tenants of the estate celebrated the coming of the New Year. Janet smiled at the decorations and chose a seat by the window where she could watch the comings and goings of the guests.

Alec moved through the company, assured and handsome in his kilt and black velvet jacket. He made everyone welcome, saw everyone's glasses filled, saw that everyone knew their way through to the dining room, where a great silver punchbowl was wreathed with flowers and full of a fragrant and heady combination of red wine, Madeira, lemonade and sliced fruit. Its scent twisted through the gathering like a wisp of perfumed cloud and infected them and everyone else in the room with gaiety, the women sitting around the walls, the clusters of people stood talking in animated groups. On the massive oak dining table, plates were piled with cold meats and bread, oatcakes and crowdie, fruitcake, flapjacks and red Christmas apples.

Iona was laughing and flirting with a group of gentlemen, her glass filled and her eyes bright. She looked to be enjoying the festivities, but Janet, hypersensitive to the increasingly charged atmosphere between the Laird and his Lady, noticed how her eyes darted constantly, kept Alec in her sight, watched

116

the way he interacted with everyone who crossed his path. She saw the effort it cost the Lady of Uishall to trust her husband, for as well as tracking Alec, she always had to know where Janet was, too.

Janet saw the hurting, too, the Laird and his wife still childless, the strain beginning to tell as another new year loomed, still empty of the gift they sought. The way Iona was entirely cold with her now, as if she secretly blamed Janet for her barren condition. The fear that crept into her eyes whenever she caught Alec speaking to his storeroom apprentice, the way she would interrupt if she felt the conversation was going on too long. And even though the rule at Uishall Castle was that the staff spoke in English, she would still overhear her husband speaking in a lower voice than usual to his storeroom apprentice and knew they talked in the old language that excluded her. When she reprimanded him for breaking his own rule, he smiled and said that sometimes, he liked to reward Janet's considerable progress in the foreign language required by her employment, by allowing her to communicate freely with him in her mother tongue.

Everyone knew about the Lady Iona's recent efforts to bolster her strength. Everyone saw the way it was changing her personality, her kindly nature gradually becoming infected by an obsessive and destructive hope that burned in her eyes with a dark, cruel light. Tonight, she had determined to be merry, but the determination was more in evidence than the merriment.

It had been a trying day for her. She would not touch the juniper branches when they were brought into the hall to be hung, and held a dainty handkerchief to her nose when she was standing near the fireplace, in case she breathed the scent from the logs too deeply. If the curse placed on her husband should ever be lifted – or if, indeed, it already had – it would be sheer folly to court disaster and risk losing any child that might otherwise bind to her and flourish.

Janet sat quietly, enjoying the spectacle, the dazzling dresses of the richer ladies, the relaxation of her household colleagues, all of whom relished this opportunity to let down their hair and enjoy for once the splendour of the castle they worked in. The men she worked with were more restless than the girls, slipping out from time to time to smoke, or steal across to the earthy warmth of Gillies MacNicol's woodshed to take a nip of whisky or *brose*[1]. She watched, occasionally sipping from the glass of punch, once or twice straying into the dining room to pick at the inviting spread. She paused to chat, too, to the storeroom mistress and Alice, and to the maids and kitchen maids with whom she had the closest working relationships.

Alec played the part of host with artless diligence, the men wanting to share in the conversations he made around business and politics, flattered when he asked their opinions. The ladies caught his eye, smiling shyly at his kind politeness, blushing if he should choose to tease them.

He gave a plausible excuse when the absence of Ruaraidh and his family was commented upon, and refused to be pressed for details of the last occasion they had stayed at Uishall. *Had he not been lured into a cupboard by a maid with a fancy for him*, some of his less well-informed guests eagerly asked him. *Why did the Laird take such exception to such a harmless dalliance*? Alec, his face tight beneath the easy smile, said the matter was closed. When some of them persisted, he said it was not a subject he cared to pursue, and one or two of them looked wryly at each other when he had gone and whispered, *So it must be true. It was the little wench who bore the child*.

Alasdair had grown to love the Hogmanay parties thrown by his father, just as he had grown into his role as a landowner's son. He was now quite at ease, the manners second nature to him, his attitude thoroughly schooled. He did not stand at his father's side all night as he used to, but moved amongst the company, speaking to everyone as etiquette demanded. Some of the younger ladies were even beginning to bestow favourable glances on him, and he received these politely and with secret amusement. He was much too young to marry, and when he came of age, he would not be choosing his bride from any local family, however well endowed, because he knew his origins would always make him a target.

Alec talked and laughed, kissed hands, turned a blind eye to the little groups who gossiped about his past and the choices he had made. He sighed as he approached another newly arrived guest. He would empty his home of half the people he had invited, were it not for the political and familial ties he was obliged to make. Despite his tactful and solicitous ministrations, he never looked at Janet, although he knew exactly where she sat.

When the dancing started, The Laird's Favours began – Alec's traditional pledge to dance with every lady in the room, guests and staff alike, and personally wish her good fortune for the coming year. This same courtesy he was careful to extend, via handshakes and conversation, to all the menfolk. Janet watched him take the floor with Iona, and thought that this time, she might not remain a spectator as she had done in the past.

II

The previous three Hogmanay celebrations had been marked by Janet's evasion of Alec's pleasant and courtly practice.

The first year, when she had only been at Uishall a few months, when Alasdair was still not fully schooled and she was still too ill at ease to allow her association with Alice to develop into friendship, she had tried to plead her way out of attending, but Alec had advised against it.

"My presence will only cause you embarrassment and discomfort," she had said. "And it will undermine Alasdair's position as the Laird's son."

"You must come," he said, and pitied her anguish. "I would not insist if I thought there might be another way to handle matters. If you do not come, even for a half-hour, you will only have to bear their censure the following year. Those I call my friends will not look unkindly on you. Stand to, for Alasdair's sake, for he will be subject to the same scrutiny, and worse. Then curiosity will be satisfied, and you will be left alone."

That first year, it had taken all her resolution to walk into the room where she knew all the company would be watching for her. When she had done her best to lose herself amongst a crowd of Uishall's housekeeping staff, she began to feel the worst was over, but one of the kitchen maids then gaily told her of the custom of the Laird's Favours, and she had been panic-stricken.

The news that the Laird would make it his business to dance with her had filled her with dread as she stood by the window, unable to join in with the conversations that seemed in any case not to need her inclusion. She had been given a glass of punch, but her hand shook so much she had been forced to place it on the table nearby, where it remained untouched.

She glanced fretfully about the room and saw that at least Alasdair had his father's protection, even though he did not seem to need it. He seemed remarkably unselfconscious about the situation and was quick, as usual, to sort out those of the company who would at least extend him courtesy, and those who would not. Although most people were aware of his presence by then, few of them had actually met him – Alec had considered that too much on top of all the learning he had to do in the first place. With his customary candour, Alec cast euphemisms and explanations aside and introduced him as his son. Iona loyally gave her support, saying Alasdair was an unexpected blessing who would do well for the Clan Macleod. Alasdair held their attention momentarily, but everyone wanted to know the rest of the story - who had carried the Laird's first and only son.

Which one is she, they had demanded eagerly of each other. They shook their heads and looked about them. They had been waiting for her, and although she escaped detection for quite a while, word got round eventually and discreet fingers were pointed. Conversation then moved naturally to Iona, and the bravery she showed. *The Laird has made a foolish error*, they said. *Even with Alec's noble blood in his veins, how could such a boy rise above his background*? They looked sympathetically at Iona; they saw through her brittle cheerfulness, though they did not guess the root cause of her unhappiness. *How could he insult her so*, they demanded indignantly. They looked at Janet and raised their eyebrows knowingly at each other. *What ruses these young strippets took to, in pursuit of their ambitions*!

Janet had been standing amongst her kitchen colleagues, wondering if she had stayed long enough for Alec's liking, when she turned and saw Alasdair approaching her, in full view of the company. Before he reached her, she turned away and hurried from the room, through the back door of the castle, where she stood in the chill night air, her shawl pulled tight around her. Despite the furious glance she had thrown him, he followed her.

"Why did you avoid me? I only wanted to wish you well for the coming year, as any son would do," he said.

"You must not associate with me if you are to be seen as your father's son," she said angrily. "You must think of your future now. Did you not see how scornfully they viewed me? Stand with me, and they will mock you and call you a simple-minded child who cannot let go his poor roots."

"You are too touchy," Alasdair said with a smile. "Everyone knows who I am, and what my father would have me become. Why hide it?" He took her hand and held it in both his. "I will not be ashamed of you," he said. "My father acknowledges you. Why should I not?"

"It is his job to acknowledge me," she said in exasperation. "He can do no other but extend me the same courtesy he offers everyone else. It is different for you."

"Do you know how I do it?" he said suddenly. "I can see that it is all a game, and I can only win if I learn all the rules. We are *all* players, mother, concealing our cards and hoping to beat our rivals by making the right moves." She stared at him and he pulled at her. "You cannot hide out here all night. Come back a few minutes," he said. "Play the game. Then you can say you have done the Laird's bidding and he can ask no more of you."

She would not enter the Great Hall with him, but hung back until she saw him safely back at Alec's side. She stayed barely long enough to watch the Laird begin his favours in the usual manner, by dancing with his Lady, before she slipped away to her room and spent the rest of the evening at her writing desk, practising the letters that were so important to her advancement within the household. But her young son's words stuck.

The second and third years were much easier to bear. As Alec predicted, the company tired of her, although a few sought her out as they would other members of the household, and spoke kindly to her. She managed to dodge the Laird's Favours by always moving away to the opposite side of the room from him, or ensuring he was busy with a partner before she left. It became another game she played, not without a certain tense pleasure, knowing everyone watched her to see what would happen if she should let the Laird take her in his arms again. She never danced with anyone.

III

This year, Janet watched Alec circling the floor with easy grace and found she could not leave. He worked his way through the ladies present, spending a few minutes with each, chatting, sometimes laughing if they said something that especially pleased him, spinning them away from him, drawing them close, and releasing them with a bow and a smile. He enjoyed partnering Alice, who was not shy with him as so many of the servant girls were, and flirted quite openly with him, so that the Laird relaxed and was not obliged to make allowances for nerves and propriety. What she lacked in finesse she more than made up for with energy, and several of the company applauded their

121

hectic turn. Iona danced too, rather flamboyantly, usually close to Alec and his current partner, catching his eyes with a brilliant smile whenever she could. Once, he even leaned away from his partner to kiss his wife, and Iona glanced triumphantly across at Janet to see if she had seen the affection that still existed between them.

Janet had not seen, for her view of the dance floor had been obscured by the not unexpected appearance of Gillies MacNicol, awkward in his best suit, his large frame dwarfing her. She nodded politely at him, and he held out his hand.

"Will it please you to dance with me?" he said, and his kind eyes were smiling, though she knew he was nervous. He had made this same approach every Hogmanay, and always she had refused.

Gillies was not the man she wished to take to the floor with, but this time, she did not like to hurt his feelings when he had been so considerate towards her since she had arrived. She had other reasons to feel gratitude. It was he who had found time to come and light the fire in her room the morning after Ruaraidh's assault, and she was sure it was he who had left the little posy of wild flowers to cheer her sickroom. Two days she had been kept in bed on the order of the physician and the insistence of Alec, who assured her she would suffer no loss of wages on account of his brother's misconduct. In that time, Alice had paid her numerous short visits, the storeroom mistress came to wish her a speedy recovery, and Gillies stoically brought wood for the fire as he always did, only enquiring at the end of the second day if she was feeling better. She had found out, too, that the juniper logs she had been treated to had not been commissioned by Alec, but had been smuggled in by Gillies. She had been grateful, though she had also worried that too effusive a display of thanks might serve to encourage his attentions. But now it was Hogmanay, and everyone was dancing, the mood was merry and there could be no harm in it. Before she gave herself too much time to think, she rose and laid her hand on his arm and he led her onto the floor, his face comically red with surprise and panic at her acceptance.

He was a clumsy dancer, touchingly apologetic for his lack of grace, and he held her carefully, taking no liberties, his manner painfully respectful. At such close quarters she felt compromised and would not look at him, concerned that he would read too much into the halting embrace in which they were of necessity locked. She focused on his shoulder, responding briefly to the few halting attempts at conversation he made, when he was not concentrating too grimly on the movement of his feet. It seemed an interminable dance to Janet, and she wasn't sure that Gillies was enjoying it all that much, either.

When at last it ended, he bowed and thanked her and asked if she would move across to the dining room to take a little refreshment. She looked kindly at him and shook her head. He looked crestfallen, but withdrew after commenting wryly that after all, it had taken four years to get her to dance with him. She stood a moment, watching him disappear into the crowd, and had half a mind to follow him and seek out friendly company. But she had barely taken a step towards the dining room when she found the Laird barring her way.

"Mistress Macleod," Alec said with exaggerated gravity, apprehending her with a bow, his face flushed, for by now he had crossed the floor a score or more times. "You may think it has escaped my attention, but you have refused my favours every Hogmanay, and offended me."

"Some would say I have accepted too many of your favours in the past," she said drily.

"I have never seen you dance at Hogmanay until just now," he said. "Perhaps you prefer the attentions of our woodsman to your Laird?"

She shook her head. "No, sir. I wished only to avoid causing you embarrassment. Gillies did not dance as well as I would wish."

He laughed quietly, seized her hand and slipped his arm around her waist. "I am glad to hear it," he said. "Besides, I have danced with every lady in the room except for you and until you accept, I cannot in truth say I have discharged my pledge." She hesitated. "Come, Janet," he said gently. "You'll not refuse me tonight."

Despite the loaded implications that the rest of the company would find in their being together, she laid her other hand on his arm, flushing, as the band struck up a new tune.

He smiled down at her. "It is time we laid this ghost to rest," he said. "They will watch us, but no matter. I will not be held to ransom for wishing to include you."

For a second they stood, and then Alec moved her onto the floor. He spoke to other couples as they circled, cheerful, throwaway remarks as if he was careless of the tiny, rather stiff young woman he held in his arms, but she felt the warmth of his hand in the small of her back, and the glow of his eyes when he looked at her. She looked around her and saw Alice, laughing in the corner with one of the grooms, and Gillies leading one of the parlour maids towards the floor.

And she saw Iona, who had quite forgotten the group of people she was standing with, and was watching them with an expression that Janet could only interpret as blank despair. Iona looked in their direction until she caught her husband's eye and he saw her reproach. His eyes flooded with sadness. His step faltered momentarily, and then Janet felt his arm tense around her.

"Tell me, Janet," he said. "Do you not think I have been punished enough?"

Alec danced the whole tune with her under the grim gaze of his wife, and at the end, he bowed formally and said, "May I wish you all good fortune for the coming year, my faithful storeroom apprentice."

"And the same wish I make for you," she whispered. On impulse, she laid her hands on his arms, raised herself on tiptoe and kissed him on the cheek, a movement so swift that afterwards, he was not sure if he had remembered or imagined it. She walked from the room, her head down, not wanting to know if anyone had seen her kiss the Laird, or seen how he responded. When she turned to look back, he had already swept another partner into his arms and was laughing with her as if nothing had happened.

Janet heard the bells tolling for the New Year from her room, as she had always done since she came to live at Uishall.

For Alec, the New Year began with accusations, weeping and an argument.

Notes:
1: *brose*: liquor made from whisky, oatmeal and honey

15.
TIGHT LINES
MAY 1836

I

Alec slid into bed, lay down next to Iona and drew her into his arms. When they were first together, this had been a nightly ritual that still had spontaneity about it, still communicated their passion and desire. But there was a holding back in him now, something he did not automatically give to her, because she had so often rejected it in recent months. Both of them had forgotten that making love had ever been about something else other than trying to make babies.

After a moment, he pushed her back into the pillows and kissed her. She stirred, opened her eyes, her face wan in the dim candlelight. He saw the blank sorrow in them and knew it would be no different to the last time, or the time before that. He tried though, every time he tried to rekindle the fire in her that previously he could so effortlessly ignite. He untied the ribbons fastening her nightdress. When she did not touch him in return, he guided her hand. At last she returned a thin smile, and her mouth met his in a kiss that owed more to token than anything else. His lovemaking was not especially sought after anymore. If she could make the baby without his caresses, without *him*, she would. It was just that unfortunately, this was what he had to do to make it happen, and her disenchantment with his efforts had finally sapped her attempts at reciprocation.

Alec sighed. It was a grim affair making love to a woman focused solely on the reproductive powers of sex. Iona was no longer interested in the gentle byways of loving, the subtle twists and turns on the journey towards fulfilment. There was business to be done. Her eyes were closed again, but not because she was feeling pleasure. She was concentrating. When she sighed, it was not with longing, but impatience. She did not want him to be skilful and leisurely, she wanted him to perform, make the baby and vindicate all her patience and faith in him, the humiliations he had forced upon her.

It was hard for him to feel enthusiastic about such a mechanical prospect. Despite the escalating tensions in the house, he still wanted to love her, and he wanted her to want him – for himself, the way she used to, not just for what he ultimately might give her. His hand probed her, seeking out some response that would connect her to his own desires. But she had already parted her legs, she was ready enough, it would do, he should climb onto her now and deliver his hopeful gift, the sooner the better, and then tomorrow they could try again.

When it was like this, it took him a long time to climax. This time, it was harder than ever to thrust away at the dead weight beneath him, and he felt like a soldier stabbing a bayonet with disinterested efficiency into a straw-stuffed practise dummy. He managed it, climbed off again, didn't bother to kiss her or hold her in his arms as he used to, because she was already turning away from him with a tired sigh and drifting towards empty, painful dreams. He didn't bother to tell her that he loved her, because more and more, he wasn't sure he did. He lay on his back and remembered how it used to be, making love with his wife instead of failing to make babies with her, and his face was wet before he snuffed out the candle and closed his eyes.

II

For three years, Janet and her son had made their lives in Alec's ancient home. For two of them, Iona had doubled and trebled her efforts to make a baby with her husband.

She had tried everything. At first, she was in control, consciously making her dealings with Janet even cooler, briefer and more physically distant than before, buoyed up by the strength she drew from her consultations with the old healer, and the optimism she felt at working with new strategies. She continued to take a variety of herbal infusions, demanded constant supplies of stag-horn jelly, repeated charms to support herself through Janet's silent and malevolent magic. To no avail.

They had started with wild carrot, and Iona worked the charm assiduously, creatively, hanging them over their bed, placing them under his pillows, even begging him to push them gently inside her, that she might directly absorb their powers before he entered her. The season for wild carrot passed and she had made the most of it. To no avail.

In the summer, Alec found himself drinking salep every evening, the ancient mother's recipe made from the dried and pounded roots of the early purple orchids that liberally peppered the wild grasses of the hills. Iona prepared it herself, using rich goat's milk, honey, herbs and spices, pressing him to drink. He came to bed at night, and the bedroom was purple with the small, heavy-headed flowers she had gathered and strewn over their bed, crushed and spread on his sex, heaped on and under their pillows.

Watercress began to appear on the table at every meal, even breakfast.

Iona searched the beaches for phallic-shaped stones and littered the bedroom with them. She visited fertility stones and embraced them, speaking her spells into the keen winds blowing around her, or hearing them echo back to her in the heavy mists of early morning. All to no avail.

Alec, compliant at first and willing to try whatever she suggested, however desperate or outrageous, eventually began to resist her constant harping. She had only one topic of conversation, it seemed, and there was only one thing she wanted to do. The night Alec could summon neither will nor energy to sire her, Iona fell into such hysterical weeping that she could not breathe, and he had to slap her to break the fit. The next day she was confined to bed, and he refused to lie with her for a week, until she had recovered her strength.

"It cannot go on," he said. "You will die for want of making a child, Iona, if you do not stop this course. You are forcing what will not be forced, and it is breaking both our hearts."

"It isn't me," Iona said. "It's her. You know it is the truth. It's the mother of your child you brought into our home. She possesses you, so I must fight her."

"Iona, she has done nothing except what you imagine in that fevered mind of yours," Alec said, as he always did. "Janet is my employee, and a good one at that. You are exhausted; your mind is not your own when you cast about for someone else to blame for the predicament we are in. And you have chosen this desperate action, brought us both to a place where we cannot do a thing but think about the child we do not have. I have other cares," he said. "There is Uishall to manage and our prosperity to maintain. No – don't be angry when I say it. We have Alasdair. I know you did not carry him, but we must learn to be grateful for him, and let it rest at that."

"Still you protect her," Iona said, seizing his hand fiercely, "even though now she is withdrawing your power to serve your wife –" she stopped and lay back into the pillows as she saw him shake his head. "This is not God's punishment," she said at last. "It's hers. She has been punishing you since the day she conceived."

"Stop," he said. "I will not listen to this superstitious nonsense."

"You are a Judas, and it is your destiny to betray me," she said. "I knew it at Hogmanay, when I saw you dancing together. And I knew that whatever I did, and however much I struggled, you would make a martyr of me."

She closed her eyes, her fingers opening and tightening fitfully around his hand until she fell into uneasy sleep.

For a long time, he sat in the darkness and watched her ravaged face. He had claimed his child, and Alasdair was already a son he was proud of. But he had lied to Iona, he had been lying for a long time - and he had been lying to himself, hiding his real motives for keeping Janet in his home behind his wife's convenient belief that he was bewitched. The conflict caused by the self-deception was now insupportable, when Iona saw through him so clearly. He still could not confront the tumult inside him, could barely admit that even as he bathed Iona's forehead, hers was not the face he saw. His act of kindness and the helplessness he felt had been borrowed from a previous occasion.

In the aftermath of the storeroom incident, there had been a bitter quarrel and he had forsaken their bed when neither of them would apologise to the other for the way they had behaved. Still blaming himself for the harrowing events of the evening, he had stolen into Janet's room in the early hours of the morning and found Alice still at her station.

"I am afraid to leave her," she had said. "Her skin feels as if it is on fire."

"You have done well," Alec said. "But go to bed now, for you must be at work in a few hours. She will not sleep alone."

He had sat beside her on the bed, his mind blank, simply aware that he was alone with her for the first time in many years. Such a wrenching feeling went through him, it tore through the fabric of lies and forced him, if only for the next few hours, to recognise his misery for what it was.

He felt again the rush of fear when Alice had run into the dining room. He knew, even as he pushed back his chair, not even bothering to excuse himself to his astonished guests, that this was about Ruaraidh.

The kitchen was preternaturally quiet when he raced in, everyone's eyes riveted on the storeroom door. When he threw it open, he saw his brother's hands already on her. The rest was all snatched impressions. He remembered Iona, who faced then what he still could not acknowledge. All the time he had been shouting at his brother and berating the kitchen staff and his wife, he had been conscious of Janet, needing the help and comfort he could not give her.

His hand trembled as he bathed her face and wrists. He had not touched her for years. Now there was nothing to stop him, not the malicious censure of the kitchen staff, not the fearful jealousy of his wife, not the guilty desire he had so strenuously repressed. He kissed her wounded head. Her hand was hot and lifeless in his, and he didn't know if she could sense that he was close. She opened her eyes once during his vigil; they rested on him and he smiled.

"I am watching over you, *Seonaid*," he told her, "and I will chase away the nightmares."

She closed her eyes; she had not seen him. Her insensibility emboldened him to lie beside her, and once he had taken her in his arms, he could not go back to his more seemly position at the bedside. He talked again, confessing things that made him weep. At last he left, before the servants were about their business, for he could not be discovered at her side.

16.
STRIKE
JULY, 1836

I

Gradually, Alec came to understand the dying process of his marriage, that he and Iona now wrestled with separate pains and could no longer touch each other's. He had been brought so close to her obsession, and felt such guilt for being the cause of it, he could not summon the strength to knock down the wall he had built for his own protection.

He took comfort in Alasdair, whose inheritance was secure. Ruaraidh would be unlikely to survive more than a few years, and Ciaran was already dead – a loss that the now invalided Margaret had barely been able to support. Maglavat would now pass to Ruaraidh's surviving son, Jamie, and Uishall would be Alasdair's. Whenever he made love to Iona now, which was much less often than it used to be, it was as if he was lifting the corpse of their hope into his tired arms, and he felt the child they would never make like a dead weight at his centre.

He spent long hours staring from the window or riding over the hills. He had taken to reading in the library late at night, wandering the castle, unable to confine himself to the bedchamber where his wife waited for him with increasing hopelessness. One night he found himself standing before the portraits of his ancestors. Soon, his face would hang among theirs, and he wondered how he would be remembered. He sometimes found he had strayed to the bottom of the tightly twisted spiral stair that led to Janet's room, and he stood there frozen, a man who did not know which way to turn. Finally, he would creep to bed in the early hours, and lie awake until dawn.

As his marriage continued its painful self-destruction, Janet was no longer the quiet, unassuming presence he could deny. Now he found pretexts to seek her out, easily done when Iona contributed less and less to the running of the house. And as the balance between them began to shift, Janet looked at him more often, spoke to him more often, and knew she comforted him when she deigned to smile. He would see her now and again with Alasdair, and feel with a sharp pang his absence from their little family group.

The distances between them began to shrink. She had done nothing, yet she held him in a grip of rising want that would not let him go. In the end, he fought constantly against her, and knew the hopelessness of his struggle.

Iona was now past anger and jealousy, all done with desperation. There were no more arguments, no more visits to the spey-wife, no more fits of weeping. There was no more striving, and there would never be any children. She knew that now. Six years of trying, an accumulation of dashed hopes that had eventually become too much to bear. She had thrown away all her charms, given up all the medicines and consigned her collection of fertility stones to the garden. She had all but lost her husband. Her acceptance was expressed through utter lethargy and depression, and it was Alec who became fretful as the passion for his wife died and the echoes of his love for her faded. He lay awake beside her and his misery was so deep, she felt she was drowning in it.

"Go to her," she said at last, her voice breaking the folds of the heavy darkness that pressed in on them that night.

He lay still, his back turned to her as the words penetrated, and she did not see the way his eyes closed, or hear the thud of his heart that betrayed him. It was a gift so selfless, so longed for and so tainted, that he did not dare move or speak, so afraid was he of accepting what she offered.

"I know what you must do if you are to bring peace to that tormented mind of yours, even if you do not."

"I swore my faithfulness to you the day we married," he said. "It stands."

"She's haunting you," Iona said. "There is no point in denying it any longer. You cannot eat, you cannot work, you wander like a lost spirit through the house, our bed offers you no comfort."

Now he turned to face her, ready with his indignant protestations, but she pressed her fingers to his lips. "You will not rest until you take her, and know she cannot bear you a son again, any more than I can. You must do it, because otherwise you will kill the last of our love with all your doubts and longings, and we will never know a moment's peace. So go. You have my

131

blessing. It is the only thing we have not tried. I will not ask, I will not bear a grudge. Only satisfy yourself that she has no more magic in her body to bear you children than do I." She stopped, laid her hand against his face, and kissed him. "And when it is all past, perhaps we can be faithful and loving, as we once were."

"Iona –"

"You cannot love me while you are possessed," she broke in. "You have not loved me since she came, and you won't again until you set us free of her."

It was here at last; and now the moment was upon them, he understood its inevitability. Iona had given him his chance; now he could know, once and for all, if Janet could work a second miracle. But too many other desires were already at work in him, his guilty longings suddenly unchained by his wife's desperation and her failure to understand.

She pushed at him, thrust the candle into his hand. "Go now," she said, her voice harsh, her words hasty with failing courage. "I will not wait on you like this another night. Force her once more if you have to. And don't return to me. I could not bear it. You will not share my bed again until she is banished from your thoughts and our home."

He stood in his nightshirt, a pale glimmer of indecision in the darkness, and then he was gone.

II

He walked through the castle, the candle shining in his hand. He ached inside, his heart, his mind, his spirit broken by suffering, want and the wretched bravery of his wife. He did not stand like a lost man at the foot of Janet's stone spiral staircase, but climbed it and padded in his bare feet to her door. His knuckles rested for a moment on the warm wood, then knocked softly.

In a few moments, the door opened a tiny crack, then swung inwards to admit him. He hesitated, then stepped over her threshold and closed the door. Her body, too, sheathed in a white nightdress, both of them glowing like ghosts in the dim light. He set the candle on the writing table by the window and at last let himself be swallowed by her eyes. His hand touched her face and a sob rose in his throat. The pain seemed to swell and burst inside him as she returned his gaze.

"Janet, do you fear me this time?"

She sighed. "No. But I fear your presence here and what it means."

"Tell me."

"I know why you have come," she said at last. "As you have tortured me these past fourteen years, so I have come to torture you. But have you thought through what must happen now? What if I conceive? Must I bear another bastard child?"

Her words stunned him. He had not thought it through. He had come to her, driven by his desires, finally beaten by the forces that were already pulling his life apart. He had imagined they would rush at each other, blind with passion, that he could take her in a frenzy that would enable him to relinquish responsibility for the treachery of his actions. But no; Iona had set him free, and now Janet was holding him in check, asking him to rationalise what he was about to do, asking him to consider her. The darkness of her chamber seemed to close in around him.

"You have lain with two wives and not sown any seed. If the deficiency lies in you, you know I can't promise what you would have me deliver."

"Don't speak of deficiency, mistress," he said. "You are too forward."

Her pragmatism stung him, her unflinching grasp of his motives for coming to her. She expected him to use her, she was saying, as if she had not seen the misery in his face, the helplessness she had brought him to.

"There may be something in us that creates a match," she said calmly, refusing to be intimidated by his show of lairdly temper. "And you'll do whatever's necessary to take advantage of me. If I carry your child, you might be grateful, but I have no security. It's a fair question. Will you abuse me again?"

He knew, he had expected her to try to bargain with him for some sort of improvement on her previous position, but he could not think beyond the desires that were coursing through him. He wasn't absolutely sure what she was asking of him, and there was a part of him that didn't want to know. Now their distrust was mutual and for a moment, Alec felt despair – was security all she wanted him for?

"Nothing I say will make you trust me," he said at last. "But if I must promise anything, it is not to do you wrong a second time. Will that suffice?"

It was not specific enough. "Well then," she said, and he heard the catch of hurt in her voice while he dangled on her answer. "It will have to do for now."

She stood before him patient and submissive, and when he loosed the ribbon that tied up her red curls, she felt him tremble. His lips pressed gently against her forehead.

"My sweet *Seonaid*, I –"

"No," she said quickly, panicked by the intensity of his gaze. "Say nothing you might regret when you are no longer drunk with desire."

He stopped. He was so close to her now, her warmth and scent dizzying him, but still she would not let him come to her. And then he understood. She was afraid. She had come so far in the years they had been apart, but nothing had really changed. He still held all the power, still had all the advantages. For all the distance they had travelled, they might still have been standing in the same place. He could not bear the way she was holding back.

"I forced you once," he whispered, his fingers twining through her hair. "And it has come to haunt me, that all that's followed may be my punishment for the wrong I did you. I will not lay a hand on you tonight unless you ask it."

For a long time she said nothing, only closed her eyes and rested her head against his hand as he cradled it. The blood was rushing through his body, the tension in him agony as her silence held him at bay. He did not move.

"Only let me try," he said at last. "For there'll be no peace for me otherwise."

"No peace for any of us if this try is successful," Janet said. "You say you love your wife – but what is that love worth if I prove fertile?"

He stared at her as realisation dawned. The gift Iona had made him was not hers to give. If he wanted Janet, he could not have her on the same terms as before. Security was only part of her problem. He almost reeled; he seemed to have no authority, as if she drew him into a place where all the rules he lived by had been changed, and for a moment he was frightened. If Janet conceived, the divine message would be unmistakable in its meaning. He threw himself into the abyss and knew the dark thrill of plunging downwards.

"Lie with me, and if you carry my child I will marry you." The words seemed to do nothing but pitch him further into the desperate hope that had become his despair.

"Swear on it."

"I swear."

He waited, the treachery of his promise settling around him like a heavy mantle, and he felt a piercing chill, as if he had heard Iona scream. And then Janet's small, strong hand encircled his wrist.

"You took me all those years ago," she said, and there was tenderness as well as sadness in her voice. "And even though I fought you and have wished often I could give myself to another, I was yours then and still am."

At this, he pulled her into his arms, his face buried in her neck. He knew how much those words had cost her, knowing how little he could give in return, knowing all their sad history, and everything else seemed to wash away from him, leaving only the savagery of his desire. He realised how much both of them were trapped in the past, by old motives and old knowledge, and all he wanted was to make something new with her.

He took her hand in his and kissed her fingers. "Then give me permission, Janet, and I will reward the faithfulness I did not deserve."

Her arms reached round his neck, he lifted her, and as she wrapped her strong, thin legs around him, he felt the warm crush of her breasts against his chest. To feel her close to him again was to be whisked back to the wild moorland where first he had claimed her. The time they had spent apart was suddenly unravelled, a ribbon of pain they cut between them as they came together.

His mouth found hers, and the gentleness of that first touch of her lips brought back a sudden, dazzling memory, of the first time he had kissed her and the shy, trembling girl in his arms whose trust he had abused. But this time, in this new space opening up before them, the woman did not run from him; she did not fight him, he did not need to coax or deceive. Instead, she drew him in, her mouth opening, her tongue darting out to caress his. The breath broke in him. His hands gripped her head, the poignancy of the kiss swamped by a hunger that was almost angry in its intensity. He felt the greedy wanting he had unleashed and wondered what power she worked that made his flesh thunder with such passion.

He broke away, inflamed almost beyond endurance, carried her to the bed and lay her down, stripping off his nightshirt. She did the same, wrenching her nightdress over her head and casting it aside. They were still for a moment, looking at each other, then she reached for him and pulled him down beside her.

He laid his hands on her, the places he knew, the places he remembered, the new ones that beckoned; he wanted all of her all at once, to gather her up and know her completely. He kissed her mouth, her throat; his swift and urgent exploration took in her arms, her shoulders, the dip of her waist, the length of her spine and the curve of her hips, until his hand touched her and found her ready. No dry, frightened virgin, needing all his powers of persuasion, but the woman he had awakened to desire and then kept waiting. As his hand slid between her thighs to draw out the sweet torture of her anticipation, the violent tremor that ran through her almost undid him. He moved his mouth to her breast, her nipple hardened against his tongue and when he drew on it, she threw back her head and gave a low, anguished cry. In it, he heard all the yearning of the long years she had suffered, and understood his own deprivation.

He could not wait for her any longer. He mounted her, his hands sliding under the small of her back, over her buttocks, lifting her towards him. Her head down in the pillows, red hair billowed up around her face, her eyes limpid, dazed with passion. In the moment he was suspended above her, the past was undone, for no fear clouded the purity of her desire as she arched towards him. She wanted him; that was all. There was a powerful jolt inside him, an agonising moment of surrender as he found her, entered her and felt the sharp, sweet shock of knowing her again. She cried out and welcomed him, came for him, begged him rake again the wound he had been the first and only man to open.

His movements were deep and strong and in a few moments, it was done. She felt the surge of his climax through the fading throb of her own, and her body lifted, capturing the last fragments of ecstasy that beat between them. He hung exhausted over her, awed and trembling, unsure if she would prove to be his saviour or despatching angel. She smiled and stroked him, soothing him. He moved to her side, smoothed the hair away from her face. A great weight seemed to have fallen from him, even though the outcome of their union was by no means certain. At last he understood that ever since she had come to live in his house, she had done nothing but torment him with what he thought he would never again possess. She lay at ease in his arms, fitted against him as if she belonged there.

"What are you, elf or fairy, that you bewitch me so completely?" he said. "That I am here with you, risking my future, my marriage, on a wild gamble?"

"I am no witch, no spell-maker," she said, amused. "You think that we can wield the power that makes a child. There is no mystery to it."

"There are practicalities to consider now, beyond the question of whether or not you will conceive," Alec said ruefully. "This is not a situation I want known all over the house. Can I trust your silence?"

"My business is my own," Janet said.

"You serve me faithfully, beyond everything I deserve. I will be fair to you, whatever comes of all our trials."

"You were a faithful husband up to now," Janet said after a moment.

He rolled onto his back. "Ah, Janet," he sighed. "Don't spoil it by bringing up my guilt, for I feel it keenly enough without your help. If you conceive, I'll release Iona on the promise I have made to you and help secure her a new mate." He looked away from her, for he had made it sound easy, when he knew it would be the opposite.

"And if I don't?" she persisted.

He looked sadly at her. "Then I will have no choice but to pick up with her, and try to make the best of it. I am already divorced, and she will not agree to set me free." It occurred to him briefly that in that case, he would make Janet his mistress, but he knew already how miserable that would make all of them. The present situation would only be survivable if it was temporary. He paused. "My life is not so simple as yours. It's true, I am compromised, as you once told me, by wealth and position and the expectations of others. It will not make it any easier for us to be together –"

When he saw her despair, he drew her towards him, and his kiss was deep as she clung to him. "*M'eudail*,"[1] he whispered, holding her face in his hands. "Whatever I feel for you, it is extreme folly for me to make these choices when I already have a wife. You know this without my even saying it. In giving in and being with each other, we could end up hurt worse than we have been already."

"I would not give this up," Janet whispered fiercely, "for all the hurt it may bring in the end."

They lay quietly together, a sober aftermath as the realities of their situation began to pull at the edges of their contentment, and then Janet looked down on him with troubled eyes.

"If this is to be business and not love, we must agree terms before you come to me again."

He stroked his hand through her hair, hearing his own fear echoing in her voice. They would not last the course if they abandoned themselves to the intense passions that had just consumed them, and were then forced to part. He brought her face close to his but she pulled back.

"Here is my proposal," she said. "We may meet for the next few months, but there will come a time when, if it has not happened as you hoped, you must accept the way things are and return to your wife. And then our contract will be concluded, and we can at least say we had our chance to love, and took it."

She looked anxiously at him, afraid he might misunderstand the common sense she tried to show. But he nodded, tilted her chin and kissed her, sealing the pact. "Such a grave face before me now," he said gently. "And suddenly so practical in your dealings with me," he went on, his voice light. "Tell me, strange little mistress, now I have accepted this proposition, will you take no pleasure in our transactions?"

She turned her face archly away, feigning boredom. "None at all, if they yield nothing but wasted hours in fruitless toil."

He laughed softly and rose to this deliberate provocation, turning her onto her back, planting playful kisses on her tender throat, his hands moving over her body. "There's pleasure in this," he whispered. "Don't lie to me, little Janet, for I feel it in the way you tense against my hand."

She smiled and kissed him, and brought his hand to her and he laughed softly at the candid way she told him he was right. He felt so happy, Janet in his arms, her eagerness for him to please her as he roused her again to desire.

"Your passion is as strong as mine," he said, when he had proved his point and she was ready to yield again. "I think we shall enjoy the business we must do."

When he had gone, Janet lay alone in her ruined bed and wondered what would happen if she did not conceive. She could not help the feelings that now poured from her – she loved him, wanted him, ached for him. She would do anything for him, and anything to get him, and she prayed aloud for her love to be graced with a child so that she might hold him to his promise. She trusted in the feelings he had shown her, but struggled with the reality they faced. Now she was vulnerable, because he had touched her need, felt it vibrate through her, and heard its echoes in his own breast, and she knew that if she lost him again, she would never recover.

Notes
1: *M' eudail*: my treasure

17.
BROUGHT TO BAY
AUGUST 1836

I

The eastern sky was a painterly swathe of cerise and aquamarine, a rose-coloured sun at its centre, the early morning air damp with dew. The hunting party set out from the castle, making its way along the track that wound by the shore of the loch, and then climbed steeply into the bracken-covered hills. A small party this morning, Alec and Alasdair, their gamekeeper Joshua, two white Eriskay ponies, Solas and Kilda, and two deerhounds, Tamlyn and Meg, trotting amiably at Alec's side. The eldest, Tamlyn, stood thirty-two inches at the shoulder and his wiry brindle coat contrasted with the grey one of his sister Meg, who stood a couple of inches shorter. Their claws clattered impatiently on the rocky path, their long thin noses raised eagerly to the early morning air, restlessly looking about them for open country and possible quarry.

The hounds were Alec's pride and joy, his main pastime when the cares of the estate were not pressing on him. From time to time, his hand rose to pat them affectionately, but he seemed preoccupied this morning, subdued and not inclined to make conversation.

Joshua, however, was not so taciturn, and since Alasdair was still being trained in the art of stalking, he had good reason to talk to the young man, showing him how to look for marks on the ground or droppings, signs of the recent presence of the deer they sought. A mature stag was their quarry for today, seen limping in the valley the previous afternoon and thought to be mortally wounded by a poacher's snare.

"He will be an easy take for the young dog, Meg," Joshua said, "for she has run for but one or two hinds and is still learning. She has always looked to Tamlyn for the kill."

Higher in the hills, the need for silence arose, and they moved quietly through the thick bracken, Joshua ahead, the dogs leashed now, quivering in anticipation of a chase. They stopped at length to rest and Joshua wriggled a little way ahead and pulled out his spyglass to see if any beast was moving in the distance. Father and son stayed back, allowing him space to interrogate the land and interpret its signals. Alasdair, not insensitive to his father's silence, had noticed a change in him in the past weeks, and guessed that financial concerns were at the root of his mood. His mother seemed tired, and was not spending as much time with her son as she usually did. He did not suspect that the uncharacteristic behaviour of his parents was connected.

"You have been to see Ruaraidh," Alasdair said eventually to his father, in the lowest voice he could. "For the first time in over a year. Has something happened between you?"

Alec turned to him, his clever son who seemed to intuit more about the world around him than he was given credit for. "What makes you say that?"

Alasdair shrugged. "You have been to Maglavat, not ten days since. The Lady Margaret continues poorly, and the Laird is away for further treatment. And now the factor is coming to dine tonight. Is he borrowing from you?"

Alec sighed and looked out over the hills. He was acutely conscious of the fact that they were lying below the little knoll where he had first taken Janet, and it seemed that she invaded his thoughts at every moment; even the landscape seemed to belong to her. But his son was right; other concerns also lay at his door, waiting for resolution. At some point, Alasdair would guess, or would have to be told what was happening between his father and mother. He was silent for too long and at last he felt his son's hand on his arm.

"Will you not confide in me?" Alasdair leaned forward. "I have a mind to listen to some of the cares that afflict the estate – to see if I can find remedy for them." He smiled engagingly at his father. "It will be good for my training."

Alec smiled back. "It's true, there are several matters that need my attention, but all of them should be the concern of my brother, whose deteriorating health means that he is decreasingly able to meet his responsibilities as Laird."

He glanced up. Joshua was still scanning the hillsides, muttering to himself. The non-appearance of the injured stag was of considerable concern to him.

Alec turned to face his son. "Well then, in a nutshell. The estimates for the costs of building the new castle at Maglavat were far less than the final bill, and the returns on rents and livestock will barely accommodate them. One of the reasons Jack Macaskill dines with us tonight is to examine the discrepancy between the figures – he does not trust the builder, and thinks he may be slipping in additional costs. That's one."

Alasdair thought for a moment. "Where is the original estimate?"

"We do not have it. The builder says it lies with us, but even so he should have copied it. Jack swears it was last with one of the suppliers who were marked to cut the granite blocks, but that man says the builder has it." Alec shook his head. "We could be running between the builder and half a dozen others for months before we get to the answer – if we ever do. And if Ruaraidh had been more interested in making sure the costs did not run away with him in the first place – but there, it is a pointless occupation, wishing my brother had less of the spendthrift about him, and more in the way of acumen."

"And the rest?"

"There are the medical bills for the Lady Margaret, who needs almost constant care and medicines from the physician. And there is Ruaraidh himself, beset with the glengore, who will do nothing but deny the seriousness of his condition, even while he slinks off to indulge in lengthy and expensive medical regimes that do no good because the root cause of his problem is still not under his control." He sighed. "The whisky has made us rich, but the land seems determined to undercut its profits, whatever strategies we adopt. And I confess, I am running out of ideas to make it pay its way."

"What are your thoughts so far?"

"I had considered giving him a loan, if the estate's resources will stretch to it, so that we can increase the numbers of sheep and cattle –"

Alasdair shook his head. "I would not enter on such a course."

His confidence amused his father. "Why not?"

"The sheep are not the long-term future of our land," he said.

Alec waved his hand across the vast expanse of wild heath and hills before them. "And what else would you say it is good for? The tenant farmers can hardly turn to crops if they are to yield greater profits from the acreage."

Alasdair creased his forehead. "I'm not sure yet," he said. "But the sheep farms in Australia and New Zealand process much greater numbers than we can. In a few years, they will outstrip us, and that will drive down the price. The sheep will be finished."

Alec looked at him. "Did you love the land and care about its future so much when you were struggling with poverty on Eilaster Glen?"

Alasdair shrugged, gazing out across the hills. For a moment, his father thought he was offended, but then he said, "Whether I am rich or poor, the land does not change. What changes is what people try to do with it. What has changed for me is that on Eilaster Glen, I could only suffer the consequences of other men's decisions. Now I could be the man others will look to for their futures. That changes how I see it." He stopped. "Aye, I probably do think differently about the land now. But I love it just the same as I always did."

"It's a wild land," Alec said. "It will not be tamed to the advantage of either rich or poor. We try to turn it to profit, we try to change it, harness it. We can go so far, but then it seems to say to us, you must accept me as I am, for beyond this, I cannot change."

"Perhaps that is our mistake," Alasdair said. "Perhaps we will discover that the key to its riches lies in its wildness."

Alec sighed. The conversation seemed to have turned itself back to the problems he wrestled with. "Come then, give me your opinion," he said. "Do you think Uishall would be at risk if it should divert some of its riches into Maglavat?"

Alasdair weighed his words then said, "I would think carefully about the amount you spend on such a gamble, seeing as the beneficiary is so inconstant a character."

Alec laughed and was rewarded by an angry glare from his gamekeeper. The spyglass was shut with a snap.

"Well, Joshua, what can you see for us to hunt today?"

Joshua shook his head. "There's no sign of him. But away there –" his knobby finger pointed to a distant rise – "there is a group of hinds. If our approach is careful, we may see the stag that minds them. The sun is behind us and the wind favours us – best to go now."

They roused themselves and began to move cautiously through the bracken, at times lying flat to pull themselves along the ground, through the heather and over the raw peat. The dogs mimicked them, their breathing shallow, still not free to run, still not in sight of anything to chase.

Alec moved behind the gamekeeper, his expert stealth the result of years of practice. Ruaraidh had never had the patience for the stalk, complained of the discomfort when they were forced to wade through streams or crawl over wet ground. Alec loved the hunt, but today his mind was crowded with other things that were a constant threat to his concentration. The sight of the stag would focus his thoughts, drive out the distractions that were plaguing him.

He had already spent more nights than he could count with Janet. His fall was fast and furious, his confusion over what to tell his son – if anything – profound. It was a strange kind of infidelity he practised. It threatened to snap the threads that bound him to his wife, yet had begun to weave the linking strands between father, son and mother that had never been made. If there was damnation in the course he took, he could not help but feel that somewhere there might be redemption in it, too.

"Here – here!" The sudden hiss from Joshua froze them into place. They had been moving a good few hundred yards by now and were suddenly upon the grazing hinds, perhaps only three hundred yards distant. They were concealed in a narrow gully, any sound they made masked by the tumbling stream beside them, but to get any closer meant a move onto the open hill, and the risk of being spied. The hinds looked peaceful enough, but raised their heads from time to time and looked anxiously about them, as if they sought a missing member of their party.

For some time, the three men lay and watched cautiously over the edge of the ridge.

"Now – over there," Joshua said urgently after a long while, and Alec shifted his gaze to the right of the herd. "You see the stag? He's lying down, but this is not the injured man we saw yesterday."

There was a low whine from one of the dogs; the more experienced Tamlyn was quiet, but Meg, younger and more excitable, had seen the stag and begun to strain at the leash that held her.

"Patience," Alec said softly to the bitch as he took the spyglass from Joshua and studied the stag.

"I know this beast," he said after a few moments. "He has rutted here these past four seasons. But he was gored last year, and this year I saw him challenged, and it seemed he did not stake his claim with quite so much authority. Perhaps it's time to give a younger stag the opportunity to claim these hinds." He glanced down at the dogs, both now staring fixedly at the stag. "If we loose them now, it is more than likely he will run uphill. That is our best chance."

"He is a big beast for a young bitch," Joshua said in admiration. He bent to Meg, furiously concentrating, and scratted her ears. "Can ye handle him?"

Alec grinned. "With Tamlyn as her partner, she will do us very well," he said. "But this is too soon a start for them. The sun is still behind us and will give us some advantage, but the stag will be aware. If he starts to run early, we'll lose all sight of him once he clears that rise."

"There's heather just ahead of us," Alasdair said. "If we take the dogs through it low, we might make some progress before we cut them loose."

"Aye," Joshua said. "That's our best chance. Macleod and I will handle the dogs. You keep your eye on that beast. If he moves, you must signal, and we'll take our chances."

It happened in seconds. They had barely wriggled their way into the dense heather when the stag's head turned in their direction. Meg let out a single yelp of pure frustration. Joshua cursed and pulled sharply on her collar, but the damage was done. The stag was already getting to his feet and further stealth was futile.

"Slip them!" Alec cried. "Away!"

Freed of leashes at last, the dogs streaked off through the heather, bounding in magnificent loping strides towards their quarry. Alec, Alasdair and Joshua stood to watch the chase.

"He's running up hill," Alec said. "Tamlyn will cut him off."

The stag was already labouring as the dogs closed the distance, racing down the slope then leaping the burn at the bottom almost in unison and beginning to climb the other side. They split, Tamlyn galloping in a wide arc to the right, Meg going left to create a pincer movement. At the widest point of their separation, the stag turned in desperation and began to charge down the hill between them.

"Downhill," muttered Joshua grimly. "Now we'll see what Meg is made of."

The dogs changed direction in a fluid movement that brought exclamations of delight from the stranded hunters, and began to run downhill on either side of the stag. They overtook it and then closed together. Alec's heart was pounding as it always did, as dogs and quarry faced each other. The contest was by no means one-sided. Alec had buried many deerhounds, gored or crushed by beasts that had fought and won the day. The stag's heavy, powerful bulk could only stop its downhill run with difficulty. It put its head down and charged, so that both dogs were forced to leap to the sides to avoid the thrusting antlers. As they regrouped, the stag turned and again tried its luck uphill.

In response, the dogs ran to left and right, then came together too fast and collided with each other in front of the stag's heavy ascent. Another yowl from Meg, a furious thrashing of tangled legs as the dogs struggled to right themselves. Alec groaned.

"That young fool," he said in tense exasperation. "She'll lose the kill if she doesn't follow Tamlyn's lead."

"No - it's all right," Alasdair said. "Look."

The dogs had halted the stag's escape and the great beast attempted to charge a second time. But the chase had taken its toll. Tamlyn bared his teeth, and Meg leapt clumsily onto the back of its neck. Her teeth gained purchase, but the stag threw its head back and she tumbled off with a howl.

The men began to stride down the slope. "Has he wounded her?" Alec said to Joshua. "He has fourteen points, at least."

"He might have," Joshua said, stopping to pull out the spyglass. "But I can't see blood, and she's on her feet. Meg yelps at anything, as we've already heard."

Tamlyn rushed forward as the stag reared its head, and closed his jaws around the throat. The stag tossed him, but he held on, even though the force of the beast's thrashing knocked him off his feet.

"He has him!" Alec cried. "It's all done. Meg will finish. Quick, quick!" he shouted at the bitch, who had made another unsuccessful lunge and failed to connect.

At this, Meg saw her partner struggling and in a single leap, caught the stag's ear with her teeth and pulled savagely downwards. The sudden movement caught the beast off balance and its neck broke clean. Meg leapt clear as the stag fell. Then she stood back, panting extravagantly, looking rather surprised at what she'd just done.

By the time the hunters joined the dogs, both were lying down on the heather next to the stag. Alec squatted down to stroke them, checking both for wounds and finding nothing but a long, thin scratch on Meg's neck from one of the antlers.

"A fine job," he said to Tamlyn. "And you, young Meg – a good, clean kill, decisively taken in the end. We will make a hunter of you yet." He glanced across at the gamekeeper. "She's been nicked, but nothing we can't cure with a little bathing. Our young bitch is blooded."

He stood and surveyed the kill. Joshua had finished Tamlyn's work and gashed open the neck with his knife, in case there was any life left, and he and Alasdair had begun the gralloch[1]. The stag's eyes had already glazed. Alec's hand ran down the broad chest and found a hard knot of flesh where the old gore injury had healed.

"It went deep," he said, looking up at his son, his fingers probing around the scar tissue. "He will have sustained damage to the lung with this. That's why he could not make good his escape. It was a good fight."

On the rim of the hill, the group of hinds stood and watched in silence, as if they understood they were bereaved.

"They always watch," Alasdair said uneasily, when he had withdrawn his bloody hands from the body cavity and the thin white membrane that encased the guts had been slashed open on the heather – lunch for the hoodies already beginning to appear on the surrounding rocks.

"They're not watching us," Alec said. "They're mourning. He's taken care of them all season and sired them. As much as he felt the pride of ownership, they felt themselves possessed and safe." He smiled. "But you know women, Alasdair – they are resilient creatures, and inconstant with it. They will watch and weep for him today, but by tomorrow another, younger stag will have claimed them and they will have forgotten their dead paramour and be content."

Alasdair gave him an odd look, then bent over Meg, drew his bloody thumb down her long nose and went down to the burn to wash his hands.

In less than half an hour, the stag had been hoisted onto the waiting Solas's back, and the walk home begun, the pile of entrails and the blood staining the heather the only signs that things had changed.

II

Back at the castle, the carcass was unloaded and winched up in the skinning shed to be decapitated, skinned and sawn. Alasdair stayed with Joshua to complete the task, while Alec took the dogs back to their kennels. He tended Meg's superficial wound before the pair of them were rubbed down and watered and left to rest.

Crossing the stable yard alone, preoccupied again with thoughts of the forthcoming meeting that evening, and thinking he must strip off his wet and muddy clothes and bathe directly, he collided with Janet on the cobblestones as he made his way towards the back entrance. She was hurrying towards the kitchen door, head down, and when she walked into him, she looked almost frightened to be so rudely halted.

Her shock was lost on him after the exhilaration of the hunt; there was no one else about and on impulse, he took her hand and led her quickly across the yard, trapping her teasingly against the wall that curved to form a nook where one of the towers rose. Now in shadow, they were both safe from prying eyes, and his blood quickened as he moved close to her. He had never laid a hand on her outside her room; his own daring pleased and excited him, and he hoped might provoke a little audacity from her in response.

"Less haste, my sweet mistress," he said, amused at her panic. "No one is here to listen to our conversation, or spy on where our secretive hands may dare to wander. Where have you been that necessitates such a rush to make up lost time?" He tilted her chin, forcing her to meet his gaze, and saw that her face was streaked with tears, her eyes filled with such pain that she couldn't hold his gaze.

"Janet, what's happened? Has someone –"

"No, no. It's nothing," she said. "Forgive me. It is just the situation we are in. There is gossip amongst the servants, no matter how discreet we are –"

Her voice was rising, the words tumbling over themselves in their rush to get out. She broke off, breathed deeply. "Forgive me." For a few moments she seemed to be conquering the emotions that threatened to overwhelm her, then without warning, she burst into tears.

He stared at her in amazement, all thought of lovers' games vanquished, and then drew her towards him. At once, she tried to push herself away.

"No," she said. "If we should be seen –"

Alec refused to let go. "I cannot stop the talking," he said, "and you have patiently borne much more than idle gossip in the course of our affair." He gazed at her. "Look at me. Have you told me everything?"

Janet leaned against the wall and closed her eyes. She looked exhausted, and for a moment he understood the demands he was making of her, however much she was now his willing mistress. His hands, dirty from the stalk, held her face and his thumbs stroked away the tears.

"I should be asking your forgiveness, not the other way around," he said. "There is still no promise I can make that will last beyond the stolen hours we spend together."

She wiped her eyes. "Then come to me tonight," she said. "Come to me and hold me in your arms, for that is all the comfort you can give me, and all that is needed to put the world to rights. That will be promise enough."

"Janet, I have the factor coming for dinner and will be at table late, discussing financial matters –"

She interrupted him, seizing his hands in hers and kissing them. "I have never asked before," she said. "But now I beg you, come to me tonight and I will never ask again."

He shook his head, hushing her, surprised and puzzled by her vehemence, his determination not to see her overturned. "You do not need to beg," he said. "I told you long ago that if ever you had need of me, then I would help you. Now we are lovers, I am doubly bound by that promise."

At this, she clung fiercely to him, her mouth sealed to his, and her ardour was such that he was forced to disengage from her.

"Janet, be still," he said, part maddened, part disturbed by the fervour of her embrace. His arms wrapped her, rocking her slowly. "Be still. Don't inflame us when you know we cannot quench our fires." He kissed her again, more gently, and at last she relaxed and leaned on him. "I would take you now," he said, "if time and our circumstances were kinder mistresses."

"Why wait for kindness?" Janet said. "Take me now, and passion will be served instead."

He released her with a regretful shake of his head. "This is not the time to lose our heads and risk discovery. But I will come to you tonight, and you must leave your door unlatched. Till then, draw on the strength you always seem to find, and think of this kiss for comfort's sake if the rest of the day should prove hard."

She nodded, smiled at last and scrubbed roughly at her face with her hands.

"Now go," he said, when she had made herself respectable, "and see that all is well made up for this evening's dinner. Discharge your duties well, and you will see how fast the time goes between now and when I come to you."

Her lips touched his fleetingly, a swift and heartfelt kiss that told him of her gratitude; and then she was gone, out into the searing sunlight and through the kitchen door.

Alec waited a few moments, then left the shadowed nook. The cobbled yard was busy now as he made his way towards his room. One of the stable boys, a yoke across his shoulders, struggling towards the stalls with water for the horses; Gillies MacNicol, bearing a huge basket of logs away from the woodshed. The dairymaid, Eilidh, fetching fresh butter to the kitchen. Alec smiled as he passed her; she tried to curtsey, her toe caught one of the cobblestones and she fell with a little comical cry, dropping the wooden trencher with a clatter.

He went to her as she surveyed the disaster, the butter pat squashed on the dirt, beyond redemption. She looked fearfully at the Laird.

"You are hurt?" he said, holding out his hand and pulling her to her feet. "No? Good, then. No harm done."

"I am so sorry, sir –"

Alec shook his head. "The fault was mine, for catching your eye. Quick now – fetch another butter pat, and say no more about it. I'll make it straight with the housekeeper, and then you need make no excuses to the cook."

She thanked him, embarrassed and grateful, smiled affectionately at him, and scuttled off, back in the direction of the dairy.

Notes:
1: Gralloch: dialect for gutting the stag

18.
PRIEST
OCTOBER 1836

I

For the three months following Alec's first visit to her chamber, Janet admitted her secret lover whenever he begged entry. After three weeks she bled, and it was a further week before they resumed their tryst. Another month passed, the humdrum days eclipsed by the nights, lovemaking and lovers' talk, reminiscences and discoveries, but the future a blank before them; they could not make plans, and so they seized each night, and did their best to let it go with the morning.

But after he had encountered her in the cobbled yard and subsequently gone to her late the same night at her bidding, all pretence of their coupling being a business arrangement had disappeared.

Dinner with the factor had been a lengthy business; the ledgers were got out, the accounts for both Uishall and Maglavat examined, and the financial state of both considered. It was clear that if Alec was too generous in his efforts to save Maglavat from terminal decline, Uishall would be put at risk. Alasdair was invited to express his opinions, but Jack Macaskill was an old-fashioned man who thought it a waste of time listening to the thoughts of minors, and refused to treat the contributions of the Laird's son with anything but condescension. To make matters worse for the careworn Laird, the factor was circumspect with his advice, not wanting to commit himself to any dangerous course of action. He had talked vaguely about stocking the land, and Alasdair had talked, when he was permitted, about the need for something new. Alec seemed both troubled and preoccupied, Alasdair was frustrated, and Macaskill had eventually left, a little before midnight, with no new ground broken, and all their ideas either poorly articulated, or at odds.

Alec dismissed the last of the servants and then realised that the whole evening had been coloured by his impatience to hurry through dinner, close down the meeting and keep his appointment. His concentration had faltered in the last turgid hour, and it had taken considerable willpower to remain seated before the pages of figures, trying to contribute usefully to the future of his estates.

When at last he unlatched her door and crept inside, she was asleep, her face dimly lit by the candle still burning on the writing table. For a moment he wondered if he should leave her to sleep, but he could not countenance stealing away without giving her the comfort she had begged him for. He stripped in the candlelight and she woke only when he was beside her, gently loosening the buttons on the night gown that hid her body from him. She opened her eyes with a start, drew him towards her, and it began.

He took her at once, desperate to chase away the shadows that stalked her eyes, and release the powerful desire that had built up over the long afternoon and evening. It was not enough, it seemed at moments of that long night that nothing would ever be enough, but as the hours passed, their passion lost its frantic edge and Janet and Alec crossed over the boundary they had set to protect themselves.

That night, Alec's life had seemed to crumble about him, and he sought refuge in her, for she was the only thing that grounded him amidst the outlying chaos. He felt her warmth and heaviness against him, and in her rhythmic breathing he felt the trust she had placed in him. He lay awake, absorbing the low, deep throb of her contentment, and knew that he loved her, that he had always loved her, and that whatever the cost, his life must change to admit her.

His hope of a child had waned quickly, but all the same it would be impossible to repair the damage to his marriage. His future now seemed spiked on such terrible ecstasy that he could not work out what he should do next. Once again, he was heading into difficult political territory, compounded by all the financial complications that would accompany his promise to marry a woman with no income and no dowry, and he agonised over the choices he must make. How could he hope to have a second petition for divorce sanctioned – and even if he managed it, how would Uishall bear a second fiscal battering? The weeks slipped by, as childless as they had ever been, Alec paralysed by indecision, the hurt he did not want to bring Iona, who had suffered so much already. He hung on, clinging to the last vestiges of hope that Janet would conceive, as if that would legitimise the drastic actions he knew he must take.

As for Iona, she could see her gamble had been disastrous and she had lost the contest for her husband's affection. Her pride made her stubborn and she would not let him go; her superstition still insisted his mind was not his own. She waited for the moment of empty victory when her husband would come crawling back to her with the news that no, Janet could not bear his child either, and he had destroyed their happiness for nothing.

Throughout all this, Janet worked away at her storeroom responsibilities, sometimes a little tired if the Laird had been abed with her the night before. She could now read and write and was a fair mathematician; she kept a firm hand on the flow of orders and supplies, always knew what was in the larder and what was in need of replacement. She managed the accounts, won the respect of all the traders who brought their wares to Alec's house, and began to supervise the kitchen staff. The household beat away the passing time to its familiar rhythms – Janet still read and wrote alone in her room, still conversed with her son once or twice a week, still stood stiff and cold at her door while Gillies MacNicol stacked the logs in her hearth.

The waiting pressed on all of them, Janet at its centre, spinning out all their destinies, as she had always done.

II

They were sitting in the dining room one morning, Iona in her brilliant green dress of watered silk, Alec still in hunting clothes, just back from a dawn expedition for grouse. Their painful silence, broken by the odd fragment of conversation, drifted through the open casement, where a muggy, misty morning was just beginning to cloud with the malevolent dance of a late hatch of biting midges. Alec felt the tiny stings begin about his face, and Iona rose to close the window. She was busy at the sashes when Janet entered the room.

Alec looked up and bid her come forward. His daytime dealings with her were increasingly tense, especially when Iona was close by, as he strove to maintain the professional distance required of him. For weeks now, she had not mentioned anything about the travails of the past months. She had done nothing to

153

assuage his dreadful anxiety, except to say one night, "I will tell you when all hope is lost. Until then, try to be patient and do not keep asking me."

Janet's face was pale and thin this morning, her eyes dulled by dark shadows. She came towards him, then realised Iona was with him; she stopped and looked flustered.

"Ah," Alec said, too quickly, all business with her. "You have come for your instructions regarding dinner this evening?" He did not wait for her reply, but rattled on, anxious not to prolong the disagreeable tension of being in the same room as his wife and mistress. "My guests and I have been hunting this morning with some members of the Lady Margaret's family, and sixteen grouse have just been delivered to the larder. There is venison, brought over from Maglavat last week, that you gave orders to be hung, and I hooked a fine fish only yesterday at dawn. Those will be the makings of a grand dinner for the company." He paused, did a rough count in his head. "There will be fifteen at dinner, for Alasdair is to join us, and twelve guests, I think, and all the bedrooms to be freshened up. Set Alice to the task of distributing the chores."

"Yes, sir. Thank you." She turned to go, but there was something in the hesitant way she did it that made him call her back.

"Wait. You don't look well today," Alec said. "What troubles you?"

She shook her head. "It will do another time."

His forehead creased, and now Iona was beside her husband, her face taut. "Come forward; speak," she said. "We will hear it, man and wife together."

Alec smiled stiffly and nodded his encouragement. He saw the pleading look she gave him, as if he was failing to grasp something important, then his heart thumped against his ribs, and he felt suddenly heavy, the moment of truth upon him. He understood everything in a second. She had waited to be certain, and now she did not want to tell him. She did not want to give him up – the pact they had made would separate them forever now all hope of a child was lost. Small wonder, then, that she had not rushed to break her bitter tidings.

He looked at Iona and pity, fear and tenderness seemed to all crowd in his heart at once. She had been watching Janet impatiently, but when she caught her husband's gaze, she knew, too, and seemed to stiffen in anticipation of the blow. Alec's face flickered. His throat was tight, he could not speak. Janet stood before them, and even though she was the centre of all their attention, the moment seemed to belong only to Iona and Alec, a suspension of six years of pain that would at last find resolution. So many weeks of waiting, so many questions he had heard and answered through all the long days as he cared for Uishall, educated his son and worried for his future and his wife. And all the time, there was only one question he had asked himself repeatedly, to which he cared to hear the answer. And now it was here and he was unprepared, when for weeks he had been preparing –

"Don't be afraid, Janet," he heard himself saying. "It is all at an end now, one way or another."

She faltered another moment, and then found her courage. "I thought it well enough to tell you now," she said. "I am with child, sir."

For a moment, silence hung in the great dining room as if it was a palpable force, freezing all of them in place. It broke and crashed about them as Alec uttered a strange, low cry and took a step towards her. And then he was reaching for her, gripping her hands with such ferocity that she cried out, for without her to support him, he would have fallen. His expression terrified her. His face was white, the blood was beating in his head and he was staring at her as if she had half-killed him with the news.

The rustling sound he heard behind him was Iona fainting to the floor.

19.
BAGGED
OCTOBER 1836 – APRIL 1837

I

Four years had passed since Janet and his son came to his house, and now Alec stood on the brink of all he had longed for, with the price of seizing it laid bare before him and already forfeited.

The day of Janet's shocking revelation, Iona had collapsed. The combined stress of remaining childless, struggling to hold the love of her husband, fighting Janet's growing influence and the trauma of hearing the announcement of her pregnancy, conspired at last to break her. Three months she lay ill, eaten away by strain, her strong frame wasted, her once quick and clever mind reduced to tattered ramblings. They sent for the ancient mother at her request, but her charms and remedies were ineffectual against the malaise that had set in. Iona, frequently delirious and beset by fevers, swore that many nights, a hare raced round her bed, trying to protect her from the worst spirits attacking her.

Alec sought cures for her illness as desperately as his wife had sought solutions to his infertility. The spey-wife he eventually dismissed, seeing no value in her herbal remedies and mysticism. Besides, he still harboured the bitter memories of all that he and Iona had done on her recommendations, and he could not help but suspect her of exploiting Iona's vulnerability for her own gain.

He listened most respectfully to his own physician, who had tended all the family for years, but when he said there was little that could be done, Alec sought the opinions of other healers and priests. He was briefly tempted to descend into medical cruelty with a variety of traumatic tactics proposed by them to shock Iona out of her symptoms. But in the end, he could not subject her to more torment on the slender chance it would effect a cure. He listened to advocates of dousing her in freezing water, flagellating her with sharp heather twigs, applications of leeches and even blowing, which he had endured during his own illness when first he was married to Catherine.

The spiritual fanatic who wanted to bind his wife with rope at midnight on All Hallow's Eve and lay her in the bottom of a boat finally brought Alec to his senses. The healer then proposed to row her around a small sacred island in the middle of Uishall Loch, where stood an ancient ruined pagan temple. Finally, the would-be healer righteously intoned, she would be wrapped in the skin of a freshly slaughtered ram and shut inside a stone sarcophagus before the altar, until dawn broke. Alec heard him out with growing dismay then threw him out, shouting angrily that his wife, if not mad already, would certainly be so by the time she had completed such a monstrous ordeal.

At last, he stood at the foot of Iona's bed, looked at her spent frame with tender pity, and could not find it in his heart to either abandon her, or punish her any further. He kissed Janet's hands, begged her patience and forgiveness, and took it upon himself to care for Iona until she died, which his loyal physician told him would not be long.

He sent letters to her family in Sutherland, telling them of her pitiable condition. But the winter gales were so wild that their boats could not cross the seas, and when the screaming winds relented, the snows came heavier than they had for a decade, and her family, stranded in their castle, could only grieve at a distance for their dying daughter.

Janet was removed from her position within the household, and Alice promoted to her place. Amidst a torrent of rumours, Alec charged Janet with the responsibility of assisting him during the crisis period. For the three weeks Iona suffered the final stages of her decline, Janet advised him of current estate affairs, reported his decisions to relevant parties and was messenger and runner between Iona's room and the physician's house, chief comforter to the Laird.

In the long nights Alec nursed her, Iona raved about witchcraft, the little demon that had taken her husband, was sucking the life from her and carrying the devil's child. Most distressing of all, she begged her husband not to fall further under Janet's spell and forgave him for his unfaithfulness because his mind was not his own. She repented of her pagan rites and threw herself back on the mercy of God, who, evidently unimpressed by her radical change of tune, proved as deaf to her pleadings as he had before.

Alec hardly left her side, urged by Janet to tend his failing wife, who said she had managed one pregnancy well enough without him, and would easily cope with the second now he was promised to her. She held him firm, comforting him when he was nearly broken by exhaustion, never reproaching the desolation of his grief when Iona died in his arms at dawn one winter morning.

Janet wept for him, consoled him and reminded him of the future they had yet to build together. She talked of his dependants and the child she soon would bear for him to call his own from the beginning. No longer a lowly maid with no claims on the household she lived in, she took her place beside him with quiet dignity and challenged anyone to say she had not earned it.

II

It was not hard for him to keep his promise and marry Janet, for she had proved herself a strong and loving companion in the hardest of circumstances. Apart from anything else, she had restored his pride, his self-belief, given him his family, and when the worst of his grieving was past, he looked towards the future with Janet at his side.

He arranged the marriage swiftly, cutting short his period of mourning, for he had sworn that Janet would not bear a second bastard child. He dealt brusquely with the politics of clan and class, saying that he would not act on any objections raised to the match, so the least said on the subject, the better. He scandalised them by saying he would marry his already pregnant bride at God's altar; it conferred no insult, he said, for God had sanctioned their union in the most direct way possible.

He and Janet broke the news to Alasdair, who received the tidings with quiet surprise, but said at length he had long wished that he and his parents would be united. With a sidelong glance at his mother, he added that he had for some time suspected that his wish might one day be granted.

He quarrelled again with Ruaraidh, a bitter dispute because Alec had now to support Uishall purely on the wealth of his own family and endeavours, and Ruaraidh had become too dependent on his brother's gifts to get Maglavat through the lean times.

Then Alec assembled all his staff and told them with a shocking concision and utter lack of contrition, that whatever rumours they had heard, Janet Macleod was carrying his second child and they would marry as soon as the arrangements could be made. Amid gasps of amazement, he went on to say that the marriage would take place as much to conform to the dictates of respectability as to cement the profound affection that existed between them. He warned them that one of their peers would soon become their mistress, and that they would answer to him if they took issue with it, or find alternative employment elsewhere. A few of them, who had taken the Lady Iona's part in the difficult situation existing at the castle, took him up on his offer. Janet moved into separate quarters on the first floor to await the wedding day.

The day before the ceremony, Alec knelt before God's altar, wept with sorrow one final time for the loss of Iona, and wept with joy for the triple blessing of Janet, the child she carried, and the son she had already borne for him. He asked forgiveness for all his sins, and wondered at the ways of God, for after causing so much suffering and enduring such terrible punishment, he had been delivered at last into blissful contentment.

It was a quiet wedding in the church close by his ancient home and only family attended – those who were prepared to support him in the match. He had eyes for only Janet that day, and on their wedding night, he decked the bridal chamber with candles and flowers, and took her for the first time as his wife – a poignant new beginning for them in the wake of so much suffering and loss. It seemed a deeply symbolic act to him, the baby growing between them as he possessed her, evidence of the promising future that lay before them. He cradled her belly in his hands, rejoiced in the prospect of the new life she carried, and marvelled at the lusty kicks inside her. She was his miracle-worker and he loved her at last with unfettered passion, free from the constraints of secrecy and the social divide, for this quiet daughter of the land, now elevated to the status of land-owning lady, had given him gifts and taught him lessons he would never forget.

In the summer, the Lady Janet laboured briskly and without trouble to produce a daughter. Alasdair, now fourteen, now absolutely and thoroughly his father's heir, doted on his tiny sister from the very beginning. The little bundle did not look like her father. She looked like Janet, with a haze of copper-coloured curls even when she was born. Alec held her in his arms when she was all of ten minutes old, and cried with painful joy as if he was a newborn bairn himself.

They named the baby Elinor.

PART TWO

2001:
A TALE OF TRANSITION

DECAY AND SEPARATION

I

Times change, people move through the landscape. Sometimes they leave traces behind them, sometimes they fade to distant echoes and become one with the cry of wind and the whisper of water.

The Clan Macleod of Uishall and Maglavat, still strong in the first half of the nineteenth century, eventually began to fragment and weaken. Janet and Alec passed on, leaving legacies and secrets that would not be discovered for almost a century and a half.

By the 1950s, although Uishall Castle was still the family seat, seventy years had passed, and disenchantment had set in. There was also a deeper loss, linked to preoccupation with the figures, and the indignity that comes with being dispossessed. The distillery and its distinguished single malt had long since been sold by Alasdair to finance more lucrative business interests, and production moved to a more convenient mainland location. Uishall lost its clan ties and the spirit of the place, at once bolstered by its long history and strengthened by its endurance, began to fossilise. It was now owned but not possessed, a dead tradition, not a living one.

A syndicate was established in the mid-1960s, when Lachlan Macleod, a clan member with a six-hundred year bloodline binding him to Uishall, sold the castle and estate to clear death duties on other, more valuable property. Having watched his forefathers struggle for decades to make the vast acreage pay, he decided to cut his losses. Four families – Bartlett, Keldon-Smythe, Fynn and Clarence – went into partnership to purchase the estate, with the intention of continuing to run it as a sporting castle. For all of them, Uishall became a holiday tradition and their children were raised on its myths and stories; the ancient walls rang with their laughter and arguments, and they breathed the wild island air and roamed the hills until Uishall was part of them and they were the richer for it.

The new owners had pledged to protect its natural resources – the fish and deer, the water and the land where they lived – by generating income to support the necessary conservation work. At the beginning of the twenty-first century, Keldon-Smythe is dead, the remaining partners are getting on, the children are grown up and times are changing, even if the river and the lochs, the hills and gorges, the rocks and the heather seem invulnerable to the subtle handling of time.

In the castle, the sense of the past is still strong. In the blood red entrance hall, the head of a stag, a fourteen-pointer hunted by Alec in 1836, hangs above the door to the main drawing room. The small plaque beneath it names Alec's companions that day and the dogs, Meg and Tamlyn, who brought down the stag without the aid of guns. A plaque below it, often overlooked, bears an engraving of a deerhound and the legend: *Arakan: Faithful unto death*.

The echoes of history are strengthened by the portraits hanging in the great dining room, as they have done since 1394. Here, gazing down on the people gathered around the table, their faces warmed by the glow of candlelight even in this age of halogen and electricity, are all the Lairds of Uishall, every single one of them, and a good few of their wives as well.

Alec is there, the 23rd Laird who took three wives and seemed to know very little peace in his troubled reign. His son Alasdair is there, the first Laird to be photographed rather than painted for posterity. There he is, his thin, handsome face, pale and distinguished, his eyes bright with that strange, preternatural light often bestowed by early cameras. His eyes are not troubled like his father's, but cool, perhaps, with an air of distance. A man who has seen much, but thought it in his best interests not to feel. On one of the tables, there is a smaller portrait of his sister, Elinor, who never made it to a loftier position on the walls.

Beyond the castle walls, the Uishall Estate of the twenty-first century offers three kinds of hunting, and an escape into a world of privileged manners that echoes a long-lost past. Away from the river, sporting enthusiasts may leave their salmon rod propped neatly in the tackle room and take shotguns from the locked cabinet in the gun room to pursue the furred and feathered kinds of quarry. Thus equipped, they may join the grouse, woodcock and snipe shooting groups, or the deer stalking parties moving painstakingly through the heather and shallow bogs of the distant hills. For a few glorious weeks, the salmon, grouse and deer seasons coincide, and the three can be hunted together – the season of the Macnab, for those who care to try.

For the four children of the Uishall partners – Hugh and Robert Bartlett, Trevor Fynn and Freya Clarence – Uishall was part of all their lives before they were even born. They knew the river where the salmon jumped and swam, the lochs and burns where the lithe brown trout kept watch, the wild moorland and rocky hillsides where the deer grazed. They knew the light of sunrise and sunset, when impossible clashes of golds and greens, purples and reds stained the sky, and made black and amber shadows of the drifting clouds. They knew the histories, the stories and traditions of the Macleods, and had listened in their turn to the extraordinary tale of the ugly-beautiful Italian monster – Freya's favourite, often recounted to visiting friends. Much of the old furniture – including that most romantic of pieces – is still in place.

With the turn of another century, the ancient Macleod bloodline of the Uishall Estate hangs on by a tenuous thread, held unknowingly by one of the owning families; and the tradition of hunting for pleasure, born out of the second wave of clearances, persists.

II

There are darker sides, too, to this place of extremes. Times may have changed, but the pressures of running a large acreage and making it pay are even more pronounced than they were in Alec's day. The sometimes bitter attitudes to the English landlords, expressed through poaching and vandalism, are so deeply entrenched for some, they are almost genetic. These are the serpents of Eden.

New laws have been passed that make it possible for communities to buy back the land taken from them during the clearances of the nineteenth century. The old estates, with their grand houses, fish, deer and bird populations, can no longer exist in the way they used to. Labour costs are high and conserving the natural resources is time-consuming. What should be seen as a practical measure to improve access to the land and its earning potential has instead become a political weapon brandished against the old order, even in the absence of a credible structure to take its place.

Alec Macleod witnessed the death of the old clan system, but didn't live to see a satisfactory replacement. In 2001, the very notion of there being a landowning class seemed anachronistic, a dinosaur thrashing in a mesh of high-tech lifestyles and global businesses built on information technology, underpinned by an increasingly classless society.

Where did the landowner fit in, the archaic idea of a ruling family reporting to the Crown, in charge of the people on his land, governing their activities, supervising their property and financing their endeavours? How should this tattered institution be perceived – was the aristocratic landowner paternalistic, generous and responsible, or bullying, tight-fisted and autocratic? Did it make a difference if the landowner was an aristocrat with an ancient bloodline and a tradition of responsibility for the people on his land, or a rock star with no lineage, no roots, but all the money in the world? Did owning huge tracts of land make any sense at all? And even more perplexing – if the people on the land took it back and took the landowner out of the mix, where would they get the money that had gone with him to finance its husbandry?

As Hugh, Robert, Trevor and Freya grew older, completed their education, found careers and beat out the rhythms of their lives in cities far removed from Uishall, they felt its pull ever more strongly, and were bound to it with increasing passion. They also began to feel that perhaps, despite their powerful love of the place, they might not be able to inherit their fathers' treasure.

1.
BELLY UP

I
APRIL

It should have been easy. All he'd had to do was frighten him. How hard was it to frighten little Frankie? Little, weasly Frankie, with his loud talk and big boots and big ideas that never came to anything. Stupid little Frankie, with his ridiculous shredded-wheat hair, bragging about the contacts in high places he had, the sly winking that drove everyone to distraction, sounding off in the pub until he either got himself into a fight, or fell over before someone had the chance to deck him. Well, he wouldn't be annoying anyone anymore, not in this life.

Ally ran through the heather – stumbled more like, his feet snagging on the roots, the treacherous potholes and abrupt drops concealed by the tough, bushy ground cover. He was getting too old for this kind of caper. The moon was bright, the stars pale imitations of the dazzling glory they could achieve on a peat-black winter's night. He longed for his bed – God in heaven, even the snoring of his wife would be welcome tonight. He ran the long slope up to Janet's Knoll, skirting the double granite gravestone eerie in the moonlight, and eventually the heather cleared, changed to tussocks of peat topped with stiff, pricking grasses, rising out of softer, bare patches of black ground that sprang dully under his thudding boots. The going was no easier. His chest heaved, his breath rasped – too much whisky, never enough exercise – and sweat ran down his neck and belly.

How many times had he been sent out onto the moors on business – and done it, no bother, without screwing up? All he'd had to do was frighten him. He'd done that, all right. Scared him to death. Whatever Frankie had been up to over the past few weeks, they'd never find out now. MacInnes had wanted him warned off, sent back to his usual patch. The incident had implications for all of them. Poaching Uishall, being a thorn in the side for the toffs was one thing. But a death was something else. The law would be on their backs from the moment the body was found. He'd lost his temper and Frankie – stupid, weasly, pathetic little Frankie – had panicked. Ally swore in disgust at his own stupidity. MacInnes wouldn't be pleased when he found out. Probably kill him.

As he cleared the last rise a broken strip of grey tarmac, metallic in the moonlight, glittered dully some five hundred yards distant, at the foot of a long downward slope, in sight of the ruined houses crumbled like oatcakes into the heather. He stopped only when he was below the crest of the hill, like the good stalker he was, and bent double for a while before dropping onto his back into the heather. His mouth open, contorted in the aftermath of exertion, blood heating his face, wishing he didn't have to breathe. After a painful interlude, he picked himself up and followed the line of the single-track road a couple of hundred yards back, dropped into a shallow gully and negotiated the banks of a tumbling burn, noisily celebrating its collision with a rubble of rocks and stones. He jumped across the narrow neck where the water, forced into a narrow channel by two large boulders, dropped down sharply a few feet, before carrying on its way. At last, his legs weakened by the punishing run, he walked the length of the wire fence and turned up the long peat road that led to the house at the end of Eilaster glen. No one had seen him.

Well, at least that part had gone according to plan.

When he limped into the kitchen an hour later, his feet stinging with blisters, the clock told him it was three o' clock in the morning. He kicked off his boots and fished out a bottle of whisky and a tumbler from the kitchen cupboard. He sank the first one while he was still standing at the counter, and poured another before he collapsed on the sofa, glass in one hand, bottle in the other.

Oblivion – that was the aim. Swept away on a rising tide of the water of life, maybe it would all be gone in the morning.

II
MAY

At the height of summer, dawn in the Outer Hebrides comes outrageously early. It's a bad time of year to be up to no good, for the night offers no real cover. The sky, still fully light at eleven in the evening, has never been truly dark by the time dawn begins to gently push the sun back over the horizon. It begins to brighten at about three o' clock and the birds start to sing at about four. By five, the light is rounded and soft, caressing the hills with its golden warmth, and the sea, spread beneath the violet sky like a yearning mistress, gleams sapphire, bronze and copper and seems full of secrets.

This particular morning, a small clinker boat was drifting peacefully in the shining water at the mouth of the Uishall River, a quarter of a mile out to sea from where the granite castle sat in placid repose on the bank of the river mouth. It was six o' clock and a white mist was rapidly burning off the glassy calm of the water, occasionally disturbed by the rise of sea trout and the movement of the boat. A lone man was resting on the oars, pausing in his early morning tasks to enjoy the tranquil warmth. An idyllic spot, a place where, in a week or so, the salmon would be leaping in full view of the castle windows, daring the breakfasting fishermen to down their bacon and eggs in double quick time and rush out to catch them. Across the water, there were green hills roughly covered with grass, low white rocks with most of their contours smoothed down, beaten into submission by the tireless elements.

It was late May. This was the last of the precious time before the season began, before the guests began to arrive at the castle and the place was roused into life. Aidan Gillespie, the estate manager, and the man out on the water this morning, liked this time of year best, when the summer was still working towards its peak and the river was quiet, beset by neither guests nor poachers. When the cook had not arrived and the domestic staff and seasonal ghillies were still not occupying the servants' quarters. When the boats were painted and fitted, and there was just Aidan and Kenny, the head ghillie, and the veteran gamekeeper Angus working to an agreed set of priorities.

The three men were equally possessive about this patch of earth with its wild, unfettered beauty and tumbling waters, and the creatures that lived there. Once the guests arrived, the place no longer belonged to them. They became its servants, and earned the privilege of living here. But now, for another ten days or so, the river was ripening with moving salmon, the glens and crags were playing host to the deer; the grouse, snipe and woodcock were busy with their young, and everything was going about its business without the worry of hunters' guns and hooks. The water and the land, the sky and the castle all belonged to Aidan and Kenny and Angus, and they were the keepers of paradise.

It wasn't that the guests didn't appreciate Uishall. Far from it. Most knew how fortunate they were to have access to its waters, to be able to enjoy the comforts of the castle, to indulge in genuine escape from lives weighed down by the obligations of high powered jobs. The difference between Uishall Castle and the cities of mainland England, where most of the guests made their livings, was almost incomprehensible. For the castle guests, Uishall was a place of temporary pleasures, a place of escape. They understood its elemental qualities, but it was Aidan and Kenny, full-time residents in their tied cottages, who felt them, lived them and loved them. For Aidan in particular, relaxing in the clinker on this sublime May morning, his shirtsleeves already rolled up, his waistcoat hanging open, his sharp eyes lazily scanning river mouth and cloudless sky, it was a place he could no longer separate from himself.

He didn't know how long he'd been on the water when he noticed a large piece of flotsam trapped in a tangle of floating willow branches. It had come into view from behind a small rocky island in the middle of the sea loch, and was idly making its way towards the shore, with no particular landing place in mind. Mottled in various shades of green, grey and black, it wasn't immediately distinguishable as anything of importance, but it was a curious shape and looked like something that shouldn't be in the water. It was still some distance from the clinker boat, but the closer it got, the more it pricked Aidan's curiosity and eventually, he raised his binoculars and began to focus them.

A movement beneath the surface suddenly disturbed the mass, and loosened it slightly from the willow. It flipped and seemed to right itself obligingly for the benefit of the inquiring gaze of the binoculars. There was something about this new perspective that made Aidan's heart thud suddenly with understanding. As it came into sharp focus, he found himself looking into the swollen, discoloured face of a floating corpse, its bulging eyes almost comically grotesque, accusing him of staring.

Even the expletive erupting from Aidan's mouth had only a momentary impact on the serene calm of the morning, as if the outburst had been immediately hushed into shamed silence by a scene conscious of its own splendour. The binoculars clattered against the boat and dropped to the floor. The corpse with its hideous face bobbed gently towards the clinker, insolent in its disfiguration, as if it had a right to be a part of things. Aidan, sweating, his breakfast sandwich rebelling in his stomach, got a grip and began to haul a net from the bottom of the boat.

III

The estate manager still looked grey in the face when Detective Inspector Duncan Macrae arrived to investigate the scene. Aidan had towed the body back to the castle, where it now rested, covered with a blue tarpaulin, above the waterline on the small slipway. The smell was already approaching insupportable out in the fresh air, and Duncan could only pity the pathologist who would have to work on him back at the mortuary.

"Well, this is a grim turn-up, Aidan," he said, looking out over the peacefully lapping water. "Not what you're expecting to haul up on the end of your line. A good job it wasn't one of your guests who hooked him."

Aidan shook his head. He had won the battle over whether or not his bacon sandwich stayed in his stomach, but it had been a close call. Dragging the body to shore had been nothing short of revolting; when he had tried to grasp the arm, the putrefying flesh had collapsed beneath the army combat jacket. He would remember that sickening sensation of ooze and squash for the rest of his life.

"Any idea who it is?" Duncan asked.

"Aye," Aidan said grimly. "You can't tell by his face, right enough, but the hair's the giveaway. It's Frankie Johnson, I'll put money on it."

Duncan grimaced. "Frankie? But what would he be doing up here?"

"Causing bother," Aidan said, recovering his equilibrium a little as anger began to warm him. "The man's not fit for anything but trouble."

"He wouldn't tamper with the fish," Duncan protested. "The fish are who he's trying to save. He'll not have been about anything in that line –"

"Maybe not the fish, or any of the creatures that creep and crawl about the land," Aidan said angrily. "But the boats, the bothies, the ghillies' equipment – any of that would be fair game to him."

"Maglavat is his patch," Duncan said, squinting against the sun's glare as he looked out to sea. "Or was. They've had a lot of petty vandalism out there prior to the season."

"It's on the market," Aidan said. "They'll be trying to give the place a bad name and put off the buyers."

"Is the community not interested in purchasing the land?" Duncan asked. "The MSP's been making a lot of noise about it."

"What would the community do with a piece of land the size of Maglavat?" Aidan said scornfully. "And the grand house?" He shook his head. "It's all very well, the dream of reclaiming the birth right of our great grandfathers. But they couldn't make it pay back then. How will they do it now?"

Duncan laughed. "Well, the English landlords pay your wages, I suppose," he said. "Is that what makes you a sceptic?"

"And a good few other folks' as well," Aidan reminded him. "The community – how will it afford to buy Maglavat? You know the answer yourself – the Scottish Executive will give them a grant to buy it. And then what? The deer still have to be culled, the land managed, the river policed, or it will all go to pot. And then the community will get another grant, and another, and another, until it's all ruined, the deer over breeding and starving, all the fish poached, and none of us will get a living from our forefathers' legacy." He shook his head again in disgust. "Whatever you think of rich Englishmen, when they buy the land, they pay for it. At least there's some dignity in that. Grants don't give anybody dignity. They just give you an easy route into a situation you don't understand, that will blow up in your face when it's too late to rectify the damage."

"You'll have to harangue me about the intricacies of land reform some other time," Duncan said, smiling at the normally taciturn Aidan's sudden show of passion. "I've a dead man to bag, a widow to question and a motive to uncover."

"I'm not entirely biased," Aidan said, his tone less aggressive. "The situation we have here at Uishall isn't perfect. It's a good business, but its heart no longer beats. It's the same with all estates where the landlord is an absentee, and not on the land where he belongs. The community buys Maglavat, and what will you have then? People in charge of an investment they can't afford, and a grant system to prop them up instead of a landowner's investment. What's the difference?"

"You have a syndicate now," Duncan reminded him. "Uishall's not had a Laird for almost fifty years."

"And it's the poorer for it. Now we have money instead of a Laird, people who send cheques and keep a constant eye on the profit and loss. It's like giving a child all the toys it wants, but no affection." He shook his head, watching with grim resignation as the body was loaded into the ambulance. "This man dying is a sign of the times we live in. There's politics wrapped up in this."

"Away with you," Duncan said, waving his hand and preparing to climb into his car. "Get back to your fish and leave the mysteries of foul play to me."

IV

Hedda MacInnes caught her red curly hair back into a rough ponytail, threw the suitcase onto the bed and began to pack. She conceded that a season at Uishall as kitchen help wasn't the best-paid summer job on the island. But it would be paradise compared to standing in a fish processing plant on the prawn line for ten hours a day – or worse, slaving on the gutting line in the salmon factory in the middle of the night. Uishall was set in beautiful countryside, and while the personal privacy might not be that great, it was forty miles away from the spiteful disapproval of her parents, who had never made any secret of their feelings about her long-standing relationship with John Gibson.

"He's your *teacher*," her mother had said in anguish, when Hedda had broken the news almost two years ago. "It's sinful, that's what it is. The Lord will have no mercy."

"He *was* my teacher," Hedda had said. "I left school in June. We didn't go out together until July. We did nothing until my exams were over and we were both out of school."

Her mother had wrung her hands in despair, while her father had been surly, his eyes dark with hatred.

"It's the devil's work," he said angrily. "Not enough that he spent his last year filling all your heads with liberal tosh about

173

incomers and the politics of the English –" he broke off, unable to articulate his disgust about the nub of the matter.

Hedda had done it for him. "So what really gets you," she said, "is not that he's six years older than me, or even that he was my history teacher. It's back to the usual."

"Ach, Hedda, there are plenty nice island boys to be going out with," her mother had pleaded. "Why pick an English one?"

"Because –" Hedda had said violently, and stopped herself. They'd never stop scoffing if she tried to explain. "Just because," she finished.

Two years later, it was no better. In fact, it was worse. Hedda was still living at home during the holidays while she finished her university education in Glasgow, still fielding the petty remarks and barely veiled hostility about her choice of partner. She had left the church, thrown herself entirely into the arms of Satan as far as Murdo and Katie-Bel were concerned. John had begged her to move in with him, but she wouldn't hear of it until she could support herself.

"Will you have your own room there?" he asked her now from the chair in her bedroom, while she pulled underwear and socks out of drawers, and hunted for T-shirts and jeans and something respectable for when she had to serve in Uishall's splendidly historic dining room, with its fascinating portraits of the Macleod Lairds, and its ancient Italian cabinet, where the decanters and glasses for the malts and vintage port were laid out.

She looked innocently at him. "I don't know what you mean."

He laughed, catching her by the arm as she passed him, her hands full of knickers, and pulled her towards him. She lost her balance, fell into his lap with a cry of surprise and kissed him for longer than she intended.

"Stop it," she said after a while, disengaging herself. "It's bad enough that you're in here with me. At Uishall, it won't matter. There's a lock on the door. And yes, I do have my own room."

"Praise the lord," John said fervently. "The opportunity to sleep with Satan's daughter and commit my sin without the fear of interruption." He set her back on her feet. "Finish packing," he said. "Then we can get out of here."

He watched her. It was all still slightly unreal to him. He had sworn, probably like most of his colleagues, that he would never get involved with a student. The first year, he had kept to his promise, even though Hedda was in the fifth year class he taught. It was the second year he began to be aware that she was interested in him and then – far more potentially compromising – that he was interested in her.

It wasn't just her enthusiasm for pursuing the themes he had raised in the classes on the Jacobite Rebellion. It was something else that he had tried to shake off, and failed. They got along together. It was as simple as that. As the academic year wound to its conclusion, Hedda predictably sailed through her examinations and her place at university looked secure, he began to think about what it would be like with the school empty of her.

Eventually, the fact that he couldn't get her out of his mind pushed him towards action. He had paid a visit to the shop run by her father in Eilaster, two weeks before the end of the school year, but circumstances conspired against them, and nothing was said. He could still remember, though, the confrontation with her father, the tortured silences between him and Hedda as they strolled along the glen road, his indecision about what to do and his fear of telling her how he felt. And the anguish in her eyes when he belatedly took control of the situation and decided that anything they wanted to say was better left until they were both safe from the legitimate interference of the school authorities. That told him what he needed to know – that she felt for him, too, and was suffering because of it.

On the last day of term, when everyone was going round saying their goodbyes, she had approached him.

"I'll miss you, sir," she had said in her habitual forthright manner. They were in the corridor, students streaming in and out of doors, mayhem all around.

"Well, you know what leaving school means, Hedda," he had said, smiling.

She flushed, without knowing why, and an odd feeling went through him.

"It means that you and I are no longer student and teacher," he said, with exaggerated seriousness. "So you can stop calling me sir."

She laughed. "And it won't be against the rules."

"For us to see each other," he said, and was shocked at the way her directness had infected him. Now they were both blushing, staring at each other as it came out into the open for the first time. Looking back, it had been one of the scariest moments of his life, opening his heart to a girl six years his junior in a teeming school corridor. It was pure idiocy. His immediate reaction had been panic, a violent resurgence of doubt, and he cringed inside, dreading her response.

She could have laughed at him, said, "*What – me go out with an old git like you?*" and half the school would have heard. But she didn't. She put her hand on his shoulder, kissed him on the cheek and whispered, "I'm so glad you said that. I thought it was just me." Then he was left standing, wondering if he had just imagined it.

After that, he was on the rack for two hellish weeks, trying to widen the gap between the relationship they had had in the classroom, and the unknown quantity they would create when they got together outside. Eventually he rang her, and they went out on a Friday night, a noisy date with most of his old sixth form students there, but they had decided that they might as well start out in the open. She felt self-conscious calling him John, but he had threatened her with walking out if she called him sir. Mostly, she managed to avoid calling him anything at all – a tactic that was as subtle at times as it was infuriating at others.

They talked until midnight then John took her hand and led her onto the dance floor, both of them awkward about touching each other in front of such an expectant audience. Neither of them wanted their first kiss to be accompanied by a deafening cheer from the crowd of alternately curious and impatient onlookers, but in the end, that was the way it turned out.

The man Hedda had not called by name all evening drew her close during a slow song, smiled into her eyes and said, "Let's get it over with, or they'll never let us out of here." Hedda had smiled back, folded her arms around his neck and kissed him with a shy tenderness he would never forget. Around them, Hedda's old classmates erupted. After that, nothing parted them for the rest of the evening, whatever music was playing.

Later, alone on the harbour front, John Gibson took his new girlfriend in his arms again and said the kiss on the dance floor had been a mere crowd-pleaser. Then they kissed properly, and he asked if he could see her again, and she raised her eyes and belted him round the head, which he took to be a yes.

Over the summer, they tried to keep it light, painfully aware of Hedda's impending departure for a four-year degree course. Mindful too, of the inevitable gossip, the jealousy of not only a couple of girls from Hedda's old history set, but also of one of the teachers, who had fancied her chances and didn't take kindly to being out-manoeuvred by a younger girl. *Let's not expect too much*, they had said. *Let's just make it fun*. And it was fun. But it also became serious. They were still together when Hedda left to begin her studies, still together at Christmas, when the novelty had worn off. Still together at the end of the first year, and now it was the end of the second year, and they were still together. Katie-Bel and Murdo, still hopeful that it wouldn't last and that their daughter would be saved from the devil's clutches, were beginning to feel increasingly desperate at their daughter's determination to continue with her unsuitable match.

With her case packed, a box full of books and videos and John teetering down the stairs behind her with a small television and the video player, Hedda met her father at the kitchen door. He surveyed them with grim despair.

"A poor choice of employment you've made to go with your poor choice of man," he said.

"Aye, and you'd rather I was sweating away ripping the bellies out of salmon all summer, than working on an English-owned estate," Hedda said.

His face darkened. "Ripping the belly out of your own father," he said, with ill-judged melodrama. "And don't be thinking that just because my daughter's working there this summer, it will stop me."

"I never expect anything to stop your childish prank-playing at this time of year," Hedda said acidly. "One day, you'll go too far – if you haven't already."

She was unprepared for the sudden flash of anger in his eyes and the savagery with which he gripped her arm. She gasped and the box clattered to the floor, but what registered was something that frightened her far more than the pain.

"What do you know?" he said. "What have you heard?"

She wrenched her arm free. "I've heard nothing," she said. "Nothing that's ever made me proud to call you father. Whatever you've been getting up to on the moors, I haven't heard about it and I don't want to."

He stared at her with loathing. "The least I see of you this summer, the better for us all." His parting shot delivered, Murdo strode off towards the kitchen, his mood unimproved.

"What was that about?" John asked when they were finally on the road to Uishall.

Hedda shook her head. "It's how he amuses himself during the hunting season. A great case study he'd make for you,

177

with all your political theories about how islanders and English get along together."

"I thought that was young men's work," John commented drily. "It takes energy to go hiking over the moors at dead of night, looking for trouble."

"It depends how much hate you have inside," Hedda said sadly. "On the amount he carries, he can run his private war against the English a good while longer." She sighed. "You're not a special case, you know," she said. "You're just another one – and it's the worst thing in the world that you're going out with his daughter."

V

Marie, dark-haired, cheerful, hardworking and robust, drove the long road to Uishall from the centre of London with a light heart and Celtic rock blaring through the speakers. The car was the only place she would sing along, in the certain knowledge that she couldn't be overheard. She had just ended a four-year relationship, quit her job as cook in a busy city centre pub, and landed the cook's job at Uishall, the chocolate-dipped cherry on her liquor-sodden trifle. And after Uishall – who could tell where she'd be, or what she'd be doing. She had the irrepressible sense that life was beginning all over again.

She had firm ideas about how she was going to tackle her new position. The housekeeper, Heather, had given her more than a hint that Uishall Castle needed a fresh approach. The previous cook had been there a long time, and the current owners owed her a great debt of loyalty. In eighteen years, she had never let them down. *That didn't mean she was perfect*, Heather had added hastily, as if at pains not to paint a picture of a paragon that Marie could never live up to. *We had our problems with Christina.*

Marie was not troubled by what she heard. To her, cooking for sporting folk was not a matter of refinement. The job had to be done well, and the food had to be of a high standard, but this was not an environment where the cook scored points for delicate arrangements of a few sparse items on a plate. Her guests were hungry men and women who had just spent eight or ten hours striding across rough moorland or wading thigh-deep in a fast-moving river, and could well be going back for a bit more

178

punishment after dinner, while the light was still good. They came to the cook for nourishment, a hearty plateful of tasty food that would sustain them though their sporting ordeals, help them celebrate their triumphs, and comfort them in their one-that-got-away losses.

A generation of hunters and fishermen had eaten at Christina's table, and been quite happy to do so. Marie could picture the food. Bowls of Scotch broth, salvers piled with great slabs of roasted meat, mashed potatoes and buttered Brussels sprouts, baking trays fragrant with the scent of gingerbread, and pudding plates steaming with generous portions of rhubarb pie and custard.

But Marie was replacing the old order. She had sailed through the interview process at the castle, acquitted herself well on the test lunch she cooked for her examiners, Bill Bartlett and Heather. She proved that she understood her market, liked to see her guests satisfied, and wasn't scared of tradition. But she also showed that she was a cook with her roots in modern kitchens, and her food reflected the mood of inevitable change that was overtaking Uishall.

VI

Christina stood in the middle of the kitchen and wondered what she should do next. She had cleared out all the old roasting tins and baking trays, the patty tins for the Yorkshire puddings, the loaf tins for the fruitcakes. Most of them were years old, blackened and warped, stained and crusted up in the corners. Some had been there as long as she had. The new cook wouldn't be wanting them, she was sure.

Normally, this was a busy time for her, baking the cakes for the picnic baskets, cooking up and freezing the vast quantities of soup for the hunters' flasks, organising the shopping lists. Scrubbing down the cupboards and surfaces, the pantry with its marble slabs and stone floor, the enormous storeroom, the great cooker with its stainless steel so old and so often scoured that it was beginning to look like pewter. Then there was the Aga, with its four ovens flanking the central fire box, one hot for roasting, one medium for baking, one slow for casseroles, one warm for the plates and serving dishes. Yes, there was plenty to be done two weeks before the start of the season.

But none of it was her responsibility. After eighteen years, it felt strange indeed to not be slipping smoothly into the automatic routines. The new cook was arriving tomorrow, and it was her kitchen now, to sort out as she pleased. Christina pinched her lips together. She had tendered her resignation as a ploy to increase her salary, and it had backfired. Heather had taken it to the directors, and instead of adding to her income, they had called her bluff. She could still feel the shock, and she was still cursing herself over her timing. She'd done it in January. If she'd waited until March, they would have been less confident about finding a replacement at shorter notice. They might have given her what she wanted. Instead, they told her that they would miss her very much, she really had been a treasured institution at Uishall, but they quite understood that the demands of the job were becoming too much. They thanked her – this was the galling part – for being considerate enough to tell them in plenty of time for them to hire a new cook.

She heard that they were conducting interviews in February, and then that Marie had been hired in March. It was all over, apart from the offer of the weekend cooking, which Christina might still like to undertake for pocket money in her retirement. She had accepted, and now she was wondering whether or not she should have.

2.
CASTING
MAY

I

Hugh Bartlett, second eldest of the Uishall kids at thirty-five, leaned back in the leather swivel chair and waited for his summons to be answered. The telephone thirty miles away, buried somewhere in the airless moneymaking towers of the City of London, rang in his left ear. More than anything else, it seemed to him that the telephone had been the precursor of the modern age, the start of the cranking up of the speed of life. These days, the world jostled for space at your left ear, and constantly made its demands on you. The telephone brought the world into your home, your office, your mode of transport, your weekend barbecue party, whether you wanted it there or not. And everyone was terrified of being without it, in case the world wanted them, and they could not be contacted. The telephone had meant the death of privacy, and the enslavement of the free world.

As he waited, the scent of hops and barley brewing in the mash tuns drifted through the open window, and his eyes roved around the office and settled on the framed photograph on his desk. Not of his wife and children – he didn't have any – or any other relation, friend or inspirational person. It was a stag; a twelve-pointer, head raised, pausing in the act of grazing, alert to a faint sound he didn't recognise.

The image always made Hugh shiver. He had clicked the camera shutter a few seconds before Angus had pulled the rifle trigger and felled him. The moment had haunted him ever since. A defining moment, more dramatic, even, than the one when, standing in the middle of a student beer festival, with the best pint of bitter he had ever drunk clutched in his hand, he knew he wanted to be – must be – a brewer.

Bill Bartlett hadn't been pleased, and the announcement from his callow, hung-over son, who had described the pint of bitter with more passion than he had ever spent on eulogising a woman, was met with a good deal of harrumphing. Three generations of accountants sat at his father's back, and Hugh was obviously lined up to carry the tradition forward. But the father's vicarious ambitions were thwarted by the son's determination to apply his mind to the rigours of roasting hops rather than the cooking of other people's books.

It was the second major turning point in Hugh's life. The first had been that stag, high on the hills of the Uishall estate, looking down on Janet's Knoll, who turned his great head in Hugh's direction. Hugh, flat to the heather, his eye fixed to the gun sights, his finger sweaty against the trigger, had thought he made eye contact, and for him, the hunt was over. Instead of making the kill, he had put the gun down and reached for the camera slung around his neck.

Beside him, the gamekeeper, Angus, had turned his head cautiously, his greying moustache quivering, his eyes puzzled.

"Will you no take the shot, Hugh?"

Hugh shook his head. "Wait," he said. "Just a second."

Angus flicked an anxious glance towards the stag, found it still frozen in position. He didn't want to lose the chance, leave it limping another day. They had got within a hundred and fifty yards, a safe distance to ensure a clean kill. "He's lame," he said in the lowest voice he could. "He'll starve come winter. This is a kindness for the beast, a good death."

"I know," whispered Hugh, staring through the camera lens. "But I can't." He turned briefly towards the gamekeeper and his forehead creased. "He deserves a better death than I can give him. Do you understand?"

The seconds stretched between them, between the stag and his destiny. Hugh took his photograph and Angus took the shot. The stag was dead before he hit the ground – the good death the gamekeeper had promised. It was a long time before they moved to recover the body, and fifteen years later, Hugh had not laid the memory to rest.

"Robert Bartlett," said a careful voice in his left ear, as if Hugh might be an obscene telephone caller. Hugh briefly considered doing some heavy breathing, but decided not to get things off on the wrong foot.

"Robert, do lighten up," he said.

"Oh, hallo, Hugh. Never start off too friendly. It's a policy of mine. You just don't know these days, do you?"

Robert was the accountant Hugh was never destined to be. Robert was in fact sitting at the very desk at which Hugh would have been sitting, had inspiration not come to him in the form of a pint of ale. To mollify his disappointed father, Hugh had pleaded that Robert, a year older, then in his final year at university, would be more than capable of carrying on the family business without his younger sibling. Robert's cautious manner belied a quick and agile mathematical brain, more pure and direct in its thinking than the creative and impulsive Hugh. To his credit, the Old Man had gone along with the idea, perhaps still hoping that Hugh might yet change his mind about entering the brewing trade, grow up a bit, and realise that accounting would be the mature career choice. It was an arrangement that had worked out well for both brothers; Robert was now a partner in the business and set to step into Bill's shoes when he retired in a few years. In view of the excellence of his elder brother's performance, Hugh had been forgiven some time ago, and allowed to get on with his radical ambitions in peace.

"Are you on for the Macnab?" Hugh asked, cutting to the chase. Robert had been forewarned, the only way to get him to agree to anything. If you sprang a surprise on him, he shied like a nervous horse, and that was the end of it. Even so, Hugh heard a sigh at the other end.

"Oh, I don't know, Hugh. That's not really the point of going to Uishall, is it? I go there to wind down, cast a few flies and catch the odd fish … I'm not much of a shooter, really. And I don't like competitions. They make me nervous. It's never the same when you're hunting under pressure."

"Come on, Robert, it's not exactly a competition, is it? It's more of a challenge, and a challenge is always better when you're up against an opponent. What do you say?"

Robert's tone shifted to outright glum. "There you go again. Challenge … opponent … they're such competitive words for a place like Uishall."

"Well, if you're hell-bent on total relaxation …" Hugh paused to consider his options. He had no intention of taking no for an answer. "What if we designate a day –?"

A faint groan from Robert as the persuasion tactics began. Hugh punched air. Robert was already yielding to inevitability.

"It's such a long way off yet," Robert said half-heartedly, and with a degree of pique. Hugh probably had advanced qualifications in persuasion. Funny they'd never yet landed him a girl. "It's only May now – you can't do a Macnab until September –"

"Dad's called a syndicate meeting bang in the middle," Hugh interrupted. "It's perfect. September's wonderful up there, you know it is."

"I was thinking I might go up next month," Robert said, and Hugh heard avoidance tactics kicking in. "Aidan says the fish are moving already." He paused. "To tell you the truth, I've had a project in mind for a couple of years now, but every time I promise myself I'll get on and do it, I get caught up with the fishing, or running around with Aidan –"

"What is it?" Hugh asked. "Not the fishing records again?"

"No, although there may well be a few stray oddments floating about. It's about those four boxes of papers Dad found in the attic in the old part of the castle."

"I remember," Hugh said, suddenly interested. "So what's in them?"

"Well, we finally got round to looking through them a bit last time we were up, and it turns out they date back to the 1820s and go right up to 1874 –"

Hugh whistled. "That's the clearance period," he said. "And hang on – isn't that when Alasdair Macleod sold out –"

"It's the whole transition, from Willie Macleod setting up the sheep farms, to Alasdair's eventual realisation of Uishall as a sporting estate. I had a quick look through – there's even letters and accounts relating to Maglavat. It's amazing that place didn't take Uishall down with it at the end – Alec Macleod must have been on the edge of ruin. There's a mountain of stuff, personal correspondence, medical records, kitchen records, wardrobe requisitions, travel documents –"

"It sounds fascinating. Need a hand?"

"It will all need cataloguing," Robert said. "I was thinking we could hand it all over to Freya when it's sorted, so she could work a miracle similar to the one she performed on the fishing history. It'll be right up her street – she'll probably turn it into a best seller. Alec was divorced once and his second wife went mad before he settled down – as if he didn't have enough on his plate."

"Really?" Hugh said. "I've always wondered who worked out the sheep were never going to pay."

"That was probably later on. Uishall seemed to adopt sporting very quickly compared to the other island estates. And there's no doubt it saved Maglavat."

"Well, if you want to make a start in June, I'll be up there myself. I'm supposed to be running part of this two-day ghillies' course – something to do with a casting demonstration."

Robert allowed himself a dry laugh. "Rather you than me," he said. "Presumably you won't be reeling in any more floaters."

"I certainly hope not," Hugh said. "Aidan sounded pretty shaken up when I called him."

"Can't think why an animal rights man would be getting himself drowned up there," Robert said. "Seems such a waste." He paused. "Bit early for that kind of thing, apart from anything else. Aidan says the post mortem estimated at least six weeks in the water."

This was not where Hugh wanted the conversation to go, and he had a strong suspicion that Robert had seized on yet another change in subject for less than subtle motives. Troubling though the appearance of the corpse was, he'd already had his fill of it from his father in the course of the last few days.

"Well, look – we're getting off the point," Hugh said, determined not to fall for any more distractions. "About this Macnab. Suppose you choose a day to have a crack at it."

Robert sighed again. "It doesn't really work like that, though, does it?" he said. "If I pick Tuesday, then conditions are perfect on Wednesday, I'll be annoyed."

"Not to mention screwed," Hugh said. "Look, you could just go for it when you get the urge. You pick the day on the day, or go at it all week – your call."

"Is anyone else up for this?"

"Trevor," Hugh lied, not having secured definite commitments from anyone at the moment.

Robert laughed and began to relax. "Oh Christ, trust Trevor to get himself talked into it," he said. "Always up for anything going. Will old Cornelius be there as well?"

"I'm afraid so. Syndicate meeting, and all that."

"Anyone else?"

"Freya, of course."

"Ah."

Hugh grinned. His big brother was always touchingly embarrassed about his affection for Freya. He got on well with her, especially since he'd married someone else. He had once been more than a little in love with her, from a careful distance, but she frightened him too much. He had never declared his feelings, and was eternally grateful for the fact. Now he could admire her from afar, safe within his happy and faithful marriage, hiding behind the protection of his wedding ring.

"Will she be up for the Macnab?"

"Well, maybe not the Royal part –"

"Oh now really, Hugh, I draw the line at that," Robert protested, with a sudden, pathetic vehemence. "I'm a married man."

"You're the only one of us who's taken the oath," Hugh said with false commiseration. "But you might fall victim yet to peer pressure."

"Straight Macnab," Robert said, unwittingly giving Hugh his unconditional surrender. "What you get up to after the guns and rods are put away is your affair."

"Quite," Hugh said, who guessed that Robert had missed his own irony.

There was a small, defeated silence, then a gentle laugh. "All right then, count me in."

"Good man."

"Freya's good with the rod," Robert mused after a moment.

"Fishes like an angel, shoots like the devil," Hugh agreed. "She'll have no problem landing the salmon. I don't know how she does it, actually. Always catches, even when conditions are atrocious and nobody's seen a fish move for days."

"We've all seen her stalk," Robert said. "She's like a snake, wriggling her way through the heather. And steady as a rock when she takes a shot. I wouldn't write her off."

"Well, unless her reflexes have improved, she won't be bagging any grouse," Hugh said. "Trust me."

"Well, we'll make arrangements nearer the time," Robert said, which meant he'd had enough chat for now and really must be getting back to his beloved figures.

II

Hugh hung up, leaned forward across his desk, swallowed water from a glass encouraging him to drink the brewery's latest strong bitter, and hit the speed-dial for Trevor Fynn, the youngest of the four. Trevor had always been the black sheep, viewed with a mixture of fascination, awe and amusement by the other three, who, even allowing for Hugh's digression into brewing, had all opted for fairly conservative careers. Freya was particularly scathing about the direction his adult life had taken. But Trevor had always been the one at odds – with his father, Cornelius, with the ambitions he had, with the gifts he had been given. All of them knew how tough it had been for Trevor to be his father's son.

In his younger days, he had acquired a fair degree of fame and notoriety as a rock guitarist with a high-profile band. Those days were gone now, but not the memories, and certainly not the talent. Nor the guitar collections, the long hair – now worn in a sleek pony tail rather than permed and flying free – and the indiscriminate activity of his dick, which still seemed to require constant gratification. These days, he did a little producing and the odd gig, but mostly lent his considerable guitar skills to other bands as a session man of some distinction.

He had tried marriage once, but his sexual generosity had made him a failure at monogamy. The brief relationship had been the usual celebrity all-singing-all-dancing affair, grounded in immature fantasy. It had left him only with memories of soured euphoria and a deeply embarrassing collection of wedding photographs of a young couple so obsessively trendy they had become parodies of their own generation. At least he had worked that one out and gone for bachelor status. Only now he was acting out an alternative lifestyle propagated by a seemingly endless procession of his contemporaries – brief liaisons with a string of pretty but unsuitable partners, which seemed equally unsatisfying. For several years now, Trevor had been stuck in the same place, wary of commitment, not seeing how he could ask a woman to embark on a long-term deal with such a hopeless case. All the same, age was beginning to creep up on him, and he had not yet noticed that his needs and attitudes were changing in response.

The Bartlett brothers were, however, sensitive to the fact that Trevor was going through something of a mid-life crisis. Robert, who found racy lifestyles hard to understand, was secretly fascinated by the exotic stories about life on the road that were so far removed from the life he led himself. He had adopted a somewhat fatherly attitude to his excitable friend, and, with his accountant's hat on, did his best to protect the unwieldy collection of financial assets that had accumulated around him. Bill Bartlett still kept an eye on the Fynn banking fortune, which Trevor would inherit on his father's death. Hugh, who had more faith in Trevor than his brother, got on with him pretty well, and looked forward to the conversation as he waited for him to answer. Apart from anything else, there was one thing Hugh admired him for. Trevor was a brilliant shot. If he had a gun in his hand, no flying bird was safe. And despite his lack of angling skill, there was no question that he would enthusiastically seize the Macnab challenge.

When the receiver was lifted, Trevor's end was throbbing to the strains of a good quality rock outfit. "Hey," he said enthusiastically. Trevor was always enthusiastic. "Just hold it – " There was a pause, the music seemed to get louder, then stopped abruptly. "Did you catch that? I've just laid down five tracks with the String Grizzlies. Producer was a wanker, but I think we got away with it." He stopped, and there was the sound of him falling extravagantly into a leather chair. "Anyway, great to hear your voice."

"Likewise," Hugh said. "Any new girls in town?" he asked, and then thought, stupid question – with Trevor, they were always new, or nearly.

His answer being predictable, they talked totty for a while. Trevor was at least up front about the endless beauty pageant that pumped and rolled across his sheets. He never told you that this was the girl, that he was in love, that bells were ringing and this was the big one. Hugh had dated far fewer girls, and rather hoped one of them *would* turn out to be Mrs Right. But it would either happen or it wouldn't, and his life was rich enough to make him relaxed about either eventuality.

"Got a proposition for you," Hugh said after a few minutes, when they had finished talking about recent girlfriend number three, who was called Amanda, and the indefatigable Trevor was about to start on guitars. "Uishall syndicate meeting September – Macnab challenge for the kids, while the grown-ups sort out the business – you, me, Robert, Freya."

"Very juicy," Trevor said at once. "Who's cooking this season?"

"New girl called Marie. Christina will be working the weekends."

"Oh good, a *girl*," Trevor said, and Hugh knew what would come next. "Probably single," he plotted, "if she conforms to classic castle cook profile. Come on, Hugh, give, give – the full profile, if you please."

Hugh laughed. "I haven't met her yet. But she's capable, and she didn't insult anyone at the interview. She cooked a blinding lunch for Heather and Dad. That's all I can tell you. Except that she's thirty-five, which makes her older than you, and therefore much too old."

"What am I, a cradle-snatcher?" Trevor said, affecting outrage, and then sighed. "You know me too well, old friend."

"I do indeed."

"Doesn't automatically make her a dog, though, does it?" the incorrigible Trevor said, brightening at the thought. "We could be on for the Royal, if the totty's up to scratch."

"That's up to you," Hugh said. He shook his head in amused exasperation. Now Trevor had his out-to-shock hat on, there would be no getting any sense out of him. The defence mechanism was so transparent that Hugh hadn't the heart to tell him that none of them fell for it any more.

"Robert's already backed out of that part – and I had to work to get him interested in the sport."

"Hmm. You'll have to raise the stakes if it's just you and me and we're on for the cook." He laughed delightedly. "Do you realise, Hugh, that this is the first time in eighteen years that we've actually been able to even *dream* about a Royal Macnab? Christina's Saturday relief was the most awful old boiler I've ever seen –"

"You're a terrible old shag," Hugh said. "And I didn't say I was joining you on that one."

"Oh come now, Hugh, don't be shy. I can give you plenty of tactics if you're the victor – I won't be churlish in defeat."

"I'm not committing myself," Hugh said quickly. "And neither is poor Marie, of course – a minor point. But if you insist, I'll throw in a bottle of the widow if you persuade her to yield *and* your seduction is an honourable one, unblemished by false promises."

"Vintage." Trevor pressed the point, hugely enjoying the conversation. "I want my accomplishments recognised."

"Yes, well, that rather depends on performance," Hugh said drily. "And we won't be in a position to judge that, will we?"

Satisfied that his rewards were commensurate with the level of effort required of him, Trevor was overtaken by a further thought. "Well, Freya's certainly out of the Royal frame unless she's turned queer on us," he said with glib certainty. "Has her shooting improved?"

"Not since last time. But even if it had, none of us can hold a candle to you when it comes to the grouse."

"I'd better get some practise in," Trevor said. "No harm in maximising my advantage." He paused. "Tell you what – I could even offer to help Freya out. I think I can afford the risk."

Trevor was generous to a fault.

III

Freya was out with a client when Hugh called, but she rang him back in the afternoon. She missed him, because he was sampling a new bitter with his master brewer, and she left a message to say he'd better call her before four o' clock because after that, she'd be away for the next three days. Hugh just made it, unwillingly dragging himself away from the best part of his job.

"Busy time, Freya?" he asked. As well as all the Uishall holidays, the four of them had all done school together, at a trendy unisex boarding establishment. But Freya was strictly one of the lads, a keen competitor – she'd had to be, learning to shoot and fish alongside them, refusing to be outdone by the boys. It was a habit and an attitude she had never lost.

"Absolutely," Freya said. "New author last year, big launch, all the critics banging on about promise, awards and all that. Eighteen months later I'm sitting here like a spare comma waiting for the follow-up book, before everyone totally forgets who she is and cares less. She hasn't a clue what she's got, or what she's about to lose."

"Bad luck," Hugh sympathised. "I thought the message sounded a bit breathless."

"Well. That's the way it goes sometimes. And before I forget, have you heard about Maglavat? It's up for sale."

190

Hugh caught his breath. Maglavat was smaller in acreage, with a less distinguished salmon river, but far superior deer and grouse populations.

"Anyone interested yet?"

"That's why I wondered if you'd heard. Natasha Tang has requested the details." Freya was immensely satisfied by the gasp of incredulity this piece of news elicited. "A buddy of mine in estate agency tipped me off. Says she wants to continue her crusade to stamp out the evil of hunting, and take it into the Scottish islands. Didn't Trevor say anything?"

"He probably doesn't know," Hugh said. "He's been buried in a recording studio with the String Grizzlies – what? Don't ask. Well, that *is* big news."

Natasha Tang was arguably Britain's richest rock star, and – a lesser claim to fame – an ex-flame of Trevor's, before she'd discovered his passion for shooting. Militantly vegetarian and pro-animal rights, she had begun to buy land up and down the country, banning all forms of control and running a highly emotional – and inevitably illogical – campaign against blood sports.

Freya was dismissive. "I always believe that in the end, common sense prevails about these things," she said. "Natasha Tang is full of cause and empty of brain – and she'd never cope with the climate." She laughed unkindly. "What a hoot, her clambering over the moors in her sparkly stiletto boots, trying to outwit the poachers. They'll run rings round her. It's not going to happen, is it?"

"You might not be giving her due credit –"

"She's a fashion victim," Freya cut in, and Hugh was surprised at the hostility in her voice. "Her money might give her some power, but she's at the mercy of her personality, her image and her laughable IQ. A year or two, and she'll have forgotten all about Maglavat and be saving Bengal tigers and picketing Indian nuclear power stations instead. I know these types," she added, with more than a trace of bitter disgust. "They keep writing proposals for books that are going to save the world in a variety of extremely suspect manners, and sending them to me." She stopped. "And the worst of it is, I have to take them seriously, for no other reason than that the reading public recognises their names and will buy the book anyway, however stupid or inept it is."

"You really are having a bad day," Hugh said, and both of them laughed.

"I'm sorry, Hugh – she's really not worth getting all worked up about, is she? What did you call for?"

Hugh outlined the Macnab.

"That sounds fun," Freya said, which meant, *so a fight to the death, then?*

"Well thanks for that," Hugh said. Her keenness for the sport was cheering, and healthy, after Robert's reluctance, and Trevor's immediate and predictable preoccupation with the new cook. "I only got Robert on board by upping it to a Royal, so he at least gave in for a quiet life. And Trevor promptly started machinating to bed the cook – poor girl. He'll get his grouse and stag, no doubt about that, but he's the iffiest man I've ever seen on the end of a salmon rod."

"He'll be bringing the bottle, of course?" Freya said slyly.

"Of course," Hugh said. "Never seen him here without it. Pity it doesn't age in the bottle – it must be twenty-five years old now, if it's a day."

"We've all got our weak points," Freya said, then paused. "So I suppose you've all automatically written me out of the Royal part?"

"Well, Freya, unless you've suddenly decided you fancy women, and the cook does too, it's a bit of an outside call, wouldn't you say?"

"Has having two tits and no dick ever cut me out of the mix before?" Freya said shortly. "All we need here is a little lateral thinking."

There was a brief silence and Hugh waited, intrigued.

"Look. Here's what I'm going to do. I don't see why you chaps should have all the fun – assuming you can meet the Macnab requirement in the first place. I'm going to instigate a Ladies' Macnab, so I get the chance of a shag as well."

Hugh slapped his knee and laughed. "Freya, you're marvellous," he said. "You've just upped the entertainment stakes a hundred per cent."

"All we have to do is nominate a suitable candidate with commensurate standing to the cook," Freya thought aloud.

"Head ghillie?" Hugh suggested. "That's the obvious one."

"No. Far too easy. If I pull off the Macnab, I want a *climax* to the achievement, not an anti. Couple of drams and I get to spend the night in a dismal annexe room with someone who hasn't washed his socks? I don't think so, Hugh. I want to *enjoy* my perk, not suffer it." She thought a moment longer. "Aidan," she announced firmly. "The estate manager will be a fitting challenge."

Hugh laughed again. "Perfect," he said. "My God, girl, if I think you've got the slightest chance of getting laid with that great bear of a fellow, I'll help you myself."

"You can donate the grouse," Freya said drily. "Don't lie, I know quite well what you'll all have been saying about my shooting."

"Book yourself some sessions on the clays," Hugh advised her. "It'll be worth it. Get Trevor to coach you. He actually offered when I spoke to him this morning."

Freya snorted. "Certainly not. If I ask him for coaching, he'll – well, you know exactly how he is. Totally obsessed with that widget of his. Do you think we should warn the cook?"

"Her name's Marie," Hugh said. "Dad was very impressed. Still going on about the pudding. I must admit, I don't think it's fair that she should be the unwitting victim of Trevor's attentions. We'll have to see if it's in the rules."

"Oh, *rules*," Freya scoffed. "Don't be so stiff, Hugh. If I can invent a Ladies' Macnab, you can invent a fair play clause."

"She's probably quite capable of taking care of herself," Hugh said. "And she might be quite keen. She might have all his records. Why spoil her fun?"

"To save her from being another addition to the Fynn collection," Freya said. "It's a personal crusade of mine. Yes, I know Hugh, we all love him dearly, but I don't know what all these women see in him. I think he bangs them over the head with a brick and they wake up in the morning and wonder what on earth they've done."

"Well, strictly speaking, Freya, if we're going to warn Marie, we should also warn Aidan of your designs."

This stopped her. "That's a point," she said. "In that case, cancel the honourable intentions. You couldn't warn Aidan. Poor man. He'd be frightened to death."

Hugh said goodbye to Freya and turned his attention to business matters – and at least one more pint of that masterly bitter ale. He paused only to send a brief email to Trevor and Robert: *Freya on for the Royal – Aidan final catch of the day. Any takers for bets?*

Then, having set his Macnab challenge in motion, with all four of them signed up, he could afford to forget about it for a few months and get on with the business of making a living.

In truth, he felt a bit of a hypocrite. He wasn't quite sure why he had even set it up at all. But it would be fun. And it would certainly be an interesting contest. Trevor had never landed a salmon in his life, Freya couldn't shoot grouse for toffee, Robert was a good all-rounder, but a meticulous planner and agonisingly slow – and Hugh? He glanced briefly at the photograph. Hugh had never yet pulled the trigger that had killed a stag.

3.
WEIGHTED
MAY

I

Natasha Tang threw the Maglavat estate prospectus onto the floor and took a sip of mineral water. After a moment, her personal assistant, Felix Steele, picked it up with a barely perceptible flicker of disgust. From her reclining position, she stared dully out across the back of the white hessian fabric sofa to the towers and buildings lining the Thames. Natasha's sleek, jet-black hair, cut in a harsh angular shape to exaggerate the Oriental accent of her features, framed a delicately sculpted face with startling green eyes.

"What's for lunch?" she asked in a bored voice. When she spoke to the press, her voice had a quality of whiney do-gooder about it, the helpless little girl struggling vainly for truth and justice against a cruel and unfair world. Off the record, it wasn't like that at all. There was an odd sense of reproach in it, as if there was some terrible wrong in her life she could never put right. She straightened a long, graceful leg and one of the three huge white Persian cats dotted with studiedly casual elegance around the room, crept onto her lap. After treading protractedly, the cat settled down and curled itself into a ball. Her hand rested automatically on its head and stroked it with more disinterest than affection. The cat, too haughty to purr, shrugged and closed its eyes.

"Goat's cheese grilled with roasted peppers and salsa," Felix said. "Your favourite."

"I hope the goats are the free range kind."

"They live in innocent bliss on the lower slopes of the Dolomites," Felix assured her. "Where the rumble of agricultural machinery is never heard. They're so free range, they practically milk themselves."

Natasha shot him a sharp glance, but his face showed only rapt, politically correct enthusiasm. Sometimes, she suspected him of playing jokes at her expense, but he was too clever for her to catch him. Then again, Felix might be a rogue element, but he met the criteria, increasing her charismatic appeal. He was a vegetarian – a prerequisite if you were going to enter Natasha Tang's charmed circle of personally appointed employees. And he was gay. That made him doubly right-on.

"What's the best meal you've ever eaten?" she asked, testing him, her voice deliberately listless, as if she might not be paying him full attention.

"Aubergine stuffed with free-range pecorino and baked in peppered vine leaves," he said automatically. "You've asked me before. I ate it on a Greek island" – he resisted the temptation to describe it as free-range – "with Roy."

She sighed. "Is everyone happy with my choice of lunch?"

"Of course," he soothed her automatically. He looked through the Maglavat brochure, wanting to apply his talents to something more intellectually bracing than ego stroking. "So – are we interested?"

"Oh, I don't know," she said. "There are pluses and minuses, aren't there?"

"We ought to see it," Felix said. "The castle looks wonderful."

"Yes, it does look rather amazing." She rolled over and snapped her fingers in the direction of the desk. The cat fell gracelessly to the floor, bestowed a withering look on its thoughtless mistress and stalked off huffily, its tail waving in the air. On the way out, it stretched its great length, then placed its front paws against the hessian sofa and made scratching movements. Felix glanced down at it, then dutifully brought the prospectus back over to Natasha. She flipped to the picture of the Great Room, wainscoting and oil paintings, most of them quite valuable, included in the sale, sofas big enough to get lost in.

"Cost a fortune to run," was her only comment.

"So does everywhere," Felix said, looking over her shoulder. "Look at the running costs for the house in Devon – it couldn't be worse than that."

"Scottish weather," Natasha said, shivering. "And the islands to boot. Mark my words – it could be *a lot* worse."

"And the history is fascinating," Felix said. "It used to be part of the neighbouring estate, and it's been in the Macleod family for hundreds of years –"

"We're becoming quite the little scholar, Felix," Natasha said, managing to convey boredom and bitchiness in equal measure. "Of course you are conveniently forgetting that the history of this barbaric place is bound up in the deaths of thousands of blameless animals, hunted for their meat and skins. And if I *do* buy it, Felix, we shall be throwing all that sad history out of the window and beginning a new era of civilisation, freedom and respect."

"What would you use it for?" Felix interrupted her, a barb of irritation scratching at the slick of politeness he had always to cultivate for her. "A retreat? Or were you thinking of converting the stables into a recording studio?"

"Possibly," Natasha said lazily. "But what I'll certainly do is use it to launch the next leg of the Crusade."

"Oh," Felix said, and this time his lack of enthusiasm was detectable.

Natasha's eyes swivelled towards him. "You're not going to tell me you don't approve of my Crusade?"

"Oh, not at all," Felix said smoothly. "It's just that this place is so remote and the elements are up against you – it might be a bad place to try to do it effectively. Whatever it is you're planning to do," he finished lamely.

"Well, that's really for me to decide, don't you think?" she snapped, and Felix thought it wise to change the subject.

"Can we make it secure?" he mused, slipping into the mode of conscientious planner of her personal security. "The public road runs very close by, in fact right past the front door, and you can't block it off – there are villages all the way along that strip of coast."

"Re-route it," she said offhandedly, with the air of one who is accustomed to getting one's own way.

"I don't think so," Felix said seriously. "Look at the aerial shot – the sea on one side, rocks on the other. You'd have to blast it away, like they did to build the castle."

"Hmm." Natasha studied the photograph. "We just need guards," she said with determination. "Give 'em shotguns. That'd give the simple rural folk something to talk about." She paused, then flashed a devious smile at him. "And it would be *very* good publicity."

All she ever thinks about, Felix thought savagely, and turned away to look out of the window. How could someone this good at music turn out to be so shallow and so self-obsessed? He had wanted the job more desperately than any other he had ever applied for. And now he had it, his dream come true appointment had destroyed forever the image of his cherished rock star idol. Natasha Tang, who used to write witty, intelligent lyrics before her politics invaded her music, was nothing but a walking ego. God, how he hated her. And how betrayed he felt.

After a moment, he placed the prospectus neatly back on the desk. Maglavat looked a wonderful place to him. He thought mournfully about the forthcoming lunch. Natasha didn't give a stuff about the free-range goats. She didn't want to know that the nanny goats all had to be kept in milk in order to supply her with free-range cheeses, thereby necessitating the regular slaughter of the billy goats, which were then sold as meat. As long as someone else was eating the meat, that was all right. She had never come to terms with the fact that all the pretty, furry little creatures she wanted to save still shat and pissed and had bad breath. Felix grimaced at the rod he had made for his own back. He had come out about being gay at his interview, to impress her. But he had lied about being a vegetarian.

Right now, he could murder a bacon sandwich.

II

Later, Felix lay in bed and wondered why the hell he was still working for Natasha Tang. He drew up a list in his head and ticked off the minuses. He despised her. That was a big one. She was his personal fallen idol, tumbling off her pedestal with a finality that still hurt him. He couldn't believe he had got her that wrong. He hadn't played any of her music within a short time of unmasking her as an image-driven fraud. He was always travelling, being run ragged by the press, by booking agents and recording companies, by the endless, silly errands fabricated by someone who was so rich and so rudderless, she could barely function anymore. He missed Roy, who was still with him, despite the upheavals and separations of the last eighteen months, and he now bitterly resented the long gaps between the short and emotionally intense reunions. If he stayed much longer, he worried that the relationship would be endangered, and Felix would do anything to avoid losing Roy.

Roy, it had to be said, was more pragmatic about the situation. He didn't see it as a threat, only as a testing time. The times of separation were hard, but they passed; the job would pass; in time, everything passed. Whatever changed, he and Felix would stay together. Roy was a talented chef and ran his own restaurant, so his days and nights were as busy as Felix's. It wasn't as if either of them was moping around without the other. Roy thought Felix should worry less about the relationship and more about himself. He looked as if he needed feeding up. A vegetarian diet clearly didn't suit him.

If he were going to walk out on her, he would have to set it up carefully. She was known for her spiteful retributions if any of her handpicked team decided she wasn't good enough to work for. She could make it hell while you worked out your notice. And the notice could be long – a couple of months at least, while she agonised over a replacement she could trust more than the departing incumbent. If she was about to go on tour, you could be tied to her for much longer. Roy said he was paranoid – she was only a woman, what could she do? She couldn't even buy birthday presents for her mother without help. That was enough minuses to be going on with.

Come on, Felix told himself severely, *what about the pluses*? The pay was good – very good. The kudos was high. The travel – well, he travelled all right, but he didn't seem to see much of the world, for all the planes he'd climbed into and the luxury yachts he'd sailed on, and the coaches and trains that carried Natasha's complicated entourage from Europe to America, from Canada to the Far East, from Asia to Australia and back again.

The food was terrific – he'd sent Roy cookbooks from all over the world, eaten in all the best places. When he'd trotted out the best meal of his life for Natasha, it wasn't the truth. He'd eaten the best meal of his life on one of her American tours, in New York. It wasn't so much the food as the occasion – Natasha had flown Roy out for a surprise weekend, paid for everything. She was good at that, he conceded – the grand gesture. Of course, there had to be something in it for her, and she usually got a lot of feelgood press from her extravagant treats. But it was so lovely, such a brilliant surprise to see Roy three thousand miles away from where he was supposed to be, he forgave her the exploitation. They'd done the MOMA, then picnicked in Central Park on cheeseburgers and jelly doughnuts, and Felix had confessed about the vegetarian thing, and sworn Roy to secrecy. Roy laughed about it until he almost choked, and it was still one of their favourite memories, that sunny lunchtime, courtesy of the world's most public vegetarian, wolfing down ground beef and melted cheese under the trees. He had been genuinely grateful, and he had a feeling it would be the first thing Natasha would throw in his face when he told her he was quitting.

Natasha took everything personally.

In the midst of this reverie, a high-pitched sound split the silence of the suite of rooms. Felix was out of bed before it stopped, and understood the noise with his gut before his mind translated it into a scream. Fear flooded through him as he threw himself towards the bedroom door and rattled down the wrought iron spiral staircase that separated her rooms from his.

Pictures of the last time he had heard her scream like that stroboscoped across his memory in the ten seconds it took him to lunge down the stairs and throw himself at her door.

A house in Milan, near a recording studio. A girl with a knife who had broken into the bedroom and stood in front of Natasha, weeping, making slashing cuts across her own thighs and arms and breasts, because she couldn't be like her. When Natasha tried to stop her, the girl turned the knife on her and would have used it had Felix not arrived. He remembered the terror on Natasha's face, the empty desperation on the girl's as he broke her grip, the agonising minutes that seemed to go on forever before the *polizia* arrived and bundled her away in the ambulance.

He had felt genuine pity for Natasha then, as the raw underbelly of the glamorous rock star life revealed itself. Ever since, her morbid fear of death had intensified and her passion for animal and vegetarian causes had turned to obsession.

He burst into Natasha's room. She wasn't in bed and his heart seemed to leap in a fresh spasm of fear as he shouted her name. He registered one of the cats, looking past him with startled blue eyes. Then he saw her, standing in silk pyjamas in the bathroom, and the source of her distress was immediately apparent. A spider of fairly impressive proportions was crawling up the wall.

You stupid bitch, he thought, collapsing against the wall, his breathing ragged from the fear and the sprint, and the scream that had galvanised him. Last time, it could have been murder.

200

This time, it was a spider. Felix tried to speak gently, only partially succeeded.

"Natasha, you can't do this," he said. "I thought you were in real trouble." He dropped his upper body forward, his arms braced against his knees. "Try to scream in proportion to the scale of the problem."

"I'm sorry," she whispered, and the apology alone alerted him to the fact that things were not right. She turned towards him and her face was streaked with tears. Felix tried to deliver the sympathy she wanted, but she was trying to commission it too early. He sighed deeply and took off his slipper.

"Here –" he said, and began to approach the unlucky spider.

"Don't kill it," she said.

He dropped his arm, closed his eyes in irritation.

"Natasha, it is very late, the spider is distressing you, and there is no one from the press to haul you over the coals for cruelty to living things. I am not going to ring them up. Do you have a better suggestion?"

"Put it outside," she said, and her voice was shaking now, barely audible. "Please, Felix. Don't kill it."

He didn't really want to handle the spider; he wasn't too keen on them himself. But then he looked down. At his feet, the Persian cat was watching the spider with wide blue eyes, its expression one of evil glee, and he realised that if he bottled, Natasha would be forced to witness a senseless killing by a cat that was certainly not in need of additional nourishment. He shooed away the cat, found a piece of paper and a glass, caught the spider, put it into the corridor, and watched it scamper away towards the lifts. When he went back inside, he found Natasha hunched up on her bed, shivering.

"Can I get you anything?" he asked, more gently. There was a silence and she shook her head. "I'm sorry," he said at last. "I was in Milan, too. I have the nightmares just like you do."

She looked at him with huge eyes and Felix got onto the bed and took her in his arms, pulling the quilt around them, cradling her head against his chest. She started to weep. Felix stared ahead, trying not to let her anguish invade him, giving in to unfolding events.

"Were you dreaming again?" he asked her, and she nodded. He kissed the top of her head. "All over now," he said quietly.

After a while, she raised her head. "I don't suppose you'd make love to me?" she said in a small voice.

He laughed softly, shaking his head, and began to stroke her hair. It was attention seeking, and both of them knew it. "No, Natasha." It wasn't the first time she'd asked, but he'd only go so far when it came to earning his salary. "But I'll stay with you. That's my best offer."

She accepted without quarrel, a sure sign the question hadn't been asked in the belief he would answer in the affirmative. She snuggled up against him and when she was drowsy, she said, "Felix? You really are gay, aren't you? It's not that you just don't fancy me?"

"Remember Roy in New York?" She squeezed him yes. "I wasn't faking."

Natasha fell asleep held fast in Felix's arms, still troubled that the world didn't always turn in her direction.

III

Hunched over the old Uishall record books, Robert was planning the salmon strategy for his Macnab offensive. Now he had got over the way he had been manipulated by Hugh into taking part, his love of research and preparation had come to the fore. His pet theory was that if he could correlate data on weather conditions – similar patterns of rainfall, sunshine, temperature and so on – he could deploy tactics used by fishermen in previous years, with all the advantages of modern angling equipment to support his efforts. Not that he was a gadget man – that was Trevor's department. Robert believed in fair play and tradition, the ancient game of wits between angler and salmon, played out in an atmosphere of mutual respect.

Although the current syndicate had owned the estate since the 1960s, the river records went back to the 1870s, almost to the original sale of the land by Alasdair Macleod. River levels, rain or shine, wind direction and strength, number of fish landed each day, on which beats, to what weights. Taken over the 130-odd years, the records told another story, too, of declining fish populations, the changing attitudes of anglers, the growing popularity of catch and release. The early record books listed catches and weights only, with a column for anglers to write general comments. Most of these referred to conditions, especially if the fish was big, or the first one caught for a day or two. Rarely did these early gentlemen and ladies record what fly they fished. Forty years later, around 1911, a new record book added a column specifying fly. From then on, the fishermen dutifully scribed their choices – Dusty Miller, Silver Wilkinson, Stoat's Tail, and then later on, the yellow and orange Ally's Shrimp, or teams of black and silver flies fished with a Muddler or Goat's Toe on the dropper.

Robert loved the records. He loved adding to them when he caught, painstakingly noting down the information, not just in the Uishall book, but again, in more detail, in his own fishing journal. He liked to imagine a man like himself, a hundred years from now, poring over the books and picturing to himself the personal dramas of fish landed on Willie's Twist, or the Long Neck, or, more intriguingly, Simon's Dibble. If Uishall still existed by then. If anyone still cared.

September was a lovely month there. Often clear and dry, it made fishing tougher, but the heather on the hills, the gold and crimson light of late afternoons, the warm breezes still catching at the trailing threads of summer, made it magical. He knew Freya would use light tackle – she always did. Robert was tall, and could handle a long, heavy rod with comparative ease, but the river at Uishall was kinder to anglers with more subtlety and patience. Freya never needed patience when it came to salmon – she would have her fish quickly, probably leave it until late in the evening, a dead cert to enjoy if she had spent the day bagging her deer and – would she? – her grouse.

Robert flicked the pages. He knew many of the entries by heart. This summer, so far, was similar in weather pattern to 1894, a year when most anglers kept their fly selections to themselves. But one obliging young lady had landed an eighteen-pounder – her first fish – and was obviously determined that the moment should go down in history in all its glorious detail.

"Stalked the Whipper's Pool early morning for two hours," she wrote on the evening of September 2nd, her handwriting shrunk down to try to fit into the small space allowed for comments, and Robert could hear her breathless excitement.

"Teased him a decent while with a good old Jock Scott then switched to a Lady Caroline. Daddy suggested the double hook, but I stuck with the single. Terrific whoosh as he came up, very sudden on the take, ran in circles rather than a distance. Almost snagged on boulder, but line held firm. Landed after a

*good hour worrying away at end of line. Arm very tired. Daddy
held the net. Great fish. Ate splendidly!"*

Robert smiled. On the Whipper's, eh? Not a good spot in
recent years. Freya was the only one who caught there. He made
a mental note of the fly, and went to look up the dressing. He liked
the idea of honouring such an emotionally charged catch by
going to the same pool with the same fly – or as close as he could
get – and maybe replicating the experience. It was the biggest
fish that month, too. He looked at the name: Annie Ferguson. His
forehead creased then his face relaxed into an intrigued smile.
Surely not? How come he had never made the connection
before?

He went to the bookcase and pulled down a brand new
book, a labour of love, written by his father, and published
privately by Freya's father – a history of Uishall from 1870.
Trevor's father had financed it, but done none of the work. The
old photographs of the Castle before the extensions were built,
the proud ghillies with their massive catches in the 1920s – it was
all there, even the documents transferring ownership from
Lachlan, the last of the Macleod Lairds. He turned to the index,
compiled with much cursing and swearing by Freya, sought the
name and looked for the page of text.

No, his memory hadn't been playing tricks. Annie
Ferguson, proud recorder of the only salmon she ever landed,
had died the following year in tragic circumstances, aged only
nineteen. Annie was one of Uishall's ghosts. Now and again, she
appeared on the river, or strolling along the front of the house.
Her involvement was suspected in one or two landings of salmon,
when distracted anglers swore their net had appeared out of
nowhere, or they had felt a helping hand on the rod when the
playing of the fish was beginning to tire them. Robert had never
been favoured with a sighting, but he had heard all the stories,
and their sheer number had at least partly held his natural
scepticism in check. With the record book open before him, her
sad story acquired new poignancy. That fish must have meant a
lot to hold her here over a hundred years after her death.

Robert pursed his lips, thinking. Women were good
anglers, always seemed able to steal a march on the men.
Maybe it was the much-vaunted pheromones, maybe it was just
their patience, or the fact they could land a fly on the water with
more teasing delicacy than their male counterparts. With salmon,
it was all about seduction. Oh, you could catch plenty in high
season when the fish were hurling themselves at anything that

moved, but the interesting catches, the ones you stalked, coaxed and wooed to the end of your line – those were the real rewards of the sport. Robert had caught many, but only a handful of them were memorable. If the Macnab was going to be worth doing, it was worth doing well. Robert would take up the challenge in honour of Annie Ferguson and her prized fish.

IV

Felix put the phone down for what seemed like the fiftieth time that morning and allowed his head to drop into his hands. In her usual capricious fashion, Natasha had decided to pay a visit to the Maglavat Estate and wanted to go there immediately. The agents handling the sale were polite, but firm – they understood her wish to spend a night at the castle, but could not guarantee there would be room there until they had spoken to the owners. When they didn't get back to her office within half an hour, she insisted Felix rang Maglavat direct. The owners were out stalking and no one could handle the enquiry.

"It's because they know what I'll do with it," Natasha said, working herself up into an indignant fury. "They don't want me to buy it."

Felix sighed. "It's been on the market for eighteen months," he said. "I would say they're desperate for someone to buy it."

"Then why are they blocking me?"

"They're not blocking you, Natasha; they're out for the day."

"Shooting," Natasha said with revulsion. "Killing innocent living things."

"They'll call back later today," Felix said, not wanting to get embroiled in one of Natasha's emotional outbursts about the wrongs of hunting. *Why didn't she just stick to what she was good at?* he thought despairingly. His eye fell on the tomato and feta salad, dressed with honey and basil vinaigrette, perched self-righteously on the table. There was never enough bread to go with it. He wished there were one – no, two – of Roy's fat, bleeding fillet steaks, char grilled to medium-rare perfection, sitting alongside it. Eighteen months of vegetarianism had made him perpetually hungry, not to mention bloodthirsty, obsessive about what he wasn't allowed to have.

"It's only one night," Natasha said petulantly, not about to let him off the hook.

"I'm sure we can work something out," Felix said. "We might be able to fly up another day –"

"Your job is to manage my itinerary, not set it," Natasha spat back, and he sighed and gave it up.

She'd been like this ever since the incident with the spider. This was what he always got for his sympathy. This was how she punished him when she had shown him her weakness and he had been kind to her.

At least they were going. Felix would never have put himself down as an Outer Hebrides man, but the photographs in the Maglavat brochure had moved him. Wild hills, great expanses of space sighing with the freedom of the winds, blue, all-encompassing ocean. Not the prissy little pseudo sea of the English Channel, but the untamed Atlantic thundering all around, possessing the land in its passionate embrace, lapping its shores with sometimes tender, sometimes savage waves. He had been reading it up, bought books on the island and its history, borrowed library books about the hunting and wildlife that took place in those extraordinary landscapes. What excited him even more was that Roy was madly jealous when he told him where he was going at the weekend.

"Tell me what it's like," he had said. "No, really. I want to know. Manchester is beginning to get to me."

"What's got into you?" Felix had demanded with amusement. "The great committed urbanite? How would you survive without clubland and Asian food?"

And then, to his utter amazement, Roy had said, his voice soft with yearning, "Just think of the space, Felix. Aren't you sick of other people telling you where to go and what to do all the time? I know I am. How many decent restaurants are there in the islands? Not many, I'll be bound."

"How many rock stars want to live there?" Felix had retorted. "Bearing in mind that this is a pipe dream as far as Natasha is concerned. I'm a PR man. I know no other life. I'm looking at the equivalent of Alcatraz with Natasha if she's stupid enough to write a cheque, or unemployment. Death is preferable to either."

The conversation had unsettled him, partly because he was afraid that Roy might be making the same mistake as Natasha, falling in love with an idea when he had no grasp of the reality. He promised to tell him all about it, and leave no stone unturned in his efforts to paint a truthful portrait.

But for now, there were the logistics to figure out – getting Natasha there, getting her settled, getting all the information she didn't know she needed, getting her to see the wisdom of going no further with her enquiries. To Felix, Natasha and Maglavat made no sense as an equation – it simply didn't balance. He had only to look at the photographs to know that such a landscape would blow wide open Natasha's naïve visions of the way wild creatures got along together. Never mind the hunters with their guns, stalking the deer and shooting the grouse, or the anglers hooking salmon and trout and despatching them with a brutal blow to the head. There were the eagles and merlins hunting rabbits and wrens, hooded crows tearing lumps out of newborn lambs, buzzards scavenging the corpses, black backed gulls snatching puffins out of the air, gannets diving for fish, hedgehogs stealing eggs from the rare ground nesting birds. Natasha would be forced to accept that Nature was not a matter of sweet, furry and feathered creatures living together in mutual respect and harmony, and was in fact a constant spectacle of bloody, armed combat. Within a short space of time, she would hate the place and be planning improbable rescue strategies like rehabilitation programmes for raptors and vegetarian schemes for mink.

"What's the problem with the castle?" Natasha said again, determined not to let the subject drop. "Explain it to me."

"It's very simple. There aren't any vacant rooms until the Saturday night. If you fly out on Friday, you won't be able to stay there – you'll have to spend a night in a hotel."

Natasha considered this for a moment. "Well, what's so terrible about that?"

Felix looked up sharply. She had her lazy voice on, the one she used when she was feigning disinterest in something. He was instantly suspicious, and another dark cloud seemed to loom over the distant prospect of Maglavat. What was she up to?

Natasha, idly leafing through a magazine, said without looking up, "No-one will know where I'm going, and when we get there, no-one will know who I am, anyway. Book in under our usual alias, and we won't have any trouble. It will give us a bit more time to see the island, and we can fly out on Sunday."

"You can't fly out on Sunday," Felix said. "The church forbids it."

"The church will have to make an exception," she said, her tone sharpening.

Felix dropped his pen onto his secretarial pad. He was being wound up and fool that he was, he was rising to the provocation.

"The airport will be closed," he said. "There are no public services on a Sunday. You can't catch a bus, or buy petrol. You will not be able to travel."

She stared at him with loathing, then began to smile in a manner contrived to increase his fury.

"Well. We must be tolerant of the local customs," she said sweetly. "Especially if we are considering becoming natives. You win, Felix – Monday it is – the day of our glorious return to our fair capital city from the far-flung wilderness of the north."

"Monday you are supposed to be in Paris recording the last song for the forthcoming album. The musicians are booked, and so is the guest artist. The arrangements were made months ago."

"If we don't make it, I'll do a separate vocal track later," Natasha said, enjoying the way she was effortlessly leaping the obstacles Felix set before her. "Modern recording technology is *very* sophisticated."

"You will offend the guest artist," Felix said. "And miss a golden photo opportunity." There was a frosty silence. "I'm just reminding you of your professional responsibilities," he said pleasantly.

Natasha shrugged, but was nettled. "The guest artist is my third choice," she said sourly. "Hardly top-drawer."

"Your first choice is on tour, and your second has just been operated on for cancer," Felix said. "Rejecting you was nothing personal." He paused, then said, "However you feel about this, Natasha, negative PR that makes you look less than polite and respectful to your fellow artists is never good."

Natasha stood up, slapping down the magazine. "We'll fly direct to Paris from Maglavat on Monday morning," she said flatly. "Please make the necessary arrangements, Felix, and remind me why I gave you the job."

"I can't make any arrangements until I speak to Maglavat," Felix said, and the hole in the bucket scenario had played itself out.

She let out a long, tense sigh. "I'm going to the rehearsal room," she said suddenly. "I don't want to be disturbed. I'm working on an alternative harmony for the closing section."

However casually she did it, Felix knew it was significant that she made certain her mobile went with her. If she was really working on a song, all forms of communications technology in the rehearsal and studio spaces were unequivocally banned.

4.
SNAGGED
MAY

I

It was bound to be difficult. Marie, in her chef's whites, curly hair scraped back into a ponytail, was unpacking the shopping. Working alongside her, in skirt, blouse and pinny was Christina, who had buried her feelings of demoralisation, and decided to reassert herself as mistress of Uishall's kitchen.

"There's the three fridges," she was saying, moving with lightning speed from one to the other. "Meat, dairy, fruit and vegetables," she rattled off, pointing briefly to each one in turn. "And three freezers, one in the cook's larder, one in the storeroom, one in the game larder. Plus there's the big fish freezer for the guests' salmon and the breakfast kippers – that's out in the fish store. I'll show you that later."

On this new tack, Christina was beginning to feel that having a new cook in was no big deal after all. It was still her kitchen. She knew it inside out, and she would still be working here two days a week, which gave her rights. It would be just the same, except she wouldn't have to do nearly as much work. She could superintend things, take charge, then sit back and take the credit. She flew around, pulling things out of boxes, carrier bags, heaping them all onto the table, chattering all the while about where things went and how things worked.

Marie watched in growing bewilderment as Christina began to put things away in the familiar places. Then a flash of light seemed to illuminate the scene for her, and she understood how things were going to be if she didn't do something fast. Another half-hour and the shopping would all be away where Christina wanted to put it, and she would have lost her territory before she had even claimed it.

"Wait, wait," she said, doing her best to sound friendly and cheerful. Christina stopped, a bag of carrots in one hand, a cabbage in the other. "I've already done some thinking about where I want things to go."

Christina's face set. "Och, it's much easier if we keep things where they've always been," she said.

"Easier for you, maybe," Marie said, and Christina's open rebellion against the new order began to falter. Marie smiled, took charge of the carrots and cabbage and put them back on the table, but there was a steely glint in her dark eyes. What Christina didn't realise was that Marie had already spent a day in the kitchen, looking at the layout and planning changes. She had sat at the table and drawn up her lists, and looked out of the large windows onto the sunny, calm waters of the river mouth. An odd feeling had come over her, a certainty that she was going to be happy here, and that the kitchen would be a special place to work.

Once she had got it right.

"The meat is going to be in the fridge in the storeroom," she said firmly to Christina. "All the soft fruit and vegetables will go into the chiller. The root vegetables and hard fruit will go into the storeroom in the baskets. The dairy will go into what used to be the meat fridge. It's smaller and makes more sense, so the cooked and raw meats can be separated properly in the bigger fridge."

Christina looked at her in astonishment. In eighteen years, it had never occurred to her to change anything.

"Well, it seems a lot of unnecessary trouble to go to," she said.

"The fridges are all empty at the moment," Marie pointed out. "It's no trouble at all."

"Well," Christina said, and all the energetic efficiency of a moment before seemed to fade and transmute into a wooden resistance. "You know best when it comes to the kitchen, I'm sure."

Marie was angry now and having difficulty hiding it. Mixed in with the awkwardness was a hint of pathos, as if Christina was suddenly expecting sympathy. Marie was not interested in playing emotional games. She hadn't got time to waste propping up Christina's flagging self-esteem, and she had plenty to keep her busy for the next day or two, before she even started to cook. She decided to be brutal, get the fight for her kitchen over and done with, and hopefully Christina would get the message, sulk for a bit, and then get on with what had to be done.

"Look, I appreciate you offering to help," she said briskly. "But I think I need some space to get everything organised. Why don't you get some lunch back at the cottage, and when you come back, I can talk you through the new system."

Christina stood, letting the insult smart, tears and fury warring inside her. A new system! Things put away where she'd never be able to find them. She folded her pinny neatly and hung it over the back of the kitchen chair – *her* kitchen chair; it had been there as long as she had – then looked at the table heaped with shopping. She sighed as the winds of change blew around her. As she turned to leave, she noticed a pile of cream cartons waiting to be put away.

"I'll just put these in the new dairy fridge before I go," she said. "They'll spoil on this warm day." *Fancy leaving them out*, she thought indignantly. *These young ones, all systems and no common sense. The kitchen would be a shambles inside a week.*

"Thanks," Marie called from the larder, where she was busy with the vegetable baskets.

Christina put the cream neatly into the new dairy fridge that used to be the meat fridge, on the top shelf. In the last carton, she made a short gash with her thumbnail as she put it in, positioned over the cheeses on the next shelf and the butter packs below them. She smiled at the greasy mess it would have made by the time Marie opened the fridge again.

Christina was through with open warfare. Guerrilla tactics had taken over.

Marie spent an hour and a half unloading all the shopping, sorting it into wet and dry stores, then moving surplus stocks into the storeroom – the sugars and flours, the jams and chutneys, the biscuits and oatmeal, vinegars and oils, mustards and cereals, chocolate and honeys.

Christina came back, markedly less co-operative than she had been before. She parted grudgingly with her information about breakfasts – what time, what they consisted of – and was just as niggardly about sharing her knowledge of staff lunches, afternoon tea and evening dinner. Marie was exhausted by the time she had wrung out of her everything she needed to know to make a start. Eventually, Christina left. It would be ten days before she was wanted in the kitchen again, on Marie's first day off.

As Marie began to draw up a schedule for the next day, the kitchen telephone rang.

"Hallo? Who's speaking there?" said a male voice.

"It's Marie, the cook."

"Ah, I'm glad I caught you," said the voice. "I thought you sounded too young and friendly to be Christina."

Marie opened her mouth, then thought better of it and opted for silence.

"I'm one of the syndicate members," the voice went on helpfully. "Sorry, I should really introduce myself before I start talking, shouldn't I? My name's Trevor Fynn. I'll be coming up to the Castle in September."

"Oh I see," Marie said, her tone immediately guarded. Company directors were not usually in the habit of ringing up employees to pass the time of day.

"I'd heard there was a new cook starting, and I wanted to say welcome on behalf of the members, and I hope things work out for you."

"Well, thank you," Marie said, her suspicion in part overridden by surprise. "I can honestly say my first impressions are favourable."

"And you've got help this season, am I right?"

"Yes, a kitchen assistant," Marie said. "She's arriving any day now, full time for the season. I think her name's Hedda."

"That's terrific," Mr Fynn said. "I've said for years we should stretch the budget to accommodate some help for the cook – it's a long haul to the end of the season otherwise. Now, be sure to let us know if there's anything you need. There's a lot of old equipment that needs ditching, I know that much – just let me know if you have any trouble sourcing replacements and I'll sort it out with Heather."

"Heather's been very helpful already," Marie protested. "I'm sure that won't be necessary. But I appreciate your interest." She stopped, then let her guard down a little. "It's refreshing, to say the least."

"Well, that's great," Mr Fynn said. "I'm sure you'll settle in and I'm looking forward to eating your food. Your reputation has preceded you, I can tell you that much."

After a few more pleasantries, Marie hung up, more puzzled by Mr Fynn's motives than pleased with the compliments. Why on earth would a director ring up to welcome her to Uishall, when all the formalities had already been dealt with?

II

Cornelius Fynn, crenellated, crusty and cruel, had harboured feelings of disappointment about his son even before Trevor was old enough to truly merit them. Had Cornelius not been heir to a large banking fortune, it was doubtful he would have bothered to have any offspring at all. But his vast wealth necessitated a family line to inherit, so he had resigned himself to siring an heir and hoped that his first shot resulted in one of the right sex. He was lucky there, and his delicate wife, Phylicia – too weak-willed to resist the combined assaults of his gruff proposal and the greedy bullying of her father, a Northumberland landowner with ship building interests – had delivered a son three weeks early. Since then, his experiences of fatherhood had been downhill all the way.

He didn't like Trevor the first time he saw him at the hospital, and failed to notice or respond to the radiant happiness of his wife. This in itself was remarkable, as Phylicia had never demonstrated radiant happiness since the day she had married him, so he had never seen it before, nor would again. Oblivious to this unique event, he complained loudly about his son's scrawny limbs, disturbing puce colour and squashed head. His wife, worn out by a long, punishing labour and an unpleasant aftermath involving a lot of stitches, promptly burst into tears, creating an unbreakable bond in Cornelius's emotionally challenged mind between children, crying, frustration and disappointment.

Trevor was a frail child – *weedy*, his father barked at anyone who asked, or tried to pass comment – who hated sports, shrank from fights, caught every childhood illness possible, and preferred the company of girls. All that, combined with his clinging affection for his mother – *each as pathetic as the other*, Cornelius thought bitterly – convinced his father that his son had the makings of a first-class woofter. And quite simply, that would not be tolerated.

Even the discovery that Trevor was something of a musical prodigy did nothing to mollify him. A rugger star, a marine in the making, a boy with the glint of filthy lucre in his eye and an obsession for making more of it – all those were things his father could have understood, been proud of and nurtured. But the sight of his son seated at the piano or picking at his first guitar did nothing but fill him with despairing rage.

So he took the boy in hand, and made Uishall his training ground. Long, bracing walks over the rough moorland, especially, it seemed, in cold, nasty, wet weather, when the other children were permitted to stay indoors and keep warm and dry. Long, distressing coaching sessions wielding salmon rods and learning the intricacies of casting, the process ending in the grim realisation that on top of all his other manly failures, his son was a useless fisherman as well. But finally, Cornelius's efforts were rewarded when he put a rifle in his son's hands for his first shooting lesson. Trevor's natural brilliance behind a gun was evident from the first time his father, on the point of giving up and abandoning him to the world of music, girls and woofters, put him on the clays. It was the closest he ever came to showing approval for his son, who until then had been starved of all paternal affection. For Cornelius, it came close to being an emotional moment.

Having proved his prowess on the clays, young Trevor was introduced to death. Lots of death. Cornelius judged death to be character building.

Trevor's father killed things with an admirable detachment, whacking salmon on the head with a large, lead-filled priest, shooting grouse out of the sky and taking the stricken birds from the gentle mouth of his inexplicably faithful black Labrador, Mab.

Trevor met death on the outside, and then met it again in the kitchen, where Christina stood over the sink, grimly reaping scallops with business-like thrusts and sharp twists of a short, sharp-pointed and thick-bladed knife. Like Cornelius, she was impressively unimpressed by the piles of dead creatures she methodically gutted, boned and skinned, then froze or hung in the capacious larders. The first time Trevor watched her shelling scallops, she put the newly eviscerated mollusc in his outstretched hand and he felt it throb, a single, strong pulse in his palm like a heartbeat. He started, dropped it, and Christina laughed unkindly at his distress. He worried for hours afterwards that the scallop had still been alive.

"Things live, things die," Cornelius gruffly told his small son, by way of explanation. "That's the way of the world."

Trevor was sorry that it was, but knew better than to say so. He put it down as another example of failure on his part to come to terms with the fundamentals of living, and his exhausted and nervous mother did nothing to disabuse him of the notion. Perhaps neither of them was a good enough match for the world according to Cornelius.

Trevor tried to accept the harsh, unvarnished truth of life and death insofar as it applied to the animal kingdom, and thought that his father's detached brutality must be the right way to deal with it. But when all four families were holidaying at Uishall one summer, something happened to open Trevor's eyes, and for the first time, he saw his father as others did.

On a particularly hot and sunny day, Christina was boiling the live lobsters for supper. Trevor, ten by this time, was already struggling with the problem of loving the living creatures, indigo blue, unearthly and fascinating, while simultaneously adoring them, scarlet, dead and delicious on his plate. Christina had had two enormous pans of boiling water on the cooker, and had despatched a dozen lobsters with her usual efficiency. The pans had been emptied and scoured and put away when there was a sudden commotion in the scullery, and Trevor heard his father coming through the door. There was a clattering sound, swearing, and his father's mocking laugh, then squeals from Freya, who was cleaning mussels at the sink with her mother. Trevor went through, partly from curiosity, and partly because Freya sounded scared.

It transpired that Cornelius had arrived with a latecomer for the lobster feast. He had been out in the boat with Christina's husband, collecting the last few pots in the bay. Three were empty, but the fourth had trapped a marvellous specimen. Cornelius, red in the face from the boat trip, and rather the worse for wear from the several drams he'd downed along the way, had come in brandishing the lobster, and dropped it on the tiled floor. The heavy claw had snapped off. Cornelius had picked up both lobster and claw, and was now chasing Freya round the scullery.

Trevor arrived just as Freya's mother, Lillian, pulled off her rubber gloves and slapped them onto the draining board.

"Cornelius, that lobster is still alive," she said levelly.

He stopped teasing Freya and looked at her in surprise. "So what if it is?" he said. "It's just a bit of fun. Isn't it, Freya?" Freya screamed as he launched another playful jab at her. The lobster waved its legs and surviving claw. "You're not going all animal lib on me, are you, Lillian?"

Lillian was not timid like Phylicia. She held out her hand. "Give it to me, Cornelius. *Now.*"

He held the lobster high above his head. "Shan't," he said, acting the schoolboy. Trevor watched curiously. Suddenly, his father didn't look terrifying anymore. Just bullying and stupid. Lillian, all quiet dignity concealing a rising fury, was making him look like a fool.

"What's your problem, Lillian?" he sneered, keeping the lobster aloft.

"My problem is that the lobster is still alive," she said. "It has been thrown to the floor and mutilated. It is a living creature, not a plaything. It needs to be killed quickly." Cornelius was unmoved, even though Lillian's voice was shaking. "And you're giving out unforgivable messages to the children about how we treat creatures that are still alive. Show some respect."

"You're being cruel," Freya suddenly burst out. "You've hurt it. Give it to Mummy."

Trevor at this point felt some sort of obligation to stand up for his father.

"Dad says they don't feel pain," he said, disastrously, to try to comfort Freya. She gave him a look of utter disgust he never forgot.

"That's not the point," Lillian said. She held out her hand again and Cornelius, the taunting smile growing sour on his lips, lowered the lobster in his hand, and then dropped it on the floor again, staring at her all the while. He threw the claw into the sink and marched off. Freya burst into tears.

It was only in later years that Trevor understood the peculiar expression warping Lillian's features at that moment. She bent down, picked up the lobster and his claw, and looked at both children.

"Come with me," she said. "Freya, stop crying. That won't help him."

Back in the kitchen, she got one of the lobster pans out of the cupboard and set it to boil. The lobster she set gently in the sink and covered it with a wet towel, where it sat quietly, stunned by its recent adventures.

"If we are going to kill things for food," she said to Freya and Trevor, her tone mildly lecturing, "we do it as quickly and cleanly as we can, so the creature doesn't suffer."

Trevor looked at the floor.

"Your dad's awful," Freya said suddenly. "He's *cruel.*"

217

Trevor cringed. "He didn't mean it," he said. "It's just the way he is."

But the word *cruel* stuck. He couldn't get rid of it. It was as if Freya had suddenly opened his eyes to a blinding truth. His father was cruel. Trevor wasn't. His mother wasn't. His father was what was wrong with the world.

"The thing is, Trevor," Lillian went on, more kindly, "whether or not the lobster feels pain is not the issue. It was suffering – taken away from its home, put in a hot, dry place, and then treated unkindly. It's what that says about *us* that matters. Would you like to be treated like that?"

"No," Trevor said in a small voice.

The water came to the boil and Lillian picked up the lobster and his claw and dropped them both in. Immediately, she looked better. Trevor watched the colour change from indigo to scarlet. As if reading his mind, Lillian said,

"I think this is the kindest way to do it because it's very fast. Some people put them into warm water and bring them slowly to the boil, some people put them in the freezer so they get colder and colder and go to sleep. We don't really know, do we? But I think this is best."

"Is it cruel of us to eat them?" Trevor asked.

Lillian smiled. "No. Nature is full of creatures that eat each other and are eaten in their turn. I love eating lobster, just like you do, but I like to think it's had a happy life before, and I like to make sure it suffers as little as possible when it's time for it to die."

Trevor never forgot that afternoon, just as he never spoke of it again. He maintained a lifelong affection for Lillian, and her words about suffering acquired a more poignant meaning for him when a few years later, his mother began to die of cancer. In the long months she lay in bed, while the disease painfully sucked the life from her, he often thought about blameless creatures and unnecessary suffering, and wondered what his mother, like the lobster, had done to deserve it.

III

Freya set the heavy 12-bore on her shoulder, waited for the spring of the trap, and swung the gun in a wide arc as the clay pigeon rocketed into the air. She fired as the clay soared to the peak of its trajectory, fired again as it began its descent, and watched it sink untouched to the ground.

"*Shit*."

She reloaded, said, "Pull," to the trap operator, waited again, aimed again, missed again. The swearing got worse.

It was her competitive streak that had made her contact Trevor in the end. He had been touchingly thrilled that she had thought of him, and immediately took her in hand. She had wanted to go to a more modern shoot, but Trevor didn't want her using automatic set-ups. This was new territory to her, but familiar to him, and it put her on edge. Trevor had explained that if she was in charge of the automatic foot switch, it was just one more thing to worry about. The old-fashioned way was the best, with someone operating the spring-loaded handle. And he would only set one trajectory at first, across the gun sights, forty yards range. The shoot was set amongst scrubby woodland, and offered a natural setting for practice.

"You're overshooting," Trevor said unhelpfully from behind her. She picked up the amusement in his voice, and her mood darkened further.

"I know that," she said testily. "What I need to know is how to stop doing it."

"Follow through," Trevor said, grinning. "Shoot at the sky, not the clay."

She turned to him. She had always known this would be a bad idea, and she cursed Hugh for putting it into her head. "What are you talking about?"

Trevor stood up and came up close behind her, pulling and pushing her shoulders and arms into what he considered a more suitable posture.

"Christ, Freya, you're tense as hell," he murmured. "Stop beating yourself up about this. You'll never shoot anything if you don't learn to relax."

She moved angrily away from him. "Stop that right now," she said. "This is a shooting lesson, not a groping spree."

Trevor grinned innocently and stepped back. "Look, no hands," he said, ostentatiously raising them, relentlessly good humoured as ever. Freya's tension increased. She couldn't learn anything from this man who was so unfailingly successful at winding her up. She missed another three clays.

"Change the trajectory," Trevor instructed the operator at last, while Freya slumped dispiritedly onto the low stone wall. "Lower, a less sharp curve." He squatted down in front of his disgruntled pupil and she raised her eyes and glared at him.

"This isn't helping," she said.

"Listen to me," Trevor said. "You're too hung up on the clay. I used to be. You automatically fix on it and stop, however much you don't mean to. You have to understand it's moving all the time, so you can't fix on it. Learn to aim in front of it and don't look at it directly. Keep it in the corner of your eye and look at the bit of sky about two feet in front of it. You fire the gun, the shot goes out, and the clay gets there *after* you fire. It's logic. It's just doing it that's hard."

She sighed, her expression softening a little. "I know. And I'm grateful you're trying to help. I just don't like being such a hopeless case."

"You're not hopeless," he said. "And if you crack this, you're in with a good shot at the Macnab. Think about that night of passion with Aidan you've promised yourself —"

Freya punched him in the chest and they both broke up into laughter, hanging onto each other for support.

"Think about how much you want that big, hairy man between your thighs," Trevor said, trying to make his naturally soft voice sound husky and animal. Freya hit him again.

"Stop it," she said, between gasps of laughter. "You're dreadful."

"That's better," Trevor said quietly, a few minutes later, when they had laughed themselves into a companionable silence. "You've got to relax before we do anything else."

Freya raised her eyes. He couldn't help it. Whenever he spoke to women, whatever he was saying to them, he always sounded as if he was trying it on. He didn't know any other way. She got to her feet and handed the gun to him.

"Talk me through it again," she said.

She watched in admiration as Trevor hit four out of the next six clays. She was quite sure he missed the other two on purpose. He talked about keeping the barrel of the gun moving, aiming at the sky, how the clay didn't stop obligingly in mid-air while the shooter fired his shot, how the shot had to intercept the clay. Finally, he passed the gun back to her. She took it and gripped it firmly with renewed resolution.

"OK, let's go again," she said.

Trevor moved behind her. "I don't mean anything by this," he said, "but this has got to be right. Where you start from, how you stand." She felt his hands on her neck. "*Relax*," he said, a hint of impatience in his voice. "I can feel your muscles all bunching up." He worked them with his fingers and her shoulders dropped slightly. "Good," he said. "Now, the gun – *here* – your hands – *here* –" his hands covered hers, aligning them over the trigger and barrel until they were as he wanted them. "Now, set your chin – no, not like that, more like this –" His hands adjusted the tilt of her face. "Does that feel comfortable?"

"Yes," Freya said in surprise, trying to turn to him and realising she couldn't. "That's different to how I normally position my hands. It feels as if I'm more in connection with the gun."

"Good," Trevor said again. He signalled to the trap man.

"Are you going to move back?" Freya said, wriggling a little.

"No," Trevor said. "I want to see and feel how you respond to the trap firing. *Go.*"

The clay shot into the air, Freya swung the barrel, fired and missed, fired and missed.

"That's only your first try," Trevor said. "Persevere. Come on, Freya, you're not a quitter. You have to follow through. Shoot at the sky, not the clay."

She straightened her shoulders. She missed again.

"OK, let's try this," Trevor said at last.

"Try what?" she said, her tone sharpened by disappointment. "This isn't working. What else is there to try?" She was expecting too much, that Trevor would somehow have a magic formula, and cure her overshooting with a simple but brilliant insight. She saw now that it wasn't going to happen.

"Again," Trevor called to the trap man. He stood close behind Freya as she racked the gun, let his hand drop from her shoulder. She tensed at once, not trusting him.

"Shoot at the sky," he said, low in her ear. "Concentrate."

She fixed her eyes on the patch of sky above the trap, but as soon as the clay was fired, her eye was drawn inevitably to it. As she followed it with the gun, she felt Trevor's hand graze the side of her breast. She swung the barrel in fury, incredulous at his opportunism, fired – and high in the air, the clay shattered

221

into a thousand fragments. Trevor jumped backwards, grinning, as she stared open-mouthed at the shards dropping from the sky, and then turned to him in outrage.

"A hit," he said levelly, studiously nodding towards the patch of sky where the clay had been broken. "A bullseye, no less. Well done."

She turned on him and he backed off, shrugging, holding up his hands.

"What?" he said.

She reloaded. "That was a fluke," she said, furious with him, with herself, for being taken in by such a cheap trick. But she knew it had worked. That jerk of irritation had pulled the gun away from the magnetic attraction of the moving clay and fixed it on a point somewhere in front. She felt as if someone had opened a door wide, right in front of her, that she had never seen before. Trevor had hit pay dirt.

Freya hit the next three clays while Trevor sat on the low wall, being careful to say nothing. He hadn't played strictly by the rules, but Freya could shoot now, and the Macnab was really on.

At the end of the session, Freya broke the gun and pocketed her last few cartridges. He could tell she was elated.

"Good job," she said, then surprised both of them by throwing her arms clumsily around him. "Whatever the dubious nature of your methodology, you've done what no other instructor has ever been able to do. I thank you from the bottom of my heart. I owe you a big one."

She walked towards her car, thinking that that was probably the worst thing she could ever have said to someone with a mind as literal as Trevor's, and her heart sank as he called to her,

"I'll take you up on that."

She turned back. "What?" she said suspiciously.

"Fishing lesson," he said, and she relaxed immediately.

"You're on," she said. "About time I did something about that casting action of yours."

IV

Marie woke in her room late in the night and lay listening to the water lapping against the jetty. She liked the fact that even when she concentrated, on calm nights like this she could hear nothing else. She lay for a long time, soothed by the water and the languid movements of the curtains as an occasional breeze pushed idly at them. But sleep seemed to be eluding her as she lay and turned over the events of the past few days, hoping she would nod off again.

She had got to know Aidan, who was often outside the kitchen windows, busy with the boats at the jetty, or walking his deerhounds; the dogs paid homage to the old castle traditions, and he never missed an opportunity to share his extensive knowledge of the breed with anyone who might express an interest. He lived alone in the large white house up a lane behind the castle and could always be tempted by the smell of baking coming from the oven as Marie batched up fruitcakes to wrap and store in the larder, and chocolate sponges for the freezer. She had even started to make scones and pancakes in the afternoons, as the castle got busier with arriving staff, knowing that food was as good an ice breaker as anything. Aidan in particular had a sweet tooth, seemed to have a critical interest in food in general, and was a willing guinea pig when she was trying something new.

Her assistant for the season had arrived, and they were getting on well. Hedda MacInnes was bright, receptive and good company, and Marie had already worked out that she was capable of taking on higher levels of responsibility than the job allowed. They would make a good team if things worked out. The presence of Aidan and Hedda went a long way to mitigating her poor relationship with Christina that had started badly and seemed to be getting worse.

Ingredients and kitchen equipment were going missing, and Marie had quickly worked out that if Christina knew what she was planning to cook the next day, something would go wrong. Cake tins wouldn't be there, or spices would have run out, even if they had only been bought a few days before. Essential elements of the electric beater or food processor would have vanished.

Marie had been on her guard ever since the incident with the cream carton; given the resistance Christina had put up on that first day, her initial reaction had been suspicious, and she was ashamed of herself for thinking the older woman would do something so petty. She had discovered the short, neat slice in the carton after only a few minutes, cleaned up the mess, transferred the cream to another container – and said absolutely nothing.

She had quite enjoyed the following day, when Christina had cheerfully asked how the reorganisation had gone, and had finally been driven into opening the fridge to check if her handiwork had been discovered, confirming all Marie's suspicions. Watching her colleague peering into the fridge and failing to find evidence of the little crime she had committed had given her a great deal of malicious satisfaction, even while she understood that this was the beginning of a long game.

So now, things were going missing. Even though Christina wasn't yet working, she always managed to pop into the kitchen, cheerily asking if she could beg a bit of mixed spice or a wee bunch of parsley, or a couple of eggs or whatnot, and asking what Marie was up to. The simplest thing was to lie. If Marie was planning to make gingerbread, she told Christina it was going to be fruitcake. Then the glace cherries or ground almonds would take a hike, and not the crystallised ginger or black treacle. The next day, when Marie was looking for something else, Christina would arrive with her pretext for nipping into the cook's larder, and the things she couldn't find the day before were mysteriously back in their places. It was tiresome, but it was also fascinating, and Marie had resolved not to make a scene about it until either Christina tired of not getting a response, or she caught her red handed.

Marie sighed impatiently as her predecessor and weekend relief drifted into her thoughts and then dropped anchor. She moved the covers aside and levered herself reluctantly out of bed. She wasn't going to get any sleep with Christina on her mind. There was cold bottled water in the storeroom fridge. Perhaps a change of scenery and a gaze out of the kitchen windows while she quenched her thirst would put the night to rights.

She padded down the corridor, past Hedda's room, into the old part of the castle. In the Macleods' day, the current laundry room had been the scullery, where the kitchen maids scrubbed the pots and pans and washed the fine dining room china in a deep wooden sink. Through the kitchen lay the storeroom, still with the original wooden bins for potatoes and root vegetables, and the racks for the fruits that were stored in wicker baskets.

As yet, Marie and Hedda were the only two people sleeping in the castle. Heather lived a short drive away in the village by the ancient church; the domestic staff were due to arrive tomorrow, and the ghillies were already arriving from the mainland and other parts of the island, and taking up residence in the annexe. It was like boarding school, Marie thought, as she made her way towards the storeroom, the boys all separate from the girls.

Suddenly, she stopped. She could hear faint noises coming from behind the heavy storeroom door and recognised the sounds of someone rooting through the fruit baskets where the bananas, apples, pears and oranges lived. The door was closed as Marie had left it, and now she lifted the latch quietly and pushed it open. The figure before her was bent over, red curly hair hanging down her back, tied neatly with a ribbon, and her movements were swift and agitated. Marie smiled, relaxing, her kitchen partner obviously having the same trouble sleeping as she was.

"Hedda," she said quietly, hoping she wouldn't startle her. "Do you want some water to go with whatever you're fishing out of those baskets?" She yawned and turned to open the fridge, expecting an answer, pulled out two bottles of water and turned back to the racks.

Hedda had gone.

"Hedda?" Marie called out in surprise, her voice low. "Where did you get to?"

She looked out into the kitchen and along the corridor, but there was no sign of anyone. For a moment she stood there, puzzling over why the normally companionable Hedda had declined to join her in some late night comfort chat. She hadn't even acknowledged her. She shrugged, returned the other bottle to the fridge, closed the door, crossed the kitchen and went back to her room. She drank the water and was asleep five minutes later.

5.
BLOODED
MAY - JUNE

I

Duncan sat in the oppressive gloom of the small sitting room with the growing feeling that he had only just got into this situation, and already he could see no way out of it. Opposite him, Frankie's wife, Sunny, stood by the window, too bitter to dissolve into tears over her husband's untimely and unpleasant death, too exhausted at the prospect of having to raise the two small kids on her own to feel anything but an annihilating self-pity. The sunshine outside looked depressingly bleak as she watched the children arguing in the garden, and turned listlessly away. She had no energy for conflict today; no energy, it seemed, for anything.

"The social will help you with the money side of things," Duncan said, trying to pitch his remarks in a place where they might be fielded. He shifted on the grubby upholstery and longed for freedom.

"Maybe so, but they won't be much help with the kids, will they?" she said. She threw him a helpless, angry look, her long hair falling either side of her face as her head drooped downwards. She lit another cigarette and pulled on it savagely. "The stupid fucker. Always more interested in fish than his family. Always trying to save the world. Always wasting his time being a stupid fucker instead of doing something useful."

Sunny's long-suffering martyrdom was thoroughly convincing, and a demoralising dead-end. Duncan knew she didn't know anything, but he clung to the faint chance that she might know something without realising it. He had never known her to get involved in any of Frankie's animal liberation schemes, never helped him in his manic marches across the moorland. But then, she had never hindered him either. Her lethargy extended to doing nothing in either direction, making Frankie a freelance activist, unfettered by anything except the nagging and whining she inflicted on him whenever he set foot in the house. But beneath her contempt for him there was loyalty. She might not help him while he was alive, but she certainly wouldn't grass on him now he was dead.

"Do you know what he was doing out at Uishall?" Duncan asked hopelessly.

"I don't know and I don't care," she said. "He's drowned and I'm a widow with two kids who fight all the time –" She broke off to wave a hand towards the sounds of dispute, littered with expletives, coming from the garden. "And now I know he's never coming back – how will I tell the difference? He was never here in the first place, except between plotting his missions to save the fish."

Duncan, never a popular man in this house, saw the uselessness of prolonging the interview. When he had come to talk to Frankie in the past, it had at least been more entertaining – Frankie argued and slithered round things like a wet ferret, always slipping out of his grasp whenever he came close to bagging him. At least he got a chance to practise his interrogation techniques.

"I'll need to look through his things," Duncan said, his tone slightly firmer as he tried to get back to business and dig them both out of the pit this woman was wallowing in.

She waved her hand again, this time towards the back of the house. "Everything of his is in the rooms through there. You can burn anything you don't want."

"Sunny, going through Frankie's things is something you're going to have to do yourself," Duncan said, and walked out of the room, leaving her staring back at the garden. As he opened a door, he heard her rap angrily on the window and shout a string of threats at the children if they didn't shut the fuck up. A sheepdog with wonky eyes and a limp, tied up in a neighbouring garden, joined in for the hell of it.

Duncan sorted through a handful of papers in the kitchen, stuffed behind and into an ancient and greasy toast rack, and found nothing but unpaid bills and strong letters from the council about rent. He looked in the bedroom Frankie had shared with Sunny, and found only clothes. In the children's bedroom, he found broken toys and old apple cores and crisp packets and dirty socks and sweet wrappers; shoved under one of the beds, there was a box covered in Noddy and Thunderbirds stickers. He opened it, and his heart lifted all at once. Inside, there was a pile of correspondence and photocopied letters written by Frankie, painstakingly clipped together. A signature caught his eye, and he raised his eyebrows in puzzled amazement. He gathered it all together and went back into the sitting room. Sunny looked as if she had taken root by the window. Now he had something to go on, Duncan could afford to be a little more generous.

"You can't bury him until we know more," he said.

She nodded briefly, her back turned to him, and he saw that other emotions were now at work. He laid a hand on her shoulder and was relieved when her stiff posture gave way and she began to sob convulsively. It was better out than in. Duncan let her cry for a while, his arms uneasily around her, then guided her to the sofa and sat her down. He went into the kitchen, put the kettle on and came back with a cup of tea.

"Look at the state of us," she moaned. "He'd never get a job, refused to go on the gutting line. Oh, he was far too good for the gutting line, wasn't he? It was way beneath him. All we heard about was his principles. What did his principles ever do for us?"

"There are some letters," Duncan said, showing her the box. "Do you know anything about them?"

She glanced at it. "Fundraising," she said bitterly. "That was him trying to get money together for his good causes." She looked at Duncan. "And if he ever got any, we never saw it. He didn't count his family as a good cause, that's for sure." She started to cry again, and Duncan sighed and stood up.

"I'll take these away to go through them properly," he said. "Sunny, you're going to have to try to get yourself together a bit. This is going to be a tough time – not just losing Frankie, but all the implications of how he was found." She said nothing and he sighed again. "I'll send in Annie from over the way," he said. "She's out there now, wondering what the news is."

Duncan drove away with the box of letters on the seat beside him. A grim job, breaking bad news. But he had left with a new lead, and the detective in him soon superseded the concerned citizen. Sunny would have to frame herself and sort out her own problems – nobody could do that for her, not even the capable, interfering Annie. Duncan had more pressing concerns now. He wanted to know why Frankie Johnson had written several letters to Natasha Tang – and why she had bothered to reply.

II

Hedda was in the dining room, setting the table for breakfast the following morning, when John came up behind her and slid his arms around her waist. She smiled, broke off briefly and leaned back against him. It was late, close on eleven o'clock, as the guests had been tardy vacating the table when dinner finished on their first night. The rest of the girls were away to town for a start-of-the-season drink, and Hedda and Marie had offered to do the late-night tasks so they could leave a bit earlier than usual.

The preparation period was over and the season was officially open. Uishall booked its weeks from Wednesday evening to the following Wednesday morning and Heather had briefed Marie, Hedda and all the girls about who was coming in, any particular requirements they had, who would be sleeping in which rooms. Two of the directors were here, Hugh and Robert Bartlett, brothers, both very nice, and the other six were regular season-openers at Uishall. Robert had come for the fishing, Hugh had already discharged his duty – contributed to a course for the ghillies on offering better service to the guests. Dinner had gone well, despite the brief panic over losing the meat for the main course. It had eventually been discovered tucked neatly – and *pointedly*, Marie thought – into the *old* meat fridge, in the box at the bottom, right at the back. Hedda had been let in on what was going on.

John had already decided that the dining room was his favourite place in the castle. He had spent a good deal of time walking the gardens and wandering the rooms, while the girls scurried about making beds and cleaning bathrooms, setting flowers in the great porcelain vases, brushing down the heavy damask curtains and polishing pictures and silver. The dining room impressed him with its heavy oak table and twelve carver chairs, the massive oak sideboard with its ostentatious carving, the Macleod tartan carpet and the walls recently restored to the same blood red as the imposing entrance hall. But what he really liked about it were the portraits of the Uishall lairds, hung on the walls, dating back to 1394.

He let his gaze roam over the walls until it settled on a figure that caught his interest.

"Who's this?"

Hedda didn't even bother to look up. "I thought you'd spot her before long," she said, concentrating on laying cutlery, close to finishing a long day.

His interest was sufficiently engaged to make him walk over to the wall and stare up at the face looking out at them. Hedda plonked the cruet into place, raised her eyes at last from the snowy white of the tablecloth, and tracked his gaze.

"Well, ask me, then," she said, amused, as the portrait swiftly deflected John's interest. "I do actually know about her. That's Janet, wife of Alec Macleod, 23rd Laird of Uishall. She's interesting because she was a tenant's daughter who ended up marrying the laird. It caused quite a stir at the time."

"How did she swing that one?"

"Heather can probably tell you – she pointed her out to me on the first day, because she thought we looked alike."

John turned and looked at her, then looked back at the portrait. The artist had evidently spent some time on capturing the mass of red curls that tumbled from her head and refused to be tamed. But he had also caught an interesting quality in the face that transcended her fairy-like beauty and hinted at something that went beyond intelligence and into the artful.

Hedda wound her arm around his waist. "You're good at people," she said. "What do you see?"

"There's a likeness, isn't there?" he said. "But don't you think she looks driven? As if she had to work for him?"

Hedda grinned wryly. "She probably did," she said. "The gap between Laird and tenant was massive – she was definitely on the wrong side of the peat cuts." She paused. "So he must have wanted her, too."

John whistled. "Think of the practicalities," he said. "Taking a wife without a dowry would knock a big hole in the Laird's finances, not to mention all the etiquette considerations. There was still a class system." He looked at the portraits. "Which one is Alec?"

Hedda scanned the walls. "That one – there. The handsome one."

John laughed and pointed his finger accusingly. "Aha!"

"What?"

"You'd have fallen for him, too."

"Maybe I'd have fallen for his money," Hedda said. She hesitated. "But yes – he's attractive. I wouldn't have turned down a roll in the heather with him."

"Should I be jealous?"

"No, because he's dead," Hedda said, grinning, dodging John's swipe at the back-handed compliment. She looked again at Janet, who had won the Laird's heart. "She's very beautiful."

"And very clever." John cocked his head, eyes flicking between the portraits. "What an interesting couple," he said. "A man ruled by the heart, falling for a woman well beneath him. There's something of the libertine in him, don't you think?"

"You said a moment ago that Janet looked driven. Perhaps she had him in her clutches. Maybe he was blackmailed."

John grimaced and shook his head. "I don't see how that could happen," he said. "What else did Heather say?"

"That she outlived the Laird and their son Alasdair owned Uishall for twenty years after his father's death. She had the fountain in the courtyard built in Alec's memory. She nearly went mad with grief and everyone feared she would die of it. She never married again and was buried at his side."

"Ah, the tragedy of true love," John said. "It always ends in death and madness." He kissed her playfully. "Why do we do it when we know it can only lead to suffering?"

"Oh, please," Hedda said. "But do you know what? They aren't in the churchyard in the village, where most of the Macleod lairds are. They're buried on Janet's Knoll, on one of the hillsides overlooking the castle. She gave explicit directions when Alec died for both of them to be laid to rest there – it must have had very special significance for them."

John stared at her. "Of course! I was up there today," he said. "I walked all around the castle while you were in the kitchen with Marie."

"Did you read the inscription on the gravestone?" He shook his head, and she quoted:

"We end as we began – God's judgement came."

"Really?" John said. "Now that *is* interesting."

III

Robert contemplated the pile of papers before him with a mixture of fascination and dismay. His initial impression had been correct. Nothing was filed, the date order of everything was random, and builders' quotes were mixed in with physicians' reports and personal correspondence, wardrobe requisitions and kitchen orders, accounts for tradesmen and rent books for the crofters. It seemed Alec Macleod and his family were avidly keen communicators and took every opportunity to put their thoughts and wishes onto paper. A tattered scrap was covered in clumsy script with the name Alasdair Macleod, written over and over again with seemingly laborious concentration, as if he was learning his letters. Robert allowed himself a sardonic smile. There was no doubt about it – Alasdair was a person of some determination, the kind who would let nothing stand in his way.

Robert stood, laid the letters in the top corner of the desk, and decided he needed a glass of wine to help him on his way. He went down into the kitchen and fished out an unfinished bottle of Chablis from the chiller. On his way through to the dining room, where the wineglasses were kept in a cupboard underneath the window, he almost collided with a tall, fair-haired younger man going in the opposite direction.

"I'm so sorry," Robert said. "I wasn't expecting anyone to be about at this hour." He looked interrogatively at him, not recognising him.

"John Gibson," the stranger supplied helpfully, and held out his hand. "I'm a friend of the kitchen helper, Hedda MacInnes. She's just in the still room, finishing off."

"Ah," Robert said. "Are you working here too?"

"No – I'm on holiday. I teach at the secondary school in town."

"What subject?"

"History." John indicated the walls with his hand. "This place is certainly lifting with it. We've just been discussing the portraits."

"Really?" Robert said, in a markedly more interested tone of voice. "Uishall's a fascinating place. In fact – have you got a minute? Not going to meet Hedda just yet?"

John shook his head. "She'll be a little while yet. I'm afraid I don't know –"

"Robert Bartlett," Robert said, shaking his hand again. "One of the directors. I've come up to fish for a couple of days. My brother's here, too, he was helping out on the course they ran yesterday." Robert thought for a moment, then said, "I'm also trying to sort out some stuff – if you're a historian, I think you might find it interesting."

Robert lifted two glasses out of the cupboard and pointed the way upstairs. "Have you had much of a chance to have a look around the place?" he said.

John nodded. "I've had a wander while the girls have been getting all the rooms ready. I've just been listening to the story of Janet and Alec Macleod and I was thinking it might be fun to do a bit of investigating."

Robert turned back into the dining room and went to Janet's portrait. He stood before it for a moment, and then smiled delightedly. "I think it's very good fortune we've bumped into each other." He led the way upstairs to the old study, set the glasses down on the bureau and poured out the wine while John went straight to the heap of papers.

"You can see I haven't got very far," Robert said. "I've literally just started."

Five minutes later, they were already losing themselves in Uishall's past. The pile of papers littering the desk was nothing less than a treasure trove – a heap of jumbled materials, each with its own story to tell.

"The frustrating thing is, I can't be here most of the time because of work commitments back in London," Robert was explaining as John sifted through invoices and letters, not knowing anything about the people who had written them. "I was going to take them home with me, but I really don't want to transport them. And if I have to rely on holiday time to catalogue this stuff, I'll be an old man before it's done."

John raised his head and looked at him. He didn't want to appear over eager, especially on such a brief acquaintance, but Robert seemed to be asking him something.

"Well," John said. "I'm going to be spending a fair amount of time here. I'm familiar with the period, if not the people. If you trust me to handle it, and keep it within the castle, perhaps we can agree on some sort of system, and I'll start the job of sorting –"

"Would you really?" Robert said, a trifle too eagerly for a man versed in the arts of caution. "I mean, I can't honestly believe my luck – it would be marvellous if we could work on this together,

233

might even get it done in a season if we're lucky. You can ring me up and report on anything interesting that crops up."

"The holiday is six weeks long," John said, "but I'll be here at weekends until the end of September, when Hedda goes back to university."

"You could keep on coming back if there's a spare room," Robert said. "I'd have no objection, and I'm sure the other directors would be more than grateful that you're working on the task." He paused, then said, "Hedda MacInnes, did you say?"

John nodded.

Robert pursed his lips, then said carefully, "I gather her father's one of the people who – ah – cause us aggravation over the season, poaching and vandalism and such."

John flushed. "She hasn't got any truck with that –"

"No, I'm sure she doesn't," Robert said. "Poaching is more to do with a particular attitude than anything else. She wouldn't be working here if she had it."

John nodded, but the draft of a letter written by Alec Macleod had caught his attention, and he held it between them so Robert could read it, too.

June, 1833

My Dear Catherine,

It was with considerable delight I heard of your impending marriage to Lord Ferguson, and I beg you to accept this silverware as a gift from the Lady Iona and myself with our good wishes for a happy and long-lived union.

I have made final settlements with your father over the question of your former investment in our marriage, and the last ties between us are now severed.

May I also wish on you both the blessing of children, for such you have long been denied, through no fault of your own. I hope you also find it in your heart to forgive me one day for the untruthful charges I laid against you, when I did not understand the nature of the circumstances. I pray that this marriage will give you everything that the Macleod match could not.

Your humble servant
Alec Macleod

"What's all that about?" John said.

Robert's forehead creased. "I'm a bit rusty on this," he confessed. "Heather's much more au fait with the history of this place. But from what she's told me, Catherine Macdonald was Alec's first wife. Before her, he'd had an affair with a young tenant, Janet, who had a son by him. It sounds as if he divorced Catherine on the grounds of infertility. But his second wife didn't bear children, either, and when she died he took Janet as his wife. It appears they had two children together, Alasdair, the bastard child who succeeded him, and Elinor, born just after they were married."

"Ah, the peasant maid made good," John said with a dry smile. He looked at the letter again. "Alec seems to have been a man of good conscience."

"It depends who you listen to," Robert said. "The stuff I've found so far suggests he had a lot of enemies, including his brother, Ruaraidh, who was Laird of Maglavat. Uishall suffered a lot of financial difficulties, sheep raids and boundary wrangles – everyone who thought they could claim a piece of him was out there to take him, it seems."

"If Alec was infertile, and not his wives, Janet may have lied about Alasdair's father to trap the Laird," John said.

"It's a possibility. But contemporary accounts insist the physical likeness between father and son was so marked, it couldn't be anything other than a blood tie. And then there was Elinor."

"Who was Lord Ferguson?"

"He owned land on Skye and Benbecula, but was resident on Mull. Catherine went to live in the mansion there, a few miles from Tobermory, and never returned to Lewis."

"Children?"

"Four," Robert said. "The Lady Catherine was certainly not infertile."

Hugh had arrived at Uishall with Robert the previous evening, and since then, the two of them had spent most of the time apart. The ghillies' course was over now. Hugh was an instinctive fisherman, which meant that he had never spent a lot of time thinking about his techniques. Freya, a much more lucid public speaker, a better fisher, and much more articulate at describing tactics and strategies, would have been a far more sensible choice. But Freya was a woman, and there was still a certain old-fashioned streak of thought dominating Uishall. The ghillies were all male, so were the majority of the members, and so, therefore, were the attitudes. So Hugh had got landed with the job of demonstrating casting, to give pointers on teaching techniques. Despite his reservations, that part had been fine in the end. It was the man running the course who had given him the grief.

Tom Forsyth was a product of modern thinking, which automatically made him an anachronism. Simply by being there he was undermining what made Uishall special, and Hugh had listened to him with a sinking heart. There were some things that were never meant to go together, Hugh thought sadly, as he stood at the back of the room. Fishing and marketing were two of them.

Tom Forsyth had come down from one of the development agencies in town with the aim of getting his course delegates to see salmon fishing as a process that could have business principles applied to it. Hugh had shifted irritably on his feet as the island clichés were trotted out to the considerable bewilderment of his audience. Service. Quality. Profitability. Sustainability. Expertise. Tom might be describing how you approached the running of a retail business or a factory, for all the connection his words had to the place and the activities that made up the spirit of Uishall.

"Your guests look to you for expertise," he said. "Your job is to harness your knowledge and deliver it, to impress on them the quality of the service they are receiving. All you have to remember is one thing. Knowledge is power."

Hugh passed his hand across his eyes and excused himself, partly because he had to get ready for his part of the day's proceedings, but mostly because he was in real danger of smacking Tom Forsyth in the mouth if he didn't leave.

As he threaded line through the rod rings and tried to run through his spiel in his head, he was increasingly distracted by what he had just heard. Uishall had its problems, but nothing Tom said was going to be the slightest help in solving them. Tom was a cosmetics expert, hired on European funding. He knew nothing about the harsh realities of running an estate, everything about slick, superficial touches that were called *solutions*. He had set out his stall to teach in a day things that could never be taught in a lifetime.

Although Uishall struggled to make a profit, it managed to generate substantial sums of money that went into the island economy. The current political climate accentuated the antagonistic feelings between estate landlords and locals, and the old prejudices were coming out of the closet, the wicked English stealing the land from the ancient clans. It was all very well, laying the blame where it wasn't deserved – an easy ticket to ride for an uncertain island economy rocking precariously on the global commercial ocean. The sporting estates were the exception to the rule – they made money out of wild moorland which would otherwise lie wasted, or become prey to the suspect charms of windfarm developers. But the ethos of sporting estates went against the political grain, so Uishall struggled to get any of the European funding that was lavished on far less sound business propositions which met fashionable economic criteria.

The people in charge of the money discounted Uishall on the mistaken grounds that it was run by rich people with endless resources to pour into its vast acreage and fine castle. If there was a buy-out, the community would have to make it pay, with only grant aid to support its efforts.

The new breed of people taking an interest in the land simply didn't understand it. Education, full of good intentions but hopelessly strangled by political correctness, was too wrapped up in modernity. Hugh remembered glumly the last group of Land Management students who had visited the estate the previous spring. Fresh from the south of England they had come, where over hundreds of years, rural land had yielded to change, was receptive to management and had adapted to suit the whims of its owners. It had allowed itself to be planted and dug, refashioned into hollows and dotted with copses, turned into artificial nurseries and killing fields with the needs of the sportsmen considerably met. So Uishall, with its fierce independence and implacability, was a puzzle to them. Why couldn't they populate the hills with deer? Why couldn't they breed pheasant and increase the estate's profitability? Why couldn't they build more access roads, drain the land, introduce species, employ more people? Aidan had done his best, but they thought he simply lacked imagination, and ought to go into education. Uishall needed marketing, they said, and Aidan had tried to keep his temper. Before they set out on their walk along the river, Aidan had asked the group if any of them had a problem with blood sports. Eighteen out of the twenty-five of them had raised their hands. He stared at them uncomprehendingly. He was on a losing wicket before he had made his first delivery.

Alec Macleod, that gifted manager of the land in the 1830s, had struggled. His father before him had. His brother Ruaraidh had all but lost Maglavat. Alec's son, Alasdair, had made the switch from sheep farming to sporting estate – one of the first Lairds to do so. And that had been the magic formula. For over 150 years, it had been the magic formula. It wasn't perfect, but it was a dead cert, the only thing that had consistently generated income from wild, ungovernable terrain. It was the economically sustainable ideal the development agencies were still searching for, it was the earliest form of an attempt to manage and preserve the precious environment, and it was right under their noses.

But Uishall's sustainability had been got at a price. Now it made money – just – but its heritage had become forfeit. It could not be replaced by the counterfeit heritage pushed by the tourist boards, replicated in ghastly knick-knacks that had about as much soul as the factories where they were produced. You couldn't knock up a few pieces of carved stone, or a replica wooden candlestick, or run off a few yards of tweed, and tout them as heritage. The locust plague of tourists that swept across the mainland every summer and left nothing in their wake but the hollow gift of money, took another piece of Scotland's true soul every time they paid for it. The knife plunged in a little deeper until the whole country began to take on the appearance of a theme park. Every year, he saw more clearly the price the Macleods had paid for Uishall's survival. It didn't need marketing. Uishall needed its heart back. It needed a Macleod laird.

He was still brooding late at night as he strolled along the front of the castle with his chocolate Labrador puppy, Belgian – a joke name conferred by Freya which had stuck despite all subsequent attempts to call him something more sensible.

Robert was standing on the jetty, looking out over the water while his bitch, Belgian's sister Ruby, indulged in a spot of late night swimming. Hugh tossed a stick into the water and with a joyful bark, Belgian plunged in and went after it. There was some good-natured fighting between the dogs when they both arrived at their quarry at the same time.

Robert smiled. "I suppose Trevor will be bringing that incorrigible spaniel with him in September?" he said. "I know they never seem to grow up, but she really does take things to the extreme." He paused for a moment. "There must be something in it, you know – that dogs take after their owners."

"She's very loveable," Hugh said. "Apart from when she gets over excited and chews something that's yours. I suppose you could say the same for Trevor. He's always had crazy dogs. Remember when we were all students and he brought that dope with him?"

Robert was already laughing. "And we were all sneaking around on the first night, smoking it in the stables so we wouldn't get caught. Amazing we didn't burn the place down. And that bitch of his – was it another spaniel? God, it was, you know – found the packet and ate the rest of the resin while we were all out of it? I'll never forget the sight of her wobbling towards us, with her eyes all glazed and her legs shaking. I seem to remember it sobered us all up rather fast. Freya was petrified. She thought we'd killed her."

Hugh raised his eyes. "Didn't Trevor come up with something about poisoning to cover up the fact that his spaniel was stoned for two days? Cornelius would have hung him from the rafters if he knew. All that ex-army stuff he used to bark about hippies and drugs and attitude." He paused. "I never saw another man who seems to have spent his entire life being angry."

Robert grimaced. "In a way, you can understand how difficult it was for him when Trevor turned out to be so different," he said. "And the older he got, the more open he was about his rebellion. But he became successful on his own terms, and I always thought that would count for something." He stared out over the river. "What I can't understand is where all that came from. With that father of his, and his mother so timid and proper – how did he end up so extrovert – and such a hit with women?"

"It must come from somewhere. Got anywhere with those papers of yours?"

"As a matter of fact, yes. I've run into the kitchen helper's boyfriend – he's a history teacher, of all things. Looks like I've found a willing accomplice."

The dogs were back on dry land, dripping, tugging the stick between them with a good deal of growling. The two men watched them in silence for a while.

"They used to run deerhounds here, you know," Robert said. "And hunt with them, too. Alec Macleod kept a dozen. What a sight they must have been, leaping over the moorland. Seems to have been a pretty keen hunter. Did hawking for grouse, the whole bit."

"I keep meaning to book myself on a course for that," Hugh said. "Never seem to have the time, though. Might be a better bet for Freya when she's going for the Macnab, eh?"

"She's no worse at shooting than Trevor is at casting," Robert said. "Well, better turn in, I suppose. I'll go in through the gun room and rub these two down." He whistled, and strolled towards the door.

V

"The rod in your – "Freya broke off, her brow furrowing, then stood back to survey her pupil. In front of them, the broad river flowed silkily into a languorous swirl by the near bank. Trevor stood upstream from it. Something wrong with him, the whole way he was standing, the rod stiff in his hand, his face a picture of desperate but unfocused concentration. Freya studied him, then her eyes cleared and she looked at him in exasperation.

Confident, easy-going, infuriatingly enthusiastic Trevor was tense. That's why he was unrecognisable. Now Freya thought about it, she had never seen him fish. He always went off on his own, away from the others with their fluid, confident casts and their easy chat over their failures to catch. Since they were children, Trevor had never let anyone see him fail. She bit her lips. She owed him the lesson, no question about it, but this was strictly business. She couldn't afford to get mixed up in any complicated psychology – there was enough of that to deal with in her day job.

"Look," she said, coming up behind him. "It's fishing, not a battle. I've never seen you so wound up. You look like I did on the clays."

He turned to her with an uneasy grin. "It just doesn't feel right, me with a rod in my hands. It never has. Every time I do it, I can hear my father bellowing in my ear. I don't associate it with having fun."

"Well, that's what we're here for," Freya said. "Come on. First rule of having a good time is loosening up." She hesitated, then laid her hand gingerly over his, curling it round the rod, painfully aware of the fact that Trevor always took physical contact the wrong way. She was still smarting over the way he had cured her overshooting and was determined to conduct her own lesson without resorting to anything that smacked of groping.

"You need to feel the rhythm of the cast," she said. "That should be easy for you, with your musical background. Isn't there some kind of guitar analogy we could use?"

He looked blankly at her and shook his head.

"Well then, let's make a start. Pull some line off with the left hand," she said. "Come on. I'm not doing everything for you. You need a good length out, to load the rod. A short line won't do it – you won't get enough forward momentum to work it. But that doesn't mean you try to throw it out to the other side of the water. Your optimum distance is ten to twelve yards. Got it?"

"Ah," Trevor said a few moments later. "That *does* help. I usually try to cast short, because it seems easier."

She watched as he pulled line off, then threw the rod back with a jerking motion and punched it forward. The fly crashed into the water like a stricken bomber, and sank.

"OK then, every fish in the immediate vicinity has just had the fright of its life," Freya said. "Keep your arm slack and let me lead. Don't do anything."

She lifted the rod gracefully into the air and flicked it forward, her arm barely moving. The line sailed out in a fluid uncoiling motion and the fly landed gently and drifted downwards out of sight. Freya regarded it with satisfaction.

"That's called a kiss," she said. "You above all people should understand that."

He laughed at this and began to relax. "You're trying too hard," she said. "It's a man thing. Think you have to hurl the line out three hundred yards – that's not catching fish, that's trying to

241

impress your fellow anglers with what a macho hunk you are. You need much less force."

By the time she had cast the rod half a dozen times for him, Trevor was beginning to work with the rod. After four or five attempts on his own, his critical teacher interrupted him.

"That's better. Now let's stop for lunch. It's difficult to keep concentration when you're having to make this much effort."

Half an hour later, they were comfortably settled on a rug, the remains of a pork pie, pickles and fruitcake scattered untidily over their plates. There was still a glass of wine left, the sun was warm, the light overcast, and Freya was beginning to fancy her chances. She stretched out lazily - but her eyes never lost their grip on the water.

"Robert and Hugh are up there this weekend," she said jealously. "What wouldn't I give for a day on the Uishall right now."

"This has helped, you know," Trevor said. "I'm beginning to see the appeal of fishing for the first time."

"Well, the best time of day is still to come," Freya said. "There are fish about for sure, and once the light starts fading, they'll start to move. I'd like you to catch something before we're finished." She shifted slightly and poured out the rest of the wine. "You should leave the bottle behind in September," she said. "Seriously. All it does is put you under pressure."

"It's sort of part of the ritual," Trevor said. "I pack the tackle, I put in the fly box, I pick up the bottle. It's like a talisman."

"Well it's not brought you any luck these last ten years," Freya said. "Apart from the fact it's a bloody good malt and I want to see it opened, it's the kind of thing that'll stop you ever catching anything just because you know it's there. Perhaps there's a curse on it. I'd spend more time worrying about what's in that fly box of yours if I were you."

Trevor sat up, reached for it, and opened it. Freya squinted across at the contents. "They're all wrong, you know," she said. "All you need for trout are the little black ones. All you need for salmon are stoat's tails."

Trevor frowned. "Aren't those black as well?"

"Exactly. Coloured flies are to catch fishermen. All you have to do is think about women at cocktail parties. If they haven't got a thing to wear, all they need is a little black dress. Apply the same principle, and you'll catch fish every bit as easily as you catch women."

"You always catch," Trevor said. "What's your secret, Freya? Women have to help a chap out now and again by sharing a few of their secrets."

For a second, a shifty look crossed Freya's face, then she rolled on her back, shrugged lightly and stared at the sky. "I just make the most of my natural advantages," she said, and looked meaningfully at him.

Trevor stared at her for a moment, then said, "You don't mean –" and looked at her with renewed fascination. "I thought it was just one of those fishing legends." He stopped. "So what exactly – no, forget I said that," he said, at a look of outrage from his companion. "This is definitely a situation where you could give me too much information," he said.

There was silence for a while. Freya's mind was wandering pleasantly over various memories of fishing days at Uishall, the four of them strung out along the lower length of the river, or drifting a hundred yards apart in the small clinker boats on the loch at the far end of the system. The time Trevor was convinced he had hooked a fish, only to discover he was pulling a huge and very angry crab towards him instead. She smiled to herself, Trevor too scared to get it off the hook – how old would they have been then? Ten? Twelve? – and poor Hugh practically taking a ducking while he did the honours and got his fingers nipped. Robert modestly accepting the praise of his father when his first salmon came to the net. Cornelius dragging Trevor over to the scene of victory, unable to suppress his angry disappointment that his son had yet to catch anything. Freya frowned. Was that the time she finally saw a tiny gleam of defiance in Trevor's eyes? Or was it the time he burst into tears and ran away towards the lodge, and wasn't allowed to eat supper with them that night for making an exhibition of himself? She felt then what she had always more or less felt for Trevor – pity and infuriation that he didn't just pull himself together and get on with his life in the way he wanted to. She was relieved that he seemed at last to have respected the distance she had put between them, and that they had got through the day without him trying to hit on her.

She turned her head. He was sitting up, undoing the straps on a little canvas bag.

"What have you got in there?" she asked.

He started guiltily. "Just bits and pieces I take along as extras," he said.

Freya sat up. "Come on," she said. "Out with them."

A few minutes later, she was staring at an astonishing array of lines and fluorescent flies that had obviously cost him a fortune, and had lured him with a variety of wild and false promises, like inconstant mistresses. There were flavoured oils to smear over flies and create unmissable nibbles out of their barbed hosts, an outrageous steal from the coarse fishing camp. Trevor laid it all out before her, with comically solemn precision, as if he was confessing his sins to a stern priest.

"You know all this stuff isn't going to help you," Freya said.

Trevor glanced drily at her. "As you so eloquently put it," he said, "I don't have quite the same *natural advantages* as you."

Freya shook her head. "The more nonsense you put between you and your fish, the further away you get from him."

"I know."

"So why do it?"

"It's like the bottle," Trevor said helplessly.

6.
BREAKING COVER
JULY

I

"There's a lot of stuff here about Alec Macleod," Robert said, looking down at a small, heavy, black leather-bound book. "He was ill just after he married Catherine. Looks like it was pretty serious."

The study, illuminated by a dazzling purple and gold sunset and two pools of light cast by 1920s desk lamps with green shades, seemed laden with the past, as if every time they came into it, they entered a place that remained suspended in time.

His companion looked up. "What have you got?"

The task Robert had set himself, and that John had eagerly become involved in, was becoming something of an obsession. The pieces of paper were slowly giving up their secrets, the information gradually piecing together into an intricate picture, the personalities emerging from the notes and letters, the household trivia. Alec's passion for the deerhounds; Ruaraidh's mystifying and costly compulsion to order chocolates from Europe, evidenced by the stack of delivery notes and invoices; the hideous treatment programme he endured. The Lady Margaret's declining health; the Lady Iona's complicated medicinal requirements. Janet's signatures on the earlier storeroom requisitions and inventories subsequently followed by that of one Alice MacPhee. The ignominious sacking of woodsman Gillies MacNicol for theft, recorded tersely in the staff log book in September, 1839. Alasdair's refusal to honour payment for a shipment of mainland sheep he had not requested. On and on the scattered fragments went like a paper trail, each a teasing clue to be slotted into a precise part of Uishall's unravelling tale.

"This is the physician's notebook," Robert said. He turned to the front, and a slip of paper fell onto the desk. "Oh now, what's this?" he said suddenly, noticing that it took the form of a brief note addressed to Alasdair and dated 1867.

"'My Dear Alasdair,'" he read aloud. *"'Now I am retired from practice, it occurs to me that certain questions you may have regarding your family background may be answered here. The last generation has passed on, and perhaps it's time to spare confidentiality in the interests of peace of mind. Your servant as always – Hector Rose.'"*

"This could be useful," John said. "Sounds like there was a long-standing connection."

Robert nodded. "Judging by this, he tended the Macleod households for years, and carried the book between here and Maglavat." He was silent for a moment, searching for the entry that had caught his attention in the first place. "On February 10th 1825, a few months after his marriage to Catherine, Alec took a bad fall from his horse and tore ligaments along his thigh. There were multiple minor cuts and he went down with a fever."

"Sounds nasty."

"I'd say so. It looks as though complications set in early and frustrated the diagnosis. Listen to this:

"'My patient has now developed symptoms suggesting internal damage – a high fever plus swelling in the groin and testicles. Some of the cuts are weeping pus. Yesterday, I felt a sharp protrusion in the centre of an angry, almost purple welt near the groin and with tweezers, was able to extract a long, fine splinter of sheep bone with a jag at the end, which caused dreadful pain and tearing during removal. Since then, he has complained of severe, stabbing pains. In the evening, I prescribed a sleeping draught for the Lady Catherine, who is quite beside herself with anxiety.'"

Robert flicked the page of the notebook, its thick leaves covered with dense black writing, a large and florid hand that was legible and gave eloquent expression to its author's thoughts. He read ahead for a moment, absorbed.

"Good lord," he muttered after a moment. "The good physician is not very happy on this page." He read again:

"'It seems my careful explanations to the Lady Catherine regarding her husband's condition have been in vain. While I was away tending Ruaraidh in Maglavat, the lady took it upon herself to call on the services of a local healer.'"

John laid aside his own document, a terse letter from a livestock dealer on the mainland addressed to Alasdair. "I've been reading about these people," he said, amused. "Spey wives were still in great demand, although I would have thought their appeal lay more with the lower classes than the educated aristocracy."

"I think Catherine panicked," Robert said. "Her husband was suffering, the physician didn't seem to be doing much – perhaps one of the servants had suggested it to make her think she was doing something useful." He sighed and made to close the tantalising notebook. "I really shouldn't be doing this," he said with a wry smile. "This is a big enough job as it is, without the pair of us getting side-tracked by every single item we pick up."

"No – you'll have to go on," John said. "What remedy did the old healer suggest?"

Robert gave in, none too reluctantly, and opened the book again.

"*I have come across this woman on several occasions. While her remedies are in the main innocuous and her potions do very little harm whilst not doing a great deal of good either, on this occasion I could well have done without her interference. I may now be forced to watch a further decline in Alec's condition thanks to her ill-judged use of blowing.*'"

"*Blowing*?" John interrupted him. "What was she thinking?"

"I've never heard of it before," Robert said.

"It was an old Highland trick they used to treat swellings," John explained. "A hollowed-out sheep or cow horn, with a small hole made in the pointed end. A ballan, they called it. The healer placed the large end over the affected area and sucked hard through the hole to create a vacuum. It was supposed to draw off any liquid inside the swelling. Some people swore by it."

"Sounds ghastly," Robert said. "Just listen to the physician's reaction:

"*I returned from Maglavat following a most disagreeable consultation with Ruaraidh. I found the Lady Catherine in some distress and went directly to Alec's chamber, where I found him in such acute pain I had to give him morphia. The foolish woman had used the ballan directly on the testicles. They are now so distended, Alec can barely gain any respite from the pain; it's a miracle he did not go into shock and die.*'"

"I don't suppose there was much they could have done in those days anyway," John said. "But blowing on already infected glands could have done real damage."

Robert was still reading. "A few days later, he has a roaring fever and delirium, and the doctor diagnoses

247

septicaemia. On the night of February 22nd, the family sits up all night and a minister comes to give the last rites. Catherine has to be sedated and Willie Macleod is rewriting his will."

"Poor Catherine wasn't much of a tower of strength," John commented. "Doesn't seem to be quite his type, somehow. I wonder why he chose her?"

"He didn't," Robert said. "Remember the documents of transference? His father pushed him into the match for political reasons. The Macdonald bridal dowry included livestock and grazing that gave the Macleods control over extensive machair land to the north of Uishall. The Macleods used infertility as an excuse to annul the marriage, but it was probably more driven by the fact that they weren't very happy."

"Ruaraidh was already married with two sons," John pointed out. "The family bloodline was secure."

"He was also a bad lot. The laird feared all the family's wealth would be lost if it was handed to him. Alec dying must have given him serious cause for concern."

"So what happened?"

Robert returned to the notebook. "'*Alec's fever broke at lunchtime today,*' the physician writes on February 23rd. '*Although he was in good spirits within only a few days, it was a month before he was fit to make the journey to Edinburgh for his convalescence.*'"

Robert fell silent a moment then said with sudden animation, "Listen to this. There's an additional note, written a month later:

"'*There is an incident I omitted to record at the time. Entering the castle gates one morning, I was accosted by a crofter girl with striking red hair who begged for news of the laird's son's condition. On being told that he was doing very poorly, she became extremely agitated and pressed a small bag into my hand. It contained a rough chunk of crystal and a bunch of herbs and she urged me to place it beneath his pillow to combat the evil forces that had been set to work against him. She only let go of my arm when she had secured my promise that I would do so. As I turned to go in, she said, "Sir, they put the droch shuil upon him - ask him to forgive them," before running away down the track.*'"

"That must have been Janet," John said. "The family had cursed him with the Evil Eye. Did the good doctor do as he was asked?"

Robert turned the page. "Here we are:

"'I must confess that Alec's condition was so desperate that night, I took the herbs and crystal from the bag and slipped them under his pillow when the family was at supper. I had nothing left but prayer in my medical arsenal and felt that anything was worth a try. I'm sure the charms had no bearing at all on Alec's condition, but it was nevertheless the next day that his fever broke and he was out of danger.'"

John whistled. "Ah, you see, the old ways still gave even the medical professionals pause for thought." He turned the story over in his mind for a moment, then said wryly, "It would be useful to know if it was the same spey wife in all three instances, and how many ways she was prepared to divide her loyalties and her charms for the sake of making a living. Poor Alec, caught between the conflicting concerns of his neurotic wife, a superstitious crofting maid who loved him from afar, and a family with a grudge. It's amazing he survived at all."

AUGUST
II

Felix stood in the kitchen at Maglavat, a soothing glass of port in his hand, and watched the sun set royally on the flat calm of the sea. He badly needed to see something serene. It was Saturday night, Roy was rushed off his feet in Manchester and couldn't talk until later, and it had been a day full of tension and unpleasantness.

They had finally made it; the original trip had been cancelled following a lavishly apologetic telephone call from the Laird himself. Natasha, mollified by his charming manners and excessively complimentary remarks about her music, accepted an invitation at a later date, when Maglavat was quiet; she could stay in the main suite, and really appreciate the atmosphere of the castle.

And at last, the later date had arrived and they were here. Natasha was finishing dinner; the food was excellent, so to compensate for the lack of things to complain about, she had run the staff ragged with a range of complicated requests. Iced water with twists of lime *and* lemon, an extra heater for her room, a blind to fill the minuscule gap between the curtains when they were pulled and didn't *quite* close, help with turning the tap on the bath which really was *too* stiff for her delicate wrists, and so on. Clearly, thought Felix with a mixture of exasperation and amusement, none of them had seen the considerable muscle she used on stage to wield an electric guitar. She carried on, alternating between a courtesy to the staff so false it set Felix's teeth on edge to hear it, and petulant irritation if one of them dared to suggest that nothing could be done about whatever problem she had so assiduously identified.

Having made her point – that she was fabulously rich and deserved to be taken seriously – Natasha was now busy charming the socks off her host. Henry Towers, current bachelor Laird of Maglavat, seemed to be rather taken with her. She was asking questions about the property, telling them about her plans for a recording studio, and hinting at the fact that once Maglavat was hers, she could work wonders for the island economy. As one of the guests was a notable at the main development agency in town, this was heart-warming conversational fare and everybody was lapping it up with relish.

Felix had excused himself early, having already arranged with Henry to drive the rest of the coast road first thing in the morning, while the guests were breakfasting.

"Do you want a top-up?" a voice asked him, and he turned reluctantly away from the window. Roger the chef, portly, smiling and red in the face from the evening's work, was standing beside him, bottle poised for pouring.

Felix hesitated, then gave in. The port was very good.

"She must be murder to work with," Roger said, and went back to laying out the grilling trays for breakfast. Felix watched him arranging proper butcher's sausages and felt his loyalty to Natasha begin to cave in. She had tried to insist that meat was to be banned from the kitchen during her visit, but Henry, though affable and polite, would have none of it. If Natasha would like to explain her position to his hungry staff and try to persuade them that anything less than a cooked breakfast was going to be the order of the day, she was welcome. The chef looked up, saw the hunger in Felix's face.

"I thought you were a vegetarian," he said.

Felix grinned with less shame and more wickedness than he wanted to feel. "So does Natasha," he said, thinking at the same time what an idiot he was to confess his most important secret to a complete stranger. "If she knew otherwise, I'd be out of a job."

Roger laughed. "I tried it once, for a girlfriend. I lasted a week. I was foul-tempered, tired all the time and she wasn't worth it. I gave her the push, walked into the nearest restaurant, and ordered a T-bone steak. It was the most liberating night of my life. I can still taste it now."

"I really admired her before I started working for her," Felix sighed. "I said whatever it took to get the job. But it's hard work sometimes, I'll tell you."

"The staff eat after the guests, at nine thirty," Roger said blandly, cutting thick slices of black pudding and laying them out on a baking tray. His grin was particularly devilish when he saw Felix, helpless in the face of raw temptation. "Come on. You know you want to. There's always plenty. As long as you don't go back on duty stinking of bacon."

Felix smiled. "Cheers." He felt a sudden thrill at the thought of his first taste of forbidden food in months. He looked back out of the window, but the mood was broken now. There were all sorts of things happening inside him, not just to do with meat. Something devastating had taken place at the airport and he knew it was over between him and Natasha. She had been no worse than usual, but somehow he had seen it – her spoilt nature, her disdainful treatment of people she considered beneath her, which was practically everybody, the thin supports holding her together on the outside, while her fear of practically everything ate her alive from the inside. He had always understood this before and pitied her, but today he had seen her for what she was, and had rejected her. He felt as if he had just fallen out of love.

"I think it's going to be a long night," he said, sipping at the port for comfort. "If Natasha's still awake at this hour, it means she doesn't want to go to bed."

"Enjoying the attention, eh?"

"You could say that," Felix said, and then fell silent. In a way, that's what it was. Natasha wanted to keep the guests hanging on her every word because she didn't want them to leave and breach the shield she had built from them during the evening. Sometimes it happened this way. He could hear it in her voice. Natasha didn't want to go to bed tonight because she feared the dark and being alone in a strange place.

He had thought, when she had been shown to her room, that this time, it might be all right. The view over the rocky bay to the distant mountains, the four-poster bed, the thick carpet that felt like velvet under their feet. But that was before the weird housekeeper, Morag, had started talking about ghosts.

"This was the Lady Margaret's chamber," she had begun, bustling about the room, her short, heavy frame full of robust energy as she heaved in suitcases, pulled back curtains and checked everything was in order. "She was the Laird's wife way back in the mid-nineteenth century, a sparkling, healthy young woman whose health went right downhill once she was married. Quite a beauty in her day, always out riding and walking. You can see it for yourself – that's her portrait, hanging on the stairs. A gentle soul, too, never harmed a living thing all her life."

Felix saw the way Natasha responded to this information, automatically drawing a favourable comparison. His smile was brief before his mood crashed as the housekeeper went on,

"It was a tragedy when she passed away. The Laird – well, he was so sick himself with syphilis he barely even noticed. And he had made her a victim of his own wicked excesses. Through there – the room that you'll be in, Mr Felix, that was where the physician slept when she was needing care. She died in this very bed."

Natasha blanched.

"I'm sure they've changed the mattresses since then," Felix said.

But this was not the half of it. Natasha might conceivably have coped with sleeping in the deathbed of someone so close to her own heart, but the next part of the engaging story ruined any such hope.

"My great-great-grandmother was born in the village in 1840," Morag went on. "Her Aunt Annie used to be a servant girl here in the castle. Annie died of syphilis in 1837, the same year as the Lady Margaret and the Lady Iona of Uishall. The laird raped her when she was just fourteen. He raped most of the maidservants in the castle – a monster of a man, Ruaraidh Macleod was."

"Really?" Felix said with genuine interest. "So servants really were at the mercy of their employers in those days. You don't realise how much until you hear stories like that. Did your great-great-grandmother escape the same fate?"

"Oh aye. Ruaraidh was dead before she was born, not two years after he put his own wife in the ground. And not before he'd all but ruined his poor brother. Alec – he lived over at Uishall – was fond of Margaret and tried to protect her, but there wasn't much he could do. She died a terrible death, raving and poisoned."

Natasha shuddered. "Poor woman," she said, and the housekeeper nodded.

"She still comes back here," Morag said, looking vaguely and disconcertingly dreamy. Natasha stared at her. "Many's the time we've seen her, standing at the window, looking out over the sea. She might watch over you, Miss Tang, if she's a mind to. She sits at the end of the bed and watches you while you sleep. She has a fancy for folks in trouble. I think she wants to look after people the way her husband never looked after her."

"I'm not troubled," Natasha said.

The housekeeper nodded. "The Lady Margaret will find you if you are," she said. "Oh don't you worry, it's not at all frightening. She's a kindly soul."

"Oh, how nice," Natasha had said faintly, and now Felix, swallowing the last of the fine port in Maglavat's shiny kitchen, thought with dread of the coming night. He bade Roger goodnight, climbed the staircase to the room that adjoined the Lady Margaret's, and settled down to wait for the screams.

III

So this is the wonderful Natasha Tang, Hugh thought with fascination the next night, when Maglavat had decided to pay court to its ancient neighbour and invite the visiting owners. The laird of Maglavat, Henry Towers, was as fashionably profligate as his distant predecessor Ruaraidh Macleod, though rather kinder of heart and not prey to disease. He had made a mischievous point of inviting over his hunting neighbours on the grounds that it would make sense for Natasha to meet the people who managed Uishall in advance of making her decision to purchase. When Natasha protested that she had no wish to meet the barbarian hordes, he tartly observed that when she was the owner of Maglavat, she could have whoever she wished to dinner, but as she was merely an interested prospective buyer, that privilege still accorded to him. She was so astounded at being spoken to like that, she simply nodded her agreement.

"Rather bizarre of him, don't you think?" Robert had said mildly as he and Hugh drove over the mountains through the rich gold and green haze of early evening. "I thought he was trying to sell the place. Natasha Tang's probably the most likely candidate he's had ever since it went on the market. I'd have tried to dig up a few vegetarians. Make her feel at home."

"It's not that easy, laying your hands on a few obliging vegetarians at short notice," Hugh said, laughing. "Well, Henry's kept things ticking over, but he's obviously not a hunting man. He's only been there – what? A couple of years? You have to really love a place like Maglavat to constantly lose money on it."

"Henry told me he'd worked out that he's not cut out for the place," Robert said. "I don't know him all that well, but the firm does his accounts. He comes over to Uishall every so often when Dad's up – he and Henry's father go way back."

"Maybe someone with a bit of passion will pick it up," Hugh said. "Is the community going to bid?"

"It's looking like it. Henry's trying to split it – get the community to buy the land, so he can sell the house and sporting rights independently."

"But the house and sport are the two components that earn the money," Hugh said in surprise. "Doesn't the community want to generate income from their investment?"

Robert cast a dry look at him. "From what I can gather, the community wants the nationalist thrill of reclaiming their land, but it depends whether they've got the smarts to make it work. Maglavat's beautiful, but at the end of the day, it's a pile of rock and heather. As I understand it, the community can buy it with help from the Scottish Executive, it will cost a fortune, then they can claim development grants on it for as long as they please, and hopefully create some sort of viable strategy. It'll be left to the owners of the house to employ gamekeepers if they want to keep the wild populations viable. It's risky, you know, for Maglavat, if this is the route they take."

"Natasha Tang would buy it as a single entity," Hugh said.

"Well, yes she would, but to then not manage the resource is tantamount to destroying it."

"I'll be counting on you to keep your temper," Hugh said. "If what Freya says is true, and she's going to try to ban hunting on it, I'm probably going to have to be held down."

Robert smiled indulgently at his younger brother, then said, "Almost forgot – Henry's got someone else staying this week who might be worth talking to."

"Who's that, then?"

"Peregrine Thornfield – a valuer from Sotton & Chambers. Henry's having the contents valued for insurance purposes – thought this chap might turn up something that would incentivise a buyer."

Natasha seemed nervous in the company of meat eaters, as if she expected them to turn their sharpened carving knives onto her. But after a few glasses of claret, she was beginning to provoke the company into a debate about killing for pleasure. Beside her, Felix, who had quizzed Hugh and Robert eagerly before dinner about how the estate system worked, looked stressed, as if he was anticipating trouble.

Hugh watched and listened as Natasha argued her case. He looked out of the window, across the wild hills, and tried to imagine Natasha, with her urban upbringing and magazine psychology, in charge of a place she didn't understand. She wouldn't have it that the hunters, too, loved nature, but with their eyes open rather than shut. Whatever was the world coming to, he thought, then sighed. The world was coming to Natasha, and people like her, who couldn't accept death as part of the natural order of life, and wanted everything to be neat and tidy in the garden.

He tried to keep his mind on the debate gathering momentum over the table, but found all he could think about was the fascinating idea of Trevor in bed with Natasha. How on earth had he kept his passion for the shotgun secret? What had been the attraction? He glanced across at Robert, who was better than he was at suffering someone he clearly thought to be a fool. He could tell that Robert wasn't paying much attention to the conversation either – Natasha had been holding the floor for quarter of an hour now, and there was no point trying to contribute until she paused for breath. To anyone else at the table, Robert looked to be entirely entranced by the verbal grace of the woman speaking, but Hugh knew he had switched off and was wrestling with a more interesting problem.

The boxes of papers were slowly giving up their secrets about the past, but one glaring omission had emerged that was perplexing him. John had come across a castle inventory dated 1830, but the meticulous listings, which recorded everything from the velvet curtains to the candlesticks, from the paintings to the teaspoons, did not include the Italian cabinet, the fourteenth-century piece in the dining room that had held so emotive a place in the heart of the Uishall Clan Macleod.

"There must be some pages missing," Hugh had said, when Robert told him of the absent ugly-beautiful monster.

"It's a bound copy," Robert said, shaking his head, "and the pagination is intact and consecutive." There was a pause. "I can't understand it. The single most valuable piece in the castle, and it's not there."

"That's probably why," Hugh said. "Alec probably decided not to advertise it. A thing like that would attract a lot of jealousy – and from what you've said, he wasn't exactly popular to start with, was he? It would be a real coup, carrying off something so precious to the clan."

You couldn't just carry off a thing like that in a raid," Robert said, amused. "You'd have to drug the entire household for a day just to get it out of the dining room." He thought for a moment. "Maybe it's been catalogued somewhere else."

"Maybe it wasn't there at the time of the inventory," Hugh said. "What if it was away being polished or something, or needed a repair? And they didn't include it because it was out of the house?"

The problem was tormenting Robert so much that he had cornered Peregrine Thornfield over pre-dinner drinks and explained it. A tall, fleshy, rather serious-looking man with silver-framed spectacles, kindly grey eyes and a slightly flushed face, he listened intently, asked some questions, and then suggested he drive over one afternoon when he had finished at Maglavat. The upshot was that after hastily conferring with Hugh, Robert had booked Peregrine Thornfield in to value the contents of Uishall and look over the 1830 inventory.

"I think you'd find our hunting friends here would argue that man is also an animal, and it is therefore not an anachronism that he would choose to hunt."

Robert and Hugh snapped to attention. Henry was speaking, which meant Natasha had finally decided to let someone else in on the conversation.

"*I* don't choose to hunt," Natasha said. "I have exercised my powers of choice."

"So have I," Hugh said testily.

"No, no, you misunderstand me," Natasha patronised him. "Animals don't have the privilege of intelligence, they only have instincts. The human responsibility is to exercise the intelligence of the species in order to suppress the instinct."

"You can't suppress instincts," Robert said. "That amounts to control, which you profess to oppose."

"There is no control on any of my land," Natasha said. "Everything is free to live in harmony, without interference."

Hugh leaned forward. "You're assuming that control of the land is something recent that can easily be reversed," he said. "But people have been managing the British landscape for thousands of years. It's impossible to just hand it back over to Nature and not suffer the consequences."

Felix shifted in his chair. It seemed as if he was holding his breath as he listened. Natasha had not often met landowners, and was not used to hearing the other side of the argument. She held up well in media situations, where she made statements and avoided the indignity of debate with people she considered her spiritual inferiors. But the Bartlett brothers were not about to be fobbed off with the arguments of someone who rarely stepped outside the urban environment. Felix reached for the wine bottle and filled his glass. He had listened intently to the discussion but had so far not contributed to it, and Natasha was beginning to notice his lack of moral support. When the subject of instinct had come up, something vicious and sudden had risen in his heart, but he had managed to fight down the dizzying urge to speak. *If I'm not brave enough*, he thought, *let someone else do it. Let someone else show her that buying Maglavat would be a massively destructive act, the inland equivalent of an offshore oil-spill.*

Before breakfast, he had driven with Henry to the end of the road, a wildly dramatic single-track strip that seemed so temporary, it looked as if it had been hastily rolled out across the ungovernable terrain like a carpet. Twists and turns, plunges and rises, stags grazing right by the road at one point, the hills dreamy, blue and purple in the hot haze of high summer light. Felix had felt his throat tighten as he gazed out of the windows. Natasha was still asleep after a restless – though mercifully ghost-free – night, and not interested in seeing what she might be buying. By the time Henry pulled up next to the white sand beach, Felix was in danger of bursting into tears, so overwhelmed was he by what surrounded him. The two men were silent as they looked out across the sea.

"It's funny," Henry had said after several minutes. "The people who love this place the most are the ones who don't have the money to buy it, and aren't interested in trying to change it. And that's much better than the alternative."

Felix turned to him in surprise. Until now, Henry had not struck him as an emotional man, and he thought at first he was

257

making fun of him. Henry had been charming to Natasha, but took no nonsense from her, either, and if he was hoping to sell Maglavat, he seemed anxious it should go to someone who knew what they were letting themselves in for. Natasha, who played so many roles in her dealings with people that it was becoming difficult to tell where the real person had got to, seemed to be attracted to him, and Henry had certainly been flirting with her at dinner the previous evening.

"You've fallen," Henry said. "It happened to me. I liked the place so much, I bought it," he mimicked. "But then I couldn't do anything with it. And do you know what? I've realised that that's the point."

"What is?"

"You *can't* do anything with it," Henry said. "Natasha has no connection to the place at all, as far as I can see. She only wants it so she can change it. But she'll never do it." He sighed. "I love it, and I'll always come back to it, but I can't do anything to make it pay. It's been like being married to a woman with expensive tastes I can't afford."

And then there had been the drive back to the castle, and breakfast. Felix was still hugging to himself the delight of the breakfast he had eaten that morning with the castle staff. The bacon, moist and crisp at the same time, sizzling under the grill, seduced him like a long-lost lover. Other ex-vegetarians had told him how their principles had been felled by bacon sandwiches, and now he joined them. The black pudding was rich and crisp under his knife, melting in his mouth like a French kiss. The sausages, fragrant with spices and black pepper and the sweetness of meat and herbs, yielded their flavours as he chewed. Felix felt as if he had been invited to an orgy with all his favourite partners. He was unutterably grateful to all the pigs that had been sacrificed so he could taste such profound, exquisite rapture. Roger fried him three eggs. He gave him warm butteries and a ton of butter made in the kitchen the previous day. There wasn't a single organic lettuce leaf in sight, not a cherry tomato or shred of basil or grilled pepper to be found. There was no olive oil, only lard. He sinned as only a repressed man can sin – greedily, hungrily, selfishly, hedonistically, with no thought of ever stopping. The staff watched politely at first, then with growing amazement, at the amount he put away. He ate with such voracious, naked, carnal pleasure that they began to wonder if they were missing something.

Afterwards, Felix had sat on the front wall of the castle and rang Roy, who thought he'd been taking drugs.

"It's over, Roy," he said. "I don't know how I'm going to do it, but it's over."

"Now listen," Roy had said, briefly afraid of his reckless tone of voice. "You can't make decisions like this on the basis of a plate of bacon and black pudding. For God's sakes, calm down first and think about what you're doing. She'll probably throw you off the battlements."

"I don't care," Felix shouted, still high on animal fat. "I mean it, Roy. I don't care."

Roy laughed. "What's it like there?"

"It's wonderful," Felix said, staring out over the sea, flat calm under a painfully blue sky. His voice was suddenly quiet, serious. He missed Roy, wanted him here at his side, sharing it. Five hundred miles away, Roy felt it. "I'm coming back for you," Felix said. "If you're serious, I'll find somewhere for us."

There was a short silence.

"Do it," Roy said.

Felix had still not come down from that giddying phone call. He had been on edge all day, his mind racing. Now, he sat at the dinner table listening to the mood turning to acrimony, and waited for his chance with terrible dread.

"My foxes don't kill other people's chickens because they don't need to," Natasha was saying. "Fostering the land can be done."

"Don't foxes kill for pleasure?" Henry said. "And I know they do well on the land in Kent and Norfolk, because there are massive bird populations – and that, I'm afraid, is down to the estates getting it wrong and vastly overstocking for the shoots. You can't get away from that – you can't drive two hundred yards in Norfolk without encountering game bird corpses – the carnage is dreadful, never mind from the guns, and it's because of wrongly-engineered populations."

Natasha beamed at him, but Hugh brushed the point aside.

"The foxes on your land scavenge," Hugh said, and Robert shook his head in dismay. "There are too many of them because there is no control, so there is not enough food for them. The consequence of that is that they are diseased and starving. Those are not options most living things would choose. And it's a cruel thing to force on creatures that have no choice."

"It's better than killing," Natasha said. "Anything's better than killing."

"Not always," Hugh said. "Controlling populations means the survivors live healthy lives with abundant food and strong progeny."

"Wild animals deserve to live out their lives and die a natural death –"

"Ah," Hugh said, his increasing anger becoming harder and harder to conceal. "The romantic ideal of Nature's creatures living a full life span. Do you know what that means in practical terms?"

"I'm sure you're going to tell me," Natasha said.

"Yes I am. When animals in the wild get old, they can't find food for themselves. Some of them get arthritis, like humans, or go blind, or stiffen up and can't escape predators so well. A trout that can't see insects in the water starves. A fish caught by an angler never suffers a drawn-out death."

"You're making it sound," Natasha said, "as if every hunter in the land goes out with only noble intentions and has no interest at all in killing, just the conservation."

"That's a fair point," Robert said. "I think the kind of hunter who likes to rack up scores and kill indiscriminately is something of a dying breed. But I'd be a liar if I said that there was no sense of exhilaration accompanying a successful kill that is cleanly done and has brought no suffering to the quarry." He stopped, trying to articulate the sentiment. "It's something you've worked for, it's a contest you've fought and won. It's quite difficult to describe if you've never done it."

"That's something I'll never understand, however much you dress it up," Natasha said. "Taking pleasure in killing." It sounded as if she was about to burst into tears, and for a moment there was a silence.

"It's not pleasure," Hugh said, frowning. "It's not the kill that gives the pleasure. That would make it sadistic, which it isn't. It's the pursuit that gives the satisfaction, and if you like, the thrill." He stopped, grinding to the same unhelpful conclusion as his brother. It wasn't something that could easily be conveyed, especially to someone who had made up her mind that hunting could not be sanctioned on any grounds at all.

"Well now, how about opening the port?" Henry said smoothly, standing up and dropping his napkin onto his plate. "Tempers seem to be running a little high."

Robert, who was sitting next to him, caught his eye with an ironic smile. "You knew they would," he said in a low voice. "That's why you invited us."

Henry threw up his hands. "I confess," he said, grinning. "Like to see what people are made of. Like to see if they can keep their heads in an argument."

Natasha looked outraged. "This isn't a *game*," she said. "The killing of innocent creatures isn't something to *joke* about."

Henry raised his eyes. "The one I'm fond of is the carrots," he said. "Something about vegetarians having to kill six thousand small furry creatures for every acre of carrots they plant. But it's all right, as far as the vegetarians are concerned, because we don't have to look at all the corpses." He looked at Robert with a Machiavellian leer. "Does that sound about right?"

Robert gave him a warning glance, then said kindly to Natasha, "I think what Henry is trying to say – badly – is that humans and animals have always had to compete for space to find food. However we go about the business of staying alive, other creatures suffer. There's no such thing as being able to lead a blameless life."

"We eat what we kill," Hugh said. "So it's not wasted."

"I'm sure that would be a great comfort to whatever comes within range of your hooks and guns," Natasha said.

"What about Catholics?" Henry said, the bottle of port poised in his hand.

Everyone turned to look at him.

"*What*?" Hugh said.

"I mean – it illustrates the principle perfectly," Henry went on cheerfully. "There are far too many Catholics. Most of them are poor and live in the most dreadfully appalling conditions and have more children than they can afford to feed. So there are children living on the streets, people living on rubbish dumps, prostitution, drugs and robbery are rife – all the social diseases people like you and me are protected from. If we extend the analogy, their landlord – the Pope, are you with me? – turns a blind eye because he thinks his job is to populate the world with Catholics. Whether or not they're in good condition is irrelevant to him, as long as he's got lots of them. Now, our principles don't allow us to cull them, which would be the humane thing to do, and their landlord won't allow them the means to help themselves – birth control – so they have to put up with it. Apply the same logic to animals living on a country estate, and being put out of their misery if they're sick or hungry or living in overcrowded conditions is actually a better deal."

There was a dangerous silence. Natasha actually looked stunned by the low level that had descended over the conversation, sensing that her arguments were in danger of not only being derailed but of being lost to an unfamiliar logic. She was trembling, convinced that Henry, after all his kind attentiveness, was trying to humiliate her. She didn't know that Henry's idea of a successful evening was to simply stir controversy, and then set himself the task of making everything all right again.

"Henry, that's outrageous," Robert said. "We can't possibly have a serious conversation about this if you're going to go off at ludicrous tangents."

Henry roared with laughter. "Robert, how can you possibly have a sensible conversation about this anyway?" he said. "Any of you? Miss Tang is never going to agree with you, and you are never going to agree with her." He turned to his guest, and his eyes were suddenly gentle and serious. "Miss Tang, are you truly serious about buying Maglavat?"

"I wouldn't be here if I wasn't."

"Why? Because you love it, or just because you can?" Henry leaned forward. "My dear, you will wage war against Nature here and fail. The land is too savage, too independent. You can't change it, and neither can the politicians who want to bend it to their will."

"You just don't want things to change," Natasha said violently.

Henry shook his head. "It's not that," he said. "I know you think me irreverent and doubtless irresponsible, but the only thing that works here appears to be sport. I don't say that that's the only thing that ever *will* work, but I am saying nobody has yet come up with something better. That's why I've been defeated. There is no other way to generate income from this land on the scale that the estate manages. It is a sustainable proposition. I am not a sporting man, so this is not a place where I can be happy."

Henry reached across the table and took Natasha's hand, and Felix stared in disbelief at the way she accepted the intimacy. "You will not be happy here, either, which is why I don't want you to buy it. Maglavat works only as what it is. A lot of people are going to waste a lot of time and money before they come to the same conclusion. I can afford to wait a little longer for a buyer who isn't going to come here deluding him or herself about what will and won't work. Maglavat ain't broke, although I soon will be, so there's no point in anyone trying to fix it."

"Look," Hugh said. "Henry's right. You can't come to Maglavat and not cull the deer, for example. Their territorial instincts mean you can't just relocate them when they get hungry. If you don't cull, they over breed and then they starve and then we're back with the situation you've engineered on the lands you own in England. And I'm not prepared to see that happen here."

"So if I come here, you'll fight me?" Natasha said.

"I won't have to," Hugh said. "The land will fight you." He smiled ruefully. "And I'm afraid the land will win. It always does."

Natasha looked down. Henry was still holding her hand. The wine, the candlelight, the unexpected turn in the conversation had conspired to confuse her. It seemed that ever since they'd arrived, Maglavat had worked some odd spell on them. The place was beautiful, she could imagine herself swanning around the castle with no problem at all, but yes, there was something untamed about the land that she feared. She didn't trust their arguments, but thanks to Henry and his unsavoury guests, she was beginning to feel that she might be able to abandon her grand gesture and still save face.

She raised her head. Felix had been acting strangely, being short with her, not responding to her when she tried to find out what was wrong. She was suddenly tired and cross and felt vulnerable, too. She moved her hand away.

She turned to Felix. "You're not being very helpful here," she said. "I keep animals myself. It's not as if I don't know how to take care of them."

Suddenly, Felix's heart was beating wildly again. It was his second chance. If he blew it this time, there wouldn't be a third. Still seated at the candlelit table in Maglavat's magnificent first-floor dining room, he scented freedom.

"Natasha keeps cats," he said quietly.

"Well, well," Henry said. "Quite the conservationist. What sort of cats?"

"Persians. Pure-bred. White." Felix said. He looked very odd. "Three of them."

"Felix?" Natasha said, frightened of the way he was looking at her. "What's wrong?"

"Do they hunt?" Hugh asked.

263

Natasha shook her head. "I keep them inside in the London flat," she said. "They're well-fed and they don't need to hunt."

"But hunting is a fundamental instinct for a cat," Hugh said. "Besides, they've enjoyed a centuries-old partnership with humans. They get the thrill of the hunt, the humans keep the mice out of the larder."

"What's their temperament like?" Robert asked.

Natasha laughed nervously. "Well, you know pedigrees," she said lightly. "Quite irritable sometimes, a bit touchy and neurotic –"

"Unpredictable?" Hugh asked. "Bite people, scratch them?"

"They don't scratch," Felix said suddenly, looking at Hugh. "Ask her why."

Natasha stared at him, as the scale of his treachery began to dawn on her. He felt her eyes burning into the back of his head and he turned and faced her again. His whole body was flooded with adrenaline and he felt drunk with the rush of it.

That was the moment. The moment he lost Natasha's trust, the moment he lost his job, the moment he felt as though he was flying and falling at the same time.

Hugh was looking at Natasha. "Are you claiming that you've trained them out of their instinct to scratch?" he asked curiously. "How on earth –"

Natasha shook her head, paralysed. She was still staring at Felix, and – almost unbelievably – he was staring back.

"She has their claws pulled," he said, his voice a perfidious whisper. "It keeps the furniture nice."

Much later, Natasha lay awake in the shadowy light of the first-floor bedroom. She would probably get no sleep at all tonight and it was already light outside. She turned her head to look at the clock. It was four-thirty and she was no longer angry, no longer upset. She had come to her room in a state of shock, then exploded into a terrible temper and spent an hour trying to come up with a chastisement vindictive enough to punish Felix for what he'd done to her. And then things had changed and the night had changed into something she had been completely unprepared for, and now she was simply exhausted, all passion spent, as if she had been through a metamorphosis.

Henry had spent the rest of the evening with her, having seen how hurt she was by Felix's sudden and unwarranted betrayal. It was still a puzzle to her that she hadn't been able to switch off the fact that she liked Henry and was attracted to him, despite his playful and disrespectful attitudes.

Henry, who had hurt her feelings at dinner, who couldn't be more opposed to her views and beliefs, had thoroughly upset things. He was the first person who had stood up to her and made her think. He hadn't tried to belittle her; he had talked about what he thought. Most people who disagreed with her called her stupid and short-sighted, another idiot rock star with millions, a guilt complex and the notion that because she was famous and privileged, she had a right to change the world. But it hadn't taken Henry to expose that vulnerable side of the way she lived her life. It had taken Maglavat.

"Henry?" she had asked him, sometime during the second glass of brandy. "Should I buy Maglavat?"

"No," he said, smiling. "You should concentrate on what you're good at."

"You're patronising me."

"Yes I am," he said easily. "Because you don't need to be told. You can't change the world all on your own." He looked critically at her. "And parts of it are very beautiful, just as they are. Perhaps you should focus on those from time to time."

Now, she turned restlessly in bed, trying to work out what she should do next, if Felix would apologise, whether or not she should keep him. And Henry. She was still trying to work out Henry. Henry, who was infuriating and played the same games she did, piercing her with his humorous, intelligent eyes, but not letting her see anything of him that was valuable or truthful. Henry, who had that instinct for performance, who was handsome and who she wanted, but couldn't allow herself to want on account of his incorrigible personality. She closed her eyes, hit the mattress in her frustration. She wished she hadn't sent him away. But she had been right to. She wished they had kissed. She wished she had turned off all her principles and taken him to bed. Oh, God she wished –

"Are you all right, my dear?"

"I'm tired."

"It's time to sleep now. Everything will seem different in the morning."

Natasha opened her eyes. For a moment, she felt strange, not recognising the unfamiliar space. The room seemed to be full of shadows, one in particular at the foot of the bed, obscuring the dim light nudging at the curtains. Natasha tried to move her foot, and found it was trapped, as if someone was sitting on it. She realised her heart was beating very fast and her breathing was shallow. She tried to sit up, but her body was rigid from head to foot, and a swift, violent sensation like an electrical current was sweeping through her. It passed and she gasped, still paralysed, eyes wide, staring into the room.

"If you follow sadness, all you find is anger," the voice said. "Don't keep turning away from the happiness in your life." A gentle voice, and Natasha felt the weight on the end of the bed lift suddenly. She sat up. There was a woman, how much of her Natasha could see and how much of her she was imagining was open to question, but she seemed to have a beautiful, kindly face with eyes that looked both wise and suffering. Her skin was very pale. Her dress was long and her hands were folded over each other at the waist. Natasha's heart was hammering so loudly she thought she would faint.

Her body suddenly seemed to relax, and she lunged for the light. The figure faded with leisurely decorum.

It wasn't until much later that morning that Natasha found Henry and described what had happened to her during the night. He listened attentively and seemed hugely entertained.

"So she stood by you –"

"No – no, I felt someone sitting on the bed. I thought I saw a shadow –"

266

Henry looked positively delighted. "A real supernatural experience," he said. "It sounds like you're one of the privileged few to have had a visit from the Lady Margaret. You'll write about it, I know you will." Seeing her still troubled face, he modified his enthusiasm a little. "Sometimes strange things happen here. But there's nothing to be frightened of. It's just the past getting mixed up with the present."

"The housekeeper said someone might come to me –"

"Oh, well, you shouldn't have taken that at all seriously," Henry said, smiling. "Superstitious housekeepers tell everybody that they're going to get a ghostly visit. It's all part of the Maglavat experience. And Morag does do it very well – she is rather good at spooking people. I should pay her extra for her undeniable talent."

Natasha grinned uneasily. "Have you ever seen her?"

Henry hesitated for a moment, and then nodded. "Quite a while ago, something similar happened to me." He smiled at her aghast reaction. "The Lady Margaret seems to home in on sad cases," he said, and just for a moment, his smile became rueful.

And with those words, Natasha *saw* him, understood that he had tried to make the connection, helped her touch just a little piece of truth. It was a second only, then Henry was talking again.

"Think of her as Maglavat's unpaid social worker. You should be flattered. What did she say to you?"

"She told me –" Natasha stopped suddenly, as if she had only just heard the words. "She told me not to turn away from the happiness in my life."

"Did you understand?"

"I think so."

"She must be a very intelligent ghost," Henry said.

7.
GRALLOCHED
AUGUST

I

On Sunday mornings at Uishall Castle, the only smell permeating the spacious, sunny kitchen is the sweet, smoky fragrance of roasting beef and its traditional Sunday lunch accompaniments.

The guests breakfast late on porridge, boiled eggs and toast. Then, weather permitting, they stroll along the river or read the Saturday papers, this being Sunday, and no fishing allowed, and no Sunday papers delivered to the island until Monday. So the guests linger and idle in and around the castle and wait for the great clock to strike twelve. Then one or two of them might wander down to the kitchen to sniff appreciatively at the roasting joint, choose the wine for lunch and ask about the pudding. They might pause to chat to the cook while she is sorting out the roast potatoes, or making the sauce for the cauliflower cheese, or greasing the patty tins for the Yorkshire puddings.

At one o' clock precisely, the dinner gong sounds and the guests, by this time enjoying aperitifs in the drawing room, come through to the dining room and take their seats. After a pause, the beef appears, borne by one of the girls, resplendent on its oak platter, crusted on the outside, Yorkshire puddings nestling along its flanks. For a party of ten, the number at table this particular weekend, the joint of beef is massive. Sirloin on the bone, fifteen pounds of it, enough for the guests and the staff, and then enough for some splendidly bloody beef sandwiches for Monday's picnic. It is a magnificent beast, the Uishall Castle Sunday joint. When it is carved by the head of the party in the dining room, the long-dead Lairds in the portraits seem to come to life and scent the air, as if they would love to be included in the company gathered expectantly around the great oval table. The Japanese tempered steel blade slices elegantly into the joint and the blood runs – another perfectly judged triumph for Christina, that veteran of the Sunday lunch.

On Sunday morning, the first job for the cook, before breakfast, is to lift the beef from the meat fridge and stand it on the table, in all its raw and naked glory, in its roasting tin, bone-end down. There it rests and comes to room temperature before being sprinkled with Malvern salt and cracked black pepper and reverently placed in the oven at exactly eleven o' clock.

Christina prides herself on her no-nonsense method of cooking the beef. The oven very high, *very* hot indeed for the first ten minutes, then lowered slightly and left. The roasting tin to *just fit* the joint, to preserve as many of the precious juices as possible. The beef comes out at twelve-thirty and the greased trays for the Yorkshire puddings go in. The roast potatoes out and into the hot cupboard. The cauliflower in, coated in its rich Gruyere and mustard sauce, to brown. The petits pois on top, dressed with butter, salt, black pepper and the tiniest sprinkle of sugar. The beef lifted carefully onto its warmed salver, covered loosely with foil and left to rest. The juices from the roasting tin drained into a small saucepan and the tin thoroughly deglazed with stock and red wine. The onions finely sliced and sautéed and bubbled up with the juices, sometimes thickened with a little *beurre manie* to absorb the excess fat. The fresh horseradish grated, with much smarting of the cook's eyes and nose, and infused with cream, lemon juice, sugar, salt and black pepper.

It is the most anticipated meal of the week, that great joint of beef, that *fuck-off* piece of beef as Marie grinningly, and *disrespectfully* describes it.

Which is why it is of especial concern at eight-thirty on this gently sunlit Sunday morning that the joint of beef is nowhere to be seen.

Christina had arrived in the kitchen, eight-fifteen prompt as usual, tied her pinny neatly round her waist and gone to the new meat fridge to pull out the beef. It was impossible to miss a piece of meat that size, or to confuse it with anything else. It could not be the pork fillet lined up for Monday, that will be beaten thin then rolled with slivers of Gorgonzola and baked with basil and tomatoes, or the venison steaks that Marie will braise and serve with chocolate sauce and her own rowanberry and apple jelly. The beef dwarfs both of them. Or would do, if it was there, as it should be, for comparative purposes.

At first, Christina was merely annoyed that the beef was not in its usual place. She tutted self-righteously at Marie's lack of organisation then went to the dairy fridge. It was always a possibility that if pushed for space in the meat fridge, Marie had squashed the monster piece of beef into the only available space and forgotten to tell her. But it wasn't there, either.

Christina checked all the fridges without finding the Sunday joint. Now she began to worry that somehow or other, it had been dumped into one of the freezers by mistake – a scenario that, at this late stage, spelt disaster, since defrosting would take at least twenty-four hours. But the freezers, too, were innocent of all traces of the missing beef.

Worry turned to panic as Christina searched the storeroom, the game larder, all the fridges and freezers – again – and even ran out to the fish store to check the cavernous chest freezer. Her weekly pride and joy was nowhere to be seen. She began to wonder if there had been a mistake on the butcher's order and it had not been delivered – but it would be impossible for even Marie to miss such a glaring omission, and besides, the butcher, well-versed over decades in assembling the order for the lodge, would have queried the omission.

After half an hour, Christina was close to tears and it was only ten minutes before she had to begin cooking the breakfast. She had taken a fierce and competitive pride in her ability to produce the meals and baking required of her on Saturdays and Sundays with terrifying efficiency. When Marie came into the kitchen on Monday morning, all was ship-shape, scrubbed and clean, with a little signature left to remind her of who had done the work – the remains of the apple crumble, spooned neatly into a little dish, which Marie was expected to eat as a sign of respect.

The girls, running about on their morning duties, delivering morning tea and clearing the sitting room of glasses and ashtrays from the night before, could offer no explanations or help. They looked blankly at her when she told them. Was she pulling their legs? What did she mean, the Sunday joint had gone missing?

With five minutes to go, Christina swallowed her pride and went into the staff quarters to knock on Hedda's door. Happily, Hedda was awake and answered readily, although she was careful to screen Christina's view of the interior and protect her from the controversial sight of John sleeping to one side of the double bed.

"Christina?"

"I'm sorry to trouble you, Hedda, but the beef joint is missing. I know it sounds ridiculous, but I've looked everywhere and I can't find it. Has it been put somewhere?" Her breathless voice stopped as she looked into the girl's kind blue eyes with desperate hope.

Hedda looked puzzled then shook her head. "The meat was delivered as normal on Thursday and I put it all away," she said. "The beef was definitely there." She paused. "How very strange. Perhaps you'd better ask Marie."

This was the last thing Christina wanted to do, but she crossed the hall and knocked on Marie's door, while Hedda watched with worried interest.

"Perhaps someone's stolen it," she said, her eyes suddenly bright with mischievous excitement. "Maybe one of the ghillies sneaked in and carried it off to eat at home."

Marie had been out the night before and was not very pleased at being disturbed with what seemed to be a fatuous question. She eyed Christina with irritation, yawned, then said she'd pull on some leggings and see if she could find it. Christina, now actually in tears of frustration, humiliation and mortal dread of having to face the guests with the news that there would be no roast beef that day, went back to the kitchen to put on the porridge and boil the eggs.

The gong had just sounded when Marie came into the kitchen and asked for the full story. She reminded Christina that she would be the one to take the rap if the beef had really gone missing. Christina, contrite and upset, refreshingly desperate to please, talked rapidly about how she had discovered the loss, where she had looked and how she couldn't imagine what had happened. Marie watched her, listening carefully, then relented a little and offered to look in the cavernous storeroom and check all the fridges and freezers to make absolutely sure. There was an outside chance that a member of staff had stolen it, which would be extremely awkward. If she failed to turn it up, there were a couple of chickens in the freezer that could just about be thawed in time in the microwave. In the meantime, she suggested, the practicalities of the situation had to be addressed, and Christina had best get on with preparing the potatoes and making the apple crumble. Marie interfering in her routine and actually giving her instructions completed Christina's misery.

At this point, Hedda appeared in her dressing gown and put on the kettle to boil. She listened sympathetically to Christina's anxious re-telling of the story, apologised for not taking it seriously when Christina had knocked on her door, then said kindly,

"I'll tell you what – did you look right at the bottom of the freezer in the fish store?"

Christina shook her head miserably. She was too short to reach the bottom without running the risk of toppling inside it.

"Come on," Hedda said. "Let's just take a look and make certain it's not there."

They walked outside and across the cobbled yard, Hedda in her slippers, taking the lead. She heaved up the heavy lid and bent over, rummaging through the whole frozen salmon, the bags of langoustine, the lobster and scallops. She eventually emerged, her hands raw with frost, her face a picture of regret.

Christina, numb with confusion, wondering how on earth this beautiful Sunday morning had turned into such a nightmare, went back into the kitchen to find Marie standing at the kitchen table, arms folded, watching the door for her reappearance. In front of her, standing proud in its roasting tin, in all its raw and naked glory, was the Sunday joint. Christina gasped and gaped at Marie in complete bewilderment.

"Where was it?" she said faintly, trembling from head to foot.

Marie shrugged. "Where I found it," she said. "Next time you drag people from their beds on a Sunday morning, make sure it's with good reason, and not because of your own carelessness."

Christina flushed. "But Marie, I looked everywhere –"

"Perhaps the kitchen is haunted by a malevolent ghost," Marie said, and turned to go. "Now if you don't mind I've got some sleep to catch up on. You're lucky I found it in time."

Back in the staff quarters, she found Hedda waiting outside her room. "I'll fill you in later," she said. "Right now both of us have got better things to do." Her workmate grinned and slipped back into bed.

"Christ, where have your hands been?" he said.

"The fish freezer," she said. "So I stink of kippers as well."

"Passion killer," John said with a grin, although his next words confirmed that he had other things on his mind anyway. "I forgot to tell you what I found out last night," he said. "Alec Macleod sustained a severe injury just after he married Catherine, then he nearly died of septicaemia. His testicles swelled up like balloons, and an old spey-wife came along at his wife's request and did blowing on him, which compounded the villainy."

"God," Hedda said. "Poor Alec."

"So – I did a bit of research, and it turns out that when the testicles become infected, they swell, and it's called orchitis, and the heat from the swellings can cause infertility. Alec had infected cuts around his thighs and groin, and that's where he got the septicaemia. I think, as a theory, it stands up."

"What does that mean?"

"It means that Janet's son was born a year or two before he fell ill, and that Alec was almost certainly the father. But after the illness, which is when he discovered he couldn't get either of his wives pregnant, he could have been infertile."

"Would the physician have known that?"

"Not necessarily. They knew about blood poisoning, but once a patient recovered, they only looked at sexual performance. As far as the physician was concerned, if Alec could still get it up and perform, there was no reason why he couldn't impregnate her. And he'd already had a child, of course."

She looked at him, suddenly curious as a new thought occurred to her. "But – he married Janet because –"

"Exactly," he said. "I told you she was clever."

Sunday lunch that day did not go well for the agitated Christina. The roast potatoes were undercooked, the cauliflower overcooked. The Yorkshire puddings did not puff up to their usual self-important glory. The cheese sauce was too thick, and there was a watery residue in the bottom of the gratin dish; the gravy was over-seasoned and the apple crumble caught. Nobody came down from the dining room to thank her afterwards, although one of the girls passed on a discreet message from one of the guests that the beef, though tolerably well cooked, was rather cold. Christina cooked her way through the debacle, hot and flushed, watching the clock as its hands crawled their way around its face, and longed for release.

II

Detective Chief Inspector Duncan Macrae picked up the hand bell in Maglavat's great entrance hall and jangled it vigorously. His eyes swept the walls as he waited, taking in the paintings, mostly non-descript Victorian depictions of ancient Greeks engaged in mild forms of debauchery, Dionysian scenes of parties and drinking, bunches of grapes, flagons of wine, unconsciousness, revelry, groping men and semi-naked women. It didn't seem quite the thing to have hanging on the first walls visitors to the castle would lay eyes on. Duncan raised an eyebrow, looked further along the wall and discovered a copy of Hieronymus Bosch's triptych, *The Garden of Earthly Delights*, which added an unexpectedly sober, judgmental tone. Disappearing in a graceful arc up the stairs was a series of engravings depicting various hunting scenes – deerhounds closing on a stag, a Peregrine falcon swooping down on a fleeing grouse, a fisherman drawing a salmon to the net.

"I've heard it all before," a deep and jovial voice greeted his examination of the interior décor. A tall, elegantly dressed man with a broad grin creasing his handsome features was approaching him, hand outstretched. He nodded at the paintings while he shook Duncan's hand in a firm grip. "I used to think I really ought to get rid of them, or at least move them to somewhere less conspicuous. But when all's said and done, they've been here over a hundred years, ever since Ruaraidh Macleod built the castle. You see this one here?" He pointed to the painting of the Peregrine falcon and grouse. "The hawker in the left corner? That's Ruaraidh. His portrait is hanging in the drawing room, so there's no mistaking him. And here?" He went back to one of the other paintings, indicating a male figure, stocky, with thick, black hair, pressed up against the back of a fleshy woman; he was holding a flagon of wine in one hand and the woman's breast in the other. "See the likeness? That's him, too. It says quite a lot about the man, I always think. I'll say one thing for these paintings – they're damned good icebreakers in these liberal times. Very few people take offence."

Duncan smiled. "I don't know much about the history of the place, and sometimes I think I should," he said. "But it's good to see you again, Henry. It's a long time since we've had cause to talk."

Henry inclined his head and made an educated guess on the reason for Duncan's visit. "Poaching, is it?" he said. "I have to say that takes me by surprise. There are really only a few fools about these days, Murdo MacInnes and his cronies who insist on dragging the past around with them. But nothing new since this drowned chap turned up." He sighed. "It's all just push and shove you know, but I do wish that these fellows would at least get the story right if they're going to pick on the landlords. It's tiresome more than anything." He paused, gazing up absently at a particularly lurid painting of what appeared to be a Victorian gang-bang, with Ruaraidh taking an enthusiastically active role in the proceedings. "I assume that your visit is to do with poaching, and not connected to the fact that Natasha Tang is staying with us."

Duncan sighed. "Despite popular mainland opinion, our local police intelligence does rise above tying messages to seagulls' legs and using semaphore," he said. "But she is, in fact, the reason I'm here."

Henry's eyes opened wide. "Really?" he said. "But how intriguing. Is she engaged in criminal activity –"

Duncan raised his hand. "Henry, you know better than to ask me questions like that," he said. "Is she available?"

Henry scratched his head. "Well," he said doubtfully. "She's in, but she didn't have a very good night. Her PA seems to have done a bunk after the most extraordinary performance at dinner last night, and after she went to bed, she seemed to think she saw a ghost."

"How taxing for her," Duncan said. "So how many flunkeys does she have left?"

"Actually, that would be me," Henry said. "I seem to have taken her on in his absence," he added, looking rather puzzled by the notion, as if he had only just realised it himself. "The two of them arrived together, travelling light. I don't think either of them expected him to leave. I believe they're flying somebody else up to take his place for the journey home. He seemed all right, too."

Natasha did indeed look rather drawn when Duncan was shown into the upstairs sitting room, a room that would be massive in an ordinary house, but looked understated in the context of Maglavat Castle. He looked curiously at her, this woman who was rich beyond belief and just as famous.

She had been extremely disconcerted when Henry told her about Duncan's arrival, had even suggested leaving prematurely. Henry, enthralled by the whole affair, at once dissuaded her.

"Duncan is a very clever man," he said. "If you refuse to see him, or even try to tactfully avoid him, you'll bring out the worst in him." He smiled encouragingly. "Whatever he wants, I can't imagine you know anything that dangerous. He'll be gone in less than an hour, and then I'll make some lunch. Peregrine's working on the second floor, so we won't be disturbed. He's rather intense, you know. But doing a brilliant job. Asked for a plate of sandwiches to be taken up so he wouldn't have to stop."

Natasha was beginning to feel the lack of sleep she had suffered the previous night, so her mood was not quite as compliant and peaceable as it had been in the early hours. It seemed that as soon as she had begun to make important decisions about what directions her life should take from now on, Duncan had turned up to remind her of the past. She thought about being affronted by Henry's slightly pushy agenda, but then decided against it. She really was too exhausted to be cross with him. And a quiet lunch would be soothing after having to meet the Chief Inspector. She was still worrying about how she should play it.

Duncan intimidated her from the moment she set eyes on him, which made her automatically defensive and aggressive. She could always sense if people took no interest in her work or views. Natasha did not figure on Duncan's scale of priorities, except as someone who had something he wanted. She was not in the habit of giving things to people who only wanted to use her.

She felt vulnerable without Felix, who hadn't been seen since his dramatic exit from the dining room the previous evening. She wouldn't admit it, but she missed his gentle nature, his comforting hugs when things were going wrong. This morning, there had been a note tacked to her door, which simply said:

"*Natasha, I think it best for both of us that I resign with immediate effect. I am leaving Maglavat but will be spending a few more days on the island. We can close any unfinished business back in London.*"

And there it was. A cool, distanced, measured dismissal of her, even hints of telling her what she could and couldn't do. There would be no point losing her temper with him, trying to force him to stay with her until she'd found a replacement. Her anger would have no power over him anymore. She still couldn't understand his sudden and brutal unkindness, after all she'd done for him. She could feel, far away in her mind, the beginning of a song about it. If she couldn't do it privately, she would humiliate him publicly with a chart topper. She was comforted. These days, while her popularity crested, Natasha's songs were always hits.

"I'll try not to take up too much of your time, Miss Tang," Duncan said, easing himself into one of the squashy sofas when Natasha had chosen her own place, curled up on another sofa. He looked around the room. "Is it true you're thinking of buying Maglavat?"

Natasha inclined her head.

"Have you had any contact with the local people here since your arrival?"

"None at all, apart from the staff, of course." She paused. "Who I will be keeping on, naturally, should I decide to buy."

Duncan leaned forward. "You're aware, of course, that buying land here on this kind of scale inevitably leads to contact with those who might seek to undermine your ownership?"

Natasha laughed dismissively. "You mean the poachers."

"Indeed. The wild resources here – the deer and salmon in particular – are considered valuable. People like yourself, with views about blood sports, tend to complicate the equation. Landowners find themselves caught between people who wish to destroy the resources and undermine their wealth, and people who wish to question how they choose to manage their estates."

"What's your point, Inspector?"

Duncan pulled a small wad of letters out of his pocket. "These are my point," he said, handing them to her. "It appears you have engaged in correspondence with Frankie Johnson, who is well known on the island for his sentiments regarding animal rights."

Natasha looked briefly angry as she took the letters from him. In the first place, she had forgotten all about them. In the second, they seemed so far away from her now that having to renew her connection to them seemed both trying and fatuous.

"I told him to destroy these," she said. "I warned him it could lead to trouble if they fell into the wrong hands."

"Quite," Duncan said. "Fortunately for you, they fell into mine."

"This might be an island, but the last time I looked, the UK wasn't a police state," Natasha said with an arrogance that only served to nettle the patient Duncan. "I don't have to apologise to you for who I choose to correspond with."

"Why did he contact you?" Duncan asked.

"I reserve the right to remain silent," Natasha said.

Duncan smiled pleasantly. "That's your prerogative, of course," he said. "I wish I could say that my interest in these letters was nothing more than idle curiosity. But the situation is more serious, and your co-operation would be appreciated at this stage. There's a good chance we can clear this up if you tell me what I need to know."

Natasha hesitated. "He wrote to me about an island policy regarding the culling of an endangered species. It seemed a typically callous and short-sighted proposal, and he wanted to know if I would support his efforts to fight it."

"With funding?"

Natasha fidgeted. "Yes, with funding. I sent a very small amount at first, but then he seemed to have used it responsibly, so I sent more. I deal with a lot of groups who share my views. Felix handled the correspondence –" She stopped. "Felix was my PA," she said. "He's just resigned and I'm afraid I can't tell you where he is."

"When did you last hear from Frankie?"

"I really can't remember. But it was a long time ago – early spring, maybe even the end of the winter. Every time I've tried to contact him since, I haven't been able to get through."

Duncan regarded her steadily for a few moments, then said, "Frankie's body was washed up in the river mouth on the Uishall Estate in May. He'd been in the water for about six weeks."

Natasha went pale at this unexpected news. Duncan watched her with interest. It wasn't Frankie's death, but the possible personal repercussions that moved her.

"I'm sorry to hear that," she said. "But I can't imagine that his death had anything to do with me."

"I didn't say it had," Duncan said. "On the other hand, it's difficult to imagine what he was doing out on the moors so early in the year. Frankie was a summer activist, working against the poachers by destroying their nets, and working against the estates by vandalising their equipment. He wasn't liked by either side, but the estates are unlikely to have tried to hurt him, unless they could get him legally. The poachers have a different attitude. I wondered if he might have been working to a brief if he was out so early?"

Duncan waited out the extended silence that succeeded this question. Natasha's mind was working so furiously it was practically audible, desperately wondering if she ought to call her lawyer, but not wanting to sound as if she had done anything knowingly with criminal intent. He sat quietly, not helping her, until it was obvious she needed it.

"Was it connected to Little Pricklies?" he prompted eventually.

Natasha flushed, and then sighed. "You've seen the letters," she said, realising it was useless to try and deny the organisation's existence. "All right, then, Inspector. Yes it was. He wrote to me originally describing the plight of the island hedgehogs, and saying that a big cull was being planned because they had been classified as vermin."

"I see," Duncan said heavily, and pinched his lips together to keep his face in correct order. Despite his best efforts, Natasha was on the defensive again.

"He told me there were mink trapping cages up on the estate lands," she said, "and the mink were subject to an ongoing programme of slaughter. He wrote to me and suggested that he could take the cages and use them to catch hedgehogs instead, and then help rescue the hedgehogs and relocate them."

"Ah." Duncan said.

"Really," Natasha said, "the people on these lands seem to think it's their right to just kill everything that gets in the way of them making money. The only reason they take care of the deer and the sheep is so they can eat them in the end."

"But if they weren't going to be eaten, they wouldn't be here at all," Duncan said. Animal rights were not his concern. Frankie's business on the moors was. "It seems to me, Miss Tang, that Frankie was rather economical with the truth when he wrote to you about the hedgehogs," he said. "Did he say anything at all about the ground nesting birds that sparked the concern about the hedgehogs in the first place?"

"No. But it wouldn't have stopped me helping him. I am a firm believer in finding alternatives to killing things wherever possible."

Duncan fought down the instinctive riposte that nature was never so obliging as to provide simple, one-sided solutions to problems. He might not be an environmentalist, but that much he did know.

"The ground nesting birds include very rare species such as the corncrake," Duncan explained. "Hedgehogs have been eating their eggs for several years now, ever since they were introduced, so that the populations of the already endangered species have been significantly and adversely affected. As most people know, hedgehogs are not in particularly short supply. Some naturalists feel that the cull is an acceptable sacrifice to make."

"Relocation –"

"This is not my area," Duncan said, raising his hand to stop her from launching into a tirade. "I have the job of investigating the death of a man in suspicious circumstances. This at least explains why he was where he was. But I still have to consider the possibility that foul play was involved, which I'm sure you'll agree is a much more serious problem."

Duncan took his leave a few minutes later, having ascertained that Miss Tang's involvement had been purely by proxy, and motivated by naivety. He might be in touch with her later, he told her, but he would be careful to keep her involvement to a minimum. That Frankie had exploited her ignorance about the island's ecosystems did not surprise him; that Natasha had not bothered to find out didn't surprise him either. He said goodbye to Henry, who was already in the kitchen cooking lunch for his guest, and drove away with the images of Frankie's recovered body heavy on his mind.

Frankie had sustained a blow to the head that might have been inflicted by a third party, but might equally have been the result of his fall – or was he pushed? – into the water. The wound was ragged and irregular, suggesting it might have been torn on a rock, and the pathologist's report hypothesised that Frankie's head was in a downward position when it received the injury. Duncan had a pretty good idea of who would be able to fill him in on the details, and drove the road back up the island with the intention of visiting that veteran of the clandestine hill operation, Murdo MacInnes.

III

Felix woke late in the morning, and lay for a moment in the large bed remembering where he was, and why. The wall opposite was beyond bright with a repugnant seventies-style wallpaper, a brash geometric flower pattern in pink, purple, brown and orange that served to remind him graphically of just how much he'd had to drink the night before.

He had made the decision to leave Maglavat immediately following his exit from the dining room. Ten minutes later, sometime after eleven o' clock, he was standing in the kitchen, his bag packed, calling for a taxi. With the prospect of a forty-minute wait ahead of him, Roger had got out the port again, poured a couple of glasses, and proved an appreciative listener while Felix related the tale of what had just happened upstairs.

Robert and Hugh had departed shortly afterwards, and the house soon fell silent apart from a brief appearance by Henry, asking for coffee and brandy to be sent up to Natasha's suite.

"Hey up," Roger had said, when Henry had requested his best brandy. "Totty bottle coming up."

Felix grinned. "He's got no chance," he said. "Not now he's upset her."

By the time Henry had settled onto Natasha's sofa to play agony aunt to her tortured rock star, Felix had climbed into the cab and was away from the castle.

He shook Roger's hand warmly and turned to look out over the sheltered bay the other side of the low granite wall.

"You're going to come back, aren't you?" the chef said.

Felix nodded.

"What will you do?"

"Nothing until I speak to my partner. For the moment, I need to find a bed for the night."

"Ask the cabbie to take you on the Eilaster road," Roger said. "There's a pub there with extended opening hours on a Saturday night. They've always got a spare room. It's pretty basic, but the food's good and there's plenty of it. She might even fix you something up for a late supper if you ask."

This information, though important in his present circumstances, was not nearly as interesting as the fact that emerged in the course of conversation that the pub in question was for sale. It seemed unreasonably fortuitous. He rang Roy again, who told him to go in with his eyes wide open. Any eulogising nonsense would be met with derision, he said firmly. Both of them were still astonished that in the space of less than twenty-four hours, Felix had lost his mind, lost his job, and now seemed about to lose his head.

He had expected the taxi ride to give him the chance to assimilate the craziness of the action he had just taken, but the cabbie was cheerful, talkative and had no intention of letting him slip away into the country of his own thoughts. Just over an hour later, the taxi was pulling into a shabby car park with weeds growing through the thinly scattered gravel. It was set in the crook of an L-shape formed by the building, a grim, grey affair without a sign. If it had been depressingly modern in the 1970s, a concrete deformity crouched hideously at the feet of the noble, ancient landscape that sheltered it, it was now simply depressing. Felix looked through the glass door, where a dim yellow light beyond told him that the bar was still open, and thought of Maglavat's gracious old-fashioned luxury with longing. He felt like Pinocchio, green and smiling, waking up to the real world for the first time. The cabbie said he would stay, just in case there was no room, in which event he would be happy to drive his passenger on to Stornoway. When Felix ventured inside, his overnight bag hitched on his shoulder, he found a half-dozen or so drinkers at the bar engaged in surly conversation, and a rather forbidding landlady.

"It's very late of me to ask," Felix began, "but I need a place to stay. Have you got a room?"

"Well, now," the landlady said. "All the rooms are being decorated, but there's one spare – a big single with a bathroom. Will that do you?"

Felix hesitated and glanced up at a large blackboard propped against the back of the bar.

The landlady sighed. "If you're hungry, there's a T-bone steak I can grill."

Felix grinned. It seemed to be an omen. "Marvellous," he said.

"That'll be thirty pounds, then. How do you like your steak?"

"Rare," Felix said promptly.

The landlady disappeared towards the kitchen and Felix went outside, despatched the cabbie, then returned to the bar and ordered a double malt from the landlord. The local men ignored him and carried on talking.

"Duncan will be about before long," one of them said, shaking his head. "You'd better have your answers sorted for him, Ally, when he comes."

A short, stout man perched on a barstool raised his glass to the speaker. "It's you he'll be looking for, Murdo, not me. I'm just one of the messenger boys."

"All season we've not been out," Murdo said, "because of your stupid clowning."

"I didn't know he was going to be there," Ally said. "Any more than you did."

Murdo leaned forward. "No, but I wouldn't have killed him for it, would I?"

"I did nothing to him!" Ally protested. A sudden kick from one of the other men hushed him abruptly, his eyes sliding towards Felix in warning. "I did nothing," he said again, his voice sunk to a whisper, his voice monotonous with telling a story he had already recounted a hundred times or more to the same audience, who seemed to think some comfort would be found in its constant repetition. "I came over the bank and he saw me. I shouted at him because he looked to be near the net stash, and he was lugging something. The next thing, he lost his footing and fell. It was a fifty-foot drop to the rocks. When I looked down, his neck was twisted – I've seen too much death not to recognise it when I see it. There was no point in hanging around."

"Why not just tell Duncan what you know?" one of the others said. "They'll have the pathologist's report. It's death by misadventure, or something of the sort. They can't put you in prison for that."

"We don't *help* Duncan," Murdo said, and the group fell silent.

When the steak arrived, Felix found that he was ravenous again. Halfway through it, his phone rang. The signal was poor, but there was no mistaking Roy's voice.

"Aren't you in bed yet?" Roy asked.

"No, but I'm in the pub," Felix said, "demolishing a T-bone steak."

"Marinated?" Roy asked. "Garlic?"

"Umm, I don't think so. Hang on –" he took a mouthful and chewed thoughtfully.

"Disgusting," Roy said. "I can hear every mastication."

"You're filthy," Felix said. "No, there's no garlic," he said, after he had swallowed. "Just char grilled, with a watercress, mushroom and lemon cream sauce on the side. A splash of cider, too, I'll be bound."

"What's it like?"

"I just said, didn't I?"

"I don't mean the steak. I mean the place."

"I haven't tried the fish," Felix said in a throaty whisper, and was rewarded by an exasperated sigh.

"Come on, Felix -"

Felix stood up. "Hang on – you're breaking up all the time. Let me go outside a minute."

In the car park, the connection strengthened slightly and Felix sighed with relief. This kind of conversation was hard enough without the phone going into malfunction mode.

"Well, it was pretty dark when I got here," he said, lowering his voice, "so I haven't seen it in daylight. But so far, it's pretty grim."

"That's as honest as I could wish for," Roy said. "Is it busy?"

"No. Four locals who look like thugs whispering at the bar. Deserted apart from that."

"Yum," Roy said. "Sounds like a hopeless case."

"I think it might be a bit over-ambitious to take this one on."

"What do they want for it?"

"No idea. They're not exactly chatty. I'll have a look round in the morning and then ask them over breakfast. Really, Roy, I think you'd be miserable here. I know you want a change from Manchester –"

"I want a challenge. Something we can work on together."

"Look, there's taking on a challenge, and there's doing insufferable penance. Let me find somewhere else. I'll do some scouting, but then we ought to come back together."

"I had the restaurant valued," Roy said, his voice suddenly quiet. "I got them in a month ago. The report came today."

Felix swallowed. This was serious.

"Go on, then," he said.

"Not as much as I'd hoped. Three quarters of a million tops –"

"What the hell did you think it was worth?"

"Well, I was hoping to go over the million mark, city centre location and all. But if we put it to auction –"

"Oh now stop, stop," Felix said. "You're being more reckless than I've just been –"

"This is a golden opportunity," Roy said. "Don't you dare start losing your nerve after such a fantastic display of strength."

Felix laughed and shook his head. "Look, I'm drunk and drained and I need to sleep," he said. "I'm going to finish my steak, which is getting cold because of you, then I'm going to bed and I'll call you in the morning."

And so he slept and now he had woken, his head heavy and his eyes sensitive and aching from the bright sunlight outside. He threw back the curtains and found himself gazing out over a sea loch stretching away to the east, dotted with small, rocky islands and framed along both sides by low hills and inlets. The water was mirror-calm that morning, the sun glazing its surface. In the shallows, a curlew was wading. Felix stood for a long time with his back to the room then turned to face it.

It looked no better. The ghastly wallpaper, the cheap bedding, the nasty green tiled bathroom – all conspired against him. But in contrast, the view outside was inspirational, as affecting as the majesty of Maglavat's seascape, and just as close.

He showered, ate another cooked breakfast and then, while the landlord was laying the fire, asked why it was on the market. He was in the lounge bar, a small, cramped space with too many sofas, tables and chairs squashed into it.

"No customers," was the unvarnished response.

"Oh," Felix said. "Why did you buy it, then?"

"Because we were looking for a country pub in a peaceful location," the landlord said. "But we wanted quiet, not dead."

"You had people in last night."

"Aye, we get the poachers," the landlord said. "And the drinkers. But no one else. We thought we could bring in the local families, build up the food side and take in the tourists. It's happening, but not quickly enough. We'll be collecting our pensions before this place takes off."

"Where will you go if you sell?"

"Our daughter's just emigrated to New Zealand," he said. "I fancy a change of scenery after this." He paused. "You can see for yourself what it's like. It needs youth and energy – and a lot of hard cash. And then you still might not get the return on your investment."

"Have you got any interest?"

"Well, the council are thinking about buying it up and turning it into a sports hall," he said. "It's the only pub for miles around, so it would be a shame – but on the other hand, there's no sense in running a business that doesn't make money. If the demand isn't there, what's the point?"

Felix sympathised with his plight, but kept staring out over the loch. In the midst of this pleasant occupation, his mobile trilled.

"Felix?"

His heart leapt wildly.

"Natasha?"

"I'm just packing to leave," his ex-employer said, deliberately cool. "We're on the afternoon flight to Edinburgh. You left your personal organiser last night. Would you like to pick it up from Maglavat – or say goodbye to me at the airport?"

In the few seconds he spent considering his answer, he realised what she was doing. She had thought of something, some devilish punishment that he was going to have to face. And she was right. He should face her. He had made his big dramatic gesture, then run into the night. He owed her the chance of revenge.

"I'll come and say goodbye, Natasha," he said. "I'm truly sorry for the way I behaved. I can't take it back, but I'd like to say goodbye properly."

"Well then. Three o' clock if you make it. Otherwise I'll leave it at the Information Desk."

She sounded very organised and calm about it, but there was something else in her voice that he couldn't quite place. Contrition occurred to him, but it didn't fit with his lengthy experience of Natasha. No tears, no recriminations. Perhaps she was saving those for when she saw him. Perhaps she'd invited the press and they were going to witness the scale of his treachery while Natasha ranted at him in the Departures lounge and the cameras flashed and clicked. She had also said *we*, he realised, as he found himself hitching a ride up to town with the landlady who had fed him so generously. Had someone been flown in from London, just to escort her home, or was she expecting him to accompany her?

IV

He arrived early at the airport, bought himself a drink at the bar and amused himself by watching the passengers disembarking from the Inverness flight. By the baggage carousel, a blonde woman in jeans and a Harris tweed jacket stood with her eyes fixed on the people climbing down the steps from the plane. She looked agitated as she waited, and he saw her react when a tall, athletic-looking man with sandy hair appeared, a red plaid shirt tucked into black jeans and a heavy leather jacket slung over his shoulders.

Felix watched, interested. The man was looking for her, too, and when he saw her through the glass, he leapt the last four aluminium treads and quickly strode the short distance to the doors. His way to her was not clear, however, blocked by several passengers greeting their own friends, relatives and business associates. She stood still, waiting for him, and Felix saw she was close to tears. The man dodged round people, almost collided with a child hell-bent on throwing herself into her grandmother's arms, and finally reached her. He dropped the jacket to the ground, and said a single word:

"Lily."

Felix swallowed some of his whisky and found there was a lump in his throat. He watched them kiss, then she was in his arms, head cradled against his chest, held fast, sobbing. There was real pain in the way she wept – it was the kind of reunion that was as painfully intense as the separation that had preceded it. He wondered what their story was.

Someone standing at the bar next to Felix, eyes turned in the same direction, said to his companion, "Christ – isn't that Jared Bell?"

Around them, the people laughed and chatted, hugged and exchanged small talk about the flight, the weather, the short delay, and waited for the creaking rumble of the luggage carousel. One or two nodded in their direction, but the couple seemed entirely apart from the hubbub, as if they cared about nothing else except that at last they were together.

Felix glanced away and saw, to his amazement, a press photographer hurrying across the seating area. For a horrible moment, he thought this was the start of Natasha's diabolical vengeance, but instead, the photographer lined up the couple in his lens and the flash popped. All the memories of hustling Natasha through international airports, besieged by the press, especially when the object of their attention was distressed, shot through his mind. The man raised his head, but kept his arms around the woman, shielding her, and there was profound anger in his eyes.

Before he knew what he was doing, Felix had got off his chair, walked briskly over and put his hand on the photographer's arm.

"I'm going to have to ask you to leave," he said. "You are violating a personal security area, and photographers are expressly forbidden." The photographer stared at him, his mouth open. "You are contravening a private agreement made with the airport authorities."

"What are you talking about?" the photographer said. "This man's just been released and he's a news item."

He was a rookie, probably local press, not very slick or on the ball. Felix reached inside his jacket and flashed his ID. "I am in charge of security at this airport for the next two hours," he said. "My client is entitled to protection and if you don't leave immediately, you will be arrested and your camera confiscated."

"I was briefed to come here –"

"And I was briefed to make sure you didn't," Felix said. He stood between the photographer and the couple. The man was watching him, his arms still screening the woman. "Now, are you going to leave while I'm asking nicely, or do you want me to make a scene?"

"It's a fucking scoop –" the photographer shouted, and made the mistake of trying to push Felix out of the way. In a second, his arm had been twisted behind his back. People stopped what they were doing to watch.

Felix cocked his head at him. "Get my point?"

"You're an arse," the photographer said, shaking himself free and walking angrily towards the doors. Felix watched him, and then followed him, knowing he would probably try for a shot through one of the glass walls. Seeing Felix at the door, he ducked out of sight behind the building. Felix sighed and turned back. He couldn't protect these people from what happened once they left the terminal, but at least he could try to let them be reconciled in peace, just for the first few minutes. He knew from bitter experience that if the press wanted them, the press would get them, one way or another, sooner or later. He could have given the photographer Natasha as a sweetener, who would be turning up at any moment, but now he was free, his loyalty to her had revived sufficiently to banish any impulse to act on petty spite. He owed her that much.

They were still there, the man's head bent over hers, a single unclaimed bag still making its way around the carousel. Eventually, an attendant lifted it away and put it discreetly onto a trolley, and the carousel shuddered to a halt. Felix went back to his whisky, wondering what the man had done to attract the interest of the press. He had turned back to the bar when a voice beside him said,

"Thank you."

Felix turned to see the man he had protected, the bag slung on his shoulder, the woman's hand held in his. She looked a mess, her eyes red, her hair tousled, her expression somewhere between pain and happiness. She nodded her agreement, but seemed incapable of speech. The man held out his hand and Felix shook it.

"My pleasure," he said.

Then they were gone, the man's arm around her, walking out of the door and into the car waiting by the entrance. A fast escape. But even so, Felix saw the photographer's car pull out a few seconds later and follow them as they drove away. As if to echo the memories that were crowding in on him, Natasha chose that moment to walk through the doors. She was wearing sunglasses and a heavy silk scarf, thrown elegantly over her head and around her shoulders. He downed the whisky in one and went towards her.

"You're travelling alone?" he said, immediately concerned.

She looked at him with a sarcasm he knew he deserved. "No," she said. "As a matter of fact, Henry's coming with me – just to Edinburgh. Someone's going to meet me there for the last leg." She looked embarrassed for a moment, as if she had forgotten that this was all because of Felix.

He looked awkwardly at her. Before, there had seemed to be so much he wanted to say to her, all of it negative, but now she was standing in front of him, he couldn't think of a single thing, except,

"I owe you an apology. What I said last night was unforgivable."

Natasha smiled thinly. She had spent half the night trying to come up with something vicious to do to him, but in the end, she had lost the will. Henry strolled over to them, tickets in hand.

"Ah, hello there, Felix. Where did you end up last night?"

Felix told him.

Henry whistled. "Never been there myself," he said. "Bit of a poachers' den."

"Yes, I gathered," Felix said. "Not a very salubrious joint. But a wonderful location."

"Heading back yourself?"

"Er, no – not for a day or two. I need time to – make plans, think about the future. This seems as good a place to do it as any."

"Have you told Roy?" Natasha asked.

Felix nodded.

"He'll be missing you," she said.

Felix stared at her. This was not at all what he had foreseen. He felt like a climber scrambling clumsily over unstable ground, unable to find secure footing.

"It's all right, Felix," Natasha said, astounding him further. "I want us to part friends."

"Natasha –"

"Please don't," she said. "Kiss me goodbye, then come and see me when you get home, and we'll sort out the details."

Felix nodded dumbly and held out his hand to her, but she came close and kissed him on the cheek instead. He returned the intimacy and felt emotion welling up inside him.

"Time to go, I think," Henry said, touching her arm. "They're calling the flight, and there's only the one, you know."

"I'll see you soon," Felix whispered to Natasha, the woman who had driven him mad for eighteen months, forced him into unspeakably cruel behaviour not twenty-four hours ago, and was now about to reduce him to tears of sweet sorrow.

"I mean it, Felix," Natasha said. "No hard feelings."

He smiled and nodded. "Hey, that sounds like a cue for a song," he said.

She turned and began to walk away, then stopped and looked back. "Thanks for all the hugs," she said.

IV

John pushed open the attic door, hesitated a moment, then walked through it. Filtered through the dusty windows set at regular intervals in the sloping roof, the light was soft and clear, illuminating a vast space – probably half the floor area of Uishall Castle. The roof was pitched so that only a couple of feet of upright wall supported it, and John could look through the windows, out across the battlements and turrets to the hills beyond.

He had been up here once before, right at the beginning of the season, and poked desultorily around the stacked boxes and discarded dressers, the tallboys and commodes. There was more recent detritus – discarded kitchen equipment, stores of cleaning materials and maintenance tools. The header tank for the hot water system was up here, pushed to its limits when the castle was full and all its deep cast iron baths pressed into service at the end of the day's sport. But there was old stuff here as well, mostly furniture and bric-a-brac, ancient black iron bicycles, children's tricycles and board games. The white cobwebs were draped thickly around the windows, trapping sounds in their dusty embrace, muffling John's footsteps as he made his way to the far end.

His visit had been inspired by a comment from Heather, when she had shown him the room that Janet had occupied for four years, before she married Alec. The canopied bed was still there, the plain stone fireplace, the rocking chair, the chest where she kept her clothes. The room had been carpeted, of course, because it was now used for guests, and the old rug originally on the wooden floor long since discarded and burned. It had been papered, too, with a replica of the pattern Janet would have looked on as she prepared herself for bed, or read in her chair by the fire. Small posies of wild roses in delicate shades of pink and green, each flower with a tiny yellow centre. When she changed quarters, to be married, and after the death of her husband, one item of furniture had come with her – her writing table. But it was no longer in The Lady Janet's Room, as it was still called, with its high windows looking out over the mouth of the river. There, it had been set by the window – he could see the depressions in the carpet left by the feet. It had been removed to the attic some ten years ago on the request of a guest who wanted floor space for yoga, and what had begun as a temporary removal had become permanent.

While they were standing in Janet's old room, Heather had described the missing writing table – simple, with barley twist legs, a galleried back and an inkstand – a standish, as they called it back then. Two drawers for paper, envelopes and quills.

He had broken off his spell in the study that morning to see if he could find it, abandoning for the moment an interesting correspondence involving Alasdair and some livestock dealers. The Laird, as he then was, had refused to receive a shipment of two thousand head of Cheviots, and was now locked in ferocious wrangling over who was to pay for the return shipment of the unwanted cargo. The copies of Alasdair's letters stated categorically that he had not ordered the sheep, and therefore had no intention of paying for them. All the other estates were buying the breed, one of the responses wheedled. It must have been a mistake – but perhaps a fortuitous one, if he should come to his senses and actually accept them. John was still intrigued by Alasdair's refusal to purchase the sheep – he already knew that Alec's son had spearheaded the shift to sporting on the island, but the thinking behind the decision was absent. What had made a man, initially reared on the poor lands of Eilaster, reach a decision that further devastated his people's prospects, and flew in the face of current thinking?

Now, John moved slowly through the jumble of the attic storeroom and tried to find the writing table again. Heather had already suggested that if he was successful, it should be restored to its original position. There was nothing immediately obvious. Chairs stood next to each other, not matching, turned indifferently towards the room as if they had fallen out a long time ago and had nothing further to say to each other. Chests and tables were pushed together, sometimes piled up one on top of the other, with small boxes perched on top. Paper napkins poked out through one, another held wine glasses, another assorted china – the remainders of dinner services that had been broken and not replaced over the years. John coughed when he disturbed the thick layers of dust.

Nothing resembled the description Heather had given him. He was on the point of giving up when he spotted a small door in the end wall, half-hidden behind a pink velvet chaise-longue. He looked curiously at it, realising that it must lead to another section. Then he wondered if this was the place where

Robert and his father had found the boxes of papers that were now in the study. He heaved the chaise-longue out of the way and tried the round wooden knob. It was locked.

For a moment, it seemed that he would be defeated, but he glanced above the door, which was only as tall as he was, and saw an old key hanging from a hook. Feeling like Alice in Wonderland, he reached for it. A few seconds later, he was turning the key and then the door opened with an unreasonably loud creaking of hinges that made him jump after the dust-blanketed hush that had preceded it.

This part of the attic was much darker, and his eyes took a while to adjust to the lower levels of light. There was only one window, and that was at the far end. But eventually it became clear that this area had been purposely created to be dark. It was full of paintings. Some canvases were wrapped roughly in brown paper, others were stacked together, others still in heavy, ornate gilt frames. Mostly oils, but there were watercolours and etchings, too, a large collection of wildlife portraits in a leather folder tied with ribbon. There were landscapes, dark with the colours of the moorland and the angry sea, bellowing stags, swooping eagles. A couple of studies of Uishall, fancifully set in a kinder landscape than reality admitted. Portraits, presumably of Lairds and their families, too many to set on the walls of the reception rooms and public areas. He gazed for a long time at a huge canvas, a family group depicted in solemn attitudes around the great fireplace in the dining room. Immersed in this new diversion, he grasped both top corners to pull it forward, to see what artistic treasures lay behind it – and there was Janet's writing table, he knew it was, small and neat, plain but for the barley twist legs, standing against the bare wall, uncovered.

He gasped with the delightful, unexpected shock of his discovery, then carefully slid the large painting along the floor until his access to it was clear. He touched it, his hands sliding over the lip that ran around the sides and back, and then lifted it cautiously. It wasn't too heavy, he would be able to drag it through the door then carry it along the attic and down into the study. Being careful to replace the painting and ensure its slightly altered position was still protected from the dim light, he seized his prize and retraced his steps.

Getting down the staircase was tricky, as the table was awkward to handle and he couldn't find his footing. He found himself back on the second floor, with the prospect of negotiating another staircase before he could deliver the writing desk to the study. On impulse, he stopped, turned into the short corridor and carried it to Janet's old room.

He lifted the latch and carried the table into the middle of the room, then stopped. Where would she have had it? He looked around, then placed it directly in front of the window. At once the room seemed charged, as if it had noticed the long absence of this valuable item and understood it had been restored. John stepped back, brought the straight-backed chair in front of it, then cast about. Above the fireplace was a candleholder. He lifted it down and then with his sleeve, rubbed away the dust on the writing table. There was a grouping of dark circular marks by the inkstand, like fairy rings. He stroked his finger over them and felt the slight change in texture, dry oiliness where candle wax had dripped down and pooled. His breathing shallow, he set down the candleholder over the most pronounced of the marks, and it fitted. A thrill ran through him.

He sat down at the table. The hairs on his arms rose and he shivered, as if suddenly he had called her back and for a second, she had acknowledged him. She would have sat here often. When she arrived, she was uneducated. To do her job, she had to be literate, and she would have had to learn English. She would have put hours into the task, copying, practising, understanding, learning the arts of written communication. He had seen the samples of Alasdair's early lettering. None survived of hers. Just her neat, small writing in the inventories, her signatures on the storeroom books, invoices and orders when she was Alec's employee, and her written instructions to Alice when she was lady of the house. John could see her strength in the writing – strong, deliberate letters, expertly executed in her small, tidy hand.

He opened the top drawer with difficulty – it was obviously years since anyone had touched it – and found it empty. He tried the second, which opened easily, but was no more forthcoming. He stared at its empty, gaping mouth and then grinned sardonically to himself, the magic of the moment fading away. What else did he expect? He wasn't going to find her here. Janet had taken her secret to the grave. The writing paper and quills would long since have been used or thrown away, the drawers filled and emptied a thousand times by the minor necessaries of succeeding castle occupants.

He sighed and felt the hollowness of disappointment as he pushed the top drawer closed. It stuck again, taunting him, refusing to let him go, and he pushed again, impatiently now, freeing the drawer too quickly so that it closed itself with a smacking sound as if it, too, was annoyed. He leaned forward, his elbows on the tabletop, and then he heard a dull clatter just beneath. Tentatively, he pulled at the drawer again. This time, it slid out in a fluid movement and came to rest, fully open, against his hand. He bent down and peered inside.

The clatter he had heard had been the falling in of a slender piece of wood that formed the back of the drawer. He reached his hand inside and pulled it out with his fingertips. A thin piece, cut without joints or grooves. His forehead creased, then he pushed his hand back into the drawer and it went further in than before, touching a solid piece of wood about six inches further back. The loose piece was a false back. He thrust his hand inside the exposed cavity, his fingers scrabbling in the space to left and right.

There. He touched it, curved his hand around it, and slid it towards him, the feel of textured leather under his fingers. And something else. Something flattish, cloth under his fingers this time, not leather. Not a book, either – a shape, something hard and unyielding beneath its protective layers. He pulled it forwards and then gazed down at his finds.

V

As John was revelling in the thrill of his discovery, Peregrine Thornfield was on the ground floor of the castle, standing before the ugly-beautiful Italian monster. He had been studying it for a long time with his stern but kindly eyes, his silver-rimmed spectacles glinting in the sunlight pouring through the windows, his hand running from time to time over his straight greying hair. Beside him, the 1830 castle inventory clutched in his hand, Robert stood patiently, trying not to hold his breath.

After several minutes, Peregrine coughed politely and raised his clipboard. He wrote a couple of words on the pad and squatted down to examine the twin cupboard doors.

"Tell me the history of this piece again," he said.

Robert was only too happy to repeat it. The valuer listened carefully as he continued with his survey and Robert, describing the fine hairline crack along the lion's head, failed to notice the touch of pity that had crept across his face and softened the careful professionalism of his expression.

"It is a very remarkable piece," Peregrine said at length, when Robert came to the end of his tale at its suitably dramatic climax, with the transformation of the fourteenth century Clan Macleod into a civilised aristocracy, following the catalytic arrival of the piece of furniture.

Robert nodded, proffering the old inventory. "Which is why I can't understand its absence from this," he said. He riffled through the pages. "You see? Here – this section. It should be here, with the dining room contents."

Peregrine glanced across to see where Robert's finger pointed. He nodded, straightened and opened one of the drawers above the cupboard door, and found it neatly stacked with table linen.

"May I?" he asked, beginning to remove the napkins.

"Of course," Robert said. "What are you looking for?"

"To see if there's a maker's mark," he said. "And to see how the drawers were fashioned – that will help me date it accurately."

"Of course," Robert said delightedly. "It came to the castle in the fourteenth century, but it could be even older, I suppose."

Together, they piled the linen on the surface, then the valuer pulled the drawer out to its fullest extent and carefully removed it.

"Ah," he said softly, as he turned the drawer over and inspected the outside edges. He dropped his head for a moment, then straightened again and scribbled something more on the clipboard pad. There was an odd silence.

"Mr Bartlett," he said, "the reason this piece is not included in the 1830 inventory is that it was not here."

"I see," Robert said. "My brother thought it might have been sent away –"

"No, no," the valuer said, shaking his head patiently. "You misunderstand me. It was not here because *it could not have been here*."

Robert gazed at him while the words assimilated. "You mean – it was acquired at a later date?" he said faintly. He didn't like the way Peregrine was looking at him. He had the sudden, dreadful feeling that there might be a flaw in the great legend.

"I mean, Mr Bartlett, that it was *manufactured* at a later date."

"But that's impossible," Robert said. "It was hand-made. The legend is well-known. It's even documented in family letters. Surely –"

"It's a sideboard," Peregrine said, a trifle brusquely. "It is a very large, impressive and beautifully carpentered and carved sideboard, but still, it *is* a sideboard."

"Yes, I can see that –"

"Sideboards did not exist in the fourteenth century," the treacherous Peregrine Thornfield said. "They were an eighteenth century invention. But most of them, like this one, are Victorian. *Late* Victorian," he stressed.

Robert realised that his mouth was hanging open. His immediate thought, apart from the desperate hope that the valuer was a fraudulent rogue who was completely incompetent at his job, was for Freya, who loved the story of the ugly-beautiful Italian monster as fiercely as she loved Uishall, and for whom the two could not be separated.

"But –"

"If you will," the valuer said, clicking on the pencil beam torch and shining it into the other drawer, and indicating that Robert should look where the light pierced the gloom of the interior.

Robert bent as if it were the weight of his own heart dragging him down, and followed the beam of light. The legend *James Shoolbred* was punched in capital letters inside it.

"You see it?" the valuer said. "And here –" he briskly closed the drawer and turned again to the one he had removed. "I'm afraid this is incontrovertible. The dovetails joining the sides together have been machine-cut. On an earlier piece, they would have been hand-cut along a line which is always visible."

Robert lifted his head from the murk of the past and back into the present.

"I don't understand," he said.

"James Shoolbred was a very well-respected furniture maker and retailer working in London in the second half of the nineteenth century. The cupboards below – one lead-lined for drinks, the other shelved for glasses – very characteristic of the style."

"Not Palestrina?" Robert said pathetically, as the last part of the legend tottered, crumbled and crashed about his feet.

Peregrine Thornfield shook his head, then turned again to the ugly-beautiful monster and gave Robert a little time to go through the necessary grieving process.

"So what's your verdict?" Robert said, staring in horror at the brazen fraud before him.

"I'd say 1860s, Tottenham Court Road," he said, with deliberately vulgar cheerfulness. "Value – oh, somewhere around two to three thousand pounds. If it's any consolation, I've already spotted a couple of paintings that are worth far more."

"Tottenham Court Road," Robert repeated, with tragic despair. "Not even Italy?"

"The only hope I can offer is that the wood used to make the piece may have come from Italy, or been carved somewhere like Venice at an earlier date. But even so, it would not have been that much earlier. And the decorations are typically Victorian, which does suggest heavily that they are of English origin."

"Good lord," Robert said, sitting down heavily at the dining table. He sat, staring with fascination at the monster that had suddenly acquired a completely new historical identity, then gazed at Peregrine as a new truth struck him.

"Somebody lied," he said incredulously. "How extraordinary. Somebody fabricated the whole elaborate tale."

Peregrine smiled sympathetically. "It's not the first time I've come across this scenario," he said. "It's amazing how we tend to swallow everything our ancestors tell us about the past. We forget that they lived colourful lives, and had secrets they did not want discovered, and motives that were less than noble. It would be very interesting to know who made up the story, and why, don't you think? Then the truth will simply add to the pleasure of the tale," he said.

Robert shook his head again, but this time he was smiling, already attracted by the new mystery – the identity of the liar and the motive behind the tale. Peregrine, on the other hand, had moved on, and was appraising the huge solid oak dining table.

"You do realise that this is probably late fifteenth or early sixteenth century?" he said, and became immediately absorbed.

Robert was getting up to leave him when John came through the door, his face tense with excitement.

"You'd better sit down again," he said, grinning.

Robert looked at him curiously, and then saw the small black leather book and what looked like a mummified effigy in his hand and obediently sat down again.

"I've just had the Uishall myth demolished by this gentleman," he said. "I have to say that I'm beginning to be wary of what the past might have to say to us next."

PART THREE

1836 – 2002:
A TALE OF TRIALS

1.
MACNAB
SEPTEMBER, 2001

I
ARRIVALS

Trevor eased the travel bag off his shoulder, dumped it on the floor and fell onto the bed. It was good to be back. He lay looking at himself in the ceiling, where a mirror running the full length of the bed had been fitted. It wasn't the only risqué feature of the bedroom. Generations of Uishall Castle staff had called it the Sexy Room, and it had been Trevor's ever since he had been old enough to claim it. In Alec's day, it was where Ruaraidh had slept, in the company of a mistress or two if he could sneak them in. The bed posts were dressed with lace curtains; these could be tied back by slender, scarlet silk twist ropes, or the curtains drawn and the ropes used for other purposes. The flock wallpaper, striped thickly in cream, gold and maroon, was dotted with erotic paintings – some of them Ruaraidh's, some of them Trevor's.

The clash of classic and contemporary styles didn't especially suit the room, but it appealed to Trevor's roguish enjoyment of discordant elements being thrown together and forced to somehow get along. The bathroom was small, but nevertheless accommodated a handsome bath big enough for two, a shower and bidet. The floor was carpeted in white deep shag pile and the walls were covered with mirror panels. A print, a modern charcoal sketch of a naked couple making love in what looked to be a tantalisingly difficult position, hung on the wall opposite the bath.

Yet despite its carnal overtones, the room usually housed single occupants, Trevor included. It was not often offered to guests, unless they knew Uishall well and were unlikely to be shocked by its décor.

After a few minutes, Trevor levered himself up, opened the bag on the floor, pulled out a bottle of malt whisky and set it on the dresser. It was battered now, its metal top scuffed, its white, green and silver label rubbed and frayed. He resumed his supine position to contemplate it. He had bought it over ten years ago, with the intention of opening it when he landed his first salmon. The Royal Macnab was the last time he would save it. Whether he was successful or not, the cork would be pulled the evening of the contest. After all this time, it was the right thing to do.

Happy with the decision, he got off the bed and stripped off his travelling clothes. He went into the bathroom to shower under the provocative stare of a fleshy eighteenth-century blonde who seemed to be more interested in him than the dark-haired rake who was ravishing her in the painting.

Along the corridor, Hugh and Robert had arrived the previous evening, for the third time that season. Robert had immediately met up with John to discuss the progress of the paper documentation, and Hugh had walked Belgian and Ruby along the river and seen a couple of fish move. Since Trevor's arrival, both Labradors had been reunited with their great friend, Trevor's Springer spaniel, Dash.

The weather was fine and settled. Today was Wednesday and Freya was due to arrive in time for dinner. The elder statesmen would not be here until the weekend – Saturday lunchtime, and would be leaving on Monday. Tomorrow, there would be time to fish a little, walk a little, scent the air and gauge the ground. Hugh had set up the Macnab. It was his call. He looked out at the deepening indigo of the sky and selected Friday. It would be a good set of tales for the older generation to listen to when they arrived, and they would enjoy the salacious element of the Royal – whether or not anybody did anything about it. Hugh strolled along the riverbank in perfect contentment, planning the announcement he would make at dinner that evening.

II
MARIE

In the kitchen later that day, Marie was making the bread that would accompany the starters – poppy seed rolls tonight, twisted into neat little knots. With only four of the directors here, it was an opportunity to cook something different on a smaller scale. Hugh Bartlett had already requested a bottle of champagne for the pre-dinner drinks, and had asked for steaks and salad leaves for the main course, with a fruit salad to finish.

Hedda was slicing the fruit and boiling the red wine syrup when the bell rang in the drawing room.

"They're starting early, aren't they?" she frowned, glancing up at the clock in the kitchen, which told her it was only a quarter to seven. She set four champagne flutes on the silver tray, alongside the bottle nestled in its bucket of crushed ice, and left.

Marie whistled as she worked. Aidan would be along soon, hoping to lay claim to some of the cake left over from afternoon tea. Without question, Aidan was her most frequent visitor. There was not a single morning that he didn't appear in the kitchen to say good morning and pass a few moments in conversation. She liked his quiet, gruff manner and found his conversation, about the islands, about Uishall, about the changes threatened by land reform, interesting.

She had other causes to feel content. Since she had kidnapped the Sunday joint, things in the kitchen had changed. Christina had been to see Heather, and handed in her resignation. Details of her dissatisfaction were not thoroughly explored, as it seemed she was not over-anxious to elaborate on them, and Heather was certainly not over-anxious to insist on hearing them. It would be the end of an era, she said kindly to the older woman, who had been fretful for most of their discussion and had started off by demanding that she be released from her contract immediately. It had taken considerable political manoeuvring to get her to stay on for the remaining five weekends.

Marie pushed her hands into the flour bag and began to knead the dough. Christina's resignation had secured Marie as

Uishall's cook for a second season. When she looked up, Hedda was back in the kitchen, and she was grinning.

"What's up?"

Hedda laughed. "Let's just say you're going to have to be on your guard on Friday night," she said.

Marie paused in her kneading. "What's going on?"

Hedda heaved herself up onto the kitchen surface and sat there, swinging her legs like a mischievous pixie.

"Well, I took the champagne down and they asked if I'd put some peat on the fire. There wasn't any, so I had to take the scuttle out into the courtyard. When I came back in, they were talking about a competition they've been planning ever since the spring."

"What's that got to do with me?" Marie asked.

"It's a Royal Macnab," Hedda said.

"What's that?" Marie said, her curiosity piqued by Hedda's infectious glee.

"They're all going out on Friday, and the idea is that they each have to stalk a deer, shoot a brace of grouse, and catch a salmon –"

"Oh no," Marie groaned, as realisation dawned. "I suppose that means I'm going to have to cook them all at the last minute –"

"No, no, it's worse than that," Hedda said. "Probably none of them'll manage it, because it's not that easy, but if one of them does it, that's called a Macnab." She paused. "The Royal part is what the victor gets to do the same night – if the cook lets him."

It took a few seconds for Marie to understand the nature of her role in this most sporting of contests. She stared at her kitchen partner.

"So I'm quarry to them, like all the other –" she broke off, as something occurred to her.

"What?" Hedda said.

Marie smiled drily. "I've just realised what Trevor Fynn has been up to over the past few months," she said. "He rang up and introduced himself in the first week, and I couldn't work out why. Ever since then, he's called occasionally, just to ask how things are going. He's been trying to soften me up!"

Hedda laughed. "I don't think any of them seriously believe they stand a chance of pulling off the Macnab, let alone laying someone they've never even met before." She stopped. "Well, I suppose some cooks would, just for the laugh. But look –

the Bartlett brothers just won't, they're not that type. I bet it was Mr Fynn's idea. It's just a bit of fun, that's all," she said.

Marie stood, staring ahead of her, absently working the now glossy and elastic dough in her hands.

"That's not really the point," she said. She looked thoughtfully at Hedda. "Is it?"

"I suppose you could be flattered he wants to do the Royal with you," Hedda said. "He used to be famous in his day, you know. He'd have just gone for the Macnab if he thought – "

Marie stopped her. "Don't say it," she said. "What about Miss Clarence? Is she in on this?"

"They were being a bit cagey about that, but I think she came up with the idea of trying to lay Aidan if she's the winner."

"Really?" Marie said scathingly. "Amazing what people come up with when they've got too much time on their hands."

Hedda shook her head. "I'm pretty sure it's all talk," she said. "They seem a nice bunch." She paused. "You met Mr Fynn today, didn't you?"

Marie's look was caustic. "Mr Ex-Rock Star," she said. "Very fond of himself, by the looks of things."

"Well come on, then. Tell the truth. He's your man if he gets the Macnab. Did you fancy him?"

Marie gaped, threw a tea towel at her, and then laughed until she cried.

Shortly afterwards, Hugh, Robert, Trevor and Freya came through to the dining room at the sound of the gong and settled down to their first course.

"It's really not on, you know," Robert was saying in his mild way. "We shouldn't even be discussing such a thing, not even in fun."

Trevor laughed and raised his glass to him. "There speaks a married man," he teased him. He leaned across the vast table towards him and said, "Seriously, Robert, I wouldn't dream of tainting my Macnab victory with a less than honourable conquest. Hugh's put it in the rules. I like her. Honestly I do," he said, when gales of derisive laughter greeted this remark. "The fact that she's rather attractive too is beside the point. I will make it quite clear that the nature of the proposition is a single night of physical pleasure and nothing more."

He looked round the table. Freya looked angry and was trying to conceal it by raising her eyes. After a moment, she said,

"Are women always conquests to you?"

He laughed. "No, not really. It's just what everyone seems to expect of me."

"I think all of us will have quite enough on trying to fulfil the requirements of the sporting challenge, never mind anything else," Hugh said, in an effort to maintain the conviviality of the company. He rose to his feet and held aloft his champagne glass. "As instigator of the Royal Macnab contest, I formally nominate Friday as the day of reckoning."

The glasses were raised and the proposition toasted.

Freya seemed to recover her good humour and glanced across at Trevor, an expression of apology. He smiled back, accepting it. The sound of footsteps from the direction of the kitchen prompted a discreet change of subject, as two of the girls arrived bearing the first course.

The starter plates came first, and the four diners eyed them appreciatively. The rolls came next, brought through on individual plates, wrapped neatly in a napkin to keep them hot. Freya, Hugh and Robert sniffed at the aromas of warm bread and poppy seed as they unwrapped the napkins and exposed two neatly knotted rolls. Trevor, who had been side-tracked by having his glass filled, was last to open the napkin. He stared down at the plate in silence, for a moment not registering what he was looking at. Then his face split into a disbelieving grin.

"Oh, fuck," he said.

Robert looked across at him. "What?"

Trevor held the side plate forward for the rest of them to see. He had not been given two elegantly knotted poppy seed rolls. Instead, his plate bore an exquisitely fashioned dick, crisped to perfection, complete with balls and helmet, with the poppy seeds crowning the head. There was an aghast silence.

"My word," Hugh said. "I think the game's up, my friend."

Freya began to laugh, and the dining room erupted.

"So what does it mean?" Freya said, wiping her eyes. "That she wants some of what you've put on offer?"

Trevor sighed. "No," he said. "I think it means, having met her now, that she thinks I'm a dick-head."

He pushed his chair back and stood. "I have to do something about this," he said. He walked straight down to the kitchen, where Marie and Hedda, who had heard the commotion in the dining room, were busy finishing off the main course.

Trevor smiled and held out his hand to Marie. "I owe you an unconditional apology."

306

"I should think you do," Marie said, offering her hand in return.

"Sometimes these things are entertaining in the abstract, but they don't work at all when you try them in real life."

"Mr Fynn," Marie said. "It would have been all right if you'd asked first. But to exclude me from the joke until the last minute makes me another of your hunting victims, unknowingly lined up in your sights. That's what I didn't like."

"Fair point," Trevor said.

"But what's interesting is that it's such a terribly old-fashioned notion," Marie went on. "It tells me that the class divisions are still in place, and privileged people such as yourselves still feel they can make use of the rest of us as they see fit. No wonder all those old hostilities about landowners are still rife."

Trevor looked at her in surprise. "You know, I'd never thought of it in that way," he said. "Rather sours the joke when you put it like that." He paused again, and then smiled. "But I have to say it was a brilliant riposte. Well worth me making a fool of myself. Beautifully fashioned, too."

"I'm very good at kneading," Marie said, and the tone of her voice was intentionally filthy.

Trevor roared with laughter. "Friends?"

Marie grinned. "I would say so," she said. "But how close we get remains to be seen."

"And if it would be possible," Trevor said, his eye catching the cooling rack on the kitchen table, "could I have a couple of rolls to go with my starter? I want to keep my little fellow for a while."

"Until he goes hard?" Marie said, and enjoyed the sight of Trevor Fynn not knowing quite where to look.

"So what do you think of him now?" Hedda asked when Trevor had left with his new supply of rolls.

Marie poured brandy into the chafing dish and set the match to it.

"On the basis of that elegant apology," she said, shaking the pan and scraping up the crusted peppercorns into the liquor, "I might actually shag him now if he pulls it off."

III
HUGH

The day of the Macnab dawned calm, cool and misty, with the promise of sunshine later on. Hugh was up last, fixed his own breakfast and set off to meet Angus in the cobbled yard. Aidan was there, devouring an enormous bacon and tomato sandwich.

"You couldn't have picked a better day," he said. "Good conditions for all elements of the Macnab."

Hugh was about to ask if that included the cook, but he managed to stop himself. He had almost forgotten that the Royal element had been kept secret from Aidan, as he was implicated in the outcome. Aidan would quickly work out that Freya would have almost certainly come up with a scam for including herself in all aspects of the contest.

He regrouped quickly. "Are the others away?" he asked, as he slung his rifle over his shoulder and pocketed a box of cartridges.

"Aye," Angus, his old stalking companion said. "Freya and Trevor are off with Spaggers and Dash to walk for the grouse first. Robert is out ahead of you, two hours since, fishing the Whipper's Pool for his salmon. Then he'll be away over to the western corner with Kenny, to try for the grouse. He's the only one who fancied his chances on the dawn rise. The rest of you will be on the river for the evening." He paused and looked with mild amusement at Hugh. "And what about you, Hugh? If we see a fine stag today, will you pull the trigger this time – or take another photograph?"

Hugh smiled. "I don't know," he said. "It seems to be a bit of an Achilles heel with me, doesn't it? Let's just see what the day brings."

Angus smiled. "Do you not think that Freya and Trevor are up to something between them?" he said. When Hugh looked baffled, he went on, "The pair of them were whispering about the grouse when they set off, as if they didn't want me to hear. I thought perhaps he might be giving Freya the benefit of his expertise and she was too proud to let me know."

Hugh considered this. "I suggested he coach her a bit in the spring," he said. "So it's more than likely they got together.

Trevor's got the patience to coach, but you know Freya – if she doesn't get it right in the first five minutes, she's very hard on herself."

Angus shook his head affectionately. He had spent a fair amount of time schooling the young Freya in the art of stalking, and respected her determination to excel. It was Freya, too, who had liberated him from the self-enforced agony of not allowing himself to pee all day if he was accompanying ladies on a stalk. He had been brought up with a generation of island children who had never learned to swim because their parents thought it indecent to be seen semi-naked on a beach. Thus, he had endured years of respecting the tender sensibilities of the frailer sex in his charge, and suffering excruciating pain when etiquette dictated that the demands of Nature could not be met. On a stalk with Hugh and Freya, when she was just seventeen, all that had changed. In hindsight, Angus thought she might have noticed his tense expression, and the uncomfortable way he moved as he tried to find a position that took the pressure off his bladder. She had stood up, and announced her intention to nip behind a rock and pee, saying that the men were to look the other way for five minutes. At that moment, Angus thought with a violent surge of relief and gratitude that if a lady could be so relaxed about it, he could be, too. He walked stiffly down the hill to a discreet spot, and never looked back.

He chuckled at the memory, and nodded in the direction of Janet's Knoll. "Away to the north side of the Knoll," he said, "there were hinds moving yesterday evening, and a stag with them. If we stalk from the west, and skirt round in a circle, that's the best chance we have of coming upon a beast quickly. I think they may be in the gully behind."

They chatted amiably as they walked out of the cobbled courtyard and along the gravelled track. The river gleamed softly as they began to climb the steep slope of the hill that shielded the back of the castle. Before them, the hills rose and fell in elegant but irregular rhythms towards the skyline. Hugh stopped for a moment and took in the spectacle.

"We'll head into the bracken there," Angus said, pointing towards a narrow path cut by the sheep. "It gives us some cover against the exposed rise to the east. You know the stags stand there often and have a clear view."

Hugh nodded. "The wind is against us," he said. "We'll have our work cut out on this first stretch."

"Aye," Angus said. "But slowly does it and we'll make it."

The bracken was dense and tall, and it took time to move through it as soundlessly as they could. Angus, as sure-footed as the deer he stalked, despite his advanced years, never put a foot wrong, but Hugh slid and tripped several times before they had gone much above a mile.

Angus stopped at length, pulled out the binoculars and studied the hillsides, the colours of bracken and heather brightening now as the sun worked to clear the mist.

"There's no sign of them," he said. "So I think they must be behind the Knoll. We'll cut across and try to spy them from the top."

"That'll put us very close," Hugh said, "if they're where you say they are."

Angus dropped down and began to descend a steep bank ending at a rushing burn. Hugh stopped, aware that his stomach was knotting. The spectre of the first stag he had not shot rose again. The landscape seemed charged with a peculiar atmosphere this morning, as if something was about to happen. He shook himself, but the sense of foreboding stayed. It was familiar, something he experienced every time he stalked. In the same way Trevor was using the Macnab to lay the ghost of the bottle of malt, so Hugh had intended to overcome his superstitions about shooting stags. But here he was, out in the hills with his old friend, playing out the same charade of would he, wouldn't he? He sighed and was about to follow his companion, when he heard a cry.

He looked up abruptly. The sound came from the Knoll, barely a quarter of a mile away. Angus, steadily moving ahead, had not heard it. Hugh pulled out the binoculars and stood up in the bracken – a cardinal sin – and scanned the summit. The sound came again – it sounded like a young girl – a piercing yell of pain. He focused on the gravestone, standing stiff and stark against the softer contours of the hills, and his heart jumped. A girl with flying red hair was stumbling towards the rise. She cast a wild look behind her, and with a surge of horror, Hugh realised that someone was chasing her. Suddenly, she seemed to look in his direction, and he heard a frantic, sobbing shout. He couldn't hear the words as they were caught up and fragmented amongst the rising threads of mist, but he heard the terror in them, the desperate pleading. She looked behind her again, and then she seemed to lose her footing and fall to the ground. Hugh, staring in disbelief through the binoculars, saw her tumble – and disappear.

He lowered the binoculars, looked intently at the Knoll, saw nothing but the gravestone. A tentative sunray poked through a narrow gap in the mist like a pointing finger, and the Knoll was illuminated. Shaken, he scanned the grassy clearing, but it was deserted, as if the action, which he had seen entirely through the binoculars, had been a sort of magic lantern entertainment with no place in the moment he now inhabited.

"Hugh?" came Angus's sudden reproving hiss from the banks of the burn below. "What are you at?"

Hugh started and looked down, his heart beating violently. "Angus!" he said, louder than he should have done. Angus looked up at him, scandalised at the further breach of stalking etiquette. "I heard some shouts from the Knoll. Can you see anything?"

Puzzled, Angus pointed his binoculars in the direction of the Knoll and patiently worked his field of vision across it.

"Nothing but the stone," he said after a moment. "And there has been no sound, Hugh, except for the calls of the buzzard we saw being chased away by the hoodies. Was it that you heard?"

Hugh looked again, not trusting anything he saw. But the landscape was empty, and he was halfway through a stalk that his companion was anxious to continue. Eventually, he dragged his eyes away from the Knoll, reluctant to let it out of his sight, then let go of it and began his careful descent to the burn.

IV
ROBERT

As Hugh was puzzling over what he had just seen, Robert was following in the footsteps of history, and trying for his fish.

He had arrived at Uishall with the old records book, shown the others Annie Ferguson's account of her catch, and explained what he intended to do. He wanted to take the river at dawn and bag the Whipper's until ten o' clock. If a fish had eluded him until then, he would try to complete the other Macnab components, and if time allowed, try again for a fish in the evening. The Whipper's being unpopular with everyone except Freya, who had other plans for early morning, his Macnab strategy was approved. Freya, however, asked that if he did need to return to the river in the evening, that he fish a different spot and let her try the Whipper's. Robert agreed.

He was a good early riser and the weak light and thick mist that greeted him on Friday morning did not deter him. He also relished the prospect of a day at large in Uishall's splendid wilderness, with no company apart from Kenny, later in the day, who would accompany him on the stalk and the shoot. He had no intention of killing himself to do the Macnab, although he would go for it if luck favoured him. His primary interest was in the salmon, and the challenge of fishing with traditional patterns that had once brought success to a young lady angler over a century ago.

He had set up his campaign carefully. A fly tier on the island, exceptionally skilled and conversant with traditional salmon flies, had done the Jock Scott and Lady Caroline flies, tied on lightweight single salmon irons, as close to the original spec as he could get. The tier being a bit of an anorak, he had gone to some trouble to research the flies, and had added, as a gift, a small Blue Charm, another contemporary pattern, if Robert had no luck with the others and was forced to try something else.

Walking out on the river, he noted the chill in the air, and the mists that signalled the early signs of autumn. A fish splashed under the far bank, and he smiled. They were here, and moving. He felt confident from the moment he cast his line out over the water.

He fished for thirty minutes, rested, ate a chunk of Marie's moist dark Guinness cake and took a small nip of whisky from his hip flask. It warmed him and he rose and fished a further quarter of an hour, taking a pace downstream when he felt like it, not pressured by the presence of other anglers into moving a step down the river with every cast. He stopped after an hour. The Jock Scott was still on the end of his line, soaked through, bedraggled and untouched. Something told him this was the moment. He sat down on the bank as the sun began to break through the mist and pulled out the small wooden fly box he had used ever since he first fished the Uishall as a boy. He cut off the Jock Scott and tied on the Lady Caroline.

He was now poised to cast in the centre of the pool, but he waited a few minutes, watching the water where it fell over a small weir and tucked itself into a nook by the bank. There was an eddy, and in the depths of the peat-dark water, perhaps five or six feet down, he saw the gleam of a fish, holding in the current.

If he had felt anticipation for the past hour, it now flared into hope. He crouched low on the bank and moved back a yard or two. He slipped on his anti-glare glasses and forced himself to do nothing for a few minutes more, tensely watching the fractured patch of silver, wavering in the movement of the current. A few minutes of this, and he cautiously flicked a short length of line into the water just below him, well away from his quarry.

Robert was a consistent, fluent and accurate caster. He knew exactly the distance that lay between him and the salmon, the speed of the water, the rough angle of drift the fly would need to tickle the fish's nose. He was trembling a little, his hand stiff on the butt of the rod as he tried to fight his excitement. He breathed deeply, kept his eye on the fish. It hadn't moved. Then it stirred slightly and looked as if it was beginning to swim to the surface. Without realising he'd done it, Robert lifted the rod, drew off another six feet of line and flicked it out over the water. The fly landed right in front of the fish, there was a surge, a bright silver flash and a sharp tug against the line. Robert, not usually a demonstrative man, leapt to his feet with a shout. He had his take. Now he had to land it.

The salmon, not unreasonably angry at having its leisurely progress up the river so rudely interrupted, fought him spiritedly. It dived and lunged, swam at him and away from him, shot behind a boulder, tried to leap the weir, threatened to first slacken the line so that the hook came out, and then to break him. Robert disappeared into the contest, his concentration grim as he fought to control the fish and bring it to the bank. Judging by the strength of the pull on the line, it was a big fish for the Uishall – maybe eleven or twelve pounds. A hen or a cock, he couldn't yet tell, but whatever it was, it was a magnificent opponent.

After twenty minutes the fish showed no signs of losing strength, but Robert was tiring. The constant demands on his concentration, the unpredictable movement of the fish and the torque on the line were stretching him. The muscles in his arms burned. The fish was determined to continue and complete its journey to the spawning grounds, and something as paltry as an angler was not going to get in its way. Another fifteen minutes and the sun was shining in a cloudless sky, the temperature was on the rise, and Robert was sweating, his hands slippery. Then suddenly, without warning, the fish capitulated. Robert sensed the sudden dead weight at the end of the line and feared his fish was lost, but then he saw it, at ease in the water, some twelve feet distant, in the middle of the Whipper's Pool.

Robert groaned with exhaustion and for a moment dropped into a squat to relieve the pressure on his knees. Still keeping the rod tip raised, he wiped the sweat from his forehead and off his hands. All he had to do now was keep calm and the fish would be his. He began to reel in gently.

In response, the fish, galvanised by the forward momentum, applied the brakes and began to resist the pull of the line. Robert almost sobbed with tiredness and frustration, then hauled himself upright. The punishing contest had drained him and for a moment his grip faltered on the rod. He tightened it with a sudden rush of panic, and felt the heaviness of his arm as the fish tugged. The prospect of defeat loomed. If the fish kept up its second wind much longer, he wasn't sure he'd have enough strength to land it.

He staggered back, then suddenly felt the weight of the rod lift. Fearing the fish had at last worked itself loose, he pulled and felt a tired tug in response. Still there. But somehow, the rod felt lighter. He wondered if he was becoming delirious with the effort, and then thought it must be some sort of physical reaction, his own second wind kicking in. He looked out at the water. The fish was now only six feet from the bank, and at the same time the prospect of netting it occurred to him, he remembered with a terrible hollow disappointment that he had dropped the landing net behind him and then become totally absorbed in the struggle. He knew exactly where it was, three yards behind him, where he had sat to take another nip of whisky before he made his cast.

For a moment, he did nothing, the fish still resisting him, then he felt a jolt in his chest as if someone had knocked against him. He moved his foot to right his balance, looked behind him – stupidly, for he knew there was no one else nearby – and saw the landing net, right beside him, the handle pointing towards him. He cried out with joyful astonishment, not remembering how it had got there, and not caring, either. He looked out over the water, saw the fish now in the shallows, bent down, seized the net and waded a step or two into the river.

A moment later, he had scooped up the fish and lifted it onto the bank. The rod fell from his hand, the muscles in his arm relaxed, and Robert sank to the ground. A beautiful fish, a mature cock, dressed in the silver, mauve and pink dazzle of a healthy adult, its mouth open, gasping in the aftermath of the battle.

"Well landed," a voice said behind him, and with his head still sunk into his folded arms, he said mechanically, "Thank you."

V
FREYA

Freya had risen early and determined to be off over the grouse moor first, away from the more reliable guns who might put her off her stride. As she walked into the gun room to prepare her kit for the day, she was surprised to find Trevor there as well, sorting through cartridges.

"Hey," he said, smiling at her. "Going to get the worst over first?"

Freya nodded briefly. "Dreading it, to be honest," she said, pulling down the shotgun. "I'll enjoy the stalk and the fishing, but I might not even get to them if I can't bag the grouse." She paused. "What are your plans?"

"Well, Hugh's going for the stalk," he said, "and Robert's on the river. I thought I'd do it the other way around – the dead cert first, you know, get my confidence up, and then do the river thing last."

She hesitated. "What do you say –"

"We could walk out for the grouse together," Trevor said at the same time. "I swear I won't cheat or interfere in any way. But a bit of moral support might help things along."

Freya hesitated again, then smiled. "Yes. All right. I wasn't sure if it was in the rules for us to work together –"

"Forget the rules," Trevor said. "This is Uishall." He hitched the gun onto his shoulder. "You'll do it today, Freya. I've just got that feeling."

The light was soft, the mist clinging to the surface of the river when they emerged.

"Higher ground, do you think?" Freya said briskly. "This is going to take a while to disperse."

They deliberated over the map, then hopped into the Landrover and headed out towards the head of the river system, at the base of Roineabhal.

As they set off across the moor, the ground was wet in the bare patches between the tussocks, until they climbed a gentle gradient and the peaty ground gave way to rolling expanses of long, tough grasses. The brackish smell of bog mixed with the earthy perfume of the heather as they walked. Spaggers and Dash frisked about, tails up, noses down, excited at the prospect of flushing up the grouse crouched on the ground. Freya walked quickly, eyes darting, alert to every move of the dogs. Suddenly, a few yards ahead, Spaggers stopped, froze and pointed. The guns halted abruptly, lifted their weapons and waited, Trevor looking relaxed, on home ground, Freya visibly concentrating. He longed to tell her to try to calm it down, but knew he'd only make things worse. Ahead of them, there was a quick flurry, a bark, and the distinctive beat of a grouse's wings as it took to the air.

It was on Freya's side.

"Yours!" Trevor shouted.

She aimed, followed through, the bird flapping low over the heather, just beginning to rise. There was a crack from the gun, a flutter, and the bird dropped. Freya caught her breath and shouted in exhilaration. She turned to Trevor and laughed, incredulous that it had been that easy, the first bird of the morning falling to her gun.

Trevor nodded, his enthusiasm slightly blunted by caution. "Great shot," he said. "All you have to do is one more like that." He pointed at Spaggers, coming back with the bird in her mouth. "Keep your head," he said. "There'll be more of them."

There were. Trevor shot the next, which flew between them, and Freya, not wishing to be greedy in her triumph, gave the shot to him. The next bird was twenty minutes away, on Freya's side, and she missed it. Another flew to her gun, and she missed that, too. Then Trevor shot his second, and his Macnab brace was secure. Freya's shoulders were slightly slumped as Dash brought it to him and he slid it into the bag.

"Stop it," he said, as he broke the gun and packed it away.

"What?"

"Looking sorry for yourself. Come on. The dogs are running up that rise. They're onto something."

They walked for another ten minutes, Freya's excitement over the first shot now muted. The going was tough underfoot, and both of them were breathing heavily as they slogged over the ground.

"It should be this difficult," Trevor said at last, when they stopped for a moment to catch their breath and look out over the land. "I always try to remember that."

"What do you mean?"

"Well, I mean that Uishall never makes it easy for us to catch or shoot anything, and you really need to be skilful if you're going to hunt here. And that's how it should be. It shouldn't be any easier than it is for us to hunt and kill beautiful creatures."

Freya grunted. Her calf muscles were straining with the effort, her face hot, and she was uncomfortably warm, even though she had already stripped off her sweater and was down to her shirt and waistcoat.

"I was shooting on an estate on the mainland last year," Trevor went on, looking out across the loch, now far below them as they skirted the rise of Roineabhal. "The house happens to be set right on the flight path for the geese when they come to winter. And do you know what they do?"

"Go on."

"They've worked out the times when the flights are going over, and they come out of the house with their guns and stand around in the garden, waiting for them. I've seen some of them out there in their slippers and dressing gowns, I'm not joking. It's outrageous, like being at a fairground, taking pot shots at them as they fly over."

"I've never liked driven shooting," Freya said. "Too much like a massacre for me. Is that the same place where they feed the ducks on the pond all summer, then shoot them all in the autumn?"

He nodded. "I'm afraid so. You don't even have to come out of the house for that – you can stick the gun out of the window. Awful. I refused to join them last time, and went out on my own with Dash. I shot probably a tenth of the birds I would have done with them, but I hate seeing all those tragic little bodies piled up at the end of the day. I won't be going there again."

"Do you ever get the urge to write a song about that sort of thing?"

Trevor laughed. "God, no," he said. "I'm a terrible songwriter."

"Natasha Tang would."

"Well, she's more gifted than I am," Trevor said. "But she'd get it all wrong on the lyrics. She's so emotional about the subject, she can't think clearly about it."

"Did you really like her?" Freya asked suddenly.

He glanced at her. "Oh yes, for a while. She could be fun, if you could get her off animal rights, but in the end, I couldn't do it often enough. And then she discovered my dark secret, of course. It was never going to work once that got out." He paused for a moment, remembering her. "Terrific body, though. And good in bed if she'd had enough wine."

"Are you going to shoot any more?" Freya said after a moment, when they had resumed their hike.

He shook his head. "No. But you are."

She looked at him in exasperation and was about to retaliate when Spaggers made a run into a heather clump and about six birds exploded out of it and began to fly towards them.

"Up!" Trevor said quickly.

Freya had raised the gun before she knew what was happening, the birds gathering speed as they rose above her head. She fired once, at a target still five yards in front of her, then wheeled round and shot as the birds flew over her head. She lost her balance and fell into the heather, both barrels empty, the gun safe.

"All right?" Trevor said.

She nodded. "I got the first one," she said breathlessly. "I know I did."

Trevor glanced behind him and looked back at her with a grin. "You got the second as well," he said. Spaggers and Dash were both standing before them, each with a grouse in their mouths. Freya stared at them, fell back into the heather and flung her arms open to the sunshine, and smiled as if she had just been given the world.

"I could have got the first," Trevor said, holding his hand out and pulling her up. "But I'd never have got the second. I can't turn round that fast."

VI
TREVOR

The evening was drenched in the rich colours of sunset when the four Macnab contestants went into the last round. Robert was all done, and would not win. The superb sport he had enjoyed at the beginning of the day had tired him, and while he had walked out after lunch with Ruby and shot a couple of grouse for the table, he had decided not to stalk. A happy man, he had spent the latter part of the afternoon with John, going through the Uishall papers.

Hugh, unnerved after the initial stages of the stalk, had found himself a hundred and eighty yards from a Royal stag after a punishing crawl up a rocky stream bed, and once again had decided not to kill. Angus, not overly surprised, had not taken the shot either.

"Och, there's no hurry to take him," he had said. "He's marked for the cull, but he may graze a little longer in the sun. Freya will be along later, and he will be a fine prize for her. This is a pleasant spot for them, and they'll not be moving the rest of the day."

The stag had indeed fallen to Freya's gun, and now she was on the river, her favourite rod in her hand, on the Whipper's Pool, and looking for the salmon she would almost certainly catch. But with Hugh and Robert no longer contenders for the Macnab, Trevor was up there with her, his grouse bagged and his stag felled shortly before the four of them met up at the castle for whisky, fruitcake and hot pancakes.

"Freya, you do realise what will be required of you if you net your salmon this evening," Hugh had said, when they had all toasted Freya's success with the grouse.

Freya looked puzzled, and then her face cleared in horrified recollection.

"I'd forgotten all about that," she said. "But after the poppy seed prick from Marie, I'm not sure I want to find out what Aidan's response might be."

"Grateful?" Trevor said slyly, and she laughed.

"He's a decent chap," Freya said. "And a bloody good manager. But if he's got that Presbyterian streak in him – he

319

wouldn't see the Royal as a joke. I think we should preserve his dignity."

"Well, you would need co-operation on both sides," Trevor said. "Pity you can't just do these things off the top of your head – we've thought too much about it now."

"This has been a marvellous day," Freya said. "Shooting those grouse was one of those moments I'll never forget. But I'll be content with the Macnab, and never mind the Royal part. I had my Royal stag – that will serve for the trophy."

"You haven't won yet," Trevor said. He shook his head. "It's fitting, don't you think – the world's worst shot up against the world's worst angler." He bowed to her. "May one of the world's worst win."

"Now look, I've asked for a late dinner tonight, and Marie's agreed," Hugh said. "It's five-thirty now, dinner is set for nine-thirty, and nine o' clock is the official end of the Macnab. It was either that, or fishing up to early supper, breaking off, and going back until midnight. Are we agreed, that we get this over, then relax and discuss the day once it's done?"

Freya glanced at Trevor. Hugh would fish for pleasure and turn in happily. She would doubtless catch quickly. Trevor would really have to catch, or let go the Macnab without trying the magical hour before midnight, when some fish decided to move and give themselves up to an angler's patient seduction.

"I'm perfectly happy with that," Trevor said at once. "It's been a long day."

"All right then," Hugh said. "Trevor, you know the rule about red fish? Hen fish must go back, but we'll still award the Macnab for a catch and release."

Trevor nodded, nervous again.

Now, the river sparkled with ruby and gold light, the sun had all but sunk and there was a warm calm in the air.

"Well, I'm for the Whipper's," Freya said, "which I know isn't anyone else's favourite, so what about you two?" She looked expectantly at the men.

"Trevor, you should have first shout," Hugh said generously. "I'm only here for the fishing."

Trevor hesitated. He hadn't got a clue, but tried to look as if he was considering his options with great care.

"If I were you," Freya said, "I'd head for the Long Neck."

When he saw the stretch of water, he understood. It was very similar to the river Freya had taken him to earlier in the summer – the Uishall not too wide at this point and the water flowing slow and easy between the banks, with a little rush towards the far end, over a rough pebble bed. It was also the beat below the Whipper's. He sat down for a while, remembering Freya's advice.

Don't go blundering into the water like a thirsty elephant. Sit and look at it. Look for interesting creases in the water, where a fish might lie for a while, or a bubbling run where they might push themselves through the current.

He looked, self-consciously, not really that much of an expert, but relaxing more as he realised the others had now all dispersed. Robert was strolling towards Loch One, away from the fishers, Freya was casting a couple of hundred yards away, just around a bend in the river, and Hugh was beyond her, aiming for a session on the bank.

Trevor sat until it was obvious he had to do something, then set up his rod and cast over the water. The fly never made it, falling onto a tussock of long grass in a complicated series of coils, and the next thing he did was spend five minutes untangling the line and pricking his finger on the double hook. Rattled, he eventually freed the line and the fly and tried again. His second cast was surprisingly good; the fly seemed to sit for a split second in the surface film, than curved into a small eddy and sank gracefully. Trevor felt the tension mounting. Not a pleasurable sense of anticipation, but a dread that he was going to fail, as usual, and let Freya down after all her patient coaching. Despite her help, he didn't feel any different, any more confident about what he was trying to do.

He cast again, his mind drifting with the slow glide of the water, the golden glow of sunset making pockets of light in the fast bubbling current lower down. Well, he had failed before. Hugh hadn't overcome his dislike of shooting stags this morning, and Trevor suspected that perhaps he never would. Robert had never seriously thought he would compete for the Macnab, although there was no doubt that he had achieved something much more personally important this morning. Freya had overcome her demon.

He realised his line was dragging against something on the riverbed, and reeled in quickly. Never mind the Macnab. Freya would win, and good luck to her. She deserved it. He stood for a moment, watching the movement of water, felt the still warm rays of the sun on his arms, and smiled. He was beginning to understand the others' passion for fishing. It was the stillness in part, the surroundings, the sound of water. He cast again, thinking about Freya and the advice she had given him, and was jolted out of his reverie by a sudden, angry tug on the line.

Freya fished with her usual confidence, but found she was thinking about how Trevor was doing. His mood had been subdued all week. He was still joking with them and making the most of his holiday, but there was something she couldn't put her finger on. Perhaps her bagging the grouse this morning had put pressure on him. Freya felt the presence of the unopened bottle of malt as keenly as he did, and was afraid it would once again make the journey back to London in its virgin state. She wondered if something else was happening at home, that he hadn't told them about.

The day before, he had spent an hour in his room making phone calls. He was preoccupied to the point of becoming moody when he and the others took to the hills to scout the terrain and run the dogs. When Robert asked him what was on his mind, he shrugged and said something evasive about the future.

She cast out and a fish swirled at the fly just as it touched the water. She snatched the take, lost it, and swore. She really had to pull herself together. There was still a Macnab to win, and she had done the hard part. The fish were moving this evening, and with her secret weapon tied neatly to the belly of her fly, she should have no trouble finishing. She cast again and was rewarded swiftly with a savage take. At the same instant, a panic-stricken cry came from down-river.

"Freya!"

Her rod bending hard over the river, Freya raised her head. She knew instantly what that shout meant. "Oh shit," she muttered, her fish struggling at the end of the line. She hesitated, then reeled in quickly. The fish fought, but Freya had no time for an intricate struggle. She held it on a tighter line than she would normally and got him to the net in a business-like fashion. Within two minutes, the fish was on the bank, the fly was out of his mouth, and she had slid him back into the water. She put down the net and trotted off downriver.

"Trevor!" she called as she approached him. She realised he had a fish on, and picked up pace. "Don't panic!" she said. "He's well on. Keep the rod up and the line –" Her list of instructions was interrupted as she fell headlong over a heather bush and landed with a heavy thud in a damp patch of peat.

"Oh for heaven's sakes!" She got up, roughly brushed down her shirt and waistcoat and kept going.

"You're fine," she said, still heading towards him. "Just hang on."

Trevor looked round. "He's quite big, I think," he gasped.

Freya arrived at his side. "No he's not," she said, grinning. "A seven or eight pounder, maybe. But that's more than big enough for a first fish. Just keep the line tight – no, let some out, he's running again –"

For a few moments, the fish thrashed about in the water, then settled for holding in the current. The tension was terrible. Trevor hung on grimly, eyes riveted to the point where the line disappeared into the water. Still on. It was still on.

Freya cast about, and saw his landing net close by.

"I'm not going to help you," she said firmly. "Or it won't count."

"It's OK," Trevor said between gritted teeth. "Just talk to me."

Freya stood by him for a while, and then sat down on a flat rock. She talked about the way he was handling the fish, what he should do when he brought it to the net. When that looked as if it might be a while away, she talked about her job and the improved food at Uishall, and a manuscript she was reading, and her plans to fly out to America in a month or so to host a new book launch. After twenty minutes or so, Trevor began to coax the fish towards him and after a perfunctory attempt to disagree with him it acceded. He had to move back up the bank a little, squat down, still keeping his eyes on the river, rod up, line tight. Groping on the grass to his left, he felt the handle of the landing net and seized it. Breathing heavily, he went forward again, rod up, line tight, then reeled in a little. The fish's tail lifted, its nose came up. Trevor sank the net into the water, pushed it forward and under the fish, and then lifted it.

He stared at it in disbelief. Another cock, a sheen of silver with subtle dashes of magenta and indigo. Freya squatted down and admired it with him, shaking her head.

"You've done it," she said, and was immediately embarrassed and confused by the gentle way she had spoken. She tried again. "Well done!" she exclaimed, in a much more jolly voice, and beamed at him. "You've earned him. And the Macnab."

She was looking down at the fish, and then realised Trevor was looking not at his catch, the one that had got away for ten years, but at her.

Something moved inside her, not to do with the stunning triumph of Trevor's fish, or the one she had set free just a short time ago and would never tell him she had caught, or the lost Macnab. What burst upon her was a sort of understanding, a stab of brilliant light that explained everything and answered all the questions she had been asking. Freya did not have time to articulate what she felt before she realised that the conclusion of the mental process was that Trevor was kissing her. And, even more staggering, she was kissing him back. She felt him pull her towards him, she was standing awkwardly on the rim of the landing net, and he was holding her and not only didn't she mind, she wanted him to. The tenor of the kiss was not to do with his recent victory, nor one of conquest. It was a kiss of affection, and realisation.

For a moment, she pulled away and looked up at him.

"Why did I let you do that?" she asked.

"I was terrified you wouldn't," he said, and paused to consider the question. "Because," he said at length, and they kissed again.

It being almost nine o'clock now, Robert and Hugh had met up on Hugh's beat. Hugh had blanked and the two of them were now walking back down the river. They had come upon Freya's abandoned tackle and guessed what had happened. They were not, however, prepared for the sight of Freya and Trevor, standing together with –

"Good lord," Robert said.

Hugh stared. "I never thought I'd see the day," he said, looking with awe at the spectacle of Freya clasped in Trevor's arms.

"I don't mean that," Robert said. "Look in the net. That's a –"

"My God, Trevor!" Hugh yelled. "Is that really your fish?"

Freya and Trevor broke apart as Hugh came striding across the grass towards them. Robert followed him, and the two stood looking down at the fine catch. After a moment, Freya touched Trevor's sleeve.

"Are you going to kill him?" she said. "Because if you are, the sooner the better."

Trevor looked at Hugh. "Will it count if I let him go?" he said. "I mean, it doesn't matter, because I'm going to let him go anyway –"

"Did you catch, Freya?" Hugh asked her.

Freya shook her head. "I had a swirl, and missed the take," she said. "Then Trevor called and I came down." She flushed suddenly and became intensely interested in watching Trevor de-hook the fish. Hugh looked frankly disbelieving, but he wasn't going to press the point and embarrass her – not until she was ready to take it, at any rate.

"Well," Hugh said, and looked carefully at his watch. "It's past nine now, and if Freya didn't catch –" he looked suspiciously at her and she looked away quickly – "then I believe the Macnab goes to Trevor, and we go straight back to the castle and open that bottle of malt."

Trevor looked up from the river, where he had let the fish back into the water.

"Did you say I called?" he asked Freya.

"Couldn't miss it," Freya said, and grinned, the enormity of Trevor's achievement now beginning to dawn on her. "It's all right, you can admit you needed me."

Trevor shook his head and stood up. "But I didn't," he said. "I hooked the fish, and I wanted to call out, but I realised you'd put your own fish at risk, so I didn't."

"But I definitely heard you call me," Freya said. "I wouldn't have come otherwise. I'd just –" she stopped short and looked at him. "I'm sure you did," she said again. "Why else would I have turned up?"

VII
AFTERMATH

They returned to the castle in time for a quick freshen-up before dinner. Hugh spoke to Marie, assuring her that once the main course had been served, the staff were at liberty to leave the pudding and cheese out, so the diners could finish at their own pace. He was just about to leave the kitchen when Robert arrived in stockinged feet, his shirt half-unbuttoned.

"Hedda?" he said. "Is that boyfriend of yours about?"

"Up in the study," she said.

"Good. Now listen, once you've finished, I want you to join us in the dining room. John already knows the plan. We've got some interesting finds to share with you." He paused then looked at Marie. "Of course, if you'd like to come along –"

"No, thank you," Marie said automatically. "I have my own plans for the evening."

Robert nodded. "Well, that's splendid." He paused. "As for our Macnab victor, I don't think he'll be troubling you tonight."

Marie smiled. "I didn't think so," she said wryly. "But just to be on the safe side, Aidan and I thought it would be a good idea to go out for a drink."

Robert laughed, and then looked at her in horror as the words sank in.

"Oh my word," he said. "Does Aidan know?"

"Oh yes," Marie said. "You wouldn't expect me to keep my Royal cohort in the dark, would you?" She smiled. "He was very embarrassed. But on the other hand, I think you've done me a favour. He would never have had the nerve to ask me out if he hadn't had his confidence boosted by your little competition."

Upstairs, Trevor had knocked on Freya's door. She answered it in a towelling wrap, her hair wet.

"No," she said at once. "I'm starving. We have to be downstairs in six minutes."

Trevor smiled at her. "This will only take one of them." His hands were behind his back.

Freya gasped. "You're a monster," she said. "If you think —"

The sound of clinking glass stopped her. Trevor held up two nips and the still unopened bottle of malt.

"This is for you and me," he said. "To begin with. Because today wasn't just about catching my first salmon and winning the Macnab."

She stood back to let him in and he put the tiny glasses on the table and set the bottle between them.

"That's already a minute," Freya said, grinning.

He picked it up, unpeeled the lead cap, twisted the stopper and listened to the squeak of cork against glass, an emphatic pop as it came free. He set the stopper on the table, put the bottle beside it, and looked at it.

"I don't think you're going to get a genie," Freya said.

"No," he said, smiling. "He's been out already, I think." He poured out two nips and handed one to her. "I knew it would be a great moment," he said. "But I never thought it would be as good as this."

"Two minutes," Freya said.

They toasted and drank it down.

"Hell," Freya croaked, the peat-smoke fire roaring in her throat. "That's terrific. Well worth the wait."

Trevor took the glass out of her hand, put the cork back in the bottle and took her in his arms. Even Freya found it hard to be business-like when she was being kissed, although for the first time, she felt uncomfortable with him, and realised that their intimacy was a very new thing, predated by years of friendship that had not hinted to her at all of the feelings that lay underneath.

"Four minutes," she said briskly, disengaging herself, and he looked at her in surprise. "I can't get dressed in two minutes and appear in the dining room –"

"You don't have to," he said, trying to sidestep her attempts at breaking the mood. "You're not going anywhere until you're properly dressed." His hands slipped to her waist. "And I won't let you get dressed until you let me undress you."

She looked at him, his closeness to her, her state of undress flustering her suddenly, as if she had only just realised what was going to happen.

"Later," she said.

Trevor, thinking that this must be a perverse game Freya played with all her lovers, began to work open the knot in the towelling wrap cord. She didn't know why she was holding back, only that she was still struggling to get to grips with what had happened between them. He was still kissing her as if he meant it, and she felt his desire as keenly as she felt her own. She knew she wanted him and she knew that probably neither of them could wait until after dinner, but she was still unable to give in to the urge. His hands stroked through her still damp hair and she opened her eyes to find him looking at her with an intensity that brought all her instincts for self-protection hurtling to the surface. She didn't want to be played. She didn't want to make a fool of herself.

"Trevor?" Freya said, her voice suddenly serious. "Please – just for a moment. Stop looking at me like that. I almost can't bear it." She took a deep breath. "Look. I'm not the Royal, am I? Because if I am –"

He put his finger to her lips. "Oh Freya," he said. "Don't ever think that. You're not some fairground trinket I'm going to pick up and then throw away. I would never do that. I've waited too long for you."

She was only partly mollified. "All those other women?" she said doubtfully.

"You made up your mind about me years ago," he said. "And for a long time, you were right. I married young because it seemed to be the thing you did. I had to learn that one wrong commitment didn't mean every other commitment would be wrong, too. I had to do something while you worked out I was capable of change."

"When did you know?"

"Do you remember when my father came into the kitchen with a broken lobster, when we were children?"

She nodded.

"The look you gave me when I tried to defend him," he said. "I'll never forget it. It hurt so much that you felt such contempt for me. I feel as if I've spent the rest of my life trying to atone for that moment."

Freya looked at him in astonishment. "You've never told me."

Trevor shook his head. "You had to be ready to hear it," he said. "I wasn't going to risk another verbal bashing." He kissed her again. "I've never really wanted anyone but you. The timing is unfortunate, but we aren't going to do this now because of the Macnab. Do you believe me?"

She smiled and let out a sigh, and looked slightly happier. "I just wanted to hear you say it," she said, and helped him with the knot. "At least the first time isn't going to be in the Sexy Room."

Trevor laughed softly, slipped the wrap down and began to kiss her shoulders. "That," he said, "would set entirely the wrong tone, and be far too much of a cliché." Another kiss, a stroking movement of his hands, and the wrap fell artlessly to the floor. Freya coloured, naked before him for the first time, and instantly, she was awkward again, and didn't seem to know what to do.

"Well, here I am," she said, and there was a note of flippancy that was at odds with the mood of the moment.

They still hadn't got to the bottom of it. "Freya?" he said.

"I'm no Natasha Tang," she said.

He looked at her in amazement as he understood what was going on. Vulnerability was the last thing he had expected, that she would feel threatened by his past, and not be scornful of it, as she had always professed to be. "Is that what's worrying you?" he said. "That you aren't a rock chick? Because it doesn't worry me."

He brought her hands to rest on his chest and ran his fingers lightly down her spine. "What stupid things we've been afraid of," he said.

He kissed her again, his arms enveloping her. This time, their embraces were less tentative, their hands less shy as they gave in to the inevitable. His hands were gentle on her skin while her fingers worked down, faster now, opening buttons, unbuckling his belt, drawing down the zipper. He shook his legs free of his jeans and everything else and then they were on equal terms, standing opposite each other in the middle of the room, grinning sheepishly at each other.

"Come here, rock god," Freya said, and he laughed as she pulled him towards her. "I'm hungry," she wailed.

"So am I," Trevor said.

"Oh, what the hell," she said. "We can always miss the starter."

When Freya and Trevor finally arrived downstairs, the girls were away, and Hugh and Robert were almost finished with the main course. Trevor had the bottle of malt with him, two nips short.

"Ah, you've made it down," Robert said, standing up to greet them. He coughed tactfully. "Almost fell asleep myself."

"Oh do shut up, Robert," Freya said, as Hugh raised his eyes in amusement and Trevor had the grace to blush. Freya poked a spoon into a dish on the hotplate. "What's left for us?"

"We saved you some of the prawns," Hugh said.

"Splendid," Freya said.

"And the grouse are wonderful," Hugh said. "I think I had one of yours, but the other two are yours and Trevor's."

They ate quickly and hungrily, their appetites even keener than before. Just as Freya laid down her knife and fork with a sigh of contentment, there was a knock followed by the entrance of John with a sheaf of papers, and Hedda.

"Excellent," Robert said. "Now we can get on to the evening's entertainment."

"Sounds interesting," Freya said, pouring everyone a glass of wine. "But first, I think a toast is in order."

She opened the cabinet door of the ugly-beautiful Victorian sideboard and paused to pat it affectionately before she pulled out six small whisky tumblers.

"I thought you'd be devastated when I told you," Robert said.

"Well, it wasn't easy," she said. "But I rather think it's added to its charm. It's such a terrific story. And even better – we have yet to get to the bottom of the mystery."

She set the glasses on the table. "Trevor, this is your honour. We've seen that bottle of malt go in and out of that fishing bag for more years than I care to remember, so this is a moment to savour for us all."

Trevor filled the tumblers.

"Save a bit for later, eh?" Robert said. "We might be needing it."

Hugh raised his glass and everyone else followed suit. "Trevor – our Macnab champion," he said solemnly, and they all drank.

"Now then," Robert said, who seemed very anxious to get on. "As you know, John and I have been cataloguing all the papers up in the study. We've found out some very interesting things, but John has done some extra research to do with –" here he turned and pointed up at Janet's portrait – "this fascinating Lady of Uishall here."

Everyone looked obligingly at the portrait, and then Trevor said, "Hey – she looks a bit like this young lady here." He stopped. "Or is it just the hair?"

John was grinning, and Hedda looked curiously at him.

"What?" she asked.

"I'll keep it brief," he said, standing up and rolling out a piece of paper. "This is all pretty rough and needs to be drawn out properly, but I've got a good idea of how it happened. Janet, who was employed in the castle as storeroom manager, married Alec, the 23rd Laird of Uishall, in February 1837. Their daughter, Elinor, was born in May that year." He swung round and picked up the painting that was propped on a small table in the corner of the dining room. "This is Elinor, aged eighteen, just a year before she married."

Hedda sat forward. "This seems to be the only room in the islands where my hair is always in fashion," she said, and laughed. "Who was the lucky man?"

"I expected it to be local aristocracy," John said, "but then I found a letter from the would-be father-in-law to Janet, discussing the match."

He laid a letter on the table.

Your Ladyship,

I write respecting the wishes of my son, Calum, who seeks the hand of your daughter Elinor in marriage. Be assured I have tried to dissuade him from the match, as he has neither land nor title and could not furnish his wife with the standards of luxury in which she has been raised, and to which she has a right. He swears there has been no impropriety between them, and therefore no insidious reason behind their wish to marry, but that the affection he has professed for her was only admitted when she first confessed her love for him.

I do not know how this situation is to progress, except that to say for my part, I will endeavour to impress upon my son the foolishness of the course he seems set on. I would know your mind on this, your Ladyship, for we have always done honest business together, and I would not lose your goodwill on account of this most unfortunate matter.

Your humble and loyal servant
Archie MacInnes

"MacInnes!" Hedda cried.

John held up his hand. "Archie MacInnes was the factor. The link is clear-cut, right from this letter. It seems that Elinor was a rebel, and never settled into the ladylike ways expected of her. She fell in love with Archie's son, who was also his apprentice, and then refused all other offers."

"What did the laird have to say about that?"

"Alec had been dead for two years when the situation arose."

"So the Lady Janet agreed to the marriage?"

John smiled. "I think the Lady Janet would have been well aware of the irony of the situation, that her daughter had no interest in the wealth she had worked so hard to secure for her. But she also knew that love was an impossible master to conquer, and so she gave her blessing."

Hedda looked with renewed fascination at Janet's portrait. "So where do I fit in?"

"Here you are. Calum worked at Uishall all his life, and was factor for thirty years. He and Elinor had three children, all sons, all survivors. The middle one, Rossyth, was born in 1860 and married Rosalyn Drummoch in 1889. Two children, Freddie, who survived, and Sarah, who died of tuberculosis in 1902. Freddie married Jessie Mayers in 1918 and had Henry in 1918 and Fanny in 1921 –"

"Henry's my granddad," Hedda interrupted him. "He died before I was born."

"Henry married Mairi in 1939 –"

"And my dad was born in 1940," Hedda said. "Mum was born in 1945, they got married in 1975, and I was born in 1980." She stopped. "Janet is my – what – I can't work it out."

"She's your great-great-great grandmother," John said. He looked up at the portrait again, then back at the stunned face of his girlfriend. "It's quite a thought, isn't it?"

She nodded. "My father will be even more bitter when he finds out," she said quietly. "Elinor gave up the land he's so obsessed with, with scarcely a thought."

Robert laughed and raised his glass. "To our new-found Uishall descendant," he said, and glanced at John with conspiratorial glee. "But our tale is not yet told," he said. "There is someone else in this room with a Clan Macleod bloodline."

Freya looked around. "Who on earth is that?" she said. "It certainly isn't me. My family tree goes all the way back to 1674, and there isn't a Scot anywhere on it."

Robert took over.

"Alec didn't marry Janet until 1837, but she had already borne him a son out of wedlock in 1824. After two marriages, Alec realised he had become infertile and could no longer father children, so he claimed his bastard son, Alasdair, and brought him into the Clan. Alasdair didn't marry until 1861, when he fell in love with Caitlin Connaught, from Alnwick, Northumberland. They had two children, Victoria, who died in infancy, and Alfred, born in 1862. When Alasdair sold Uishall in 1875, the family moved to England, where Alfred married Emily Barclay in 1884. They had one child, Lorna, born in 1885, who married Charles Sturton in 1909."

At this, Trevor looked up. "Sturton?" he repeated.

"Ah, I'm glad you're still with us," Robert said. Hugh was staring at his brother.

"Lorna and Charles had two children, Abigail and –"

"Humphrey," Trevor said, getting up from his seat and coming round to look at the paper spread open on the table. "Go on," he said, and Freya noticed that his voice was shaking.

"Humphrey was born in 1910," Robert said. "He married Caroline Dent in 1933, and they had one child, Phylicia, in 1935."

"My mother," Trevor whispered. "Who married Cornelius Fynn in 1961, and had me in 1965."

Freya gaped at him. "But – didn't you know? Didn't she know?"

"She'd never gone into it," Trevor said, still staring at the paper. "Not that far back. And my father wouldn't have asked. She had a small fortune and he wasn't interested in anything else. The only thing my father's ever looked closely at is money."

All of them were now looking at the rough family tree scrawled out on the paper. Trevor and Hedda looked at each other, and shook their heads. Robert was grinning as he replenished the whisky tumblers and raised his glass.

"As far as I can tell," John said, "Alfred was the last of the patriarchal line. So Lorna was the only link back to Alec."

Robert smiled and went to study the portrait of Alec on the wall. "When you look at him, you can see the likeness," he said. "There are still things we don't know, of course. All sorts of unanswered questions."

John gathered the papers into a neat pile on the table and said, "Well, there are a few other bits and pieces, but that's probably enough history for one night."

"I'd like to say thank you," Robert said, and shook his hand. "We'd never have got so far with this if it hadn't been for your interest. We'll meet up again before I leave and discuss future strategy, eh?"

"Most definitely," John said. He offered his hand to Trevor. "Thank you for the whisky – and congratulations on the Macnab. It seems you have quite a lot to celebrate tonight." He held out his hand to Hedda, and they left the dining room.

Trevor sat back down next to Freya and looked round at his companions.

"This puts rather an odd light on things," he said after a moment. "The Macnab was all I wanted today, and look what I ended up with." He looked more puzzled than pleased, and didn't seem to know how to break the mood. "I thought we'd be partying tonight."

"Well we can still do that. How about finishing off in the drawing room?" Hugh said helpfully. "All these people staring at us from the walls are beginning to spook me. Besides, I want to hear about that fish you caught."

"Another toast before we go," Robert said, and looked at Trevor. "To the Laird of Uishall and Maglavat."

Trevor gazed at his friends and looked too dazed to smile. He shook his head again. "What will my father have to say?" he said, and looked suddenly amused. "He's from Old Money, you know, and he's always hated the fact that I made New Money."

"And now you've just found you can legitimately claim an ancient title," Freya laughed. "It'll confuse him for years."

Trevor grew sombre again. "Well, this really does change quite a lot," he said vaguely, and fell silent again.

"Trevor, what *is* the matter with you?" Freya asked.

He shook his head, and his smile was broader this time. "There's something up," he said, and then, annoyingly, refused to be drawn on the matter. "It's no good you hassling me," he said firmly. "I can't say anything further until next week."

Down in the staff quarters, Hedda and John poured out wine and drank thoughtfully. Janet's diary lay between them.

"It's incredible," Hedda said. "It's one thing looking like someone hanging on the dining room wall – quite another to be closely related to her."

John smiled. "I think it's marvellous," he said. "You're living proof that the past is with us all the time, constantly being reborn into different people, creating new events, recreating old ones." She gazed at him with affectionate amusement. "That remarkable woman contributed to you, is partly responsible for who you are."

"And so did the man she slept with," Hedda said, "who wasn't Alec, and who may not be such an attractive proposition."

He shook his head. "He couldn't have been all bad," he said. "Nobody who made you could be all bad."

She raised her eyes, still caught in the mysteries of the past.

"You didn't tell them about your theory," she said. "About Alec and how he died, and this –"

"They'd had enough," John said. "Poor old Trevor looked as if he'd been run over by a truck." He stretched out and Hedda lay back with her head in his lap. "I'm not sure what it actually means, in real terms, but it must be a bit of a shock to discover a link like that. The thing is, he loves Uishall. They all do. And he can afford to do something about it. Perhaps that link will galvanise him."

"Or maybe he'll work out he can make more money out of the music industry," Hedda said drily. "He's got Alec's blood in his veins, after all. And Alec wasn't a fool."

John smiled sadly. "Only about the woman he loved," he said. He leaned across to the bedside table and picked up the linen-wrapped clay doll. "It can't be a toy," he said, not for the first time. "Robert thought it was Alasdair's, but why would she wrap it so carefully?"

"Perhaps it's a keepsake from his childhood," Hedda said.

John shook his head. "From what we can tell, Janet was anything but sentimental," he said. "And it's never been touched, has it? A child playing with a clay toy would break it, chip it, get it dirty. It isn't even marked." He stopped. "And it was hidden with the diary, something she wanted to keep absolutely safe. Perhaps a charm of some sort."

Hedda shrugged, more interested in the solving of the key mystery. She picked up the diary and leafed through it. "She isn't going to tell us," she said in frustration.

"She is," John said. "We just have to know what we're looking for."

"There's masses of stuff about her job –"

"She was learning to write, remember?" John said, amused at her impatience. "She would have put anything down, just for the practice."

Hedda went forward, a thick wad of pages covered in Janet's sharp, exact letters, dismissed in a single turn.

"It's all servants' gossip and –" she broke off, reading snatches, then paused.

"Hang on. This is an interesting one:

"*August 11th, 1836: It seems our happiness will never amount to more than a series of secret meetings. This week my love cannot lie with me and my bed is empty of his warmth and embraces. I lie alone and all I feel is desolation, for without a child inside me, he will not give up his wife. Whatever curse has been laid upon him, it seems there is only one way I can mend it, though in fixing, it may break us both.*'

"So there were strings attached to their affair," Hedda said wryly. "Why am I not surprised?"

"This wasn't an ordinary affair," John said. "She wasn't the only one who stood to lose." He grimaced and read the entry again over Hedda's shoulder. "That sounds like she'd made up her mind to take matters into her own hands," he said quietly. "What a terrible risk for her to take. What if Alec *didn't* love her, and was only interested in the child?"

"She must have been certain," Hedda said. "She was pretty smart, wasn't she? She'd have lost everything if she wasn't." She flicked forward again.

"August 29th, 1836: I have cast my lot with the devil. If my love is to be damned in the next life, then I must be damned along with him if we are ever to overcome the barriers that divide us. He will not know, though my heart will break for deceiving him if I now carry the weight I would bear for him.'

"That's the one," Hedda said. "Look at the writing – it's all crabbed. She must have been crying when she wrote it."

John turned the pages ahead. "So who was it?" he said. He stopped and looked at Hedda. "Could you have done it?"

Hedda shook her head. "No. Absolutely not." She looked wryly at him. "Not even with her blood in my veins."

"Perhaps she loved the other man, too," he speculated.

Hedda shrugged and bent her head to the diary again. "Hang on – here's a name she hasn't mentioned for ages," she said, side-tracked as she recognised it. "It's the bloke who did the fire in her room from the first day she was at Uishall:

"September 20th, 1839: We have dismissed Gillies MacNicol for theft. I came upon him during the day, going through the contents of my writing table. Alec confessed to being amazed that such a steady member of his household should betray his trust. I have since found all accounted for. I am afraid now, that even though he has left the house, he will not rest until he has made me pay for the bad deed I did him.'

"What bad deed?" John said, frowning. "Was sacking him that terrible?"

"Definitely," Hedda said. "Uishall was probably a key employer. If he left without letters of recommendation, it would look suspicious at the very least." She flicked forwards, the entries becoming more infrequent as Janet's life blended with Alec's into a content that needed no confirmation on paper. And then: "John, listen to this:

"October 24th, 1854: My beloved Laird is dead. I could not save him, nor can I write the terrible manner of his death. My magic was not strong enough and I must bear the blame for his suffering and my loss. Thank God, the children were spared his pain. We have sent for Elinor. All the years we have been

married, I have waited in dread, and hoped I would be spared. But my sin has found me out, and now I must wait to join him before I can end the dreadful loneliness that already torments me.'"

John leaned back, thinking. "We're missing something," he said slowly. "That previous entry – Gillies MacNicol being sacked for theft." He shook his head. "What if he was looking for something specific? What did she have that –" He stopped, perplexed. "Why would you look for valuables in a writing table?"

2.
STALKED

I

The night was dark and clear as Alec sat on the bench in front of Uishall Castle and watched the gleam of the river in the moonlight. Beside him, the grey form of Arakan, great granddaughter of Meg, dozed peacefully, her long, elegant nose nudging at her master's foot. The air was warm as it often could be at this time of year and the bright stars pricked the sky.

The 23rd Laird of Uishall was fifty-two now, his hair grey but his eyes still bright, his face still thin, still handsome to his devoted Lady Janet. They had shared seventeen years together as man and wife and they had been happy. After their daughter was born, no further children came, but Alec took such pride in the two he had, he never wanted for more, and Janet wanted only to be at his side. Alasdair, now in his thirties, had grown into a capable man and would be a worthy successor. Father and son had run Uishall for ten years now, and its wealth mitigated the failing fortunes of Maglavat, now run by Jamie, Ruaraidh's only surviving son.

The year he had married Janet and the year the Lady Iona died had brought more suffering with the death of Ruaraidh's wife, the Lady Margaret. After years of illness, she had deteriorated until she was a pitiful sight indeed – not only her body wasted and tormented by violent shaking fits, but her mind unhinged, too. Alec could still remember her final agonies, coming so close on the death of his own wife. Her shouting and raving, her wild eyes and restless hands, her distressing attacks on the servants who still loved her and tended her faithfully, and were not always strong enough to fend her off before she scratched or bit them. Eventually, her strength failed for the last time, and when she lay weeping in bed, speaking in senseless, broken syllables, Alec rode over the mountains to comfort his brother and do what he could before she died. When she drifted beyond them on the heavy doses of morphia that were the faithful physician's last resort, Alec could only feel grateful that she had finally passed beyond pain.

He took solace in his tiny daughter, Elinor, on whom he doted. If his love for Alasdair was always tempered by a certain distance, the years they had spent apart never quite closing the last space between them, the love he bore Elinor was unstinting and emotional. He saw her mother in her, the wild red hair, the strong face, the will that matched his own and caused many a fight between them.

As the family had grown, Uishall had submitted itself to change again. While all the landowners around them had brought in the fashionable white breeds of English sheep, Alasdair had trialled them, abandoned them and stuck stubbornly to the Black Hebrideans, with which he repopulated the estate. Alec gave him his head, but could see that his son's strategy was no more successful than that of his neighbours, except that they saved on import costs. Alasdair, reluctant to admit defeat, was still brooding about what else could be done with the land that surrounded them, and on which they depended in part for their prosperity. The distillery still provided the main family income, but the land nagged at him, its failure to fulfil its potential a constant irritation. Maglavat still limped along, although its relative poverty was not so much the fault of Jamie, who did his best, but of his father, who had damaged the assets so badly his son was still engaged in repair strategies before he could turn his thoughts to profit and the future.

Two years after Margaret, Ruaraidh had died in an asylum, his face eaten away by syphilitic gummas, most of his body paralysed, his heart finally giving out as the last stage of his disease triumphed. It was over a year since he had seen his home, for he grieved for his dead wife and seemed racked by guilt, too late in the day, for the way she had suffered at his hands. Alec had Ruaraidh's body shipped home and laid to rest in the churchyard at Uishall, beside the Lady Margaret. His grieving for his brother seemed all the more painful for the lack of sadness he could find in it.

II

Through all the pains and joys and triumphs and tragedies of the last seventeen years, Janet had been by him, and made everything else that befell the family bearable. The first year had been particularly hard on her, for as well as still carrying the child, she also faced a steep learning curve in a house where her only friends were her husband and son and her former colleague, Alice.

It was during this period that Janet understood the gulf that had widened between her and Alasdair. It was not a gulf of enmity, but of knowledge, and she felt keenly the alliance father and son had formed of necessity without her. She had won Alec against almost insuperable odds, but now she had to deal with the consequences that both of them faced for choosing to marry. They stood firm while the Macleod family made clear its disapproval, while the servants showed their resentment of their new mistress, and while Janet learned how to conduct herself as the Laird's wife.

She and the Laird did not often quarrel, but when they did, especially in their first months together, when relations were fraught between everyone, she would be seized by the fear that she could never become the wife he would wish, and then Alec would feel something of the insecurity she lived with.

There was, too, a great deal for them to learn about being together, for the things that Alec had grown up with, that he had always taken for granted in the course of getting on with day to day life, were all unfamiliar to his new wife, who was not used to having servants at her beck and call, or a large house to run. Alasdair had already run the gauntlet and although he remembered his first year at Uishall as something of a trial, his nature had enabled him to view it as an interesting challenge.

For Janet, the realities of becoming Alec's wife and the transitions she underwent were more complex. Alec was still coping with the loss of Iona and the censure of his peers; she knew that her complete financial dependence on him added to Uishall's burden; she heard the uncomprehending rage of his brother, who asked why Alec did not just throw the whole Uishall legacy away and move into a blackhouse with his wife and son. She faced personal challenges, too. The switch from being a servant to having to command them; from being Alec's secret lover to standing publicly at his side; from understanding her place in the household as a worker, to being utterly overwhelmed by it as its mistress.

Alec did his best to minimise the swings he saw in her mood and confidence as she fought for recognition and respect – but he could not always help her, for if she could not stand without him, she would fail as mistress of the house.

But the months passed, the baby Elinor arrived, and the Lady Janet began to grow into her role and forge relationships with the kinder members of the household. She recovered her strength and resourcefulness, and with it, her dignity. She never raised her voice to her staff, gained a degree of confidence in her own authority and found that this was sufficient to generate a better working environment.

There was a turning point, when Uishall was entertaining a party that included a wealthy Englishman, Richard Charles. He had been given a fine room on the first floor and the services of a maid, for his own maid had been taken ill on the journey. He lost no opportunity to mock Uishall for its backward ways and sneer at how the refinements of civilised life had not yet reached the islands. Janet noticed that he was also free with his hands when it came to the maids, indulging himself in familiarities that embarrassed even his fellow guests. When one of them asked him to tone it down, he shrugged and said,

"Why the devil should I? From what I've heard, the Laird himself has a dirty record with his servants."

"You have accepted his hospitality," the guest retorted, "and your behaviour speaks for us all. Macleod will not stand on ceremony if you insult him."

"I wish I had Macleod's nerve," Charles returned. "They are feisty ones, these Scotch wenches, and give a gentleman good value when they fight. No wonder he took one permanently to his bed."

After hearing this from Alice, Janet's opportunity for revenge came sooner than she expected. Passing his room one morning, Janet heard a shriek, and pushed open the door to see Mary, the maid, extricate herself from his embrace, and deliver a resounding slap to his face.

Unaware that Janet had entered, Charles grabbed Mary by the arm and forced her towards the bed. "You have just worked your last day in this castle," he said, "but you will perform one last duty for me before you quit."

"If she has already made your bed, sir, it would be folly for her to lie on it and necessitate its being made again," Janet

341

said. She turned to Mary. "Get up, Mary, and if you are not hurt, be off and about your business."

Charles looked at her in outrage. "She struck me, ma'am, and will be dismissed from your service for insulting a guest."

"I rather think, sir, that it was you who dealt the first insult, and were deserving of the rebuke." Janet turned away from him. "Mary, I need some flowers cut from the garden," she said. "A spray for the dining room and some fragrant roses to set in my writing room. Bring them to me before you resume your duties."

Mary nodded and scuttled from the room. She could not resist, however, creeping back to hear the end of the encounter.

"Only two people in Uishall Castle have the power to hire and dismiss staff," Janet said. "One of them is the Laird, and the other one is me."

"I will take this up with the Laird," Charles said. "And you will furnish me with another maid for the rest of my stay."

"The Laird will listen to me on this matter, and he will not take kindly to one of his servants being used so." At the door she said, "Besides, there are no further maids I can put at your disposal. You will have to make do with your manservant."

Janet's championing of Mary went round the castle before the hour was out; Mary delivered a handsome vase of roses to her mistress and thanked her profusely. Janet put her to work another floor while Charles remained at Uishall, which in the event turned out to be only a matter of another day. Alice gleefully informed Alec of the incident, who chuckled to himself at the first evidence of the assertive talents Janet would develop as manager of his family home.

III

Alec had lost half his friends with the divorce of Catherine, and had said goodbye to a good few more with the controversial circumstances surrounding his marriage to Janet.

With his social calendar somewhat curbed, Alec absorbed himself in the task of running the Macleod businesses, and he seemed to grow in stature with the woman he loved at his side, and the two children they had forged from their passion. Janet had met and answered every challenge, and not a day passed when they did not feel gratitude for their contentment after enduring so many years of separation.

She took to the sporting life of Uishall with the skills he remembered first seeing when she poached salmon from the river with her father, and shared his enjoyment of the deerhounds and the hunt. The first time she fished at his side as his wife, she cast deftly over the water and said, "And whose fish shall it be should I land one?" And he saw the girl he had wanted so many years ago, and the woman he had at last been brave enough to claim.

She was fond of the dogs, she was fond of the children, she liked Uishall, was a capable household manager and an interested participant in his business affairs. They travelled to England and Europe, and Janet was interested in everything she saw and fascinated by everywhere they went, and grateful for the opportunities Alec had given her. But her passion she reserved for Alec alone – she loved her husband with a fierceness and devotion that would brook no criticism of him. She had fought too hard for him, suffered too much for him and risked too much for him, to ever take him lightly, or quite believe that she was safe in his arms from the darkness of the past.

IV

Alec came back from his memories, stood up from the bench and then turned towards the river. He had intended to sit out and wait for Alasdair's return, who was away inspecting broken fences with the factor, and who would doubtless be close to home by now. But perhaps he had been cajoled into staying for dinner, and as the air was not quite so warm now, Alec decided instead to walk a little before he turned in. He thought of Elinor, away to Skye visiting friends at Dunvegan. He missed her, and dreaded the day when she would marry and he would have to relinquish her to the care of a husband.

He had hardly taken more than a few steps when a sound from the broad gravel drive running between him and the castle stopped him. He looked keenly into the shadows. The sound had been sharp and sudden, something heavy and metal clattering onto the grit. No voice came out of the darkness to reassure him or explain an accident. Beside him, Arakan stiffened and stood by him.

"Who's there?" Alec called out, sudden and loud, trying to force an answer from the darkness.

A footman appeared in the front door, which was standing open to the night air.

"Are you all right, sir?"

"Yes, yes," Alec said impatiently, for he was tense now and his quiet reverie had been disturbed. "Keep an eye out as you close up tonight, for I thought I heard someone moving near the house."

"Perhaps it might be best to turn in," the footman said uneasily. "The Lady Janet is wondering what keeps you."

Alec began to walk towards the door, then changed his mind. Arakan was listening, and there was a low, warning growl in her throat. Thinking a slate might have tumbled from the roof, the Laird decided to do a circuit of the castle, to see if the source of the noise could be found. "Aye. Very well. Bolt the door, and I'll be in directly by the back."

As he rounded the wall of the tower, just a few paces from the door leading from the back of the castle through to the main rooms, there was a shuffling sound behind him. Arakan growled again, this time a rumble of anger. Alec turned, picking up on the dog's sudden fear, but was too late to stop a strong, muscular arm seizing him from behind.

"I have you sir," a quiet voice said from behind him. "You'll not escape me now."

Alec felt the man's other arm brace against him, and heavy pressure at his side. Arakan leapt at her master's assailant and bit him savagely in the throat, but it was too late, for Alec had staggered and fallen against the wall. The man holding her master screamed and scrabbled at his side for the knife and sank it into the bitch's chest. There was a piercing yelp, she fell at once and lay writhing on the cobbles. Alec moaned in torment and reached out his hand to caress her head as she whimpered, spasmed and then lay still. He struggled to right himself and stand, but he was faint almost to unconsciousness and could make no decisive movements. He had barely felt the sting of the knife that had been thrust into his side, but he had felt the turn of the blade and its rough extraction, and knew at once that he had been dealt a mortal blow. He felt hot blood soaking through his shirt and waistcoat and running down his side, and the sudden urgent banging of his heart against his ribcage flooded him with fear. Sweat broke out on his skin. He could not think, could not reason why –

His attacker was bending over him, bleeding profusely from Arakan's bite. "You have stolen from me," he said. "All these years I have borne in silence the consequences of your theft." He stopped for a moment, his breathing heavy. "These many nights

I have waited for my chance to punish your crime and the sorrow you have brought upon me."

"Who are you?" gasped Alec. "I know your voice, if you will not show me your face. I have a right to know what wrong I did you if I am to die."

The man stood unsteadily and began to limp away. "Your Lady will know me, and remember the promise I made her. You took from me what was mine, and if I cannot have her, then at least I have killed the thief who took her."

At that moment, the back door of the castle was thrown open and the footman who had bolted shut the front door appeared. In a second, he was bellowing for help from within. The Laird was carried inside and taken to the library, and laid on the chaise-longue.

For years afterwards, the servants would talk in hushed tones of the single terrible scream that rent the candlelit gloom of the downstairs rooms when the Lady Janet ran into the library and was confronted with the sight of her stricken husband. At once she began to shout instructions at everyone, for water, for bandages, for towels and sponges. She tore open his shirt, bathed the ugly, gaping wound where the knife had twisted, tried frantically to stem the bleeding. She had to be dragged away from him when the physician came thundering in an hour later, his horse left lathered and steaming in the cobbled yard.

He brought with him news as well as his medical bag. "They have found a wounded man not two hundred yards along the drive," he said, bending swiftly to Alec and examining the wound. "His throat is torn and he is unlikely to live."

"Arakan bit him," Alec whispered. "She fought for her Laird until he killed her." He closed his eyes against the pain of the memory.

"Who is he?" Janet said. "He will not slink away to the Devil without first feeling the wrath of my own hand."

The physician was trying to apply pressure to the wound. "They are saying it is Gillies MacNicol, an ex-employee of the house."

At these words, Janet turned white.

"Alice!" the physician said, turning to the housekeeper. "Help the Lady Janet. She will fall." He looked at Alec's face, cold and sweating, already grey with approaching death.

"Macleod," he said in a low and urgent voice.

Alec's eyelids flickered. "Tell me the truth," he said, his breath coming in shallow gasps. "I will not survive this blow."

The physician shook his head. "I wish I could say otherwise. But your lung is torn and you are still losing blood. There is no time to send for the minister."

Alec smiled faintly at this. "If I were of a mind to seek absolution, he would not give it me in any case."

"Are your affairs in order?" the physician whispered.

Alec grimaced. "All. Only care for my wife, for she thinks too much of me, and cannot see a life beyond that which I give her."

"It will be done. Alasdair will do his duty, you may depend on it."

"For the rest, I am a sinner and will be damned. I will make my own negotiations with God. But I will die with my love at my side, and that will be my final blessing."

She came to him, pale as death herself, and took his hand.

"The physician says it is my time. The man has done for me, and I must ask you –"

"What did he say?"

Alec shook his head. "Only that I had stolen you from him," he said. "I rather think, if I am clear in recollection, that it was he who thought to steal from you."

"And I expelled him from our house, for I feared he would harm us if he remained." She looked agitated. "I caught him going through my papers," she cried out, as if it was necessary to defend herself. "What else should I do but dismiss him? If I had known –"

"Hush, hush," Alec said. "You have done no wrong. We could not keep a thief beneath our roof." His voice suddenly sounded dry and cracked like dead wood. He shook his head. "He said I had taken what was his." He looked at Janet and his fingers moved feebly on her cheek. "He brought the logs for your fireside," he said, as if a memory had suddenly risen in his mind. "Perhaps he was in love with the lady whose fires he lit."

"If infatuated he was, it was not confessed to me," Janet said. "He carried logs and swept my hearth. If he should presume to love me on so small an account, he was a fool."

"Ah," Alec said, and gave her a sad smile. "And I would forgive any man for being jealous of the lady it has been my privilege to love." He closed his eyes, and when they opened and rested on her face, she trembled for the sudden doubt she saw in them. "But I could not forgive it if she returned his love with promises of her own. You would not –" he said, and stopped. "When you were not my Lady Janet, you would not have –"

She shook her head vehemently. "I have never confessed love, nor given it, to any man but you," she said.

He closed his eyes in sudden anguish. "Forgive me. I should not even question –" He stopped again, his eyes moving restlessly around the room. "But I have a confession, and I must make my peace with you before I die. I never told you, Janet, that when we made our pact to become lovers, I broke my side of it."

She leaned forward and stroked his forehead. "How?"

"I told you I would only marry you if you bore my child," he said. Her hand trembled suddenly. "But if you had not, I would have married you in any case, because we had already suffered too long, each without the other."

There was nothing else he could have said that would have caused her heart to break as it did then. *Then we are both betrayed*, she thought, and wept for the fears each had hidden from the other.

She massed her courage. "There is something you must know," she said. "Elinor –"

"Elinor," he said, and a sob broke from him.

"Don't – don't," Janet said. "We will send letters. Take comfort she is spared, for she could not bear to see you injured so." She tried again, dashing tears from her eyes as she tried to steady her voice. "Listen to me. The day I found Gillies MacNicol looking through my papers –"

"I remember."

"He thought I might have –"

He shook his head at once, silencing her. "I did not make my confession to force one from you," he said softly. "There is enough pain here, is there not, without adding to our sorrow?"

"Elinor –"

"Elinor is her mother's daughter," he interrupted, his eyes holding hers. "She is her mother's daughter, and that is all. I saw you grow with her, and she was delivered into my arms from your confinement, and she has known no other father." His fingers pressed against her lips. "Never speak it, Janet," he whispered. "Never burden me with the suffering you bore on my account, because I was too slow to confide the steadfast nature of my love. Elinor is a daughter we have made between us, fashioned from our natures, and I love her beyond measure."

He stopped again. "Tell her to live as her mother lived," he said, his fingers tightening on hers. "With spirit, and with no fear for what the voice in her heart might say to her. For all the happiness I ever had is due to the courage you had in loving me, and never giving up till you had won me."

"I will tell her," Janet whispered.

"Come closer," he said. "I cannot feel your hand in mine."

"Forgive me," she said again, as if her life depended on it. She laid her head against his chest, and for the last time felt his hand weave into her hair.

"Peace, peace," he said. "I will not leave you so distressed. From being a maid, you always took the course that was meant to bring us together. You have been faithful when I was not, and waited for me when only you understood how much I loved you. You have borne my cruelty when I deserved nothing but your condemnation. And I have tried to atone for my wrongdoings with every day that has passed. But if it gives you peace, I will forgive you."

3.
SIRED
AUGUST 1836 – SEPTEMBER 1839

I
AUGUST 1836

Gillies MacNicol pushed open the door of the woodshed and paused, listening. Sunshine slanted through the horizontal cracks in the rough timber walls, alleviating the gloom with dusty bars of light. The earthy, nutty smells of soft wood chips spread on the floor and stacks of drying logs settled in his nose, the light scamper of a mouse's dainty feet ran into his ears. Familiar warmth of damp half-light, familiar scent of musty forest, familiar sound of a quick escape. But still, he could tell. There was a slight charge in the air that was different. Someone else was in there. He smiled, suspecting one of the stable boys stealing a quiet nap, and stepped inside, the great wicker basket in his arms waiting to be filled with logs for the castle fireplaces.

He went to the back of the shed, seeking the seasoned wood that would burn the best. Tucked into a cosy corner here, there was a small stove that he could light in the winter if he was working in the cold. A heavy wool blanket was thrown over a pile of straw and wood chips, where he could rest undisturbed if the duties of the day allowed. He knew too that castle staff seeking to steal a snatched moment of privacy sometimes availed themselves of his thoughtfully placed facilities. The intruder of the moment was there.

He went about his business for a while, lifting down the large logs that would burn in the great fireplaces of the hall and dining room, laying them methodically in the basket. A few more and he would have sufficient to begin his rounds. But the identity of the person – he was sure there was only one person, or he would not have stayed – resting on his rude couch was intriguing him, and in the end, curiosity got the better of him. He poked his head cautiously around the woodpile and his heart dropped. His mystery visitor was a woman, sitting upright on the blanket, watching him with bright, nervous eyes.

"Mistress Macleod," he said in amazement. "I never thought to see you in so low a place as this."

Janet smiled. "Well then, I have surprised you, Gillies MacNicol. You have often paid visits to my room, bearing logs for the fire. I thought it time I repaid your civility with a visit of my own." Her voice rang high and shaky against the low, even tenor of the musty gloom.

He shook his head. "The kitchen maids and stable boys cavort on this couch. It is not good enough for a lady such as you to sit on."

She stared at him, her eyes shining with tears. "I am no lady," she whispered. "Do not make the mistake of raising me higher in your esteem than the lowness of my birth and actions testify."

He hung in the space between couch and woodpile, and the silence between them was tense with his efforts to understand. He could not fathom what she wanted of him. He did not hope, he did not dare to hope, that she had at last divined his feelings for her, the torture of constantly bottling up the emotions he wanted to spill at her feet, and beg her humility and acceptance of his love. She had never spoken to him; she had never cast her eyes in his direction for longer than an instant, except on one occasion. When he had gone to her room after the Laird of Maglavat had tried to rape her, she had watched him constantly, fearful that he wished her harm, when all he had wanted to do was gather her in his arms and protect her from all the hurt the world had thrown at her. He stood and stared at her.

Janet shifted uneasily on the blanket, her hands knotted in her lap, and he was so blinded by his own thoughts he did not see that she was afraid, and thought only that she was shy.

"I have brought nothing with me to make a fire," she said, and her mouth shook as it tried to smile, "except my own warmth."

And then, even if she had wanted to, even if she had wanted to break the will that had brought her to him, she could not have stopped him. He took the two steps it needed to reach her and knelt at her feet. He did not see her swallow as he laid his hands on her, his face close to hers, all confusion and wonder and struggle. When she turned her face away, he tried to control the desperate fervour of his kisses, but the tide was upon him and he was helpless before its urgent sweep. She was trembling

350

now, but he did not notice. He did not notice her hands trying to stop his from pulling at the buttons on her dress, the way she writhed at first to stop him pushing them inside her underclothes to seek her breasts. It was as if she did not want him to touch her, and through the rage of his desire, he felt the sudden stab of puzzlement. He thought it merely female modesty, and knew he should only give her a few moments to grow accustomed to him, but anything that barred his way through to her was impossible to bear. Not being over-used to women at such close quarters, he did not heed her sudden cries of protest, and thought the sounds she made were those of passion, not denial. He did not know what she was thinking; he did not know that he was scarcely less welcome in his attentions than the Laird of Maglavat. Her clothes were open, for he must see her, his hands were pushing at her skirt. He had forced her back onto the blanket and now he unbuttoned the rough trousers he worked in and mounted her. Her hair tied tightly back, crushed beneath her. He did not know what she was feeling as he thrust roughly into her, his wonder at her trampled by his lust. He only knew that he was with her, in her, and his violent movements were at last bringing him release from the frustration of not having her. His eyes were closed in heated rapture as he heaved. He did not see her clenched fists as he shouted out the triumph of his climax. He did not see the way her eyes closed in agony for what she had made him do, because of what she wanted from him.

But when the first ecstatic shock was over, he felt the dull, slack weight of her body beneath him, and the way she began to push at him as soon as he was still. And then he saw the way her face was suddenly closed to him, the way it always was when he came to her room in the course of his duties. He recognised the change and was stupefied by it, as if a door long closed to him had been briefly opened and then slammed shut. He struggled to his feet in bewilderment, still poleaxed by the force of his release but confused now, chastened by her evident distress, which he could not understand, though he tried.

She stood, she pulled her clothing straight, she buttoned up her dress and smoothed her hair. He watched her with a terrible shame as it began to dawn on him what he had done to the object of his infatuation. She looked at him as if he was an empty space.

"Janet," he faltered. "Forgive my haste and clumsy manner. I have long wanted to hold you in my arms and now I am amazed that you have come to me, and I have treated you disgracefully –"

"It is no matter," she said, her voice trembling. "It is done and finished now."

It took a moment for him to register the words. He caught her arm, appalled at what she said, and she shook his hand away.

"You caught me unawares!" he cried. "Surely, after all the ways you have been wronged by others, you cannot be so harsh a judge of me. If you knew how long I had waited – how often I have wanted to confess my love – I was not prepared to find you –"

She stood before him, hearing out his desperate protests with frightening glacial calm. It was as if he had not said anything at all, and all his words had bounced off her exterior, as if she was suddenly made of ice, and all feeling had deserted her.

"Will you give me your word that you will not speak of this to anyone?"

She tried to soften her voice, but he saw now, too late, that she considered herself defiled, and his astonishment froze further attempts to dissuade her from the abrupt decision she had made. He nodded, speechless, before the sound of footsteps clomping across the yard alerted both of them to the danger of discovery.

"Is this all the explanation you will allow me?" he asked.

For a moment, she looked as if she might relent, but then her face stiffened and she was once more the untouchable woman he had loved in silence and not known how to reach.

"You have read too much into it," Janet said, and for a moment he thought there was a little compassion for him in the way she spoke. "But now you must go back to your work and forget." And gathering her skirts around her, she ran to the door, slipped out of the woodshed and walked across to the dairy.

Her legs were shaking as she leaned against the wall at the back, a quiet place where no one could see her, and she sank down and hugged herself in anguish as she wept for the course she had taken. Five minutes she allowed herself to spend her grief, twice as long as it had taken Gillies to violate her. Then she controlled the sobs, forced them back inside to wait the moment when she could release the last of them, ducked down her head and walked into the sunshine.

She was hurrying across the cobbled courtyard when she collided with Alec, just back from the hunt.

OCTOBER 1836 – AUGUST 1838

Gillies bore the swiftness of her rejection with outward stoicism. Despite his hurt, he kept his promise, hoping his loyalty might win back the brief affection she had shown him. It was several months before he understood why she had come to him, and the anger that engulfed him then would never leave him.

When the Lady Iona fell ill, he noted Janet's absence from the storeroom and her close association with the Laird, but still did not connect them. He saw Janet pale and tired, the late hours she often kept, running errands to the physician, making up medicines and balms for the patient. Once, he came into the drawing room and discovered the Laird weeping, and Janet holding tight to his hands. He wondered then what their relationship might be, if Janet had done the honest thing and rejected him because of the love she still bore the Laird, but still he did not think the worst, despite the rumours flying round the kitchen.

He brought the logs to her room and often she was not there, because she watched late over the fading mistress of the house, sharing the burden of nursing her with the Laird and the physician. Sometimes she was dismissed, when Iona woke and knew her, and began to shriek accusations. When she was in her room, and needing the warmth and comfort of the fuel he brought, she was exactly the same as she had always been, and the fleeting passion they had shared was all the more puzzling and painful to remember.

When the Lady Iona died and the Laird was pitched into grieving, Gillies noticed, along with everyone else, that still Janet did not return to the storeroom, but instead was charged with supervising the funeral arrangements. She was required more and more by the Laird, who entrusted her with a growing number of tasks that kept her away from the busy kitchen. Gillies began to watch and wonder where she was, a wrongful sense of ownership beginning to possess him. When he delivered wood to her room, increasingly he found it empty, and his suspicions that she sometimes slept somewhere else fanned the flames of jealousy that began to burn inside him.

One night when Janet's room was empty, he stole along the upstairs corridor to the Laird's room, listened at the door and heard the sigh of skin against sheet, of breath exhaling in the closed spaces between entwined flesh. He knelt and looked through the keyhole, so desperate was his need to know. He saw the Laird moving with slow and tender strokes on the woman beneath him, and remembered with bitter anguish his own brutish imitation of the act of love. Her red hair spilled on the pillows like an offering. She whispered an endearment Gillies could not catch, her dainty fingers stroking through the Laird's hair; the Laird stopped his movements, kissed her, then held her close against him and took her with deeper and more urgent intent. She cried out, a long, rising sound that ached and broke above them as if the Laird had cleaved her with his love and in sundering her, made her whole. Gillies squinted at their rocking, the way she rose to meet him, her body all alive and tensile; he remembered her protests on the rough bed in the woodshed, her dead weight beneath him, and knew the difference in the sounds she made. He saw her small, white hand clutching at the mattress in her abandon, remembered the same hand pushing at him in the aftermath of his release. He saw the passion she had denied him, and his need and loss racked him as he gazed upon the man who had usurped him.

But still, that revelation was nothing to the sense of betrayal that flooded him when the Laird called all the staff together and announced his plans to marry Janet. The amazement in the room was audible, but the marriage proved to be only half the scarcely believable tale. When the Laird said, quite candidly, that Janet carried his second child, Gillies understood at last why she had come to him, and what she had wanted from him. The gossip chain ran with tales that Janet was indeed a witch, had held the Laird in her ghastly power until she had removed the competition. You had only to think of the poor Lady Iona, whose mind was quite undone towards the end, to listen to the accusations she levelled at Mistress Macleod, and hear the dreadful sanity in them.

Janet moved into another room before the marriage, and was scarcely seen until the wedding day. She needed rest and privacy, and protection from the chatter that occupied everyone's minds. The Laird was her devoted servant, and Alice the only other person allowed into her chamber. Gillies was no longer permitted to sweep out the hearth, but told to leave the basket of logs outside the door.

In the months after the marriage, Gillies watched as the Lady Janet's belly grew, and knew the child she carried was not the Laird's, but his. The secret he had sworn to keep began to plague him, and the idea of unmasking the wrong that had been done him began to take hold.

When Elinor was born, he felt such savage deprivation that he could hardly conceal it, and all the household wondered at his dark, surly mood. The baby was a miniature of her mother, the same sharp, pretty little face and mesmerising eyes. He looked and looked, and could see no semblance of himself in the product of their joining, as if Janet had magicked away all telltale traces of his contribution. She enchanted everyone, and Gillies, miserable in his rejection, envy and anonymity, almost stalked the nursery maids who were allowed to handle her, clothe her, feed her, change and bathe her, sing her to sleep, and play with her as she grew more aware of the world around her. His unspoken claim to the child tortured him as much as the Lady Janet's cold refusal to acknowledge him.

At night, he lay awake and replayed the frantic minutes when he had taken her, and then he brooded. An image began to haunt him, of Janet in her room when he came to deliver the logs, not standing at her door waiting for him to leave, but standing where she usually was when he knocked and entered. At the writing table.

Often, he would see a small, black leather bound book closed on its surface, and a quill dipped in the standish. In the past, he had wondered idly what she wrote at, what stories she would tell in the book that she never left open for him or anyone else to see. Now, consumed by rage at the way she had used him, he thought of where she might keep it, if in its pages she had mentioned his name, or written of the secret encounter between them.

He might not have done it, might not have gone looking for it, had he not encountered the Laird one evening, sitting on the bench by the river as he often did on pleasant nights. The tiny Lady Elinor was some fifteen months old by then, and this particular evening, she was cradled in the Laird's arms as Gillies approached to tether the small clinker boat to the jetty for the night.

"Uishall is a happy place to live now, do you not think so?" the Laird addressed his taciturn employee as Gillies strode awkwardly along the jetty and knelt down to pull the boat in towards the side.

Gillies leant over the side, groping for the painter. Slap of water, sting of gravel under his knees. "If the Laird is happy, then Uishall is happy," he retorted gruffly.

"She is the brightest star in Uishall, is she not?" the Laird's quiet voice, radiant with fatherly pride, said to him, as the baby sat on his arm, laughing delightedly and pulling at his cheeks.

"She is certainly one to be proud of," Gillies said, his voice thick in his throat as he hauled the painter towards the iron hook embedded in the jetty. He kept his head down, could not bear to turn and see the contentment he had already heard, the blaze of protective love in which the Laird bathed the child that did not belong to him.

"Ah, but if she grows to be half the woman her mother is, I will be blessed beyond what I deserve," the Laird said, half to himself, as the baby tugged at him and he gazed fondly at her.

Gillies tied up the boat and stood to leave. "If there is nothing else –"

But the Laird turned his gaze on him, away from the baby, and said suddenly, "She is a fine catch, my Lady Janet. Take my advice, Gillies, for my lessons were hard learned and cost me dearer than they should. If you ever find the woman of your dreams, you must see her for what she is and hold on to her, and not be a fool, as I was in my youth."

He looked down again at the baby, which was just as well, for he missed the expression on Gillies' face that would certainly have betrayed him. His woodsman stood before him, petrified like a rock, as if his heart had cracked open.

"I let her go," the Laird said, softly now, looking out over the river, the baby held against him as he kissed her head. He lifted Elinor away and looked at her, and she was momentarily quiet when she saw the grave expression on her father's face. "I let your mother go," he said, as if he could not quite believe it. "Because I listened to others, and my own ignorant voice, telling me she was not good enough to love a Laird. And I had already held her in my arms, and knew she was." His arms wrapped the baby against the cool of the night air, and he lifted his head and gazed at his woodsman. "And now, I would kill any man who tried to take her from me."

Gillies stared back, and the blood roared through his veins. He heard only the threat, was not to know the remark was made in innocence, and he stood and watched as the Laird got up from the bench with his precious burden and carried her towards the castle. From that moment, Gillies was convinced that the Laird knew the origins of his daughter, and knew himself a thief.

III

SEPTEMBER 1839

He stood hesitantly before the Lady Janet's writing room and knocked.

No answer.

His plan of action was decided. If he found her diary, if he found his name, he would confront the Laird. He was a thinner man than the one who had so lustily taken Janet some three years before. A sharper tempered man, whose easy, quiet manner had given way to bitterness and distrust. A man who had found himself caught up in a game he had not realised he was playing. Well, he would turn the tables on the players who had tricked him and see if he could yet emerge a winner.

He went straight to her desk and opened the top drawer. He pushed his hands inside, saw paper and quills, a stick of sealing wax, a bottle of ink. He closed it and opened the second. A bible, a few pamphlets on land owning issues, a periodical from Edinburgh. And underneath them, the black leather bound book he sought. He seized it, flicked its pages, satisfied that he had found what he sought, slipped it into his pocket. He closed the drawer, looked at the desk again, and found himself gazing at a miniature of his daughter set in a heavy, plain silver frame. He picked it up and studied it.

"What is it you seek?" a sharp, peremptory voice said behind him, and he turned to find her watching him, her bonnet strings hanging loose around her face, her eyes hard as stone, her face rigid with fury.

For a moment, he was frozen. He thought to drop the miniature into his pocket with the diary, but changed his mind and set it back on the table. He had thought to throw accusations at her, rant and rave, threaten her, even, to try to get what he wanted. Instead, when he turned to face her and opened his mouth, words came out that he had not expected to hear.

"When you first came here, I served you," he said. "When all the kitchen maids slandered you, I was your defender. When you would never even look at me, or pass a word in answer to

357

my questions, I waited for your trust. I did not even realise I loved you until the day the Laird of Maglavat forced his attentions on you. And still you would not acknowledge me, and still I did not share with you how much it burned me to be in your presence, and remain untouched."

He stopped. Janet was staring at him as if she had been struck dumb.

"I never did you any wrong," he said. "Apart from a single dance with you one Hogmanay, I never came within a yard of you until the day I found you sitting by my stove. Since then, your punishment has been not only to reject me, but to rob me of the child I gave you. What have I done that merits such false treatment?"

Janet swallowed, still holding herself stiff and distant, and folded her hands before her.

"It's true you did me no wrong," she said. "You were a loyal servant, before and since I married the Laird. But you were a servant always, and no more to me."

"You came to me –"

"I came to you because I had a bargain to secure," Janet said desperately. "The only wrong you did is that you were not him," she whispered, and for a moment she pitied his despair. "For I loved him from being a girl, and was denied him by virtue of my lowly birth. The husband I have now is the man I fought for."

"And was I your weapon?" he asked. "You owe me that much – the truth of your motives."

She hung her head. Her contrition seemed genuine, but gave him no comfort.

"I thought to use you, yes," she said at last. "Because you had never spoken ill of me, or done me a wrong turn." She paused. "I did not think of it from your side. I may not have taken such a course, had I realised you were sick of love for me."

"Then the Lady Elinor is my child," he said flatly.

"You cannot prove it, any more than I can disprove it," she said.

He stared at her.

"The Laird and I were lovers then, and I made sure we spent that very night together."

Gillies shook his head stubbornly. "He could not sire a child with either of his wives. You knew it, and used me for that reason."

"But Alasdair *is* his child," Janet said defiantly. "I can swear to that, for I was a maid when the Laird took me." She stopped. "And in all the time since, I knew no other man except for you."

"Perhaps you *are* a witch."

Janet laughed. "I am a woman who did what was necessary to secure her mate." She saw the look of revulsion on his face and shrugged. "So you see, I am not worth the love you have wasted on me. I told you as much the day I came to you. I took your seed but once, and knew I had done wrong by all of us. But Alasdair is the Laird's child by me, and there is no way of telling if Elinor is not his also, by some divine influence that none of us understand."

He clenched his fists. "Is there to be no comfort for me in all of this?"

"You have a good position in the castle," Janet said. "You can still protect it."

"And if I confront the Laird?"

"You have nothing to confront him with," Janet said. "For one, he will not believe you, and for another, you will certainly lose your place here for making false accusations."

"The accusation is not false!" Gillies shouted. "Will I be forced to watch you raise my child where I cannot touch her, but must be every day in sight of her? Is that the reward you offer for my service?"

Janet said nothing. She knew how that felt.

"Well then," she said at length. "We have both learned that the world is a harsh place, for we cannot always have what we would choose."

At those cool words, he came to her and seized her arm and she let out a shriek, for the look on his face terrified her.

"It is easy for you to accept then," he said, "that I am to be denied for life not only the woman I want, but the child she bore me –"

"I did not bear her for you," Janet said. "She was never meant to be yours, and she never will be."

Gillies threw her away in outrage and began to back away towards the door.

"You have insulted me, Lady Janet, and your husband has laid claim to what is mine," he said, "and I will see both of you punished before I am done."

"Then you will leave now!" Janet cried in panic as she struggled to her feet. "I will have you thrown out for trying to steal from me –"

"What business have you in the Lady Janet's chamber?" a voice thundered, and Gillies swung round to find himself face to face with his employer. In that moment he understood the hopelessness of his case, and he seemed to sag beneath the weight of authority the Laird carried, standing over him, all poised to beat him for his impudence in entering a room that was forbidden to him. He could not hope to ruin their devotion; he could not hope to be heard without being abused, for the Laird would hear no word against his Lady.

Alec looked from Gillies to Janet, sensed the tension in their sudden silence, and noted the distress of his wife.

"I heard raised voices," he said. "What has been stolen?"

Janet glanced fearfully at Gillies, and she seemed to recover herself and grow taller as she drew herself up and folded her hands before her. "I found him searching through my writing table."

Alec looked Gillies over with a distrust he had never previously shown for him, and there was profound disappointment in his eyes as he studied the wretched man before him.

"Turn out your pockets," he said quietly.

Gillies did not move. The diary hung heavy in his jacket, against his hip.

Alec looked at Janet. "You are frightened," he said. "And if I am here, you need not be. What did this man say to you?"

Janet shook her head. "Get him out of my room," she said. "He has repaid my trust with thievery."

Alec turned back to Gillies. "Turn out your pockets," he repeated, his voice dangerously low. "I will not ask again."

Gillies brought out the diary and laid it on the table, and Janet gasped in horror, for she had not realised what he sought, or truly understood the threat he posed.

Alec looked confused, then angry. "Why this?" he said, astounded.

"I sought the words she wrote," Gillies growled. "I sought proof that –"

"How dare you sneak into my room to look for private documents!" Janet broke in. She bounded forward, seized the book and turned to Alec. "Perhaps he thought –"

Alec raised his hand to silence her, still staring at Gillies. "It does not matter what he thought," he said. "He has broken the Laird's trust, and raised his voice against the Lady of Uishall." He looked coldly at his woodsman. "You are dismissed forthwith, and will find whatever work you can without my aid. Collect your things and leave directly."

Alec stood for a long time staring first at Gillies' retreating figure until it had gone from sight, and then at nothing. It seemed that minutes passed before he closed the chamber door and turned to gaze at Janet. He went to her and touched her cheek, felt how cold it was. He saw the diary clutched in her hand, took it gently from her and set it back on the writing table.

"We will think no more on this unfortunate episode," he said. She did not know if she heard hurt in his voice, or only sadness. She trembled, and he took both her hands in his and held them firm. "You are safe from whatever harm he meant to do," he said softly. "For you will always have the Laird's love, no matter what."

Gillies left Uishall that day and within a week was taken on by a neighbouring estate, where he performed the same faithful service for his new employers, without the trauma of unrequited love to burden him.

4.
WOUNDED
OCTOBER 1854 – JULY 1859

I

In the months succeeding Alec's death, Janet's grief hung like a pall over Uishall. She was beyond comfort and her son and daughter could not reach her. Alasdair ran the estate alongside the factor, Archie MacInnes, who became a much closer associate now the partnership between Alasdair and his father had been sundered. Alasdair tried in vain to rouse his mother's interest, but her weeping gave way eventually to lassitude and she became a semi-invalid, spending hours at a stretch in her room, sometimes writing, sometimes reading, most times staring listlessly out of the window. It seemed as though the effort it had cost her to win and at last marry Alec had used up all her energy, and there was no more fire or hunger to live a life without him.

On one matter she roused her strength, and that was the burial place of her husband. Half mad with grief and speaking with a lifeless voice that sounded as if it already came from the grave, she stood down her children, the protests of all their family and associates, even the household. Alec would not be buried in the churchyard. He would be buried on the land he loved, under her safe keeping, and he would wait for her there.

She chose the knoll where he had first taken her, and fought her family again, who did not understand its significance, and only saw its dreadful unsuitability for the purpose, for it was not an easy spot to reach, and digging the grave, let alone carrying the coffin there, was almost impossible. It was two weeks before Alec could be laid to rest.

Alasdair, now the Laird, and who therefore technically had the authority to overturn her decision, did his best to dissuade her, until the day he overheard two servants discussing the matter in the dining room.

"Who does she think she is, to make such perverse commands?" one of them said indignantly. "Her roots are as poor as ours, and she connived to win the Laird's favour with her cow eyes and her strumpet ways. What right has she to place him in unholy ground, and cause the family so much upset?"

Her companion shook her head in violent agreement. "It's a disgrace. By whose authority does she think she acts?"

"By the authority of the Laird of Uishall, who got it from his father, the Lady Janet's husband," Alasdair interrupted them, and they gasped in horror that they had been overheard.

"The Lady Janet has as much right as anyone to choose the final resting place of her husband," he said coldly. "She married into my father's name and earned her title, and you would do well to remember her rank and respect it, should you ever have need to beg to retain your stations."

Janet paid the gravediggers four times their usual fee and gave each of them a bag of silver coins in recognition of the task they performed for her. A year later, she supervised the building of the fountain in the courtyard to commemorate him, and then she did not want to do any more. Alasdair, who owed everything he had to the strength of his mother, despaired at her wilful decline and was afraid her grief would break her beyond mending.

"You must do as he bid you, and live again," he said one night, when the physician had been to tend her. She lay propped against the pillows, her face white and drawn, her eyes red-ringed and dull. When she only stared past him at the window closed against the wind and rain that battered at the glass, he seized her hands and forced her to meet his eyes.

"Look at me," he pleaded with her. "*Look* at me. I am the Laird of Uishall. This is what *you* have done, and you must rejoice in it and lay claim to your life again. See how you have helped the poor inherit the land."

"And I have done my task well," she said, smiling at him. "So I am content with that, and wish to rest after all my long labours."

Alasdair shook his head. "When this bout of sickness is past, I will show you something I have done, that might ease the years you have left."

When she was well, he took her to the top of the knoll where Alec lay, and she saw that he had had a bench carried there, carved with Alec's name. He had brought flowers for her to set on the gravestone, and she knelt a long time, half smiling, half weeping at the memories that crowded in on her. They sat together in the sunshine, a warm breeze blowing about them, and she told him how it had happened, how he had been made between the passion of the Laird and his young mother, and how they had overcome everything to be together. He held her hand and listened in awe to how he had begun, the circumstances of his conception, his birth and the extraordinary circumstances that precipitated his rise to fortune.

His gift was appreciated, and helped her. On the days when she was stronger, she climbed to the spot and sat there and remembered Alec, and thought of the times when they were married, when he would take her there on warm summer evenings. They would picnic and make love, his embraces welcomed now and eagerly sought, and he would be especially tender with her, as if he wished to wipe away all traces of the time he had forced her.

"You should not hold that memory anything less than dear," she had whispered to him once, a year or two before he died. "If I felt wronged then, I do not now, for what started in pain and wrongdoing has ended in this, and I would not change it."

She wrote the inscription that was to be carved on the gravestone at her death and although she at last took heed of Alasdair's words and found some happiness in her last few years, she waited always for the day when she would join him.

II

Eighteen months after Alec's death, Elinor asked permission to marry. Janet listened gravely when she heard the choice her daughter had made, and deliberated over her consent. Calum MacInnes was the factor's son, and while Janet could fault neither younger nor older man on integrity of character or diligence, she agonised over whether or not she should set her daughter free of Uishall's protection, and give her up to the uncertainty of the less privileged world beyond its boundaries.

"What should I do?" she asked Alasdair one evening. "She will give up so much to be with him, and yet I believe she loves him. Which will be most valuable to her – the love of a man

364

she has chosen when she is still so young, or the strength that Uishall has to offer her?"

Alasdair smiled. "You hesitate because she is prepared to give up Uishall and all the trappings that go with it." He paused. "But you did not fall in love with Uishall; you fell in love with my father. Uishall was an incidental. So it is with my sister. And she is older than you were when you made your choice."

Janet looked out of the window. It was true, she had not fought for Uishall, she had fought for Alec, and now he was dead, Uishall was robbed of the heart that used to beat so strongly inside it. Uishall and Alec were bound together by blood, but she was not tied to it in the same way. Neither was Alasdair. Uishall, bereft of its last Laird, seemed indifferent to the blandishments of its new one, and still refused to give up the secret of how its promise might be fulfilled.

She looked at Alasdair, the son who had acquired a legacy that might prove more trouble than it was worth. The sheep had not fulfilled their promise, her father and the other tenants dispossessed and moved aside to Eilaster for a dream of easy prosperity that had been short lived. Now the tenant farmers, richer and with more to lose, looked uneasily to their landlord for the changes that would have to come. Already they were emigrating, many of them gone to foreign shores to seek a better fortune than the one their homeland offered. The disillusion with the land, its betrayal of their hopes, was felt by everyone, from the poorest tenant, thrown off for being unable to pay the rent, to the landlords, who still could not make it pay. Alasdair brooded, still felt the obligation thrust upon him to make the land bend to his will, and remembered his father's words, that the land was its own master and would bend to no one. Janet would give her mortal remains to Uishall as her husband had, but her spirit would be with Alec, and she would lie in contentment wherever she would find him. Perhaps Uishall felt itself betrayed, too.

So Janet met with Archie MacInnes and gave her blessing to the marriage. Elinor would never suffer poverty as she had, for times had changed and fortunes improved, and Janet made sure her daughter's prosperity was secured so that she need never fear for losing the roof over her head, or want for food to put on the table.

Janet lived to see her daughter marry true to her spirit, and be happy in her choice. She lived to see the birth of her first grandchild, David, born in 1858, who followed in his father's footsteps. But she never knew Rossyth, born two years later, whose bloodline would end with the birth of Murdo MacInnes in 1940, and lead to the legacy of bitterness that the loss of Uishall began. She never knew Iain, either, who would enter the medical profession and make his mother proud.

When Janet died in 1859, the physician could find nothing wrong with her, and could only say that nothing earthly life had to offer was enough to keep her on the mortal plane. She sought her husband, and only the healing power of death could give him to her. Alasdair was still unmarried, still struggling with the burden his father had bequeathed him. Janet made him promise he would make the choice that brought him happiness. But she would not answer the question he asked the day before she died, when he begged her to tell him why his father had suffered so cruel a death. She gazed at him for a long time, knowing he suspected the truth, but fearing that confirming his suspicions would only bring more pain on those who did not deserve it. She asked him to respect her silence, and said only that Elinor had been born, like him, out of the love she bore his father.

She died with her children around her and when she fell into her last sleep, she saw Alec standing on the knoll, his arms open. Alasdair, sitting at the bedside, her hands held tight in his, saw her smile, and knew she was with him. In the bright, brief space between life and death, Janet at last earned the peace of knowing he would never leave her again.

5.
COURTSHIP
FEBRUARY – JUNE 1861

I
FEBRUARY 1861

With the marriage of his sister and the death of his mother, Alasdair applied himself even more rigorously to the task of finding an economic solution to the problems of Uishall. His tenacity was finally rewarded on a trip to the north of England to meet with his financier, who was friendly with the owner of a small estate in Northumberland.

By then in his late thirties, Alasdair had never seriously considered the prospect of being married, although now he was the lone proprietor of Uishall, the consequences of dying without an heir had begun to dawn on him. He had courted many ladies and taken many transient pleasures, but deeper involvements had eluded him. He had watched his mother fight for the man she loved, watched his father suffer for the woman he wanted. He had seen his sister weep when she thought Calum would be denied her. He had thought, with a degree of perplexity, that the passions of love had passed him by, and wondered if he might perhaps be better off without them. He had seen, too, the way his mother and father came alive in each other's presence, the spark that danced between them. Alasdair had never encountered a woman who inspired wild thoughts of throwing away Uishall, who kept him awake at nights or who made him dream of a future with a wife and children in it.

But that was before he met Caitlin.

He had been away from Uishall for three weeks, yet it had seemed to follow him. He had not found the path that would enable Uishall to pay its way. He had gone over the accounts with his financier. The conclusion was that the land still ate into their wealth, more always being given than was returned. At dinner that night, Alasdair accepted an invitation from one of the guests, the owner of a shipping business, to take in some sport before he began the long journey home.

And so he spent the day in the company of Jacob Connaught and a dozen other gentlemen, shooting grouse and fishing for grayling, a species he had not encountered before. The grayling were the pride of his river, his host informed him, splendidly distinguished, metallic fish with scales that gleamed like chain mail and flesh that tasted sweeter than sea trout. He intended to build a little business, he said, for his ghillie to run, get people to stay in the currently disused east wing of his mansion, fish for grayling, and pay for the privilege. Something a bit different, Connaught told him jovially before strolling away, a change from the usual salmon and trout.

Alasdair, standing under the trees lining the riverbank, smiled, cast deftly into the river, and stopped, thunderstruck. The idea came to him in that moment – not Jacob Connaught's small-scale enterprise, but one that took in the whole of Uishall, every acre of its wild, intractable whole. This was the root of Uishall's recent history, its rebirth as a sporting estate that charged its guests for the privileges of hunting its wild riches and tasting the ungovernable beauty of its waters and landscapes. Alasdair knew at once that this was the idea he had been searching for. The logistics would take extensive planning, the dismantling of the last traces of the tenant system, the turning of his ancient home into a place which would welcome strangers, but the idea was instant, dazzling, and the end of his quest. He fished on, his mind seized as it struggled with the enormity of the idea that had exploded on it.

But he would be dazzled again before the night of that extraordinary day was over.

He arrived for dinner at Connaught's country house, his head spinning with plans. The weather, even allowing for the fact that it was the end of February, was unusually wild, and he entered the hall with his hair blown awry, his face flushed and his cloak dripping. He handed his hat to the butler, shook the rain out of his hair, raised his head – and found himself looking into the laughing eyes of his host's eldest daughter.

He would never forget the first time he saw her. The plans that had crammed his head only moments before seemed to evaporate into a haze and become not the driving force of his future, but merely a concomitant to them. As certainly as he had found the right path for Uishall, he had also found the woman he would love until death. He stared at her speechlessly, and she told him afterwards that the sheer passion of his gaze had done most of Cupid's work even before they were introduced. After all the turbulence the day had already dealt him, the rush of understanding that he had fallen in love, after spending his life up to that point in ignorance of what it even meant, almost knocked him off his feet.

Although they were exchanging intimacies and speaking of their mutual attraction within twenty four hours, Caitlin had the sense to refuse his proposal, made only a week after he met her. She wanted a little more time, she said, laughing at him, before she could be certain that her initial infatuation was really true love. When she knew she would be spending the rest of her life on a remote estate in the Outer Hebrides, she insisted that she make the journey to see it, and satisfy herself that she could be happy there. He did not tell her, but the sensible, hard-headed Alasdair would have sold it all up and moved to the wilds of Ancient China if she had asked him. Her good sense served them well in the years ahead, through the turmoil of change that affected not just the land they owned, but the world around them.

II
JUNE 1861

When he asked her to marry him again, in April, when she had visited Uishall and professed a liking for it, she accepted, and the wedding was arranged for June. He went all the way to London to make the arrangements and choose a gift for her.

And he found it. A grand piece of furniture for the dining room, a massive sideboard from one of the most famous cabinet-makers in the English capital. A fortune it cost him, not only to buy it, but also to have it shipped, but it was worth every penny to see Caitlin's face when she arrived at Uishall as his bride and saw the magnificent offering he had made her.

"It looks old," she said in wonder, touching the proud lions' heads, running her fingers over the satiny texture of the polished wood. She gazed around the dining room, at the great windows and stately dining table, over which Alasdair had made his second proposal to her after dinner one night, in the gleam of the candlelight. "It looks as if it is already a part of this room, and needs no introduction to it."

He lifted her in his arms and carried her, laughing, to the bedroom, where he took away her travelling clothes and celebrated his love for her long into the night. As they lay together in the dim light cast by a guttering candle, they talked about their plans for Uishall, the trials that lay ahead of them, and the future. She thanked him again for his extravagant wedding gift, and marvelled at its instant fit with the castle.

"You are playing games with me," she said, "for I cannot believe that piece of furniture is newly made. I think it has always been here, and it has a long and exciting history, and you hid it from me when I came to visit with my father, because it would save you the trouble of finding a wedding gift."

He laughed. "If that is what you believe, then I would make it half the gift to you it is by insisting on the truth," he said.

She snuggled against him.

"Tell me the story of it, and I will believe everything you say from this moment on."

He kissed her, lay in silence for a while, and then began. He wove a tale of ancient history, of the 12th Laird of Uishall, Murdo, who had wanted to impress his bride. Rather, he wanted to make things up to her, for she had married him only because of her father's wishes, and did not want to spend her life buried in a wilderness, away from her family on the mainland, separated from them by an angry sea. He told her of Italian craftsmen in Palestrina and the tree they felled in a great forest of spreading oak trees, the carpenters and carvers who worked their miracles to produce the cabinet under the hawk-like eyes of their master. He told of a perilous journey, ending at Uishall with only a crack along the lion's nose to show for its long haul over mountain and across the sea.

"Were the carriers punished?" she asked sleepily, for the day had been long, and the evening had tired her.

"No," he said softly. "For to sustain no mark at all would have robbed it of its authenticity, and made the telling of the tale less truthful. How can we go through such an adventure without even a scratch to tell the world that we have lived a little, and bear the marks of our experience?"

"And did she learn to love the husband she had been forced to marry?"

"Most definitely," Alasdair whispered, and snuffed the candle. "She loved him with all her heart, for his generosity and his kindness, and for bringing her to the land, whose wild spirit she came to love with equal passion."

Caitlin opened her eyes at this to find him looking down at her. "Can you love the land as passionately as that?" she asked.

He gazed out of the window, where dawn was breaking on the horizon. He saw the hills, the river, the gravestone where his father and mother lay, and beyond them, he imagined Eilaster Glen where he was born, in a blackhouse dense with the smoke of peat, nestling like a child into the fold of the hills. He felt the struggles he had known, as a poor crofter child and as a landowner.

"I don't know," he said softly. "I have never loved anything or anyone as much as I love you. The men I know who profess to love the land seem to know nothing but pain and anger for loving something they can never possess." He sighed. "We are transient creatures, are we not? How can we presume to love something so elemental as the land?"

"But you love your home," Caitlin said. "You work for it and nurture it, and plan for it, and protect it from your enemies, and present it as a gift to those you love. Perhaps you are confusing love with passion, which is quickly spent. Love grows alongside passion, I think, and either supersedes it, or withers. And I think, too, it can take many forms. The love you bear me will not be the same as the love you bear our children, though you will feel it no less fiercely. You have known the land all your life and you have stayed by it like a faithful husband. Who is to say that it will not repay you one day and give you its heart in return?"

He was silent a moment. "I am responsible for the land," he said at length. "But that is not to say I love it. The question is, I suppose, would I give up the passionate love of a woman for the love of the land?"

"And do men who love the land have no passionate women to distract them?" Caitlin said, and laughed.

"Is the land more valuable to me because I own it?" Alasdair said. "Does it matter that I or another man owns that headland out to sea? Suppose I am a poor man, and walk every day on that headland and take in the spectacle of the sea and draw the ocean air into my lungs. Does that not make me every bit as much a part of it, and more, than the man who has paid money for it but never even turns his head to see what he possesses?"

Caitlin smiled at him. "So you do love the land," she said.

"We have talked enough," he said suddenly, stretching and lifting her into his arms. "Now be still, for this conversation vexes me at this early hour, and it is scarcely appropriate discourse for a marriage bed. If you are so sure our passion is a passing phase, then we must make the most of it before it disappears. So give yourself to me again, let us drown in hedonistic pleasures, and the land be damned."

6.
PAIRED
SEPTEMBER 2001 – MAY 2002

I
SEPTEMBER 2001

Duncan sat in Katie-Bel MacInnes' shiny modern kitchen and found his view out towards the hills flanking Eilaster Glen spoiled by the surly face of Murdo.

"What's your business here, Inspector?" his host asked him. "There's nothing you can pin on us. We've not been out all season, on account of the body Aidan dredged up."

"Well, that's sporting of you, Murdo," Duncan said pleasantly. He sighed. "Frankie seemed to find himself in the wrong place at the wrong time. We know why he was there; we just want to know who came across him."

"It wasn't me."

"So that's one suspect I can knock off my list," Duncan said ironically. "Come on, Murdo, don't make life so hard for me. I know all about the bitter game you play up on the moors all summer, putting in your sixpence worth against the landlords –"

"It's our way of saying the land should be given back to the people," Murdo said, provoked at last into answering back.

"Aye, and it should be Christmas every day of the year," Duncan said. "And with the generosity of the grants system just now, some people would say it already is."

"The grants will finish. The European funding is all set to dry up."

"Well, you've had a good run of it these past fifty years," Duncan said unsympathetically. "New houses built for next to nothing, businesses made for life – the majority of the UK should be so lucky, right enough."

"How else are we supposed to make ends meet?" Murdo said. "All the people leaving, the land so poor, the opportunities so thin –"

"So how does needling the estates help us? When they're at least going concerns?" Duncan shook his head. "Grants are a fact of life out here, there's no getting away from it. But that's not to say they should become a way of life."

Murdo shook his head. "It's the principle of the thing," he said at last.

"And what principle was Ally acting on when he found himself on the same patch of Uishall ground as Frankie?"

Murdo glared at him. "If you know all about it, why are you here?"

"Frankie had some daft idea about saving hedgehogs," Duncan said, ignoring him. "What was yours?"

Murdo threw up his hands. "Ally was following him. He thought he was after stealing the nets."

Duncan shook his head again. "So both of you intent on sabotage, for the sake of a principle that undermines someone's efforts to run a business on genuine profit and not grants? Where's the sense in that?"

"It's not about sense," Murdo said angrily. "There's nothing here that makes sense anymore. It's about being trapped by circumstances that you didn't ask for, but you can't change."

Duncan shook his head. "So why bother? The English are here and the estates are here whether you like it or not, and you'll not change it by wasting your time up on the moors indulging in petty crime. What will you do with your time, Murdo, when the buy-outs come through and the land is yours? You'll still be bitter, and you'll still have the same problems to wrestle with – how will you make it pay, and make the land glad to have you on it? Better to take the political route to achieve your objectives, or you'll find yourselves at odds with your own countrymen."

Murdo glared at him. "I'll follow my own course and take the consequences," he said.

Duncan sighed and stood to leave. "Well, we understand each other, then," he said.

II

Trevor sat in silence on the crag and surveyed the glory of the mountains that rose in a protective semi-circle around Maglavat Castle. Since discovering his family origins, he had been busy. His Macnab triumph had barely registered, for the other business that had brought him here had infinitely larger implications. Walking Maglavat's hills was something he did rarely, and he was immediately attracted to the wildness of the estate and the quirky interiors of the nineteenth century castle, so different in atmosphere to Uishall. He had walked out with Henry Towers, who was at this moment sitting comfortably against a rock, pouring out a shot of whisky from a silver hip flask.

"So – how did you leave the negotiations with Natasha?" Trevor asked, easing himself down beside his host. "I still can't believe she was seriously considering buying it."

Henry smiled. "She had an idea of what it would be," he said. "And she was wrong." He shrugged. "At least she had the sense to see it."

Trevor grinned. "Not, as I understand it, without a little help from you," he said.

Henry leaned back. "Ah, well, you know, she needed to find the right track." There was an odd silence between them. "It didn't work out between you, did it?"

"No," Trevor said. "It wasn't meant to be." He stopped, saw a look on Henry's face that suggested he had something else to say. "How about you?" he prompted. "Hugh thought he detected a spark."

"Oh no," Henry said at once, then looked confused. "Well – perhaps a spark, yes. But how it would ever ignite, I don't know." He smiled self-consciously. "I have to say I'm really getting rather fed up of castle guests turning up with their eligible daughters in tow, as if I'm some sort of hopeless case who needs to be married off." He laughed. "She's the first woman in a long time I've been seriously attracted to." He stretched out on the grass and took in the view. "Oh, I don't know how these things work. Perhaps we're just two lost souls who aren't quite ready to find each other yet."

"I never thought she was a bad sort," Trevor said. "Just a bit intense. Maybe we met at a bad time."

"I think Natasha's been having a bad time for years," Henry said. "Sometimes, you know, you can be having a bad time and not even realise it if you've never known anything else." He paused again. "And if she'd bought Maglavat, that cycle would have perpetuated itself."

"So she didn't buy it?"

"No."

"She didn't even ask you to keep it warm for her?"

"No."

"What about the wildlife crusade?"

"I think I might have scuppered that one, too," Henry said.

Trevor raised his glass. "I'll drink to that," he said. "*Slainte*."[1]

III

When John came in, the kitchen was busy with the clicking of Hedda's knife on the chopping board as she sliced potatoes for the gratin dish, and the whine of the electric mixer as Marie beat egg whites and sugar together for that night's pudding.

"Hello there," Marie said as he walked in. "Stick the kettle on, would you?" She switched off the electric beater and began scraping the white, glossy meringue onto a greased baking sheet.

John did as he was asked, then went over to the work surface where Hedda stood. He slid towards her a square white box with a clear cellophane oval in the centre. Underneath it was a black leather bound notebook.

"You never buy me chocolates," she said, delighted.

John grinned. "I bought them because I may have discovered the origin of the custom of men giving chocolates to their ladies."

Hedda raised her eyes and picked up another potato. "I thought there might be a hidden motive," she said. "So there's more to it than simply wanting to get into their knickers?"

"Oh yes."

The kettle boiled, the tea was made and the three of them took a break at the table in the centre of the sunny kitchen. Hedda looked expectantly at him.

"I presume this is something to do with your Uishall studies?"

He shook his head, opened the box of chocolates and pushed it to the middle of the table. "Maglavat," he said. "I kept coming across invoices for boxes of continental chocolates, ordered by Ruaraidh for the Lady Margaret, and I couldn't understand why there were always so many of them. He makes reference in a letter to how much his lady dotes on chocolate, but he took it to extremes, the way he appeased her craving. The only generosity he ever seemed to show her."

"Women like chocolate," Marie said, biting appreciatively into her selection. "Better than sex, some of them think. It's a well-known aphrodisiac. They would have known that then. Casanova did."

"But that isn't what Ruaraidh wanted them for," John said. "I'm pretty sure he was giving them to her for a much more insidious reason."

"How did you work it out?" Hedda asked.

"The physician's notebook describes Margaret's symptoms as they progress," he said. "It took years for her to die. Look." He opened the notebook and pointed to an entry. Slips of paper were inserted between the pages at relevant sites.

"April 24th, 1836: I conclude that the Lady Margaret is suffering from some sort of progressive illness, which is causing rapid deterioration of her physical and mental functions. She complains of tingling and loss of feeling in her limbs, she is reduced to eating nothing but broth and jellies, and tells me that there is a constant taste of metal in her mouth."

"They didn't have fillings in those days, did they?" Marie asked thoughtfully, helping herself to another chocolate. "So it couldn't have been heavy metal poisoning."

"As a matter of fact it was," John said. "Remember Ruaraidh was being treated for syphilis? And they used mercury to counteract the symptoms?"

Hedda grimaced. "Whatever were they thinking of?" She stopped. "Did Margaret have the disease?"

"Not sure, but Ruaraidh knew there was a considerable risk she could catch it from him." He turned to another page and read:

"'June 1837: The Lady Margaret is now so ill that I believe nothing can save her. Ruaraidh is distraught and begs me constantly to think of other treatments. But now I know what he has been doing, there is no prospect of reversing the extensive damage. She has barely any flesh upon her bones, her sight is all but gone and her memory is failing worse than in

previous months. The attacks are awesome to behold, and this gentle woman is transformed beyond belief into a demented creature. Her husband surely treads this self-same path to his destruction, for the same poison has been coursing through his system, and for longer.'"

"Oh no," Hedda said. "He was giving her mercury."

John nodded. "Certain schools of medical thought believed it could be given as a preventative. But what's interesting is *how* it was given."

Hedda looked down at the box on the table. "Chocolates?"

"Husbands who consorted with prostitutes risked syphilis," John said, "but the last thing they wanted was for their wives to find out, or to catch it themselves."

Marie grinned. "What a give-away that would be."

"So they fed them mercury without them knowing. Ruaraidh made sure there were always chocolates in the house because he was trying to save his wife from the consequences of his actions."

"Tragic," Marie said. "So on the one hand, you had the unfaithful husbands dying of syphilis, while their virtuous wives had to contend with not only the syphilis, but mercury poisoning as well."

"Poor Margaret," Hedda said.

"Twisted love," John said. "He doesn't sound like much of a man, but I think he suffered for his faults, even if he was too weak to do anything about them. Ruaraidh was trying to protect her from the debauchery in his character that he couldn't fight."

Marie raised her eyes. "Men," she said.

IV

At their last dinner, the celebratory mood at Uishall was slightly dampened by thoughts of imminent departures.

"God, back to whining writers and missed deadlines," Freya said glumly as she turned a glass of wine in her hands. "Not to mention the washing up and chores again." She turned to Hugh. "What's in it for you, Hugh, your return to reality?"

Hugh smiled. "Actually, I'm looking forward to it," he said. "We're launching the new bitter this side of Christmas, and I'm going to find a distributor to supply the island. About time we had some real ale up here."

"I've got a couple of live gigs," Trevor said. "I haven't done anything live for ages. Quite exciting, really – it's a new band. I'm filling in for the lead guitar – he broke his wrist last month."

"I read about that," Freya said. "Skiing, wasn't he?"

"Surfing."

"Well, I envy you your enthusiasm," Freya said. "I suppose I'm getting to the stage where I rather fancy the idea of writing a book, instead of selling other people's all the time." She stretched in her chair. "I could do with a place like this, an island retreat where I can shut all the doors, disconnect the phone and work out who I am and what I want to be."

Trevor looked up at these words. Since the Macnab, he had had the same sense of needing an anchor place. He coughed and stood up.

"Well, let's see what we can do about that," he said.

Robert and Hugh looked quizzically at him, but Freya was preoccupied and hadn't heard him.

"Aidan told me that the rumour about the rock star buying Maglavat is still going around," she said fretfully. "So it looks as if Natasha Tang is still interested."

"Actually, no, she isn't," Trevor said. "And that's from the horse's mouth."

Freya looked up in surprise. "So the rumour's wrong?" she said. "Why am I not surprised? I wonder what put her off?"

"I think she had a run-in with Henry," Trevor said, grinning.

"So there is no rock star," Freya said. "Well, that's a relief."

"Not quite right," Trevor said. "There is still a rock star in the running."

"Another one?" Hugh said. He looked at Trevor and was suddenly suspicious. "Who is it?"

Trevor coughed again. "That would be me."

The dining room fell silent.

Trevor made a mock bow in Freya's direction. "I am going to buy Maglavat," he clarified. "I am going to buy Maglavat and claim the Laird's title."

"Have you talked to Henry?" Robert said seriously. "The financial equations don't work out, whichever way you do them."

"I know," Trevor said. "I've seen the accounts. The real ones. I've decided it's worth it. I can afford the losses while I find a way to turn them into profit."

There was another silence. Freya glanced up at the portrait of Alec.

"You didn't want Uishall?" she said.

"Oh yes, I do," he said. "But as the Directors' meeting confirmed this weekend, Uishall is not for sale at the moment. And I'm very happy that it isn't."

"You won't –"

"No, I will not be relinquishing my shares, or taking any less interest. But I'm going to move here, and I have a long-term plan." He paused. "Two long term plans."

"Which are?" Hugh said, amused. "I have to say, Trevor, I haven't a clue what's going on in that head of yours at the moment."

"The objective overall is to reunite the two estates," Trevor said.

Robert stared at him. "Are you aware – I mean, do you have any idea –"

"Not really, no," Trevor said, grinning. "But you do, Robert, and you're going to be in charge."

Robert exhaled slowly, and looked pleased at the prospect of a serious challenge.

"Part of the way I'm thinking is to put the people back on the land."

"There aren't enough people to go round," Robert said. "You'll never fill all the empty spaces. What are you going to do – return to the clan system and have all your tenants grafting on your behalf?"

"No, no. Nothing quite as archaic and punitive as that," he said. "Sometimes I think the clan system was just a protection racket for the chiefs. No, I want something that acknowledges the nature of the place we live in, and supports it. Henry was going to sell the land to the people. That's not the way I'm going to go. I might well reinvent the tenant system, lay down certain rules and enforce certain codes of ethics on the land users." He paused. "And I want to create a model for economic independence, prove it can be done without high dependency on grants."

"But the whole principle of the Laird in charge of the people on his land is archaic, wouldn't you agree?" Freya said.

"All that happens here now is that the personal involvement of the Laird has been replaced by impersonal subsidy – the people turning to the comfort of cold hard cash rather than forming any sort of working relationship."

"We're absentee landlords," Hugh said. "The ethos of the Laird can work, but only if the Laird is to hand, and taking an interest."

"It's given the whole structure a bad name," Robert said. "People buying land that they never see, sitting somewhere in the South of England collecting the peppercorn rents. I mean, look at us, we come here for a few weeks every year and we do what we can, but we're not in charge of any people, there haven't been people here since Alasdair's day. If you take on the Laird's role as well as his title, the pressure to deliver will be huge."

"It won't matter whether you're here or not once Land Reform goes through," Freya reminded him. "The people can take the land from you whether you like it or not. I'd say it was a really risky time to buy."

Trevor nodded. "I'll grant you that, yes. But then again, the people will only ask for their land back if they want it in the first place, or if the Laird is abusing his rights of ownership."

"There's a lot of bad history that says some of them will want it back just to be awkward."

Trevor smiled. "I like to think people have a less destructive mindset than that. If the Laird has ideas that work, and invests in them to make it possible, and works in conjunction with the tenants rather than being in charge of them, that should earn him a few points."

"And use the castle and assets to make money for yourself," Robert said.

"Maglavat has a stable block," Trevor went on. "Natasha was thinking of turning it into a recording studio. I think that's well worth a shot – very high profile, Scottish castle accommodation, premium rates, and recording artistes from all over the world looking for a place to chill out while they work. I've got the contacts. Publicity for the island, revenue from top bracket incomes, and all the sporting rights as well. It could be a real package." He looked at Hugh. "And as for you looking for an island outlet for your brewery – why not establish a branch here? That's something else I've been thinking about. If the peaty island water works for the whisky, I don't see why it shouldn't perform similar miracles for the real ale. And if it takes off, a distillery would be a terrific slow cooker for the next generation."

Hugh laughed delightedly. "Now that really is a good idea," he said.

Freya nodded at Alec. "I wonder what your ancestor would have to say?"

"He had fewer options then," Trevor said, and nodded towards his great-great-great grandfather. "We've got the chance to paint a bigger picture." He stopped. "It's strange, isn't it, the family connections working out like that. I almost feel as if I've acquired a little sister."

"The family tree branches certainly went off in very different directions," Hugh said.

"It was Alasdair's move to Northumberland," Robert said. "All of a sudden, your marriage options are that much wider. Alasdair was a man of the Clan Macleod, but he also understood the value of survival. He didn't get obsessed by his father's traditions."

Trevor looked at Janet, soberly taking in the scene from the wall. "When you see people who were alive over a hundred and fifty years ago, and realise that they've directly shaped who you are – I tell you, it's a life-changing moment. I felt it, and Hedda felt it, too." He smiled. "So I've decided, I'm going to look after my new little sister," he said. Freya looked aghast, and he said quickly, "For heaven's sake, Freya, not like that. I mean I want to make this extraordinary Uishall connection mean something to her."

"How are you going to do that?" Robert said, interested.

"I don't know yet," he said. "But I'm going to keep in touch, and find out what she wants to do, and take it from there. She's capable and intelligent, and you've already made a friend of John." He threw his arms wide. "See what Uishall has done for us already. It would be nice to draw in the people who have blood ties."

"That would include Hedda's father, then," Robert said drily. "The dyed in the wool poacher who's plagued the estate since we were children. Your philanthropic tendencies might come rather unstuck with him."

"Well, he's a bit of an old-fashioned anomaly, isn't he?" Hugh said. "That whole mindset will die out. There's no future in it. Murdo MacInnes is a bit of a dinosaur, reached the end of his evolutionary path. There's nothing left for him but English-hating and reaching back into the past to pick up all the rotting detritus the bad landlords left behind them."

Trevor grimaced. "We're dinosaurs, too," he said quietly. "That's the brutal truth. The landowner has got to evolve, or perish in the past with the poachers."

"Well, it will be interesting to see how you solve the problem," Hugh said. "I find all this rather moving, to tell you the truth. I always felt the reason Uishall struggled was not just because of money, but because it had lost its sense of identity. That's been restored now."

"There's so much scope here," Trevor said. "Remember what Aidan said once, about one of the schemes to stock that salmon river to the north? He said there was no point putting in a lot of fish and expecting them to be happy there if the river wasn't right in the first place. You had to get the environment right, and then the fish would come anyway. Well, I think you can apply the same principle to the land and the people. Make it right, and they'll want to come, they won't have to be bribed with grants."

Robert looked impressed. "Mammoth undertaking," he said.

"I'll need help," Trevor agreed. "Lots of professionals who know what they're doing." He paused. "And a good companion at my side." He raised his glass. Freya was staring at him. "This week, I caught my first salmon, found my home, found my roots, and at last got the woman I love interested in me. I don't know what that's called, but it's a hell of a lot more important than a Royal Macnab. I'm going to be the Laird of Uishall and Maglavat, and I need a Lady. Freya, will you redeem an old has-been who was too scared to admit his feelings, and marry me?"

Freya's gasp was so high-pitched, it was almost a shriek. Her hand flew to her mouth.

"My God," Robert breathed into the stunned silence.

After a moment, Freya stood up and rested her fingertips on the table. She regarded Trevor gravely, and his heart dropped.

"Frankly, Trevor," she said, "I think you've got a bloody cheek. Proposing to me on the basis of a couple of shags is presumptuous to say the least."

Hugh and Robert looked in consternation at each other, and then at the table in appalled mortification. The silence in the dining room was ghastly.

"I have to say the shagging was very nice," she went on, "but I don't know if it's a good foundation for a long term commitment like marriage." She lifted her glass to him. "But perhaps you're not the only one who's been too scared to admit what was going on."

All the men were holding their breath, as if they had no idea what she was going to do next.

"Oh for God's sake," she said, raising her eyes. "I'm as stupid as the next woman about a good shag. Yes, Trevor, of course I'll marry you. In fact, after the way you landed that salmon, you'll have a hard time stopping me."

He gasped with the relief and sheer thrill of it, came round the table and caught her in his arms, and she struggled briefly.

"Please, Trevor, control yourself," she said, affecting coyness. "Our friends are watching."

"Oh no," he said, trapping her arms. "I owe you quite a lot for that one."

Now her outrage was genuine. "Don't you dare kiss me in public – not like that –"

"Oh Freya, do shut up," said Hugh, grinning.

V
MAY 2002

Trevor and Freya were married in the Great Hall at Uishall, overlooking the river at sunset. Marie produced a lavish buffet, and Hedda and John supervised the decorations, before Hedda changed into her dress for the ceremony – as one of the bridesmaids. The walls were hung with great lengths of Macleod tartan and huge sprays of flowers filled the giant antique vases. Juniper boughs hung over the place where the bride and groom would take their vows. In a pleasing and entertaining decorative diversion, a single length of tartan in scarlet, cerise and green hung in the centre of the wall – the tartan of the Clan Macnab, in tribute to the contest that had brought the happy couple together. The floor was carpeted in the specially commissioned Macleod tartan pattern. Freya wore a black velvet hooded cloak with a Macleod tartan silk ball gown underneath; Trevor wore the Macleod kilt and full Highland dress.

Freya was piped into the Great Hall and so moving was the spectacle and the sound of the bagpipes that there was scarcely a dry eye in the gathering by the time she stood at Trevor's side.

"I hope they don't stand still for too long," Robert murmured to Hugh during the ceremony, "or we'll lose them against the carpet."

In the early hours of the morning, Freya and Trevor abandoned their friends and the festivities and went away to spend their wedding night at Maglavat. Before the taxi arrived, they stripped off their finery, donned jeans and sweaters, and climbed to the top of Janet's Knoll.

"We'll find our own knoll at Maglavat," Trevor said, gazing at the resting place of his ancestors, as if it was a particularly romantic and attractive proposition for his new wife.

"I can hardly wait," Freya said sarcastically. "You've only just married me, for heaven's sakes. Do we really have to start discussing our final resting place now?"

"Is the Lady of Uishall and Maglavat happy?" he asked her.

"Blissfully," she said. "But rather cold, to tell you the truth."

385

"Just a few minutes," Trevor said, drawing his shivering wife against him. "I always loved this spot. I'd love to know why Alec and Janet did, too."

"Perhaps it was the first time they declared their love or something," Freya said. "Must have been quite a dramatic moment, for both of them."

Trevor sighed. "Well, I don't suppose we'll ever know," he said. He held out his hand. "Come on. A drive over the mountains, a long bath, and the marriage bed."

"Sounds delicious," Freya said.

They entered their new home by the front door, and stood for a moment looking at the lascivious paintings in the entrance.

"Jesus," Freya said in humorous disgust. "I'm going to spend the rest of my life surrounded by dirty pictures."

"You should be so lucky," Trevor said, grinning.

"Worse," his bride said, "having to make excuses for them."

"We can take them away."

She shook her head at once. "No. They're part of the place and part of the spirit of the man who built it. However odious he was, there's something about all this that seems to fit."

"Once you know that Ruaraidh had himself painted into the pictures, it's almost impossible to let them go."

They wandered through the deserted ground floor, the shiny kitchen used for the hunting guests, the private kitchen for the Laird, the office, the rod room, the gun room.

"Morag will be in to make us brunch," Trevor said. "I'm certainly not for an early start."

"So what's the plan?" Freya asked.

Trevor's arms were round her. "Well, first I ravish you, and then you ravish me –"

She laughed. "In the long term," she said firmly. "Come on, seriously, just for a moment. How the hell are we going to make this work?"

He took her hand and led her back through the entrance hall and up the stairs, to where the portrait of Ruaraidh hung on the wall.

"My brother," he said, pointing, "apart from the accident of time."

Freya sniffed. "Not much of a recommendation."

386

"But I have Alec on my side," Trevor reminded her. "And he was good."

"He held it all together," Freya conceded. "But that was a long time ago. Times have changed."

"The world is closer than it used to be," Trevor said. "More people have more money, and natural wilderness like this is increasingly attractive."

"Now you sound like a tourist brochure," Freya said.

"All right then," Trevor said. "I'll tell you what I'm thinking, and you can tell me what you think. The key to all this, as far as I can see, is creative people. Artists, musicians, writers – people who draw on what's around them to make new things. But not just them, not just literally creative people. I mean people with a will to pull off the blinkers, let go the past and look at what the future has to offer." He paused. "I mean, I'm new money, aren't I? A disreputable from a wild card profession. The clan chiefs will be turning in their graves. But this whole island is a wild card. It can't be anything other than what it is. It can't pretend, it can't change, it can't even be persuaded. So what we need to do is make it work on its own terms."

"Well, I'll write about it and make it famous," Freya said.

"That will help," Trevor said. "And I'm going to open the doors to musicians, and give them the best studio facilities they can get. That's as well as the season guests who come for the hunting."

"And what else?"

"I'm keeping the chef on," Trevor said. "I think we can do something with the food, and Roger agrees. And I've employed a PA."

Freya looked at him. "Really? Who is it?"

"Well, I had one before, but he'd be perfectly miserable out here. But Henry told me about Natasha's PA, and it turns out he and his man have hatched a plan to move to the islands." Trevor beamed. "I met him in London. He's first class. And he can't believe his luck. Their ultimate plan is to open a restaurant here, but that could be years away. So if Felix comes on board at Maglavat, it gives him and his partner a solid income while they make their long term plans."

"Well," Freya said, "you *have* been busy." She paused. "There are the wind farms, too," she said. "They're coming."

"Never," Trevor said firmly. "Not on my land. I won't allow it."

"Revenue," Freya said. "You can't afford to dismiss any option."

"No," Trevor said again. "Not while I'm here." He looked at her, and she was amused when she saw the Laird in his eyes, as if he was suddenly aware of the title he had to live up to. "The wind farms are transient, like we are," he said. "They'll chop up the birds, dig up the land and never repay the costs of setting them up. And then it'll all be over in twenty-five years, and not have worked. I'm serious. There will never be a wind farm at Maglavat." His eyes glittered. "Or Uishall, if I have anything to do with it."

VI

Back at Uishall, the wedding party was breaking up, some of the guests retiring to rooms at the castle, the others making their way back to hotels in town. In the bright moonlight, Hugh and Robert, worse for wear after all the champagne, stood at the water's edge and looked landward, to the dark bump of Janet's Knoll and the distant glitter of the granite gravestone against the sky.

"Will it always be a rich man's paradise?" Hugh wondered.

Robert shook his head. "Who knows? Either that or a poor man's hell. Maybe there's nothing in between."

"I always used to think we had to cling on to the past if we were going to save it," Hugh said. "But the future's unavoidable."

Robert smiled. "So is the past," he said. "You need a balance. Uishall has always survived, one way or another, by embracing change. People are scared of change now, because the world seems to be turning too quickly."

"Alec married his crofter sweetheart," Hugh said, lifting his glass to the gravestone in the distance. "Eventually. That was embracing change."

"Alasdair stuck to the Black Hebrideans," Robert countered. "While all the other landowners were throwing in their lot with English breeds that didn't suit the land, Alasdair stuck to his guns. And now his sheep are returning to the fold, back where they belong. He saw that change wasn't always progress."

"But then he created Uishall as a sporting estate," Hugh said. "And took an English wife."

Robert smiled. "Good for Alasdair," he said. "And at the end of the day, Uishall's still here. It ain't broke yet, so let's not try too hard to fix it."

Robert had seen a letter written by Alasdair to his wife, during a business trip to England in 1874. It seemed that having found a way to make Uishall profitable through the sporting estate concept, Alasdair came to feel he had ripped out the heart of the land and castle he loved.

"It seems contrary of me," he wrote that summer, *"to find less love in my heart for the home that made me, now the family fortunes are all secure and there is no more struggle with rents and livestock. But having made Uishall into a pleasure palace for gentlemen, I see that I have destroyed its nobility and removed its self-respect as a place that earned its living. If I could better explain the painful feelings I have when I ride Uishall's empty lands now, you might understand better. My forefathers could not make the land work and create a reasonable standard of living for the tenants and guardians of the land. But when the people left because we tried to make the land pay, Uishall's soul went with them, and I cannot find a way to bring them back. My mind is made up. We will sell and raise our children on the mainland, and try to find solace in the superficial pleasures of our wealth. Uishall is too implacable for us to master and we must build new lives and find ways to live that are less heartbreaking and less harsh. For I have come to understand at last that we love the land because its spirit will not be tamed, and if we are to truly profess our love, we should not master it."*

"Alasdair always was the pragmatist," Hugh said. "But it still hurt him to leave."

"Alec wouldn't have blamed him, though. I think he saw the writing on the wall, and he knew his son would never make himself a martyr to a lost cause. Their time was over. And selling it to Jamie wasn't a bad move, once the sports had taken off. He's the one we should be grateful for, holding it all together, for Uishall *and* Maglavat in the end."

"And how will our new Laird and Lady fare?"

Robert shrugged. "No better or worse than their predecessors, I suspect."

"At least they've got a good accountant."

Robert inclined his head at the compliment. "And they respect the past, but won't be trapped by it. People make too much of the past here," he said. "Or rather, they make too much of it in some ways, and not enough of it in others. Why do they think the past is something you can trust?"

Hugh smiled. "I suppose because once it's been written down, it seems to acquire credibility, and then it becomes true. Well, Freya and Trevor won't be auctioning that sideboard to raise funds in a crisis."

Robert laughed. "Oh heavens above," he said. "If you'd seen the look on poor old Peregrine's face when he had to tell me it was only worth two thousand eight hundred pounds. What a rogue Alasdair was, spinning a yarn like that. Whatever possessed him? Talk about turning history on its head."

They stood and looked out at the water before turning and beginning to walk upriver. Behind them, if they had chanced to turn round and look, they would have seen a thin-faced, handsome man, still in his prime, get up from the bench and walk towards the front door of the castle, a tiny baby with flaming red hair cradled protectively in his arms. He was smiling, as if he had overheard their conversation, and looked forward, as they did, to a new era of Macleod Lairds governing the land, the waters and the ancient castle that made up the substance and spirit of Uishall.

The brothers strolled in the moonlight and talked over the events of the previous season and anticipated the new one approaching. They agreed, in gently sozzled concord, that Uishall's story was a tale of change that itself changed with every telling. Economic forces wielded their fickle power and the social order broke down and rebuilt itself in response. People lived, struggled, fell in love, procreated, passed through and died. They fought for happiness. They lied to survive. Only the land was constant.

Notes
1: *Slainte*: Cheers